BEC MCMASTER

Nobody's Hero

➤➤➤—THE BURNED LAND SERIES—→

ALSO AVAILABLE BY BEC MCMASTER

LONDON STEAMPUNK SERIES
Kiss Of Steel
Heart Of Iron
My Lady Quicksilver
Forged By Desire
Of Silk And Steam
Novellas in same series:
Tarnished Knight
The Curious Case Of The Clockwork Menace

DARK ARTS SERIES
Shadowbound

BURNED LANDS SERIES
Nobody's Hero

OTHER
The Many Lives Of Hadley Monroe

one

Wastelands, 2147

THE SUN POOLED red on the horizon, the last spears of sunlight slashing across the sky, and then fading. Night was coming, and with it the need to be home. Before the monsters came out to play.

Riley slid down over the rock, easing her body cautiously onto the ledge below. In the distance, a last glimmer of light reflected off something shiny across the desert floor. It could have been merely a shard of glass half-smashed out of some old rust bucket that no longer ran, but Riley didn't think so. Once a graveyard of cars, most of them had been hauled away for spare parts, or scrap by the roaming bands of reivers.

The only things out here now were cactus, hop sage, and tumbleweed. And the sand. Always the bloody sand.

"What is it?" Jimmy whispered, peering over the edge of the tor.

Riley frowned into the distance, her spyglass in hand. Gauging the distance carefully, she leapt across a gaping chasm in the rock and landed on the very edge of the plateau. Without anything to block her view, the Wastelands stretched before her endlessly, filling the world from horizon to horizon. Her father once said there were cities on the other side of the Great Divide that split the continent, but Riley couldn't imagine it. Living out here in the barren Wastelands, in their guarded little settlement, was the only life she'd ever known.

Peering through the spyglass, her vision catapulted forward. She soon found the cause of the reflection—an old jeep, fitted with a gun turret, a pair of vigilantes riding in the tray. Heavily armored in salvaged scrap, and covered in scarred tattoos, the pair looked hard and mean. Riley swore under her breath. "Damn it."

"What?" Jimmy asked from above. "Wargs? Reivers?" Pebbles rained down over her as he shifted nervously.

"Reivers," she confirmed, scanning the desert floor. Her heart started to pound as she swept the spyglass over the canyon below. They were heading east. Toward Haven. Her sanctuary was the only settlement out this far, and the only reason for the vultures to risk the dangerous canyon track.

Riley froze as movement flickered through the lens of the spyglass. She jerked it back, disbelief flooding her with a sickening feeling as another pair of jeeps swept into view. With gasoline sources getting low, it was rare for so many vehicles to be out this far.

Unless they were planning on hitting the settlement.

Hard.

Maybe they knew about the gasoline shipment that Haven had just received from the Eastern Confederacy?

"Shit." She waited long enough to count the men – thirteen – before jerking her head up.

Jimmy's pale face came into view, his eyes wide. "Scouting party?"

Riley shook her head grimly. She'd known this day would come. This side of the Great Divide, resources were becoming few and far between. Every month of radio vigilance brought fewer settlements checking in; the previous month, the settlement of New Hope, just forty miles north, had been hit. Since then, there'd been no word from Tom and Jenny, or the rest of the settlers she'd come to know over the radio.

The kid's face paled further. "It's crazy hitting the settlement at night, what with the wargs out there."

"We're talking about reivers. Sanity's not really a priority when it comes to membership. Come on." She tucked the spyglass in her leather bag and slung it over her shoulder. "We've got to get back to the jeep and warn them." As Jimmy made to dash after her, she jerked her hand. "Don't forget the rocs."

The reason they'd been out there. Much-needed food. Not even the threat of reivers could make her forget the brace of dead birds they'd spent the day scaling the cliffs to catch.

Running lightly across the rock, she found the rappel rope they'd used to climb up to where the enormous birds nested. Hooking her carabiner onto the ropes, and then checking her climbing harness and descender, she waited long enough to make sure Jimmy wasn't at risk of falling before she took a deep breath and edged over the cliff.

"Here we go," she muttered, and leapt backward.

The descent was short and took her breath away. She was used to scaling the heights – either for sentry duty or to get at the massive rocs that nested at the top of the tor – but she'd never descended quite this quickly.

Jimmy was quick to follow, his eyes almost bugging out of his head at the drop. Riley caught him, her gloved hand riding over his harness as he safely put both feet on the ground. The red glow of dusk was starting to fade. In the east, streaks of indigo discolored the sky. They'd been out too long, but pickings were starting to get slim now that winter was edging over the continent.

Not that you'd know it, thanks to the blistering heat the week had brought.

"Leave the ropes," she instructed, slinging the pair of birds over her shoulder and starting for the jeep. The nestlings had to weigh at least 50 pounds, but she was used to hauling her weight up the cliffs, let alone a pair of dead birds.

"Here, you'd best drive." Jimmy called, tossing her the keys as they reached the jeep.

Riley snatched them out of the air and tossed the brace of birds in the tray, next to the warg cage. At seventeen, this was his first trip out foraging. By the look on his face, he'd be lucky if he didn't put them into a ditch or blow a tire if he drove. Shimmying out of the harness, she stripped off her gloves and threw them both in the back next to the cage.

The Jeep gave a coughing grunt, but finally started. With the winding track through the canyon below, they had a good thirteen-mile head start on the reivers.

Hopefully, it would be enough. She'd heard tales of what happened to people caught out in the Wastelands by the reiver gangs. Especially women.

Ignoring the cold finger that trailed down her spine, she jammed the jeep into reverse and spun backward. Tires crunching over the gravel, Riley shifted gears, hit the gas, and they rocketed forward.

"What do you reckon they want?" Jimmy asked, grabbing for the door handle to hold on.

Riley tossed him the radio receiver. "Same thing as anybody out here. Food, potable water, shelter. Women. Here. Try and contact Haven."

Jimmy played with the dial, static crackling over the speakers. His lips compressed in a grim line she didn't miss as mile upon mile of static greeted them. Finally, the line cleared, and he let out a breath. "Ranger one to base, do you copy?"

The light was fading fast, leaving bushes and rocks as shadows. Riley peered ahead, wondering whether she dared put the headlights on. The reivers weren't the only threat out there. And she'd lead them straight to Haven if she did.

But better to get home alive than crash in a gulch.

"Base, do you copy?"

Riley flicked the lights on.

A man appeared out of nowhere. She caught a glimpse of naked skin, faded blue jeans, and a mess of black hair, and then she was tearing at the wheel. Jimmy screamed as the brakes kicked in. Gravel sprayed, but it was too late. The jeep hit with a thud and the man flipped up over the hood, smashing into the front window before disappearing.

Gripping the wheel with white-knuckled hands, Riley slowly blinked as the dust cleared. Her heart felt like it was going to thump its way through her chest, and her lungs were tight. *Holy shit.*

Jimmy looked up, blood dripping from his temple. "Did we just hit someone?"

Who the hell would be out here at this time of night? Riley sucked in a huge breath, her first since the impact. The reality of the situation was beginning to sink in. "Give me the shotgun."

Ripping off her safety belt, she slid the small handgun out of the side holster that had been customized to the seat, tossing it to Jimmy. The front window was a mess, but somehow the glass still held. She couldn't see a thing through it, so keeping it wasn't an option. Wasn't as if it was going to keep the nightlife out anyway.

Grabbing the shotgun off Jimmy, she smashed the window out. The desert night was quiet. Still. Holding her breath, she scanned the horizon. Nothing moved.

"Stay in the jeep," Riley ordered. "If I give the signal, you start it up and drive like blazes."

Jimmy swallowed. He knew the drill. "Want me to keep trying the radio?"

"Won't hurt." Though she knew chances were slim they'd be heard now. Whoever was supposed to be on duty was obviously elsewhere. Maybe Warren or Viv. Both had strayed from the radio control room in the past.

Nobody else was that stupid.

Riley's boots crunched on the gravel as she stepped out, holding the shotgun warily in front of her. It was loaded with exploding rounds she'd doctored herself; no point shooting to warn when the night was just as likely to rip your throat out.

"Hello?" she called. "You alive back there?"

The taillights cast a ruddy glow. Beyond that, she couldn't see shit. And there was no answer.

"Jimmy, hand me the goggles."

He tossed them to her and she dragged them over her head, the nightscape suddenly springing to life around her with green-tinted accuracy. They'd cost her half a year's rations three years ago, when the traders came through, but they were worth it. And Riley could hunt, so it hadn't left her hungry for long.

A pair of bare feet lay motionless behind the vehicle, blood splashed across his jeans.

"M-maybe we should go. Just leave him there," Jimmy stammered.

Tempting. Riley weighed her options – and the shotgun. She was running out of time to warn the settlement. But her father had always cautioned her not to lose her humanity. The rest of the world might be torn apart and broken, but they had to hold onto their souls out here, or risk becoming just as empty as the wargs themselves.

"We leave him here and he's as good as dead," she muttered, inching toward the back of the jeep. There was no sign of the cat-shine of animal eyes out there, but they wouldn't be far away. The sun had gone, and a few stars flickered in the sky. Time for the wargs to come out and play.

Pumping a round into the chamber, Riley stepped around the vehicle, aiming it at the prone man. "Hey. You alive?"

No movement. She kicked his foot, and it rolled to the side then back with not a hint of muscular tension.

"Shit." There was blood everywhere. A massive gash slashed across his chest, and hints of bruising darkened his ribs. Thick, dark hair blackened his scalp, but his face was turned away from her. Pewter glinted on his chest. A charm of some sort, vaguely native.

Nausea flooded through her. She'd killed a man.

Not the first time she'd ever killed – but wargs didn't count. Their humanity was long gone, stolen by the flesh-hunger that ravaged them. Monsters, her father had called them. And there was no guilt in hunting down the monsters that consumed this world. Man or beast.

"He's not moving," she called, lifting the goggles onto her head. "Start the jeep. Let's get going–"

And that was when she noticed it: the ragged edges of the gash in his chest were re-knitting at an almost visible rate. *What the hell...?* She took a step closer. Wargs healed fast, but with the moon edging over the horizon they wouldn't be able to contain their beast-form like this.

Reaching out with the shotgun, she used it to turn his face toward her.

Mid-thirties maybe. Chiseled jaw. Rough dark stubble, and skin that glowed under the harsh red light of the rear lights. The kind of face that made her hesitate, just for a moment....

Then his eyes shot open, the light catching them and reflecting back silvery-red. A smile stretched over his lips, immediately devilish. "Surprise," he whispered.

Riley's stomach dropped, and she leapt back with a curse. "Gun, Jimmy! It's a warg!"

In the seconds it took to yell, the stranger rolled onto his feet. Fluid. Lithe. Almost too fast to see. Riley shoved the shotgun up, but the warg smashed it out of the way, following up with a kick that swept her feet out from under her.

She hit the ground hard. The breath exploded from her lungs and, for a moment, she couldn't breathe. The goggles were gone. Lungs burning, Riley choked on nothing, her hands still clenched desperately around the shotgun. If she lost that then she was dead.

And Jimmy too.

Jimmy! Her eyes went wide. She wanted to scream at him to get behind the wheel and get the hell out of here, but she couldn't.

"Riley! Get away from her, you monster!" Jimmy's voice, coming out of the dark like some teen crusading-angel.

No! She'd promised Mabel that she wouldn't let anything happen to him.

Her lungs suddenly opened, and oxygen rushed back in on a gasp. It burned, all the way through. A hand fisted in her hair and the stranger hauled her to her feet, dragging her back against his solid chest. His arm cut across her throat, threatening to choke her, and then he tilted her face to the side, exposing the vulnerable column of her neck. Four sharp little points dug into her skin.

Claws.

Riley froze.

"Not another step, boy wonder." The voice was rough and low. A hint of amusement edged it. "Or I'll rip her throat open."

She could just see Jimmy out of the corner of her vision, the gun pointed at them wavering as confusion crossed his face. He was too young for this shit, but he knew his orders. Knew what he was supposed to do in the event that his partner was captured.

"Get back... in the jeep," Riley told him, gasping the words. Easier to make the decision for him. "And get the hell out of here. Report to base."

Where Mabel could wrap him in her arms as he cried for the partner he'd lost. They all went through it. Out here, on the edge of the Wastelands, not a man or woman amongst them hadn't watched someone else die.

The claws pricked her and she froze, not daring to move. One cut, one bite, and there was a chance of his curse spreading - a fate worse than death.

"You're not the one calling the shots, sweetheart." A slight Southern drawl. "What's your name, boy?"

"J..-Jimmy."

"Nice lookin' warg cage there on the back of the jeep." That was definitely laughter in his voice. She could feel the rumble of it through his chest. "You ever caught a warg before?"

Jimmy's eyes rolled toward her in a silent plea. "Ah, not personally."

"You ever shoot a warg before?"

"No."

"Then be a good boy and put the gun away, before someone gets hurt." The laughter cut off as if it had never been. The body behind her stilled as the claws slid down her throat, trailing lightly over her skin.

Riley barely dared to breathe. Sweat gathered under her arms and between her breasts. When a drop of moisture slid down her throat, he followed it with his claws, an appreciative purr rumbling through his throat.

Jimmy stared through the gun sight, his hair matted with blood.

"Put it down," she whispered. "And get in the jeep."

The gun lowered. Jimmy's hands shook, and she knew exactly how he felt.

"Get in the jeep," she repeated.

Lips glided along the side of her throat. Riley shivered. "Go," she told Jimmy desperately. "Warn Haven."

"Not just yet." The warg's grip tightened as he bestowed a faint kiss against the line of her trapezius. "Do you know Adam McClain?"

Even as Jimmy shook his head, Riley felt herself stiffen. *Shit.* The mouth against her nape lifted, and his warm breath cooled her damp skin.

"But *you* do." He sounded delighted.

"He's no friend of mine," she replied stiffly.

"Where is he?"

Riley hesitated. No way in hell was she giving up a human to the monsters. Even if the man in question almost deserved it. "I don't know," she lied. "I've never seen him, just heard his voice. It's only radio contact out here. We don't exactly host a barn dance with the other settlements."

A hand slid over her hip, hauling her tight against him. Tight enough to know he was enjoying this. Riley's hands clenched on the shotgun. All he had to do was give her a chance. Just one.

"Ah, ah, ah," he whispered. "Make a move, and I'll kill the boy first. Make you watch. Better you just put it down, honey."

She lowered the barrel of the shotgun and rested it on his foot, the threat imminent. "You that fast on one leg?"

"Fast enough." His fingers dug into her, the claws almost, but not quite, breaking the skin.

She met Jimmy's eyes. She couldn't do anything with him there. "Go. Please."

"And tell them I'm looking for McClain," the stranger lifted his voice. "If he wants the woman, he'll have to find *me* this time. I'll keep her alive for a week. If he doesn't come for me by then, then I'll kill her and take someone else."

"And who are you?" Jimmy dared to ask. A tear slid down his cheek, but hope had risen in his eyes. He had a week, and he knew it.

Riley knew she wouldn't be alive by then. She'd make sure of it. There were worse alternatives.

"Wade. Lucius Wade. You tell him that. Tell him I'll be headin' east."

Jimmy nodded, taking one last look at her. "Won't let you down, Riley. We'll come for you." His hands were shaking so badly he couldn't hold the pistol anymore. It clattered to the rocks as he turned, running jerkily for the door of the jeep. He slammed it shut, the noise echoing through the gulch.

Then he was gone, the wheels screaming as they fought for purchase on the sandy surface. All she could see were his taillights, fading into the distance.

"Now," Wade murmured. "Let's you and me talk a little more about McClain."

"I've got a better idea." Riley tilted her face to meet his gaze. The predatory glint rolled through his pale eyes, but she called his bluff, hoping it was one. "You're not going to claw me up. You need me alive – and unharmed – to bait your trap. So, how 'bout I blow your foot off?"

"Then what?"

In the distance, the taillights began to fade. All alone. With a man who should've been a beast by that point. Her heart was in her throat, but Riley pressed on. "What do you mean?"

"Can't you hear it?"

Silence. The wind whispering over the desert. And, beneath that, almost inaudible to her ears, the eerie sound of something howling in the distance.

She stopped breathing. Wargs. In beast form. If she got away from him, she'd be torn to pieces. If she was lucky.

"It's beautiful, isn't it?" he mused. "Like a frigging desert symphony. Full of death, and longing... And hunger... Hear that?" He tilted his head as another throaty howl echoed out through the night, slightly closer. "There's another one."

He didn't need to threaten her. Or point out that she wouldn't get far. The night was a dark place, and a little voice whispered in her mind, *Better the devil you know....*

At least Wade was still in human form. Claws or not, that was better than being mauled to death – or raped – by one of the monstrously deformed weres.

"What do you plan to do with me?" she finally asked, shifting the shotgun off his foot.

"Good girl." His fingers closed over hers. "Now, give it to me."

She didn't want to; that was her last hope, right there. His fingers tightened, just a fraction, and Riley let the shotgun slip through her hand, sucking in a deep breath.

Wade snapped the barrel open and examined the shot. "You know lead doesn't have much effect on a warg?"

"Silver's harder to melt," she replied. "And I wouldn't look inside the casing if I were you. You don't want the chemical contents inside mixing together while it's in your hand." A direct look into his eyes. "Or within fifteen feet of me."

"What happens then?" Something that might have been curiosity shifted in his gaze.

"Boom."

"Hmm." He snapped the barrel shut and let her go. "You make it yourself?"

The sudden chill of the night almost made her want to step closer, huddle against his warmth. "What does it matter?"

He smiled. His teeth were very white in the night. "You're an interesting woman." Leaning closer, he laughed in her ear. "I might just keep you around for a while."

She smiled back. "You'll have to sleep sometime."

Wade's laughter echoed, the sound of it soft and intimate in the night. "We'll see. Now, turn around and put your hands behind you."

"Or?"

The laughter died. He gave her a dangerous look and hefted the shotgun like a club, the butt of the stock raised above his head. "Or I knock you out, and throw you over my shoulder. I'd have to carry you, but you won't be able to see where I'm taking you then, huh?"

She obeyed, grinding her teeth together. The thought of being helpless was far from appealing, but she didn't have much choice.

And she knew this land like the back of her hand. If she could escape – during the day – then she might have a chance of making it home. As if he knew what was going through her mind, he chuckled softly.

The feel of his hand on her midriff made her flinch, but he was only undoing her belt. "Relax. I prefer a little more subtlety to my seduction, and the night's about to get dangerously overcrowded. I'm not fussy, but I'm not that interested in sharing either."

She looked up. No movement on the plain, but that faint, echoing song still lingered in the air. "You want to hurry a bit, then?"

He jerked the belt through the loops of her jeans, making her stagger. "Now you want to come with me? Must be my charm."

She didn't reply, and he wrapped the belt around her wrists. Once. Twice. Thrice. Then jerked it tight, setting the buckle in place. There wasn't even a finger's width of wriggle room.

"Which way?" she asked.

"East."

"But there's nothing out there."

Wade gave her a lazy-lidded smile. "You'll see."

Faint light turned the sky ahead of her rosy. Dawn. A long time coming. Riley's feet were aching, and her hands throbbed from lack of circulation. They'd left the warg-song behind hours ago, but she still glanced over her shoulder occasionally, checking the horizon. You didn't always hear them coming.

Despite the hike, Wade seemed none the worse for wear. He hadn't bothered with conversation, and she wasn't interested in starting one. He'd tugged a duffel out from behind a rock an hour into the trek, dragging a faded black muscle shirt on and a pair of heavy shit-kickers. From the rattle of the bag, he was packing some serious heat too.

"Why just the jeans?" she'd asked.

"The better to tempt you with."

They were the only words they'd exchanged.

Exhaustion was starting to settle in when she staggered up a dusty rise. As the sky cleared, she got her first sight of what lay ahead, and stopped in her tracks.

"No way."

Icy sweat sprang up against her spine. Ahead, a barbed-wire fence stretched for miles. Signs clung to the wire with faded black hazard symbols barely visible against the yellow. She didn't come out this way often. Nobody did. But she knew where she was.

"Black River Testing Facility," Wade said cheerfully, shoving her in the back with the shotgun.

She staggered forward, then dug her heels in.

"Home, sweet home," he added. "Don't be shy. I scrubbed the bloodstains off the floor."

"It's not the bloodstains I'm worried about," she replied. "I changed my mind. I'll sit out here and wait for the wargs."

He laughed. "It's sterile. They came through and destroyed any remaining signs of the pathogen. You're not at risk. It's been over seventy years since Black River was used to weapons-test their gene-enhanced critters, and sixty-something since the meteor hit."

"Why didn't they bomb the place?" She glared up at the stark adobe buildings behind the fence.

"What would be the point? Everybody was dead." He shrugged. "And the government had other matters on their mind. Namely the Eastern Confederacy, and the enforcer bands."

He gave her a gentler nudge. Riley staggered forward, her left knee giving out beneath her. With a sharp cry, she plunged forward, unable to balance herself.

Strong hands caught her by the belt. She almost screamed as fiery pain flashed through her hands.

"I forget you're only human," he commented, tearing the belt buckle loose.

"No," she murmured, feeling blood begin to circulate through her fingers like liquid nitrogen through her veins. Too late. The throbbing sensation made her head spin. She could barely even move her arms, even though they were free now.

"You should have told me you were hurtin'." He swung her over his shoulder with ridiculous ease.

No! She kicked at him. "I'm not going into that building! Leave me out here! I'd rather die."

"So melodramatic." He kept walking, ignoring her struggles. "That's always an option, you realize, darlin'. I really only need McClain to *think* I've got you. A little hair and the scent off your clothes ought to do it, if I bait the trap right." His manner was easy, as if he were speaking about what she'd like for dinner, and not about cutting her throat.

A shiver ran through her. Any doubts about just how dangerous he was evaporated like a drop of water in the desert sun.

Glancing back over her shoulder, she could see the fence looming closer. "Why the hard-on for McClain?" *Keep him talking. Then maybe he won't kill me.*

"He's still breathing," he replied, as if that explained it all.

Ripping a piece of the fence aside, he slipped in through the gap. The scrape in the dirt showed this wasn't a recent development.

Just how long had he been out here, hiding in this godforsaken place? Watching for a chance to get at someone, and hoping they came from McClain's settlement.

The buildings loomed in the night, soaking up the soft, pre-dawn light. The stark white adobe walls looked ghostly, and the silence was unerring. Some trick of the wind kept a sheet of loose iron banging in the distance.

Creepy. She tensed against Wade, momentarily grateful for his company. And that just said it all, really.

Black River was the site of every Wastelander's nightmares. Everyone knew the stories: a hidden government facility running research into wargs, and forced *evolution*, whatever the hell that meant. Weapons testing, though the weapons had once been human. Rykker, the only settler in Haven who remained from before the Darkening, claimed that nobody even knew what shadow-cats were before the meteor struck, and *something* escaped from Black River. Now, the Great Divide was crawling with them.

Why would you even create something like that? Sometimes she thought it would be easier to live in pre-Darkening times, where you could buy your foods in something called a supermarket, or fill your car at a gas station, according to Rykker. Then she'd think about all the bad things that still plagued the world, like the Dead Zones surrounding ancient nuclear plants that had been destroyed by wildfires from the crash, or the revenant plague.

Maybe a simpler life was a better one?

Wade swung her to her feet in front of one of the buildings. Riley staggered back against the wall, too exhausted to even try running. He gave her a terse look, realized she was too tired to care, and knelt down.

Shuffling the dirt out of the way, he yanked on a smooth iron ring.

Opening the trapdoor revealed a gaping black maw.

"No." She scrambled away.

"Ladies first." He grabbed her and hauled her forward. "Mind the drop."

Levering her over the hole, Wade lowered her into it. Riley's feet curled under her as she tucked into a fetal position. She couldn't help herself; she was partly hyperventilating. The only thing connecting her to the world outside was the warm hand gripping hers.

Looking up, she stared into his pale, emotionless eyes. "Don't you leave me here." The last words broke unsteadily. "Don't lock me in."

A moment of silence. Something flickered in his eyes – not quite sympathy or compassion, but the most human reaction she'd seen in his face so far. As if it were buried so deep, he didn't even know what it was. "I'll follow you. Put your feet down. You'll be able to touch the floor."

She didn't want to let go of his hand.

Their fingers clung, entwined.

And the silvery animal-shine of a warg flashed through his eyes. His lip curled back. "Let go."

It was the hardest thing she'd ever done.

Landing on the floor, Riley knelt, breathing quietly whilst she waited for her eyes to adjust to the pre-dawn light. The room was thick with darkness, encroaching in on her, looming, *pressing....*

Looking up revealed a circle of azure-colored sky, so far away she couldn't even reach it. Riley's breath tasted thick and heavy. There could be anything in there with her. The tales about Black River were legendary.

For a moment, she thought Wade'd lied, that he was gone, but then a pair of boots swung through the hole, jeans tightening over the man's butt as he dropped to the floor beside her. Landing lightly on the pads of his feet, with his fingertips touching the floor, he looked up.

Riley smashed her knee directly under his chin.

Wade's head snapped back, and a growl erupted from his throat as he hit the floor. Riley jumped up, fingertips catching the lip of the manhole. Kicking desperately, she dragged herself up through the hole, hot sunlight staining her face and shoulders for a moment, arms straining, and—

A hand locked around her ankle. "Going somewhere, darlin'?"

Riley kicked out at him, but he caught her other boot. A hard yank tore her back through the hole, stomach scraping against the edge. *No!* She grabbed at a hank of dry grass, the brittle fibers tearing loose from the sandy soil. Fingernails raking over the gravel, she felt herself falling.

And then the world was dark again, strong arms catching her as she fell. Riley grabbed at his shoulders reflexively, his unnatural heat clinging to her skin. Hot breath curled over her face and, as her eyes adjusted, she caught the faint, silvery sheen of his pale eyes.

He was smiling.

The bastard was smiling.

It curled over his lips, slightly crooked and completely wicked. As though he'd enjoyed her attempt to free herself. "Entirely predictable."

Wade let her go, and Riley's feet hit the floor. Reaching up, he grabbed the rope that trailed up through the manhole. "Lights out," he called, then dragged the cover back into place.

The room plunged into a darkness so heavy she felt as though she were trapped in a vacuum. Her other senses intensified, and she focused on the scent of musty air, a hint of masculine sweat and wolfish musk, and the sound of denim shifting in the darkness. Her heartbeat was a ragged staccato. Wade had to hear it.

"Where are we?" she whispered.

Reaching out, she felt for anything to grab, taking slow, shuffling steps, testing each footfall before she let her heel strike the floor.

"This office opens into the psych ward, judging by the leather straps on the gurneys, and the labels on the medication bottles in there." A warm hand wrapped around her outstretched arm. "Watch where you're going."

Riley turned toward him. Her own personal psycho, but then it was better to have his company than none at all. She grabbed his shirt, clinging to him in case he left her here.

"Now you want to be friendly," he muttered.

"Don't let it go your head. It's not personal."

"You're afraid of the dark?"

"Not usually," she admitted. "But I think the phobia's starting to grow on me. Something about being trapped underground in an abandoned research facility with a bad reputation."

"Nothing's going to get to you," he said. "I'm the worst thing here."

"That's not very reassuring, you know?"

He laughed, a smoky sound that lowered into a purr at the end. "You want light?"

Her heart leapt at the thought. She'd never realized how much she relied on her eyesight, how much the thought made her feel so much safer. "Please."

He bent down, her fingers twisting in his shirt. "You can let me go, you know?"

Riley forced her fingers to open, clenching her hands into fists at her sides. The dark threatened to smother her, her breath coming as a loud rasp in the still room.

"Christ Jesus," he muttered. "I can almost taste your fear."

A witty retort died on her lips; all she could do was stand there and shake. Blue light sparked at knee level, and then a fluorescent globe overhead blazed to life, blinding her.

Riley took a deep, shuddering breath. The room was stark white, with a pristine warg cage in the corner, and piles of supplies. A comfortable-looking nest of grey, confederacy-issue wool blankets nestled in the center of the room, along with an assortment of clothes strung over a thin rope at eye level. There was a small cook oven in the corner, as well as a set of pots and pans. He must've had a generator somewhere, and a fuel supply, judging by the faint hum in the distance.

Surprisingly domestic. Wade had clearly been there a while.

Turning back to him slowly, she tried to catch her breath. Her heart was still racing, but the light had chased away the last vestiges of her panic-fueled phobia.

"You don't need a paper bag or something?" he asked. "To breathe into?" The silvery shine of his eyes seemed more pronounced. Or maybe that was the fluorescent light that made them seem brighter.

"I-I think I'll manage."

"Good." His expression hardened. Turning away, movements precise and controlled, he knelt in front of a pair of saddlebags and started rifling through them. Tension rolled across his broad shoulders.

Riley looked around. *What I wouldn't do for a wrench right now.* It might not kill him, but surely it would knock him out for a while. Enough time to escape.

Her gaze fell on the warg cage.

Good luck wrestling him into that.

"Don't," he warned, his voice cold and hard. It seemed entirely at odds with his earlier demeanor.

"Don't what?"

"Do whatever you were planning to do." Dragging something out of his bags, he turned and shot her a look that chilled her right through to the core. The monster rode him hard, staring out at her through those glacial eyes. "I can hear your heartbeat speed up."

Riley took a sharp breath and stepped back.

Wade bared his teeth at her then looked away. "It's the scent of your fear. It's... arousing."

Don't look down... Don't look... Too late. She caught a glimpse of hard, muscled thighs and the thick ridge of his cock, straining against the denim. But that wasn't the worst bit. From the look in those eyes, she realized he wasn't just talking about sex.

Riley's back hit the warg cage.

His eyelids lowered, body completely still except for the tick of his pulse in his throat. "Don't ever forget that I'm a monster, darlin'." Holding up a set of handcuffs, he gestured toward the cage. "These? Or the cage?"

Riley's hand wrapped around the cage bar behind her. "Why? Where are you going?"

"I need to hunt." He took a step toward her, warg-shine still glowing in his eyes.

"You said you wouldn't leave me here," she blurted. Funny, he might look like he was half-tempted to eat her, but the very thought of being trapped there in the dark alone terrified her more than anything.

Heat flared in his gaze. "I can't breathe without tasting your fear. Trust me, you don't want me to stay. So it's your choice, the cage or the cuffs. I won't be long. I just need to go kill something, let off a little steam. I'd rather it not be you. You still serve a purpose."

She licked her lips, looked at the cuffs. "Don't lock me in the cage."

"Hands out," he snapped.

Riley held them out, her teeth ground together. Grabbing her wrist, he snapped the manacle around it, then hooked her to the cage.

As soon as she was chained, the tension in his shoulders relaxed. "Don't miss me too much, sweetheart." Tossing her a blanket and a canteen of water, he turned and strode toward the door.

Within seconds, he was gone.

two

LUCIUS PEERED THROUGH the scope on his rifle, focusing on the narrow canyon track that led to Black Water.

A blur of movement shifted in the hot desert sand. A man in tattered clothes, crawling over the ground near the fence where they'd come in, sniffing at the air. No doubt following their scent. Whoever it was, it wasn't Lucius's scent that had caught his attention. No, it was that sweet cinnamon scent of Riley's, all hot, lush woman. More tempting than the smell of blood and animal flesh for a warg.

He'd known bringing her there would draw the attention of the settlers, maybe even McClain. What he hadn't counted on was the local wargs. The amulet around his throat kept his mind focused, his beast instincts caged in his body, trying to tear their way out. He wanted McClain. The woman was a means to that end. But the monster within him howled for her blood, her flesh. Wanting to shove her down and take her. The creature out there, prowling along his fence line, didn't have anything to fight off the surging instinct of the beast. All he'd be thinking about would be rutting with her.

One small native charm. That was all the difference between what he'd become, and that creature out there.

Lucius put the rifle down.

He could make the kill from here. Nice and quick. A bullet straight to the brain. But he was already on edge, pushed there by the scent of her fear, and the fact that he hadn't hunted for a month, hadn't let the beast off its chain. It was a constant battle of give and take, to keep his darkness leashed. He needed this to be bloody, both to satisfy the monster inside him and to make every warg in the area wary to take him on.

Sliding off the top of the building, he dashed across the shadowed yard beyond and hit the fence. It took him a second to scale it, then he vanished into a nearby gulch, moving so silently that his footsteps didn't even stir the powder-fine sand.

Circling around, he descended into the ravine that led to Black River. Odd footsteps tracked his own and the girl's. The warg, sniffing and shuffling as it hunted them. Lucius let himself make noise at that point, knowing the wind blew straight toward the creature.

By the time he stepped into the open, it was facing him, teeth bared and scraggly beard matted with dried blood. It had fed well the night before, no doubt. From the size of him, this was no creature that feared another. Lucius's eyes narrowed, sizing it up. Looked like a normal man, except for the crazy eyes, and the fact it roamed on all fours. More used to spending time in its beast shape than as a man. Some skin-shifters even became trapped like that. Maybe it was easier? Because then you'd never have to return to your human shape again, knowing what you'd done the night before. Giving it all over to the beastly half of himself might end bloodily, but he'd be nothing more than instinct then, hunger, hate, rage, *monster*... And a monster didn't care. A monster didn't feel the cold, hard bite of loneliness as he faced night after night by himself.

Maybe, he told himself. One day. But first, he had matters to take care of. Matters like revenge....

"Woman?" it hooted. "Where's woman?"

Lucius took a step toward it. "She's mine."

"Mine," it snapped, skittering toward him at breakneck speed.

Lucius splayed his hands out, letting the shiver of the beast out just enough to feel it on his skin. His fingernails lengthened, became claws. The warg was on him before he knew it, dangerously fast. No doubt fueled by human meat, and the rage of his inner monster. A dangerous opponent, when Lucius dared use only his man-shape. He smiled. *Might be an even matchup.*

He stepped to the side, claws raking across the warg's shoulders. Blood spattered across the sand, and the man screamed. Veins throbbed in the warg's temples as he turned, baring his teeth in a hiss. Pupils flashing, his shoulders suddenly expanded, tearing through his ripped flannel shirt. Thick, bulging muscles that had nothing to do with a human form. Only the obscene.

The warg roared, his face half-shifting, teeth elongating, and his eyes narrowing to thin slits. Lucius danced forward, striking out with his claws. The warg darted back, caught in half-shift. Normally, that would have bought Lucius the game, but this warg was old, clever. And he'd obviously managed to control his shifts long enough that the half-form gave him no disadvantage. Indeed, with those teeth, and his man's brain still mainly in control, this bastard had become a far more dangerous adversary than Lucius had predicted.

"Fuck it." He spun out of the way of those snapping teeth. But it was too late. Claws raked his thigh as the creature sprang for his throat.

Driving his fist up, Lucius buried his claws in the creature's stomach, using its momentum to shove it up and over his shoulder. It landed on cat-quick feet, and he barely had time to turn before it was on him again, driving him down toward the dirt.

Lucius twisted, bringing his fist forward in a solid punch. Blood sprayed the sand, and one of the warg's teeth moved. Its claws raked his gut, plowing white fire through him. Lucius ground his teeth together on a scream and twisted the creature into a wrestler's hold, one arm around its throat, his legs locked around its hips. Crushing it too close to him to do any damage. He yanked the warg's head back, bracing his forearm against its throat. The stench of its greasy, matted hair seared his nostrils along with the stink of decaying human flesh. No doubt it took its prey back to whatever it called home and ate it there.

"Leggo!" it rasped, raking at his forearms with its claws. No sound that should ever come from a non-human throat.

Lucius ground his teeth together and hauled back harder. A snap cracked through the air, one of its vertebrae. The body flopped onto his, breath rasping through its throat. Lucius twisted, making sure the neck was broken before rolling to his feet. He stunk, the warg's smell leeching into his clothes and skin. Turning away, bile burning in his throat, he ripped off his shirt and threw it away.

A fly buzzed around the body, sprawled obscenely on its back in the canyon floor. Lucius glanced at it then away, examining the low foothills. There'd be more wargs out there, but few of them ventured out during the day. It was too hot, and they mostly wore their human shapes during sunlight. Human logic would keep them in the shade near water. Only when the moon rose would they have no choice but to turn, the warg curse tearing through their bodies and bringing the beast to the surface. Only a few ever learned to control it.

Ignoring the body, he returned to his rifle on the roof, and the duffel bag of spare clothes he'd brought with him. The bloody slashes across his abdomen had stopped bleeding, beginning to crust as heat burned there. He swiped at it with a spare shirt, ignoring the pain. Sometimes pain was good. Reminded you that you were still human – or human enough.

Stripping off his jeans lessened the smell, but it wouldn't fade entirely. Not until he'd washed.

Fury simmered beneath the surface of his skin. The fight hadn't been long enough, or bloody enough. It had taken the edge off, but it wouldn't take much for him to rise to the killing edge again. He needed to go hunting.

And he needed to feed the woman.

Kill two birds with one stone.

This time, Luc took the rifle with him. One taste of sweet blood in his mouth and even the charm wouldn't be enough to hold him. He was on edge again, and he knew why. So many days, months, years alone, and there she was, invading his space with her sweet smell, and the dangerous allure of her fear.

Besides, the taste of raw deer flesh made the man in him sick at the thought. Or *not* sick. Maybe it was the opposite? Maybe the idea of craving it made him sick. It reminded him too much of what he could be.

Of what he had been.

▸————————▸ ◂————————◂

Noise echoed through the tunnels.

Riley lifted her head from her arms, her lungs seizing as she tried to listen. Wade coming back? Or something else?

Black River was notorious amongst the settlers at Haven. After the skies blackened in 2083 – the result of the meteor carving through half the Continent and sending dust clouds into the sky, joined by the smoke from the wildfires that ravaged the world – it had been abandoned as the world turned to shit. The scientific team who'd been in charge of the experiments had been trying to flee when something went wrong. Her grandfather had been part of the team that first entered Black River searching for survivors. Only three of a group of twenty had returned, raving about revenants eating human flesh and brains, about blood splashed over every wall, every surface... Her grandfather had never really recovered. He'd kept to himself mostly, though they'd had to sedate him in the end. Any sudden loud noises or bright lights could send him into a fury, where he wasn't quite sure who he hit, or tried to kill.

The other two survivors didn't last long either. One had died during the six years of the Darkening, when food grew scarce and people were forced to retreat to secret bunkers underground to survive. The other survived the Darkening, only to vanish out into the desert one night, muttering about the dead coming to life again.

Over the years, Black River became a rite of passage for local youths. Back before the reivers formed organized parties, her own father had been one of the kids who'd ventured out to see what secrets Black River owned. Or to find out what had driven his father mad, most likely. Four teenagers went in. Two came out. Nobody talked about the two bodies they never found, but the local settlements got together and passed a law. Nobody entered Black River. This entire swathe of land was off-limits.

Riley looked up sharply as noise sounded through the walls. Empty, clanking sounds that echoed from some distance away. Staying very still, she cocked her head to the side, trying to listen. There it came again. Another echo, like a lead pipe striking a wall.

She yanked hard on the metal bracelet around her wrist, skin tearing at the edges. She'd tried to undo it when Wade first left, to no avail. But this new fear spurred her on. Something was coming. Something deep in the facility. She just knew it.

There was no way she could get the handcuff over her wrist. Not without dislocating her thumb, which she was loathe to do. Her gaze strayed to the keys hanging from a hook on the far wall. She'd never reach them.

Glancing around revealed nothing long and thin with which to retrieve them. *Damn him. What I wouldn't give for a broom right now.* She glared balefully at the hook. It looked like plastic.

Breakable. She knew that. Her grandfather had collected old relics and items, anything pre-Darkening. He'd hit her once, when she played with an old toy truck and broke it. That was the last time her father let her visit him. She'd been seven.

A plan began to form. Standing up, Riley extended her foot, her hiking boot falling just short of the nest of blankets at the base of the wall. Straining, she stretched her whole body out, toes pointed, each muscle in her frame trembling. The tip of her boot landed on the edge of the blankets and Riley stilled, her heartbeat thundering in her ears. Hollow noise echoed through the wall, close to her ear. Swallowing hard, she edged the blankets toward her.

The thick wool was warm with Wade's scent. It wasn't entirely disgusting. Reminded her of a man – sweat, dirt, hard labor, and warm skin. Scowling to herself, she bent down and picked up one of the blankets, shaking it out before kicking the rest of them to the side. There was a thin mattress rolled out underneath, but Wade obviously didn't care much about comfort since the floor was hard linoleum, the blankets thin.

What had brought him out there?

Revenge against McClain? There had to be some reason for him to want the man dead, and it had been personal. The light of it had lit his eerie eyes, which meant he knew Adam McClain somehow.

McClain wasn't exactly a friend, though everyone else seemed to think him some kind of hero. His arrogance rubbed her the wrong way every time she heard his voice. McClain didn't ask people to do things, he told them as if he expected it done. For the last few months, he'd been pushing her to commit the people of Haven to him – to abandon their settlement and accept his protection. His argument was that the reivers were coming, and Haven had to be the next on their hit list.

Of course, McClain ruled one of the more old-fashioned settlements. His entire council included only one female, and that was his sister. He'd also made it quite clear that if Riley wanted a protector, she had only to ask. As if she hadn't spent the last six years of her life looking out for herself, or even earning her own spot on Haven's council.

He was a chauvinistic asshole, but he wasn't a bastard.

So, why would Wade want him dead?

And why should she care? All she needed to think about was how to escape him.

With a scowl, Riley flipped the ends of the blanket out straight, letting it settle on the floor. It took three throws before it rested against the far wall, nice and flat.

Wade had even left a pair of heavy boots behind. Riley dragged one toward her with the tip of her shoe, then hefted it. Nice and solid. Real leather with heavy soles crusted in red dust.

The boot hit the plastic hook dead-on, and the thing smashed to pieces. Riley blinked in surprise as the keys dropped neatly onto the blanket along with the boot, and the pieces of hook.

Well, what d'you know?

Grinning to herself, she grabbed the edge of the blanket and hauled it toward her. Slipping the key into the lock on her handcuffs, she clicked it, and the metal sprang open.

Free.

Ignoring the ominous clanking, she grabbed a spare pack and filled it with some of the foodstuffs he had stored in crates along the wall. Wade was there for the long haul, his provisions well thought out, if not exactly gourmet. Hardtack and dry biscuits, sourdough bread, a wheel of cheese, flour, sugar, tea, and canteens with fresh water in them. There was plenty of weaponry too. She stole a knife, testing the edge with her thumb before strapping the sheath around her thigh. An old military rifle with plenty of cartridges that looked like it had once belonged to one of the enforcers. A closer look showed they were silver shot, most likely for taking down a warg. It would work perfectly, as long as she wasn't overtaken by a roving band of enforcers, who'd want to know how she'd got it. They tended to shoot first, then ask questions.

How long had Wade been gone? Her eyes were grainy with exhaustion, but she didn't know how many hours had passed since he brought her there. A long time, she guessed. She'd napped briefly after the first flurry of trying to escape had failed. No doubt it was afternoon, or thereabouts.

Night fell swiftly here.

For the first time, Riley faltered. She knew the desert like the back of her hand. She also knew the rule number one for survival out in the Wastelands: don't get caught out alone at night. One sniff of her and every warg in the area would be on her trail.

A bottle of vodka caught her eye. With that fancy, dust-coated label, it'd be worth a fortune on the black market. Wade would kill her, but it would also dilute her scent. Maybe. It wasn't like there was any soap around. Biting the lid, she unscrewed it, then poured the vodka into her cupped palm and washed herself all over, until her skin was dry and thirsty.

It wouldn't be enough. Wargs had a fine sense of smell. Riley opened one of his packs and shimmied out of her shirt and shorts. She even swapped her own socks for his, though the boots she'd have to keep. Then she dragged an old, faded black shirt over her head. Wade's scent surrounded her immediately. His jeans were another matter; he was a large man, and she was slender. Wrapping his belt around her waist twice, she tore another shirt into strips, rolled up the hems of his jeans, and tied the strips around her ankles loosely so the material wouldn't unroll.

It would be warm outside now, but night was cold out here. She threw his heaviest wool sweater into her pack and looked around for anything else.

Nothing. She was as prepared as she was ever going to be.

And the clanking was getting nearer.

Dragging a crate into the center of the room, she reached up and eased the manhole open, peering out. The sunlight speared her eyes and she squinted, letting her vision adjust. There were two doors in the room below, but she wasn't venturing further into Black River, even if Wade was standing out there waiting for her. Whatever was making that noise was something she didn't want to run into.

Flipping aside the lid, she tossed the pack out and hauled herself up through the opening. The heat hit her immediately, shimmering on the hot sands. At least most of her skin was covered. She dragged another shirt out of the pack, wrapping it around her head and face. It would have been better if she'd worn white, but the heat wasn't the worst danger out here. And white would stand out at night like the fluorescent globes in the room below.

There was no sign of Wade. No sign of any wargs. Only his footprints, leading away toward the back of the building.

She peered toward the fence ahead, toward Haven. Time to find out if her folks were still alive. The settlement was well-guarded, but the reivers had been packing a fair bit of heat. Hopefully, Jimmy had gotten there in time to warn them.

The hot sun baked the back of his neck, his hat nestled low over his eyes. Ignoring the heat, Lucius peered through the sight on his rifle, watching the deer's ears prick. It knew he was out here. Somewhere. It just didn't know where.

He'd been tracking it for a mile. And keeping an eye out for warg tracks, but they were obviously tucked away after the previous night's gorging. He'd found a rabbit carcass — or the remains of some fur and a paw, anyway. Clear tooth marks that showed a warg in full-shift, to someone with an experienced eye. He'd been tracking them for years, even before he'd been clawed up and turned. A few hairs on a scraggly tree, the stink of urine against a rock... But they didn't come closer to Black River. They'd smell his own scent, find the body left out for the scavengers. Not much could kill a warg, and it'd make them wary.

Taking a deep breath, he let it out, smooth and slow. His finger eased over the trigger—

And a hint of darkness caught his peripheral vision. Lucius took his finger off the trigger, cursing under his breath. For a second, he thought it was a warg, but then he saw the sunlight gleaming off honey-blonde hair.

"Son of a bitch," he whispered, staring at his prisoner. Or his *ex*-prisoner.

Riley slipped through the canyon far below him with impunity, some insane turban thing wrapped around her face and head, with her hair tumbling out beneath it. The pack over her shoulders was his. The rifle too. His shirt.

His jeans. The bloody woman had somehow escaped her handcuffs, and stolen half his gear.

Lucius choked on a laugh. He'd underestimated her.

His eyes slowly narrowed, and he looked to where the deer had been. Gone. Dinner had vanished into the fading afternoon sunlight. He might have chased it, but he had larger prey to run down.

Blonde, eminently curvy prey. And a quick glance at the molten disc sinking toward the horizon told him he didn't have much time to do it.

Something caught his eye on the horizon. Dust. Like a car or a jeep. Bending low, Lucius frowned, peering through the scope. An armored jeep shot into view, a pair of heavyset men in the front and a gun turret mounted on the back. A hint of movement in the dust trail behind it — more jeeps, more men.

Reivers.

Fuck. He stood up and bolted across the rocks, throwing caution to the wind. They were following the only road out here.

And it led straight to Black River.

⇒⸺⸺⸺→ ←⸺⸺⸻◂

The shadows lengthened in the canyon. Riley traced the path they'd taken the night before, trying to check landmarks as she went. It had been dark, and the area around Black River was unknown to her, but every so often she caught the faint trace of a scuffmark. Wade moved almost invisibly, it seemed, but her own tracks weren't so untraceable.

She'd found a dead warg just beyond the fence, its dark eyes rolled back in its head, silvery light striking off the pupils. Bloody marks marred its abdomen, but the broken neck had been the thing that killed it. The sight had kept her wary for a mile, the gun lifting at the slightest sound. Wade had to be out here somewhere, but there'd been no sign of him. Only the eerie sensation of being watched sometimes.

Like now.

Riley stopped in the shelter of an overhang and waited, holding her breath. Being trapped in the canyon sucked, but it was the only way out. The scrape of something moving over the sandy track followed her. She eased the safety off Wade's rifle, pointing it toward the sound.

Hesitant footsteps followed her. Quiet. Wary.

A wet brown nose came into view, and a tan face with large black eyes. Riley eased out her breath, staring. A deer. A bloody deer. The wind was blowing toward her, not the deer.

She lowered the rifle and took a step out from underneath the overhang. The deer's legs stiffened, its knees bending as though to spring away.

"Hush there," she whispered. "Easy now."

It trembled, staring at her outstretched hand. Then its eyes widened and it looked up, behind her.

Riley spun, the rifle flying to her shoulder as a shape launched itself off the rocks behind her. Wade smashed the rifle down, landing lightly in front of her. Riley opened her mouth to scream but he clapped a hand over her mouth, shaking his head sharply. The deer was long gone.

Tension rolled through his shoulders. Eyes raking the canyon, he yanked her under the overhang. Riley froze. She might have tried to knee him in the balls, but the easy humor which usually rode him was gone. A cold, battle-hardened man stood in front of her in that moment, ready for a fight.

Something had spooked him.

"Reivers," he whispered. "Coming through the canyon. You need to follow me, and be quiet. Understood?"

Lucius Wade, psychopath warg, or a convoy of reivers?

She chose the lesser of two evils.

Easing her grip on the rifle, she nodded and let him lead her toward the sheer rock wall of the canyon.

"They're coming fast," he murmured. "Can you climb?"

"Like a monkey."

Slinging the rifle over her shoulder, she dug her toes into a narrow crevice in the wall and leapt up, grabbing a handhold. Wade shoved a hand under her ass, urging her on. She could hear him cursing as she scrambled up the rock, his warm body almost hot on her heels.

"How many jeeps?" she asked, arms straining as she climbed higher. Dragging herself over a lip of rock, she knelt on the small ledge, trying to catch her breath.

Wade's hand caught the edge and he shoved himself higher, sweat dampening the collar of his shirt. "Three."

Riley sucked in a sharp breath. Then reached for his hand.

Wade stared at her then took it, his own rasped with calluses. Their eyes met as his weight dragged at her. *Just let go and he'd be nothing more than a broken body on the ground far below....* The thought was enticing. Then she dragged him forward, onto the safety of the ledge.

Wade knelt low, peering over the edge. Dust was thick in the canyon, travelling toward them swiftly. He jerked her down, shoving a hand between her shoulder blades as he pressed her flat. There wasn't much room on the ledge. Lowering himself onto his palms, half his body covering hers, he peered below.

Hot breath curled over her ear, his thigh thrown over hers. Riley half-glanced over her shoulder, unnerved by his closeness.

"You could have done it," he whispered, his words stirring the damp curls at her ear.

Their eyes met. She knew exactly what he was talking about. "Don't think I didn't think about it."

"I know." A hint of dark humor curled his mouth. "I saw it in your eyes."

Below them, dust swirled, thick and choking. Wade's hand stroked over her back, settling against the base of her spine, but his gaze was locked on the road below, as if the movement was unconscious on his behalf. Riley's eyes narrowed. Maybe it was. Maybe not.

"What made you change your mind?" He leaned closer, breathed the words in her ear.

The first jeep shot through the curve of the canyon, one of the men laughing as it zoomed around the corner. Riley flinched, pressing herself deeper into the rock.

"I might be able to avoid the wargs out there, but not a band of reivers." Biting her lip, she added, "For all your talk, you haven't hurt me yet."

His eyes met hers. Pale, pale blue, with a hint of silver shine to the dark pupils. "You think I'm all talk?"

"No." He definitely had the capacity for violence. "I just think you haven't hurt me yet."

And he could have left her there in the dark, locked in that cage, but he hadn't. There was some trace of humanity left in him, just a hint of it.

Wade looked away, watching as another jeep shot through the canyon below, the image reflecting back off his eyes. "Don't trust me."

"I don't."

Their eyes met again. In perfect accord with each other.

"Next time," he whispered. "I *am* putting you in the cage."

Riley watched the last jeep shoot by, toward Black River. "You got another cage somewhere, do you?"

three

THE DUST SLOWLY cleared, the sounds of the jeeps fading in the distance, along with the whooping cries of the reivers.

Lucius put his hands underneath him, starting to rise when some sixth sense stirred the hairs on the back of his neck.

Riley opened her mouth and he clapped a hand over it, shoving them both flat again. Her warm brown eyes bulged in outrage, but she acquiesced. Her breath wet the palm of his hand, her chest rising and falling sharply. Another time and he might have let his gaze rove, but this wasn't the time. Or the place.

And she was definitely not the woman.

Silence settled over the canyon. The prickle along his spine grew, irritating him, like a trail of marching ants. Riley rolled her eyes toward him, as if questioning his sanity.

Lucius laid in wait.

Three seconds later, his patience was rewarded. A man stepped out from behind the corner below, carrying a heavy shotgun. He moved with the stealth of a military man, using finger gestures to direct his partner. A wide-brimmed hat shielded his face. The other guy followed on his heels, eyes roving the canyon, each foot placed with extravagant care as he tracked his gun around. Muscles bulged from his short-sleeved vest, rippling beneath the badly inked tattoo of a hawk that banded his arm.

Both of them paused. Dust stirred, the wind whispering eerily down through the canyon walls. Beneath him, Wade could feel the heat of Riley's body as she tried not to breathe.

The men lowered their shotguns. The one in the lead tugged his left glove off with his teeth, then fiddled with something on his wrist.

"Wade's not here," he muttered quietly, and Lucius's blood went cold.

Johnny Colton. In the flesh.

I thought I killed you back near Fort Lopez.

Obviously, that was one body he hadn't buried deeply enough. And if Colton was here, then Bartholomew Cane wouldn't be far behind. Colton was a dog of war, but Cane was the one with his hand on the leash.

Static crackled from below. Lucius caught a few words, enough to know they'd both been ordered back to the jeeps.

"Aye," Colton murmured, his eagle-eyed gaze raking the canyon. "Just keep your eyes open. Wade's a dangerous man."

With a few gestures to his comrade, he snapped his glove back on, put the shotgun to his shoulder again, and started backtracking the way he'd come.

Lucius waited a long time before he took his hand away from Riley's mouth. She sagged, taking a deep breath.

"You need to come with me. Now," he whispered. "Don't try to run, don't make too much noise."

"Who was that man? He knew you."

Grimly, Lucius levered himself to his feet. "An old friend who didn't know enough to stay dead."

Reaching out, he offered her a hand and hauled her to her feet. She stumbled against him, her foot having obviously fallen asleep. Unaware of her hand pressed against his chest, she tried to wiggle her boot to provoke blood flow.

"He was looking for you," she murmured. "I'm guessing it wasn't just to nurse a beer and share old hunting stories."

"That's not the question you ought to be asking."

Her full lips pursed, thoughts racing behind her eyes. "How did they know you were going to be here?" she murmured.

"Exactly."

Only one person knew the direction he was headed. Her eyes flared wide. "Jimmy," she whispered. "They got their hands on Jimmy."

Shouldering his gun, he peered up at the cliffs above them. There was no point risking the canyon track, and Black River was out of the question now. Lucky he was a man who liked to prepare for eventualities. He had two other stashes of equipment and food out in the desert. Two more hidey-holes he could tuck her up in, nice and safe. Black River was simply the most hospitable, with water and a generator he'd rigged for electricity.

"Guess your settlement dodged a bullet," he said, reaching up to grab a handhold. "He must have blurted out my name, made 'em change direction. Colton would have wanted me more than the settlement."

Riley caught his arm. "Where are you going?"

"Up."

"What about Jimmy?"

He gave her a sharp look, as if she were crazy. "I only need one hostage, and you're the prettier one. Something tells me McClain might be more interested in saving your backside than the boy's. And, chances are, he's dead."

"What if he's not? You know the reivers. Why kill someone when they might have a use for him? They sell what they don't want down south, at the borderland slave markets."

Lucius let go of the rock face and turned to face her. "What part of this situation don't you understand? You hostage. Me kidnapper."

She licked her lips. "What about all your stuff?"

"I've got more."

Anger flared on her face. Lucius watched her battle some thought, then turned back to the rock. "Follow me," he said.

"Wait!" She grabbed him again. "What if—What if I made it worth your while?"

Lucius laughed under his breath and raked her body with his gaze. "You've got to be offering something pretty damned good to make me risk my neck going into Black River against ten or so reivers and a pair of wargs."

"Wargs?"

"Colton and his friend," he snapped. "I've got some bad news for you, darlin'. Reivers and wargs teaming up? Your settlements out here are screwed."

"We got ways of dealing with the wargs."

"And the reivers? Their guns?"

Her chin tipped up. Stubborn as the day she was born, he'd bet. "I didn't think you were a coward."

Lucius laughed. "Nice try, but I don't give a shit what you think about me. I'm not here to be your hero, darlin'. I'm here to see McClain dead."

And then Colton and Cane, if he could.

Riley's fists clenched then relaxed. "You can't get near McClain, not if he stays at Absolution."

So McClain's at Absolution? Wade smiled.

"Correct," he replied. He'd seen the walls guarding the settlement, and the gun towers. Absolution was the most defensible settlement out here in the Badlands. He'd scouted them all, hunting for signs of his enemy. "That's where you come into it."

"What if I could get you McClain?" she blurted.

Lucius stilled. And looked at her.

"Without Jimmy, McClain will never know you've got me," she replied. "He won't come after you like you planned."

"Then I'll find someone else to play messenger."

"And if he comes, he'll come in force," she replied. "What if I could get him to come alone?"

"Through your magic powers of persuasion?" He glanced down again. "You're a nice little piece, but McClain's not stupid, and I don't think you've got a seductive bone in your body."

"Because I haven't used it on you?" she asked sweetly, then rolled her eyes. "McClain offered to be my protector two years ago. Trust me, I can get him alone. The man won't take no for an answer."

Well, now. That was interesting. Lucius eyed her with more consideration. She was pretty, all blonde hair, big brown eyes, and long, lean lines. Strong. A hint of curves where a woman should have them. A stubborn cleft in her chin that hinted at her personality. That was warning enough for any sane man.

And intriguing. A woman who threatened to shoot him, who somehow managed to escape his handcuffs and get herself out of Black River as easy as if she were taking a stroll? Yeah, that'd appeal to McClain. Hell, he could see the appeal of it himself.

Lucius turned his body toward her. "I get the boy back, you bring me McClain? Alone, no weapons."

"You get weapons, he gets weapons," Riley retorted. "I'm not going to lead him to his slaughter, but I'll give you a fighting chance."

"Too kind of you."

"My money's on McClain."

She'd never seen him in action. "It's a deal."

Riley hesitated, but then held her hand out. "Only if Jimmy's alive."

Lucius yanked her close to him, capturing a handful of that glorious golden hair. "You break your word and I'll make you regret it."

Riley put a hand against his chest. "You put your hands on me again and I'll kill you."

Her hair was softer than he'd expected. Lucius let it run through his fingers like wet silk. He squeezed her hand. "Done. But you're coming with me. I'm not going into Black River alone, hoping you're going to be sitting there, twiddling your thumbs, waiting for me to get back."

"I wouldn't leave Jimmy behind."

He let her go. "I'm still going to need someone to watch my back. Colton I can take, but maybe not two of them."

"You want me to go back into Black River?"

Lucius grinned, stepping back and gesturing to the rock wall in front of them. "Yep. Why? Afraid of all the monsters in the dark there?"

"There's something in there. I could hear it. It freaked me the hell out."

"Which is why you ran?"

"Part of the reason." Riley dug her toes into a toehold and heaved herself up the wall. "Mostly, I was trying to get away from you."

Wade led her around the facility. Night was falling, and both of them could clearly see the cook fires the reivers had set up out in the open, in front of the main building at Black River. Kneeling on the top of a cliff, Wade stretched out flat on his belly and peered through the sight of his rifle.

"I've got the two wargs," he said. "Eight... Nine reivers. Others must be inside." A slight pause. "There's the boy."

Riley tapped his shoulder. "Can I see?"

Wade shifted slightly, letting her lie down beside him. Moonlight silvered his tanned skin, highlighting the growth of dark stubble along his jaw. She could feel his eyes on her as she peered through the sight, a slightly uncomfortable feeling. Especially with the chorus of warg-song fluting high over the desert winds.

The camp leapt into view, men sprawled about with abandon, sharing the remnants of a meal. One of the wargs paced along the perimeter. The other was nowhere in sight. Reivers might be lazy when it came to defending their camps – or arrogant – but the wargs were obviously not.

"I don't see him," she whispered, watching the one he'd called Colton sit in the shadows of a jeep, wetting the paper on his cigarette.

"Tied to the back of the jeep," he replied, voice emotionless.

Riley swung the gun then sucked in a breath. Jimmy was hog-tied, his face swollen and black, a gag tied painfully tight through his bared mouth. One of the reivers knelt beside him and hauled him to his knees, then started dragging him toward one of the buildings.

"They beat him." She swallowed hard.

"Could have been worse."

Riley shot him a glare. The son of a bitch had the empathy of a rock. "Fuck you. He's just a kid."

Wade's eyes narrowed sleepily. "I'm only speakin' the truth. There ain't a lot of women out here. And reivers ain't real particular."

"Neither are wargs," she shot back.

His eyes darkened. She'd scored a hit, though she didn't know how. "If I weren't that particular, I'd have had you in the first hour. True?"

He wanted to force her to admit it. Riley ground her teeth together.

"I ain't touched you, darlin'. I ain't made a single move, and I could have. So you take that back, or the deal's off."

"Fine," she snapped. "You're the exception."

Wade smiled. "Did that hurt?"

"I'd like to make something hurt," she muttered under her breath.

"I'll bet."

He took the gun off her and slung it over his shoulder. Starlight glimmered behind his shoulders, outlining the stark shadow of his shape. He'd stripped to a black tank, the pewter chain around his throat tucked under the neckline. They didn't have enough weapons, but Wade didn't seem concerned.

A thought struck her. "It's night," she said. "You're not going to go all hairy on me, are you?"

A sidelong glance through those wickedly thick lashes. He stroked the amulet around his throat through the tank. "This keeps it under control. I lose this, and you better get the hell out of there."

"Colton and his friend were human too."

Wade looked away. "Colton's got one too. I can only assume he found another one. The shaman who made them for us died not long after, so maybe they found someone else."

"So that's how you stop it," she mused, her gaze running hungrily over the metal. "There'd be a lot of people out here who'd pay good money for that. We all lose friends, family...."

"You mean you shoot them," he said, watching the settlement carefully. "Before the first change."

Riley fell silent. "What else are we supposed to do? If I ever got turned, I'd want someone to kill me. We all would." She thought of her father and the sacrifices he'd made. "But if there was another option...."

"You'd what? Lock them in a cage until you got your hands on one of these? Then what?" Wade snorted. "I've seen how that game gets played, darlin'. Nobody wants a monster in their midst, no matter if they're leashed or not. They're better off dead."

Riley opened his mouth, but he cut her off with an abrupt slicing motion of the hand. "No," he said. "You talk too much. Now you need to shut your mouth and follow me. The reivers are moving inside, probably to sleep. You and I are going in under the south caves. We'll come at them from within."

Within? Riley swallowed hard then nodded. The ground surrounding the compound was too open, and the jeeps each had a heavy, mounted spotlight. They'd never get close enough, even if the wargs didn't hear them coming beforehand.

Caves it was then.

There was a small animal track heading along the cliffs that cut off Black River from the south. Wade led her along it, both of them plastered against the cliff face as they edged their way forward. Sweat drenched Riley's hair and shirt, but Wade moved as if he did this every other day.

"Not far now," he whispered. "Caves are just ahead."

"How'd you find them?" she muttered.

Wade suddenly disappeared, and Riley's heart started thumping. She hurried forward, then saw the narrow opening that disappeared into pitch black. A hand reached out and hauled her inside. Riley stifled a squeak of surprise, almost anticipating the hand over her mouth.

It didn't come.

"Keep walking," he murmured. "We'll strike a light up ahead. Just hold on to me, and don't let go."

His hand was hard and callused around hers. An odd feeling. Riley staggered through the darkness, feeling almost trapped in some airless vacuum. The only link to the world was Wade's hand, and the knowledge that his warm, broad body was just a step ahead of her. She had to fight the urge to grab hold of him with her other hand, just to reassure herself that he was there.

He stopped and Riley hovered at his side, her body trembling. "You need to calm down," he whispered. "It's a wonder they haven't heard you breathing."

Riley swallowed, her eyes rolling. "I can't help it. It's just so dark. I can hardly breathe."

"There's plenty of air."

"I know that," she snapped. "It's just so still in here. No wind. I can almost feel the mountain pressing down on me." The thought sent a droplet of sweat between her breasts. "Oh, God," she whispered. "What if the tunnel narrows? What if it collapses?"

Warm hands cupped her face. An electric presence she could almost feel along her skin as his breath trembled over her cheeks. She found she could breathe a little easier, knowing he was there.

"The tunnel doesn't narrow. I've been this way."

She could see nothing in the dark beyond his faint silhouette. But she looked up anyway. The soft pads of his fingertips stroked lightly across her cheeks.

"Where's your courage now?" he whispered. "Where's that brash, in-my-face attitude you've been throwing at me at every chance?"

Riley licked her lips. "You left me underground."

"I left the lights on."

"There was something coming. Something deep in the facility... And you left me there." Her breath was a harsh pant. She clenched her fists, hating the vulnerability. She'd always been tough. Her daddy had taught her to pick herself up when she fell, and this was no different. But she couldn't chase away the fear prickling over her skin, or the sensation that a vise was slowly squeezing her chest.

"I won't leave you here, darlin'. I promise."

Riley looked up, though the world was nothing but darkness. The words were close, whispered. But how much could she trust them? How much could she—

Warm lips brushed her own. The world stilled, and Riley froze with it as Wade kissed her. So light, almost a phantom touch, the whisper of his mouth like cool silk after the hot desert sun. Her lips parted on a gasp, and he stepped closer as if that were permission, hands cupping her face, his mouth covering her own.

He kissed her slowly, as if there were all the time in the world. As if he knew she wouldn't – couldn't – push him away. The first brush of his tongue made her shiver, her hands rising to his chest hesitantly. This was madness. She'd never felt the way she did right then. All hot and shivery, her nipples hardening into tight peaks. His tongue brushing her own, dancing with it, tempting her to kiss him back.

Before she could realize what she was doing – what she was letting him do – he lifted his head. "There now," he murmured, humor thick and lazy in his voice. "Now you're not breathing at all. Won't nobody hear us coming now."

He laughed softly.

"Son of a bitch." Riley shoved him away, her hand drifting to her lips. She could taste him still, feel the imprint of his chest against her fingertips. What the hell had she just done? Or let him do, rather? She could pretend as much as she liked, but she'd offered not one ounce of token protest.

She spun around, but the world was a wall of blackness. "Don't you ever do that again."

"Now she protests," he muttered under his breath, turning away from her. "Don't get excited. Just tryin' to take your mind off things. Looks like it worked."

Worked? Her lips burned and she could taste him still, the imprint of his touch burned into her skin. "I wasn't getting excited," she retorted. "Just so you know."

Faint laughter. Her hands balled into fists, but he was right. She wasn't thinking about the oppressive dark anymore. She couldn't get the memory of that kiss out of her head.

The sound of flint striking echoed in the darkness and a small light flared. Wade held his piece of tinder up, searching for something along the walls. "There it is." He reached up and flipped a switch. "Emergency lights. Solar-powered." Tracks of light sprang up along the walls, shooting away into the darkness. It was just enough to highlight the tunnel ahead, some of them buzzing and spitting from disuse. "Come on, princess. This way."

Riley stared ahead. There'd be more dark, more enclosed spaces. And maybe whatever had been making that noise. But this was the only way to get Jimmy back, and though she didn't have any family left, out here in the Badlands, the people of her settlement *were* family. She'd been in charge of their expedition, and she'd made the choice to hunt one more nestling, knowing the sun was sinking toward the horizon. If she'd left it alone, she and Jimmy would have gotten back nice and early, and none of this would ever have happened.

Steeling herself, she took a deep breath and brushed past him. "Call me 'princess' again, and I'll crown you."

A soft chuckle followed her down the tunnel.

The floor was worn smooth, the tunnel carved from the mountain. The light was just enough to see by. "This is obviously man-made," she whispered. "Who makes a tunnel that ends at a cliff face?"

"Someone who wanted an escape route."

"Escape from what though? What were they doing out here?" Silence greeted this question. Riley risked a glance toward him, certain she'd find him still gloating, but the only expression on his face was an intense one. "How'd you know this existed?"

Blue eyes flickered toward her. "Maybe I did some exploring when I first set up camp."

"Yet you never came across anything that might have been making a noise?"

"Maybe it didn't want to come across me." Wade glanced ahead. The tunnel ended in a corner. He put a hand out and Riley stopped, letting him go ahead. The shotgun in hand, he peered around the corner, and then slowly stepped around it. "Lights are out in this section," he said. "Strange."

Riley wet her lips. *Buck up, princess.* Somehow, her inner voice sounded a lot like Wade. "You hear anything coming?"

"Barely." He gestured her forward. "You're making more than enough noise to cancel anything else out."

Scowling, she stepped closer to him. "How far does this section go?"

"A quarter mile," he murmured. "Then there's a heap of steps that open into the lower level, where most of the quarantine cells were."

"Are there lights ahead?"

"Hopefully." A slight pause. "Though there should be lights here too. The globes can't all have busted."

"Come on then." She swallowed hard. "You're a warg. You should be able to smell anything coming, shouldn't you?"

A long, weighty silence.

"Follow me." All traces of humor had dropped from his voice. She was surprised at the brusque tone and no-nonsense nature.

Was there more to Wade than she'd first expected? Hints of an almost military efficiency kept sneaking through. As though the devil-may-care attitude was just a façade, easily worn, easily cast aside.

Footsteps shuffled and she scurried after, running straight into his broad back. He caught her by the hip, holding her still as he sniffed the air. His palm was warm through her jeans, the heat of his body seeming to leech through to her skin. "Hold my shirt," he said. "Don't make any noise. If I tell you to run, you get the hell out of here."

"What is it?"

"I don't like this." Wade breathed deeply. "Something stinks."

"Like what?" Riley could detect only the faintest, slightly musty odor.

There was a long moment of silence. The darkness only made it heavier. "How badly do you want the boy back?"

Riley's heart leapt into her throat. "Why? What is it?" What could scare a man like Wade? What would a monster fear? Unfortunately, her mind could provide all sorts of answers, here in the dark.

"You were right," he murmured. "There is something here. Something that stinks of rot."

Her breath caught in her throat. "Revenants?"

"Revenants," he confirmed. "So, I'm asking again... How much does the boy mean to you? Because I'm fairly sure we're not alone down here."

four

WHEN THE WORLD blackened and turned, the wargs weren't the only creatures to come out of the shadows. Stories had been passed down from the old folk at Haven about men who'd hidden in underground bunkers and caves near the Great Divide. Years passed, the skies cleared, and settlers began to venture back into the world. Communities began to form, and traders travelled from bunker to bunker. There was a rumor of precious minerals being found near the site where the meteor hit. Minerals that were rare on Earth, like iridium. Hundreds headed into the Great Divide, near the landing site, digging in and settling down, trying to scrape out enough to sell to the tech whizzes in the Eastern Confederacy.

And then, one day, the meteor site went quiet, where they'd been digging below to get at chunks of the meteor. All the miners who lived there never came out of those tunnels again.

The nearest mining camp sent others in, shielded by gas masks and old pre-D hazmat suits. They found every single one of the bodies down below and took them back for a decent burial. A gas leak, some claimed.

Three days later, the bodies crawled out of the earth they'd been buried in, and one thing became very clear — they weren't human anymore.

Whatever the pathogen was, it hadn't come from Earth.

Riley's breath caught in her chest, and she shook her head. "Revenants." Only one thing frightened her more than the thought of being alone in the dark. They said once a revenant got hold of you, they didn't stop to kill you first before they started eating. And being eaten alive made you one of the lucky ones.

Her fingers curled in Wade's shirt. For a moment, fear was so thick in her mouth that she thought about turning around, leaving Jimmy to his fate.

Coward.

She'd never forgive herself. But at least she'd be alive.

"Well?" Wade's sultry voice pushed at her. "Your choice, darlin'. Though I'm inclined to get the hell outta here."

"They might not smell us," she whispered, arguing with herself as much as him. "We might get past them. There's a lot of tunnels down here, aren't there?"

"Dozens," he confirmed. "But I don't like your chances."

"Why?"

"Can't you hear that?"

Riley cocked her head. Silence. "Nothing."

"I can hear something moving. They like the dark, the cool," he said. "That's why you find 'em in mines and caves. Which means they don't see real well. They hunt by scent. Best we go back."

Jimmy. She bit her lip. When he was just born, she'd been only a little girl. Mabel had let her in to see him, with his bright thatch of fine red hair and blinking, sleepy expression. He'd been the little brother she'd never had. A bit too scrawny to keep up with the other kids, he'd been mocked by the boys for his red hair. Riley had taken pity on him, teaching him the things every borderlander needed to know. How to hunt, to fight, to use a gun, knife and bow.

Heck, she'd only recently taught him to drive.

"How do we kill them?" she asked.

Silence.

"Better to ask how do we avoid getting eaten ourselves?" he said in a disgusted voice. A sigh. "We're going after the kid, aren't we?"

Riley nodded, before she could change her mind. "I'm not leaving him in the hands of reivers."

"You're a fool," he said softly.

"You're still going to help me?"

"Gave my word, didn't I?"

Another incongruity. "I wouldn't have expected that to hold."

His hand slid from hers. "You know nothing about me." He gave a jerk and his shirt tore from her grasp. Riley found herself half-reaching for him.

Fabric rustled, and she could hear his breath near her waist. "What are you doing?" she asked.

He rifled through her pack. "Need a torch," he grunted. More fabric rustled. The sound of his shirt sliding over his shoulders. "Hold this."

He shoved the gun into her hands.

Two seconds later, flint rasped and fire flickered, highlighting Wade's kneeling form. Riley caught just a glimpse of burnished skin and his tight black tank before it died, leaving her retinas scarred with the image of him.

One more flicker, and the light caught. Wade yanked a battered flask out of his hip pocket and tore his shirt into strips. He dampened the shirt, wrapped it around a stick, and lit the end. Fire bloomed. It wasn't great, but it would do.

Stuffing the flint into his pocket, he lifted the homemade torch high, the muscles in his shoulder straining. Both of them peered down the passage.

"I assume you know how to shoot? Something more than a man's foot?" he asked.

"I hunt," she replied. The shotgun's weight took away some of her fear. That and Wade's brusque tone. He moved like a man who knew what he intended to do. That was almost as reassuring as the gun.

"Hold this," he said, handing her the torch. Its heat scalded her skin, but she held it. Wade knelt and dragged the hem of his jeans up, revealing heavy boots and a knife sheathe strapped around his calf. The knife glided free with a steely rasp, and he spun it in his fingers as if learning the feel of it. Blue eyes met hers. "You see anything, you shoot it. Between the eyes if you can. Don't go for a body shot. It barely slows 'em, unless the impact knocks them down. If you can't hit the head, go for the knees. Don't leave one at your back, you'll be amazed what they can survive. So a shot to the knee, then one to the head when it goes down. Stop shooting when it stops moving, not before. Don't get within range of their hands. They're faster than you think."

"You've come up against a revenant before?"

"I used to hunt 'em." His gaze roved the corridor. Head cocked. Listening. He reached back for the torch. "Was a bounty hunter once. Out on the Rim."

"Is that how you got clawed up?"

He shot her a short look. Question time over. "Only other way to kill a revenant's by fire." He gestured at the torch in his hand. "I don't need to see. That's there to make sure they stay down."

"Got it."

He gave her his back, standing lightly on his toes, peering into the darkness ahead. Tension rippled across his broad shoulders, and his grip flexed on the hilt of the heavy hunting knife. "You get bitten, and I'll shoot you myself."

A terrifying thought. Her mouth went dry. "Thanks."

"Try not to get bitten though. I need you in one piece."

Riley shot a hard glare at his back. Prince Charming in all his glory. "Won't the wargs hear the shots?"

"Plan's changed. Do you want the boy or not?"

"Yes."

"Fine. They know we're here," he said. "The shot'll echo through the mountains. They'll think we're coming from outside."

"But they'll still know we're coming. We've lost the element of surprise."

He shot her one last hot look over his shoulder, the flames glinting off the hard sapphire of his eyes. "Darlin', your task is to survive the revenants. Then think about the job ahead."

***

Damned foolish quest.

A frown tugged his brows down, and Lucius stared into the dark as he crept along the passage. The cause for the lack of light soon became clear – every fluorescent globe had long since been smashed, pieces of it littering the floor and crunching beneath his boots.

He didn't even know why he was doing this. Why bother with the boy? He had what he wanted – a way to get at McClain. All he had to do was gag Riley, toss her over his shoulder, and head out into the desert. He'd never even give the boy another thought.

Riley swallowed hard behind him. And that, he thought, was his reason. Fear rolled off her in waves. Terrified of the dark, of being left alone, of the revenants, and she was still willing to risk this. If she could face her fears, then he wouldn't stop her. An odd mix of admiration and frustration rolled through him. The woman was hellish tough, yet strangely vulnerable. A damned tempting combination.

Besides, he'd given his word.

Something shuffled in the dark ahead. Lucius held his hand up, and the sudden silence told him she'd frozen. A little rasp sounded as she sucked in a breath.

Dust stirred. One. Two. Maybe three creatures. More behind them. Dull cataract-filmed eyes reflected the firelight. No sound of breathing – they didn't as a rule. Which meant they couldn't make a single noise. Silent predators that haunted the dark depths of the borderlands. More a soulless construct now, rather than a personality. All they felt was hunger.

His grip on the knife eased. *Come on, you bastards.* It had been a long time since he'd hunted revenants. Out on the Rim, when he'd ridden as a hunter, they'd earned fifty credits a scalp. A man could feed his entire settlement on that kind of money. Course, the risk was greater than the reward, and he'd been human then. Indestructible. Young and fucking stupid.

Lucius took a step forward, knife held defensively. He wasn't stupid anymore. He knew the monsters bit back now.

It didn't take long for them to overcome their wariness. Wasn't much to eat out here in the desert, besides the odd coyote or rabbit. Human flesh was just too irresistible, even if the scent of him warned them off.

The lead revenant loped out of the shadows with an odd shuffling gait. It moved quickly, despite the shamble, and the stink hit him full on. Lucius twisted out of the way, sinking the knife into its throat and slicing through the thick, corded muscle. He spun on his heel, torching the straggly ends of the creature's ratty hair. The stink of burnt hair made him gag, but the fire spread like a lightning strike on dry tinder. Leapt from the dreadlocks to the rough shirt the revenant wore, turning into an inferno.

The creature's mouth opened in a silent scream, and it tore at its burning hair.

"Oh, my God. Oh, my God," Riley panted. She worked the shotgun with both hands, her eyes showing far too much white as she pumped it. Strain tightened her mouth, but she aimed into the shadows and pulled the trigger.

The shotgun roared.

Lucius stepped back, kicking the creature in the chest. It staggered back into the oncoming rush of revenants, and three of them went down in a twitching, burning heap. Decaying flesh melted like wet sludge as the cleansing flames leapt from creature to creature.

The one Riley had shot twitched on the ground, a hole blown clean through its forehead. She stepped up to his side, pumped the shotgun, and blew the rest of its head off.

Good girl.

"Come on," he growled, shoving her in the back. "Keep moving. We're only drawing attention here. There's more coming."

A pair of them shuffled back in the darkness as he stepped forward, waving the torch in a threatening arc. Keeping an eye on the burning heap, he stepped past and gestured Riley after him as she frantically reloaded.

The torch was slowly dying. Lucius reached down and ripped the smoldering femur off one of the revenants before discarding the torch. The sticky flesh and rotting clothes burned a sickly green at the end of the bone, but it was light.

He arched a brow when he saw her sickened gaze. "What?" he mouthed.

He'd seen a hell of a lot of worse things in his time. He'd done worse things. The urge to survive had driven away the last of any squeamishness he might have had.

The corridor was littered with bones as they stalked down it. Mostly squirrel and coyote, but the occasional human skull gleamed in the shadows. Revenants hovered just out of sight. They hunted in packs because they were cowards at heart. One sign of weakness though and they'd be upon him, burying him in numbers, their blunt, stained teeth tearing at his flesh.

A shadowy figure swathed in rags lunged at them from a niche in the rock face. Riley shot it in the face, stepping forward grimly as she blew holes in its head. Her expression was stark, her eyes panicked. But her hands never shook.

"You're gettin' the hang of that," he said.

She gave him a thin-lipped smile, reloaded, then jerked the barrel to her shoulder and aimed at him. Lucius swung his arms up to cover his face, but the shot went wide.

Something hit the floor behind him. He looked down at the twitching creature that'd dropped from the ceiling and was silently screaming. One sweep of the improvised torch and the revenant started burning, its body writhing in sickly green flames. Lucius looked up. Son of a bitch had been waiting for him.

"You get bitten and I'll shoot you myself," Riley threw his own words back in his face, stepping past him with the gun held warily.

"That's one of the benefits of being a warg," he replied, following her. "Immunity from certain infections."

"Didn't ever think there'd be a benefit," she muttered.

He bared his teeth in a smile. "Silver linings and all, darlin'."

They reached the stairs with no further mishaps. Something had carved a tunnel just past the stairs into the cavern systems. A revenant hissed at him from the shadows, and Lucius stepped forward threateningly. It scurried backward, its milky-white eyes gleaming. He flung the femur after it, and a wall of flame surged up as it struck the creature's dry clothes and flesh, revealing a whole horde of the damned zombies in the cave beyond.

Dead eyes watched them hungrily, making even him take a step back. The skin on their faces had tightened and drawn back with death, so their stained teeth looked longer and their eyes bulged. There was nothing left of the men and women they'd once been. The pathogen that fueled their cells and made them viable again existed only to feed, to spread the revenant disease.

"Jesus." Riley wet her lips, easing up the stairs backward, one foot at a time.

Lucius eyed the pack, then followed her. "You don't usually see so many together."

"A lot of folks went missing here, years back." She took another step. They were moving deeper into the shadows now. One of the revenants crept out of the cavern, watching them with hungry eyes. "Folks from Haven," she murmured. "I keep wondering if I'll recognize faces."

Lucius grabbed her arm. "Come on. Let's move. Save the sentiment for later."

Riley yanked her arm out of his grip. "You're a cold-hearted bastard, you know?"

He looked at her. Just looked.

He knew.

"You want the boy back or not? Keep your focus. Don't let me down now."

"I won't," she snapped.

The stairs led to the basement levels of Black River. Wade flipped a switch and the emergency lights hummed to life, revealing stark white walls that were almost ghostly in the faded light. The heavy iron door slammed shut behind them, blocking the entrance into the caves... and keeping the revenants locked down in the darkness.

Each cell was sealed, the dusty door slits hiding the blackened interiors. Riley looked at them nervously. Any one of them could be hiding a revenant or two, though the majority downstairs had seemed content to wait in the caves. Something about their knee joints and stairs that didn't mix well. They could get up them, but it would be a slow progress.

"What the hell were they doing here?" she whispered. "With all these cells?" They'd passed a medical examination room, with the steel chains still hanging from the examination table. Rusty stains marred the white linoleum.

Wade's vivid blue gaze speared her. "Experiments."

"I know that. But on what?"

He shrugged, but his voice was quiet when he answered, "Wargs. The government wanted to know what they were, where they come from. And how to use them as weapons.

"They were also performing gene splicing. Trying to mix breeds. That's how they created the shadow-cat – half wolf, half cougar, a hint of something else. They thought that might have been how we came about. Who knows if they were right? Some say wargs have been here for centuries, we just hid it better then. But you can't chain a monster down for long."

The eerie cells took on a new meaning. "You think that's what happened here? The wargs got free?"

"Most likely." A bleak smile. "Bet that scared the hell out of 'em."

"You find that amusing?"

A hot look that froze the blood in her veins. A look that spoke of a lot of hurt, of pain. Of vengeance. "Yeah," he said. "I find that amusin'. Look around you, Riley. Just because we're monsters doesn't mean that we don't feel it when you cut us open. I don't like wargs none, but that don't mean I think much of humans either. Or the type of human that did this," he said, looking around.

Wade strode ahead of her.

Riley settled into a considering silence. The more she learned about him, the more she began to question everything she knew. Wargs were monsters. Everybody knew that. But Wade was an exception she simply couldn't define.

A cold-hearted prick who'd straight-out told her he planned to use her to kill a man. He was the first to tell her what a monster he was. There was no sympathy, no softness. Just the occasional moment when she wondered if there was something more to the man than he professed.

A strange yearning filled her. A need to know. To understand him. Riley glanced at his broad back, wondering if the stress was doing funny things to her mind.

They climbed through the next two levels without incident. Wade moved slower, leaving the lights off. They'd reached ground level, and enough moonlight gleamed through the windows to see. Outside, the reivers had manned their gun turrets and were sweeping the flat field with their spotlights. Wade was little more than a shadow amongst shadows.

He grabbed her arm and pressed her into the corner suddenly. One hand clapped over her mouth.

Riley froze, the gun pressed between them, and every hot, hard inch of Wade forcing her against the wall. The sweeping lights outside washed over the pair of them, highlighting the very-blue of his eyes, and the stark shadow under his cheekbones. A heavy graze of stubble lined his jaw.

"Reiver," he mouthed.

Slowly, he removed his hand from her mouth and held a hushing finger to his lips. He took a step back, urging her to stay where she was.

The shadows swallowed him. Riley held still, her heart thundering in her ears. Every sweep of the lights lit up the stark furniture in the room. A meeting room, by the look of it. Twelve chairs around a table, and an old projector half-torn from the wall.

A quiet scuffle caught her ears. She licked her lips, shifted her grip on the gun. She was out of shells, but she could still use it as a club.

Wade reappeared in the doorway and gestured to follow him. His breathing raced, chest rising and falling in a quickened rhythm. From the look on his face, he'd enjoyed the kill just a little too much. The silver charm around his neck winked at her as he turned.

The reiver lay in a twisted heap on the floor, a puddle of dark liquid soaking across the linoleum beneath him. He probably hadn't even known what had grabbed him.

Riley paused then knelt beside the body, yanking the gun from its cooling clutches. Wade was watching her when she stood, then nodded as she tossed him the spent shotgun.

He stopped beside a closed door, pressing his ear against the heavy steel. His hand slid over the curve of her back, holding her there. Pressing his lips against her ear, he whispered, "I can hear movement. The boy's whimpering."

Her chest squeezed. *Jimmy.* The poor kid.

Riley nodded, quietly cocking the hammer back on the handgun. The click echoed in the empty hallway.

Wade shook his head. "Stay here," he murmured. "I'll get him."

She caught his arm as he started to ease the handle open. Wade met her gaze and shook his head slowly.

"I'll bring him back to you," he promised. "Just watch my back."

Then he vanished through the crack in the door.

Leaving her alone with a cooling body on the floor.

The reiver was standing over the kid, swigging from a bottle. He started undoing his belt, completely oblivious to the danger that stalked him from behind.

Lucius stepped up behind him silently, grabbing him across the mouth and tilting his head back. One quick slash of the knife and the body kicked feebly, the bottle tumbling from its hand.

He caught it with his boot – thank God for lightning-quick reflexes – then eased it onto the pile of blankets the reiver had obviously taken over. His own goddamn blankets. The warg cage gleamed silver in the night, and his packs had been rifled through, his supplies scattered and torn.

The kid, Jimmy, was hog-tied and gagged. He shivered in the dark, the scent of urine staining the air. So frightened he was almost oblivious with it.

Cocking his head, Lucius listened intently. There were shouts from outside. Curses. Someone sprayed a few warning shots into the gulch beyond from the gun turret. No doubt that's where Colton and his friend would be, hunting for him.

Certain they were alone, he let the body drop and knelt beside the kid. A rough jerk and the gag was free. Before the kid could scream, he clapped a hand over his mouth and leaned close, whispering in his ear. "Riley's waiting for you."

The skinny frame collapsed in relief. A sob caught in his hand. Wade ground his teeth together; the kid was near hysterical, a mess. No use trying to sober him up, or shake some sense into him. No time either. Looking around, he lifted the hilt of the blade and dealt Jimmy a neat blow to the back of his head.

It took mere seconds to fetch everything he needed, stuffing it in one of his duffels. Then he hoisted the kid over his shoulder and headed back the way he'd come.

Riley was waiting for him as he made it through the maze of rooms. As he stepped through the door to where he'd left her, he was greeted with the barrel of the handgun. Her eyes widened when she saw the boy slung over his shoulder, and the gun lowered.

"Jimmy," she whispered, reaching out to touch his dangling legs. A suspicious shine brightened her pretty eyes. "What happened to him? What'd they do?"

"I knocked him out." At her sharp glare, he held up a hand. "Kid's hysterical. And we need to move fast. You can rip strips off me later."

"I'll hold you to that promise," she warned, a touch of her old stubbornness tipping her chin up.

"Now," he said, spinning her around. "Let's get the hell out of here. Before our friends realize the kid's missing. I'm good, but I'm not that good."

DAWN SILVERED THE sky by the time Wade let her rest.

Riley collapsed into the shadow of a rock, sweat dampening her temples. She was exhausted. Emotionally and physically.

The escape from Black River had been easier than she'd expected. Her nerves were wrung raw, expecting an ambush at every corner, but it seemed the ruse had worked. Even the revenants had given them little grief, watching them silently from the shadows as they slunk along the cave.

"It's the scent of me," Wade had said. "Makes 'em warier than they ought to be. They know I'm not human."

The thought still creeped her out. It might have been better if the revenants made some sort of noise, but all they did was watch. As if they were thinking about how good she would taste.

Riley slipped out of her boots and tipped them upside down, letting the water splash out of them. Three miles wading through a creek had ruined the leather, but better that than being caught by the wargs that were surely hunting them.

Jimmy was starting to make noise, his body jerking feebly. Wade had carried him over his shoulder as if the lanky youth were a feather-weight.

Riley knelt beside him and stroked a gentle hand over his forehead. His face was a bruised mess, both eyes blackened and one of his teeth broken. She unscrewed the cap off the water flask Wade had smuggled out in a duffel bag and tipped it to Jimmy's cracked lips. He winced then gulped at the water.

"Easy, Jimmy," she whispered. "I got you now." Every bruise was a knife to her chest, compounding the guilt. If only she'd said they'd had enough rocs that afternoon, had headed back to Haven early. None of this would have happened. Jimmy wouldn't be beaten within an inch of his life, there'd be no wargs on her trail, and she wouldn't have made a deal with the devil.

She looked up and saw Wade watching her with an inscrutable expression. The stubble along his jaw had darkened to a shadow, and his hair was wind-tossed and rumpled. Black as a raven's wing. Black as his heart.

"It was worth it," she said, tipping her chin up as she stroked Jimmy's hair off his face. "We got him back."

A slow salute of a nod. "So we did." His gaze slid over her shoulder, raking the dusty plains behind them. "But I ain't celebratin' 'til I know Colton ain't on the trail."

"What's with you two?"

She eased Jimmy's head back onto the blanket she'd cradled beneath him. He sighed and sank back into blissful unconsciousness.

Wade shrugged. "Rode with him once. Him and his master." At that, his lip curled. "Bartholomew Cane. Never did like that bastard."

"You don't seem to like anybody."

"There are some exceptions." A neutral look that could have meant anything. Wade pushed away from the rock he was leaning against, shouldering the shotgun. "Thought Cane and Colton were just men." His voice became gruff. "It's the worst fucking mistake I ever made. I swore then I'd be carving their names on a tombstone, and I thought I'd done it. Obviously, I was wrong. If Colton's alive, that means Cane ain't that far behind. He holds the leash, tells Colton where and what to hunt."

"How'd you mistake them for men?" she asked slowly. "You were a bounty hunter. You should have recognized the signs."

Wade fingered the pewter amulet around his neck. "I'd never seen a warg stay a man like that. The monsters don't always look like monsters." He stepped closer, the shotgun resting on his shoulder. The warm scent of him curled through her nose and the cool wind cut around him, leaving her in the slipstream. "Do they?" He searched her gaze, looked for the answer within.

Riley stilled. She was suddenly very aware of his large body, of the faint slick of perspiration that gleamed on the muscles of his arms. Her nipples pricked and she crossed her arms over her chest, troubled by her reaction.

He could have been any other man, but for the faint gleam of silver in his very-blue eyes. A mistake that was easy to make. One her body made every chance it could. He was getting under her skin, sinking his claws deep within her.

And she didn't like it one bit.

The thought made her feel vulnerable. On edge. And dangerously tempted.

Wade reached out and stroked her chin. Riley's breath caught. He was always so gentle, as if challenging her to accept his touch. Like a man soothing a skittish filly, seducing her slowly, bit by bit. Getting her used to the idea of him.

"We'd best be going," she blurted, jerking out of reach. Leaning down, she grabbed the duffel for something to do and slung it over her shoulder. "Your friend Colton, remember?"

Slowly, his hand dropped. Wade stared at her. "I remember."

The rest of the day was a nightmare as they walked for endless miles beneath the beating sun. Only a fool went out in this heat, but they didn't exactly have a choice. Wade's next den was hidden high in the Blaspheme Mountains.

Most of the water they gave to Jimmy, who stirred at odd moments. Wade had him slung over his shoulders again. Not once did he complain about the kid's weight as he trekked along at her heels. Occasionally, she'd stumble, and his warm hand would grab her by the elbow and steady her.

Her knees were shaking. "I don't think I can make it," Riley murmured through dry lips. The water canteen was empty. Heat pounded down from the blazing sun, reflecting off the rock pan. The world was a shimmering haze. She felt like she was in an oven.

"You drop and I'll leave the boy here and carry you myself," Wade said.

Riley shot him a devastated look. "You promised."

His teeth ground together, an edge of frustration tightening his features. "Fine." The word was grated. "I'll get the kid out. I'll get you both out." He steadied her arm, looking down at her. Something softened in his eyes. "You can do it, Riley. This is nothing compared to revenants and reivers. Don't make me think you're weak. I was almost starting to admire you."

Heat flushed through her. She couldn't stop trembling. "How far?"

"Another mile. Just one more."

This time, he kept hold of her elbow. Riley stumbled along, the afternoon shadows starting to lengthen. Most of the going had been flat, but now they started climbing. She couldn't keep up the pace, but Wade kept silent, helping her over rocks, leading her by the hand when she was sure she couldn't go another step.

One foot in front of the other.

And again. Just one more.

She didn't even realize it was dusk until he finally stopped. Looking up, she blinked to find them in front of a tumble of rocks. There was a faint slit she thought she could just slip through.

"We're here." A gentle hand settled in the middle of her back. "There's water. Supplies. I even have spare blankets."

"More caves," she muttered, but she didn't have the strength to work herself up to even a minor panic.

Wade leaned her against the rock face. "Stay here. I'll settle the kid and come back for you."

She didn't know how long he'd been, but the grip of his arm startled her awake. Night had fallen with the swiftness of a theater curtain, a thousand stars winking in the velvety sky.

"Here." There was a canteen at her lips, Wade's hand cupping her face as he tilted it back and let the cool water trail into her mouth.

Riley drank greedily. The water was colder than she'd have ever expected to find. So refreshing that it woke her up.

Wade screwed the cap back on, ignoring her protests. "You can have more in a minute. It'll make you sick otherwise." He bent down and slung her up into his arms. "Come on, time for bed, princess."

Riley's head rested on his shoulder. She couldn't even summon the strength to protest the name. Her eyes drifted shut. *So warm.* She could feel the tick of his heart beneath her palm as it rested on his chest. A hypnotic beat, but strangely quickened.

"Your heart's racing."

"Mmm," he muttered into her hair. "It's the moon."

Something about that tugged at her as wrong. She blinked. Saw the silver gleam in his eyes. A sight that had frightened her not so long ago. "There's barely a sliver in the sky. I thought the fullness of the moon aroused your inner...."

"The monster inside me?" A mocking smile, full of bitterness. He stroked a thumb over her cheek, strangely tender. "Shut up, Riley. Go to sleep."

Then he was snuggling her into a nest of blankets that he'd prepared on the sandy floor of the cavern. Dragging the blanket up, he tucked it around her shoulders. His face was oddly expressionless.

"Jimmy," she muttered.

A warm palm smoothed the hair back off her face. "I'll watch him. You just go to sleep."

She couldn't remember falling asleep. But the next thing she knew, she was freezing, the frigid desert night settling down with heavy skirts. Someone was humming, a lullaby she recognized as one her mama had sung to her as a kid. Blinking sleepily, she saw the small fire Wade must have started in a pit, and Jimmy's prone body sleeping in another nest of blankets.

Firelight gleamed over Wade's face. He'd dragged a coat on and was kneeling on the other side of the fire, slowly whittling a piece of wood. Riley watched for long moments, certain she was dreaming, her mind trying to make out what he was carving.

The knife moved with slow, steady strokes as he hummed under his breath. A curl of wood drifted to the floor at his feet, then another. A shape began to emerge. A tiny little doll. Every detail so fine and perfect it could have come from a master carver.

He finished the piece and stared at it for a long time. The humming had stopped. Then slowly he put it down beside him and rested against the wall of the cavern. Dark shadows bruised his eyes. He drew the edges of the coat tighter, then tucked his hands inside and stared into the flames.

Riley's eyes shut, and she slept again.

By the time she woke, the sun was climbing in the sky. Riley yawned, half tempted to roll over, and go back to sleep. Then she saw Wade's boots stretched out before the coals. He had the rifle leaning against the cave wall beside him, and he was staring through red-rimmed eyes at the mouth of the cave.

Riley sat up. She was sweating again, the morning sun starting to bake the air outside. Hot enough that she didn't need two blankets.

Wade's gaze swiveled to her. He looked drained, and she realized he'd been awake all night, keeping watch.

"Jesus," she muttered, shoving aside the blankets, and finding her feet. "You should have woken me."

Wade shook himself, sighing under his breath. "I can go a few days without sleep."

Riley grabbed his arm and tugged him to his feet. His large body staggered into hers, and she grabbed him around the waist before she could think about it. Wade looked down at her. So much taller, his broad shoulders dwarfing her. But graceless in his exhaustion. She could have led him around like a toy on a string.

"You can't fight in this condition," she said. "If Colton comes, you're worse than useless. Get into my blankets and get some sleep. I'll keep watch."

He must have been tired for he let her tuck him in, and tug his boots off. His eyelashes fluttered closed, and he was asleep before she could drop his second boot on the ground.

Fool.

She hesitated then brushed the silky black strands of hair off his forehead. He looked infinitely more innocent asleep, his features softened, the hard line of his mouth easing. Riley's fingertips grazed over the heavy stubble on his jaw.

Sleep had driven away all of the confusion of the day before. She dragged a blanket up over Wade's chest, turning to find Jimmy watching her through his raccoon eyes.

"Ain't that... the warg?" he rasped.

Riley scurried to his side, helping him sit up. She wrapped her arms around his scrawny shoulders and hugged him. "Oh, thank God!"

Jimmy winced and pushed at her. "Hurts, Riley."

She let him go and fetched the canteen for him. The water inside had warmed, but it was still fresh. Jimmy gulped it down, trying to drink around the split in his lip.

When it was empty, he dropped it and collapsed back into his blankets.

"Do you want food?"

He shook his head tiredly. Then turned to glare at Wade. "What's he doin' here?"

"He promised to help me get you back," she replied. Something defensive rose in her breast. "He went into Black River with me. He didn't have to. He didn't have to make that promise," she realized, even as she said the words. "He could have just thrown me over his shoulder and headed out into the desert."

Jimmy blinked through one swollen eye. "Why?"

She didn't have an answer to that.

"What's he want?"

"A chance at McClain," she replied quietly. "I'm going to give it to him."

Jimmy's eyes darkened. "We don't give the humans to the monsters."

"I'm not." Her voice hardened. "I'm just giving him a chance. I've seen McClain on the hunt. He's good, Jimmy. I've never seen a man move like that." Not until Wade anyway. "Chances are he'll bury Wade in the first few minutes."

A part of her didn't like that at all. Her breath hitched. What if she broke her word? Got Jimmy and her out of there before Wade woke? He'd miss his chance, and both he and McClain would be safe.

He hadn't moved, not even when her voice had risen. Sleeping like the dead. It wouldn't be hard to sneak out.

Wouldn't be hard for Colton to sneak in.

Riley bit her lip. She couldn't leave him there for the vultures. Her gaze shuttering, she pressed Jimmy back into his blankets. "Rest," she murmured. "I'll organize breakfast."

And figure out what she was going to do.

After a breakfast of bread and cheese, Riley took the chance to explore a little while the men were sleeping.

Sunlight spilled through gaps in the cavern roof, and the floor was creamy white sand. A long ago water course, she imagined, which had carved its way through the mountains until it formed this. The walls were washed smooth, and mustard-yellow stains marked where water had discolored the wall at stages.

Wade hadn't been kidding about the supplies. Enough long-term food items to keep a man for months, plus spare blankets, binoculars, guns, knives, ammunition and clothes. She found them packed in crates behind a curve of rock, his footprints imprinted in the sand in front of them.

He'd planned this well.

There was no sign of anyone following them. Riley climbed to the ledge of rock above the cave and scanned the desert with the newly found binoculars. Heat wavered over the rocky plains. A roc soared high overhead, riding the blistering thermals. But nothing moved over the gravelly sand.

Clambering back down, she headed as deep into the cave as she dared, past several corners and winding outcroppings. And that was when she found it. Water. Pure and fresh. Spring-fed.

It gleamed a crystalline blue from the shaft of sunlight that speared down through the roof's opening. Riley took off her boots and dipped her toes into the edge.

God, it felt divine. So cold, it startled her wits into crystal clarity.

Glancing over her shoulder revealed nothing but silence and shadows. She lifted the hem on her shirt – Wade's appropriated shirt – and wiggled out of it. The jeans were next, hitting the sandy floor around her ankles.

She kept her bra and panties on, wading out into the cool water. It struck her thighs, the cold of it leaving her almost breathless, but she couldn't wait to wash off the past few days' dirt and grime. And the blood. Definitely the blood.

"Kid's asleep." Wade's voice called from behind. "Got one hell of a shiner."

Riley squealed in surprise and dove under the water. When she came up, Wade dropped his bag on the sandy shore and reached over his shoulder for the collar of his shirt.

"What are you doing?" she blurted. "I thought you were asleep."

"Someone kept tiptoeing past like a small elephant." He paused as he saw her face, the shirt half over his head, revealing inches of hard, chiseled abs. "Please. Tell me you're not going to play the helpless virgin now." Wrenching the shirt off, he tossed it aside, his hands falling to the snap on his jeans. "I stink," he told her. "I'm covered in blood and God knows what, and I'm not standing in it one more minute. Either we share the pool, or you get out."

Riley stared at him, fanning the water slowly with her hands. "I only just got in."

"True," he said. "You weren't smelling real good either." A sudden smile lit up his face, his white teeth gleaming in the shadows. The sunlight's reflection off the water danced over his upper body in blue rippling movements. "I have soap," he said suggestively.

Soap. Her lips parted on a sigh. She'd do a lot for soap right about now. It was incredibly tempting. "What about Colton?"

"That's why I chose this place." He shrugged. "This jumble of rock is the only hill out here. I can see for miles, and there's no sign of him."

"Fine. I'll let you share my pool. On the condition that you keep your hands to yourself."

The pewter amulet gleamed against his tanned chest. Wade tugged his jeans open, enough for her to realize he was wearing no underwear. Arching a brow, he met her shocked gaze. "Darlin', I ain't the one staring."

Damn him. Riley ground her teeth together and spun around, staring at the blue-lit cavern walls. The low, throaty sound of his chuckle echoed through the area. He'd obviously recovered some of his usual spirit after the couple hours of sleep. A pity. He'd been almost pleasant when he was exhausted.

"Please," she said. "You surprised me."

The sound of his jeans hitting the sand echoed. "You hate it, don't you? The fact that you can't keep your eyes off me?"

Sometimes, she forgot he was a monster. Sometimes, all she saw was the man. In quiet little moments, like the night before, when he'd been whittling that toy, or when he carried her to the blankets and tucked her in.

And, as a man, he was a damned fine specimen.

She'd rather die than let him know that though.

"That's not the reason I watch you," she retorted. "You don't turn your back on a warg."

"Yet you've got your back to me now."

Why the hell did it have to be Wade?

Riley bit her lip. There were plenty of men at the settlement. Even McClain was one hell of a handsome devil, although they rarely saw eye to eye. Yet she'd never found her gaze lingering the way it did on Wade, and when he'd kissed her... Her nipples tightened, goose bumps springing up all over her arms and the back of her neck. Behind her, the water sloshed around her as he waded into it.

Water splashed and then silence filled the cavern. Riley glanced over her shoulder. He'd vanished beneath the surface, ripples refracting light off the water. The pile of abandoned clothes on the sand sent an odd fist of longing through her belly.

Wade's dark head surfaced first, tanned hands raking over his face as he flung water everywhere. It dripped from his elbows and the tangled lengths of his hair, sluicing over the smooth muscle of his chest. Riley's mouth went dry. Then her eye caught the pewter charm, and a shiver ran over her skin.

Not human. Don't ever forget that.

Wade looked up, a knowing little smile toying over his lips. "When I first saw what you were wearing, I wondered what the women out here in the settlements were thinking." His gaze dropped. "But there's something to be said for white cotton, it seems."

Wet cotton. Riley dropped under the water, glaring up at him. He was too close to her, all of that smooth olive skin. She pushed backward, idly fanning the water, as if she were just swimming.

Wade caught her ankle, holding her in place. His smile held nothing of humor in it now, his eyes turning molten with heat. Riley couldn't have looked away to save herself. His thumb stroked the inside of her ankle, and he glanced down beneath thick, dark lashes, as though examining the smooth length of her leg.

"It's a leg," she said, trying to make the words dry and cynical. For some reason, the last word was a breathy whisper.

"I'm aware of that."

"I'm sure you've seen dozens of them," she retorted, tugging ineffectively at his grip.

Wade held onto her for a moment, then let her go. "What do you mean by that?"

"A man like you. You'd have women all over the place."

Water spiked off his eyelashes, clumping them together. His blue eyes were burning with some emotion she couldn't quite figure. "Right. You've got me all pegged, sweetheart." A hint of anger turned his voice sour.

Riley splashed backward, uneasy with his sudden intensity. Her back hit the cool, sloped rock wall, the rasp of granite rough against her skin, sending shivers down her body. Or perhaps that was the fact that she was virtually alone, half-naked in a pool of water with a man like Wade.

She examined him in the half-light. The emotion had faded off his face, but it had been thick in his voice. Anger. Wade was angry with her assumptions. Riley frowned. "Tell me then. Since I'm obviously wrong about you. You're all sweetness and good conscience. I don't know how I missed that."

"I'm not denying my baser qualities, but womanizing isn't one of them." He edged closer, ripples circumnavigating his body. Sliding under the water until it covered his mouth and nose, he eyed her through the darkness.

Riley's breath caught.

Wade vanished beneath the water, the surge of his incoming body sweeping the water up over her skin. He surfaced in front of her, brushing his dripping black hair out of his eyes. Riley's mouth went dry at the sleek show of muscle. This was insane. *She* was insane. She knew what he was, what he could be, yet her body knew no difference. It ached for his touch, for the sight of him.

For just one more kiss....

Riley's heart gave a little flutter as he speared her with that hot look again.

Somehow, she found her voice. "You're trying to tell me you're as innocent as a lamb? Do women actually fall for that?"

"You're the one who keeps throwing it in my face about me being a warg. Limits my options. I won't pay for sex, darlin', and I ain't interested in taking it by force. The last woman I slept with was my wife."

Riley's breath caught in her chest, and her gaze dropped toward his left hand. No ring. Not even a tan line where one had been.

As if realizing he'd revealed too much, Wade swam backward, his face shuttering. The sunlight washed over him, gleaming on black hair.

"Where is she now?" Riley asked, creeping forward. Oh, God, had she kissed a married man?

"Don't know."

Curiosity pricked her. The tone of his voice was so flat he might as well not have cared. But something in his expression warned her.

"I didn't know wargs had wives."

"They don't." He surged to his feet, the water hitting his hips. A trail of black hair arrowed down from his navel, vanishing beneath the hypnotic blue of the water. Wade met her gaze, a nasty little smile tilting his mouth. "I'll fetch the soap."

Conversation over. Riley watched him wade toward the sandy shore, water running down over his bare buttocks and heavily muscled thighs. She wanted to know more. Had the wife left him when she found out he was a warg? She'd never once given thought to how it must be for them. They'd only ever been monsters to her before. But they hadn't always been so. Every single one of them had been human once.

Imagine coming home, knowing what you'd become? Knowing it would tear your family apart. A little snarl of sympathy knotted in her stomach. Her father had done as all men out here would do if clawed up – he'd bitten a bullet. But that was never an easy choice.

Sometimes, a part of her wished he'd chosen the coward's way out. Chose to run off into the desert, and that maybe, one day, she could meet him under the sun, when he was still a man. That part of her was still a little girl, longing for her daddy to pick her up in his arms, and swing her 'round.

What had Wade's wife thought when he was bitten?

Wade snatched a bar of soap out of his bag, and a thin flannel. Riley turned away as he returned to the water, troubled by the thought of him as just a man, albeit one cursed with a horrible affliction.

Just a man....

"So, what was her name?" she asked over her shoulder.

A growl echoed in his throat. "Why?"

"You were right," she said. "I know nothing about you except what I assume. I want to know."

"Curiosity killed the cat."

Riley glanced over her shoulder. Waist deep. It was safe to look. "You won't hurt me." She frowned a little, watching him lather the soap between those large, tanned hands. "You were never going to hurt me, were you?"

He didn't answer that. Just watched her as he scrubbed soapy lather over his chest. His expression hardened. "Abbie. Her name was Abbie."

Abbie. Riley tested the name in her head, a part of her wondering who the woman had been. "You loved her."

"Why would you assume that?"

"You don't want to talk about her," she said. "So some part of losing her hurt you. Did she turn away from you when you turned warg?"

Water rippled as he edged closer. Riley turned, flinching as hands caught the silky strands of her hair from behind and started soaping them. She'd taken a few lovers in her time, but that had only been sex. No one had ever done anything like this before. It was intimate. Uncomfortable. She was very close to pulling away, but something stopped her.

"I loved her," Wade admitted in a quiet voice. "More than anything."

Riley held still, allowing him to soap her hair. She barely dared to breathe. "What happened?"

"I got clawed up," he said. "By someone I trusted." He cupped water in his hands and dropped it over her head, washing away the suds. The scent of fresh lemons rose around her. Must have cost a fortune on the black market.

"Knew what was going to happen," he continued. "So I walked away, left her. I've been told she waited a few years before she married again. One of my cousins. A good man."

"Did she try to find you?"

"She knew what had happened," he said gruffly. "I was sparing her what I could." The law said that the marriage was dissolved if a man went missing for seven years – or if he turned warg.

Wade's hands ran over the straps of her bra, soothing the skin of her arms and shoulders. He had a good touch. Patient. Steady. Riley tried not to shiver, her breath coming a little quicker. His hands were so warm, his calluses rough against her skin.

Sweeping her hair to the side, over her shoulder, he brushed his fingers down over the ripple of her spine. The sensation shot right through her.

"It's been a long time since I touched a woman," he murmured. His fingertips turned questing, as if he were soaking up the sensation of her skin, content just to feel her, to explore. "A long time... since one let me."

Riley ground her knees together. She didn't know what was happening, or what to do. Every instinct in her body was screaming at her to get out of there, but the slow, hypnotic slide of his hands stole her willpower.

And something else. Curiosity. Longing. Loneliness. It was hard trying to remain an independent woman out here in the settlements. Too many men would mistake an offer of companionship for something else, as though it suddenly gave them the right to rule her life. Either that, or they'd use it – and her position on Haven's Council – to barter for something. It had been a long time.

Too long, obviously.

"Here." His voice was rough velvet. "Hold the soap."

She took it, fumbling with the wet bar as he lathered his hands together and urged her out of the water.

"I'll wash your back."

A quick flick of his fingers and her bra suddenly sagged, the edges hanging at her sides. Riley gasped, cupping her breasts in her hands, the thin, worn cotton barely containing them. "What are you doing?"

His palms slid down over her back, the soap silky-slick beneath his skin. He massaged the muscles on either side of her spine, his hands trailing off just at the indent of her hips. Gripping the side of her waist, he slid them back up, fingertips brushing against the curve of her breasts.

Riley shifted uneasily. A glance over her shoulder showed she wasn't the only one affected. She'd expected that devilish smile, the teasing gleam in his eyes, but he *wasn't* smiling. Not at all.

His gaze burned her, all the way through. A need so fierce it stole her breath left her heart thumping in her chest. And something else... Wariness. As if he was simply waiting for the rejection.

Fingertips brushed against the edge of her bra, as if asking permission. Riley tore her gaze back to the cavern wall in front of her, deafened by the roar in her ears. She had the horrible suspicion that she was going to do something reckless.

Her silence gave him the permission he needed. His touch grew bolder, stronger. Breath hot against her nape and then a kiss, just the lightest of caresses, against the sensitive skin there. Riley shuddered.

"Take it off," he whispered.

She panicked, flat-out panicked. And yet she couldn't tear herself away. "I don't think so."

Fingertips traced teasing circles on her skin. "All you have to do is say no."

Riley hesitated.

His lips trailed over her shoulder, his body pressing against hers. She could feel him through the thin cotton of her panties, huge and hard, desperate to claim her. And she suddenly realized that the answer might be yes. That she wanted it too.

Trying not to think too much, she wiggled her shoulders, let the bra slip off into the water. Adrenaline pumped through her veins, making her breath short. She tossed the bra toward the sand before she could change her mind.

"Didn't think you'd do it."

His voice was raw, harsh. For a moment, Wade's hands lightened, as if he himself were reconsidering this. As if it scared him too.

Cupping her arms over her breasts, Riley sank beneath the water again. *Idiot. What am I doing?* But something about the whole situation tempted her. This man didn't want anything else from her but this. *Just the once,* said a tempting little whisper in her mind. Both of them could take what they wanted, just the once, then walk away.

She was still undecided.

"Just so you know, the answer's 'no,'" Riley murmured over her shoulder, wondering if she was trying to prove it to herself. "But you can wash my back."

Wade reached around her for the soap in her hands, the hairs on his chest tickling her back. The faint brush of his erection stirred against her bottom, and he lathered his hands slowly, until she was barely breathing.

"You're too kind," he muttered.

The soapy glide of his hands made her arch her back. A wordless murmur died in her throat as he slid his hands over her hips and up. There was no hesitation in him now, no patient steady touch. His fingers curved under her breasts, cupping them teasingly, before darting away.

Riley sucked in a sharp breath. "That's not my back."

"No. It's not." His hands trailed over her stomach, then higher, pushing her arms out of the way.

Give the man an inch... She ground her teeth together, prepared to shove away from him, when he cupped her breasts, slippery fingers dancing over her nipples.

"You looked dirty," he whispered, laughter warming his voice. Brushing his lips against the curve of her neck, he kissed the sensitive skin there again.

A shiver went right through her. Riley tensed. She should say no. Tell him to get his hands, and mouth, off her. But it felt so good, his fingers lazily circling her nipples as he waited for her to make her decision.

Don't be a fool.

Out here, a woman made her choices quick. Death was a constant in all their lives. It could have happened to her the night before, by revenant or reiver. She had to take her chances when they came, and a sudden yearning – not just for sex, but for Wade – came over her. Dangerous men, and all that temptation....

She forced herself to relax, ignoring the quiver in her stomach, then leaned back against his chest, her breasts rising out of the water. Soap gleamed over her pale skin, his tanned hands a dark comparison as they stilled on her skin.

Wade sucked in a breath. "Christ Jesus." He cupped her, pinching her nipple between soapy-slick fingers. "You're beautiful."

Riley stirred, trying to bite back a gasp. Pressed against him like this, she could feel every hot, hard inch, including the press of his cock, rigid against her bottom. The chill of the water between her thighs melded with the molten wetness of her own body. She couldn't help herself; her hips thrust back, rubbing against him, the thickened head of his cock dipping between her thighs for one tantalizing moment.

Did she dare? The thought was terrifying, yet arousing. She knew what her body wanted. She could feel it, all hot and shivery, her breath coming in short little gasps. His hard body caged her, a delicious tease, the hair on his chest brushing against her bare back.

Wade kissed her shoulder, the rasp of his teeth bringing another gasp to her lips. "Don't," he ground out. "Don't do this if you don't mean it."

Some nameless emotion quivered in his voice. Riley wet her lips. If she hadn't heard that hesitation, hadn't realized how much this meant to him, how much he wanted it too, then she might have come to her senses. Instead, her hand slid over his. "Lower," she whispered, giving in to the temptation.

There was a moment of stillness as he absorbed her words. His own chest heaved against her, harsh breath exploding out of his lungs. "Where?"

Determined to make her complicit, to make her give her consent.

She didn't want to think about it. Didn't want to know that it was Wade. She just wanted to pretend that he was some faceless, nameless *man*. But he wouldn't let her. For a moment, uncertainty twisted her stomach, but the warm heat at her back, the hard muscle, drove her mind to other places.

Riley squeezed her eyes shut and dragged his hand lower, beneath the edge of her cotton panties. His soapy fingers slid against her wet slit, palm pressing against the tangle of blonde hair there. He held himself motionless.

"How?" Another hot whisper in her ear. Daring her.

Riley pressed his hand hard against her, writhing against his touch. The first trace of his fingers made her gasp, throwing her head back.

"Here?" He suckled the skin of her throat, his fingers drawing lazy circles.

There. She nearly died and went to Heaven. So long since the touch hadn't been hers. "Faster," she whispered, sliding her hand up, behind his neck. "Please."

The slow glide of his fingers drove her mad.

"*Faster.*"

"No. No rush, darlin'." He kissed her again, an open-mouthed wet kiss against the back of her neck that tightened everything in her body. "I ain't rushing this." Turning, he drew her into his arms, wrapping them around her bottom before pressing his lips to her navel as he forced her to stand.

Riley whimpered at the loss of his fingers. Wade watched her face respond to the rasp of his stubble against her tender breasts as he brushed his lips over her nipple.

"This is crazy," she whispered. She couldn't look away from him.

"Yes."

His hot mouth clamped over her.

"Oh, God," she moaned, wilting in his touch. His tongue darted over her sensitive flesh as if he knew exactly where she wanted to be touched. One finger slid inside her, and her whole body locked hard around it.

"Fuck," he groaned. Heat flared to life in his eyes.

Cupping her hips, he wiggled her panties down. The sensation made her eyes open wide, a hint of nervousness prickling her skin.

"It's okay," he whispered, kissing his way lower. "All you have to do is tell me to stop if you don't want to."

His mouth nuzzled into the soft blonde curls at the base of her thighs as he encouraged her out of the water, her back pressed hard against the rock walls of the cavern. Riley couldn't have denied him – or herself – if she'd wanted to.

A breathy cry died in her throat as his tongue darted into the slit between her thighs. Fingers clenching in his hair, she tried not to shudder, to lose her balance, as his hot tongue swept over her sensitive flesh. Giving a little wriggle, she felt her panties drop to her ankles, and then Wade was cupping her bottom, tilting her pelvis toward his mouth as he sucked hard.

Riley nearly screamed. "God," she whispered, looking guiltily toward the mouth of the cavern. If Jimmy heard her....

Wade suckled her clit, his tongue diving deep inside her. Slipping first one shoulder beneath her thigh then the other, he forced her legs wider, both thumbs sliding up to bare her to his touch, in a way that made her feel utterly vulnerable, completely exposed. And then he kissed her. *Really* kissed her, as if he were trying to lay waste to her.

Riley's fingers curled in his hair, as if she could control it, even in some small way, but it was just a conceit. He controlled her. He gave her what she wanted. She was used to the type of men who took, but this was entirely outside her realm of experience, and it was getting her off in a major way. She was so close, every muscle in her body tensing, her toes curling a little. Just a little more....

The sensation of his stubble against her sensitive flesh undid her. Riley shoved her fist against her lips, trying to force back a scream. Wade took advantage, tonguing her deep, tearing her apart. Her eyes went wide as sensation streamed through her. All she could see were his blue eyes as he watched her, his mouth buried between her legs. The thought tore another orgasm through her until she was shuddering, her knees going out from under her. The world narrowed and she collapsed in his arms, whimpering gently as her body flinched at the invasion of cool water between her hot thighs.

Long moments of bliss. No thought. No pressure. Just sensation. The feel of a man's arms cradling her, her head resting against his shoulder.

Wade cradled her from behind, breathing deep into her wet hair. His hips flexed, an earthy reminder that this was not done. The tip of his cock breached her clenched thighs, rode over the shivering flesh. Riley stilled. Another choice. Another moment that would change her life forever.

"You're beautiful," he whispered, his hand tracing her breast. "So strong. So wild. I want to tame you."

"Do you think you can?"

"Maybe that's the fascination. Knowing what I want to do to you, and knowing that you can never be tamed." Their eyes met as she turned her head. He kissed her lips, let her taste the musk of her own body, then bit her lower lip, rubbing it between his teeth gently. There was a slight hesitation in him. A tension within the hard steel of his arms. "You don't have to do this," he told her bluntly, letting go of her lip.

A complex man. One who had given her every choice to turn away from him, as if he expected it. As if he was already steeling himself against it.

And she knew then what her choice was going to be.

Her hand slid between them, down the wet glide of his abdomen. Wade sucked in a harsh breath as her fingers wrapped around the silken head of his cock, then squeezed lightly.

"I know," she replied.

The tension in his body changed. Fierce desire radiated in his voice. "So be it. Remember, this was your choice, and yours alone." He bit her throat, her neck, then thrust his cock against her bottom.

Riley groaned, her hand fisting around the smooth skin. Wade shuddered, his teeth grazing her jaw. She loved that she could do this to him. Make him so vulnerable. Humanize him.

But he didn't want to be humanized. He grabbed her hips, jerked her back against him. "I'm going to fuck you hard," he whispered in her ear, biting the fleshy lobe. "I want you to know that. This is not about saving the boy, about what you owe me... This is just what you want.

What I want. You want this, don't you?" His hand tightened in her hair, creating a fist. "You want me?"

Desperate, harshly whispered words.

"Say it," he hissed. His cock ground against her hips, the hair on his thighs tickling against her bare legs.

Riley's nipples tightened. "Yes," she whispered.

Some madness had taken over her mind, her flesh. She felt herself rubbing against him, his cock brushing between her thighs. Wade sucked in a sharp breath.

"No. Not like this." He turned her around, forcing her to look at him. His blue eyes burned with need. "Look at me," he snarled. "You look at me. You see me. Know that it's me. Inside you."

Riley's back hit the rock, his fingers intertwining with hers. Water rushed down his body as he half-rose out of the water, his cock sliding between them, her legs parting around his hips. He pressed against her, the blunt head of his erection slipping inside her wet opening.

She'd almost expected him to thrust home, to shove himself inside her roughly. But he paused, a strange expression crossing his face. Hands clasping hers, he lowered his head slowly, their eyes meeting.

And then he kissed her.

Softly. Slowly. His mouth dancing over hers so lightly. Riley sucked in a sharp breath, trying to stifle a moan. The man knew how to kiss. She wanted to sink her hands into the thick mat of his black hair and draw him against her, but she was pinned to the rock, his own callused hands clenched in hers. All she could do was surrender.

Wade's tongue darted inside her mouth. Tasting her. Tempting her. Riley kissed him back, their tongues dueling for one precarious second. He still wouldn't kiss her hard enough, as if he wasn't sure how much of himself he could give. How much she would let him take.

"More," she whispered, the word a caress against his wet mouth.

His hips rocked, another inch of his cock spreading her. Riley gasped, her fingers clenching around his at the shock of the invasion. He was a big man, and it had been a long time, but she bit his lip, rocked her hips. Anything for more. She needed him to take her. To give her everything he could.

"More."

Another inch. His hips thrusting lightly against hers. So in control. Riley threw her head back. *"Please,"* she whispered.

His lips slid down her throat, teeth grazing along her windpipe. "God, you're so fucking tight." A shiver ran over his skin and his elbows bent, his chest pressing against hers. He pinned her to the wall, brushing his lips against her throat. Tasting her. The rasp of his stubble sending shivers through her. "Damn you."

He thrust deep, filling her to the core. Riley gasped, her voice echoing in the cavern. Their bodies fused, his branding hers within, and she shuddered, the tremble running all the way through her. She was so close. Just the thought of what he was doing pushed her to the edge.

His mouth found hers, taking it roughly. Riley met it with a hunger she couldn't hide. She felt like she was chasing something she'd never known before. Oh, she'd fucked herself to orgasm with her own fingers, but this was more. This was... being consumed. Being eaten alive by a force she couldn't control. And wanting more. Always more. Another long, slow slide as he withdrew, then thrust hard, driving her back against the wall.

"Yes," she whispered, clinging to him.

He took her mouth, a punishing kiss that owned her. Each slow thrust of his hips was punctuated by the dart of his tongue. Wade kissed as if he made love to her entire body, as if the thrust of his hips were but one part of it, as if he couldn't get enough. And she *burned*, writhing beneath his body, pinned to the wall with his exquisite strength.

Her teeth left white crescent-moon imprints on his shoulder as the heat inside her started to tighten, to push her closer to an edge she wanted to throw herself off. It was like rappelling, only this time, there were no ropes to break her fall, and the terror of that unknown leap only heightened all of the sensation.

Wade drank of her mouth, his hips thrusting urgently, as if he could sense it. His cock rode over something sensitive deep inside, and Riley shuddered.

It spiraled through her, as hot and sudden as an electrical storm, lightning strikes shattering across her nerves. She cried out, dug her teeth against the carved column of his throat, her fingers clenching in his. His hard body anchored hers, driving her against the cavern wall, forcing the storm to build within her until she was shuddering with an override of pleasure as she came. She could feel the tension in his arms, the way his body shook. Knew he was close.

Each thrust became hard, violent. His face buried against her throat, Wade came with a harsh exhalation, a soft cry. His hips flexed as if he sought to drag out the pleasure, his breath rasping over the sensitive skin of her throat.

The world stilled. All she could feel was the burning brand between her thighs where Wade's hips were nestled, and the love-bruises on her skin. The silence of the cavern was punctuated by harsh gasps, and the steady drip of water from her hair.

Wade let her hands go, his own sliding under her ass. "Christ..." he whispered hoarsely. "Christ."

Bit by bit, the world started to intrude. And with it, guilt.

As if he sensed it, could feel her body withdrawing from his, he looked up through passion-glazed eyes. "Just let me," he murmured. "Just let me hold you for a minute."

Then he curled his strong arms around her, sinking down into the water. The cold bit at her in places and Riley wilted in his arms, her wet hair strewn across his shoulder as she hesitantly rested her cheek on it. Her heart was pounding. Bad enough admitting that she was attracted to him – but a fuck was a fuck. This... It left her feeling extremely uncomfortable, as if she was letting in something that she hadn't agreed to.

Or maybe even wanting a little of it herself.

It was easier if Riley told herself just to enjoy the sensation, the aftermath of being deliciously taken. Slowly, she trailed her fingers down his arm, tracing a water droplet and marveling at the powerful strength of his body.

A body that held her with exquisite gentleness, his own hands stroking her lower back and spine. For a moment, she could almost forget who held her in his arms. A part of her yearned to stay there, to let him hold her like that forever. Someone who admired her strength, who not only let her help him but expected her to pick up a gun and watch his back. It was only there, in his arms, that he asked for softness, asked her to be his lover.

And she liked that feeling.

Riley stared at the water patterns, lulled into a hypnotic bliss by the stroke of his hands. They chased away the guilt, the doubts, and left in their wake one burning question.

Why did it have to be Wade?

six

HE KNEW THE moment she withdrew from him.

Brushing at his hands, Riley swam backward, cold water chasing over his skin where her body had been nestled. Glancing down, her cheeks stained with pink, she started wading toward the shore.

The smooth line of her back lifted out of the water, then her hips, the pear-shaped curve of her ass. A woman's body, sleek and lithe, with just enough softness to it for a man to admire. In another time, another place, where the rationing of food wasn't as strictly controlled, she might have held a fuller, hourglass figure. A thought, swiftly detailed, flashed into his mind of taking her there. South. Letting her eat and drink to her heart's content, whilst he pushed her down amongst the pillows and made love to her.

A fool's dream.

Lucius looked away, slapping the water with his knuckles. From the stiffness in her shoulders, he knew regret was coming in to ride her hard. She'd fucked a monster. And from the bite mark on his shoulder, the soft cries she'd whimpered in his ear, she'd liked it.

"No regrets," he said softly. "This was your choice, darlin'."

He'd made sure of that.

A withering glance over her shoulder stirred his anger. Both careless and yet fully aware of her nudity, she wrung out her panties and wiggled into them, giving him another view of that full ass. One hand cupped her breasts as she fought with the wet cotton, trying to drag it up over her long legs with one hand.

"Christ," he muttered. "It ain't as if I haven't seen it... or had my fucking mouth all over it."

Heat blistered her cheeks. "I don't want to talk about it."

Lucius stalked forward, the water sluicing off his body. She glanced down then tore her gaze away, and his scowl darkened. His cock bobbed like a battering ram, barely sated. Years without a taste of female flesh, and it wanted more.

Hell, *he* wanted more.

But more than this.

Good enough to fuck once, but not good enough to mean anything to her. And that thought was a damn minefield.

You knew this couldn't be.

You know you can't have a woman.

115

But the sudden yearning took him by surprise. Grief hit him like a punch to the throat, an emotion he thought he'd long since dealt with. He'd walked away from Abbie, from his family... from everything that had ever meant anything to him. He'd even put a gun in his mouth, and thought about pulling the trigger.

Eight years should have been long enough to come to terms with the choices he'd made. Taking the gun out, he'd changed his mind. He'd do it one day, he'd pledged, but he'd see McClain in Hell first. McClain, Colton and Cane.

Vengeance was all he had left to live for.

And then... what? He'd never thought about it before, but the thought was a sudden knife to the chest. Years of hunting for any sign of McClain, following whispers and rumors. Years of fending for himself, hunting alone. He'd gotten good at pretending he didn't give a damn, but the human part of him – the man – longed for company.

And not just any company. He shot Riley a guarded look, horrified at the direction his thoughts were taking. One hit of human flesh and he was like a goddamn craver, strung out for the next hit. Wanting her to turn to him, to smile at him like she meant it, to stroke his face in a tender way. A need so strong it scraped him raw. Maybe this had been a mistake, for now he knew exactly what he was missing out on.

It wasn't just a dull memory anymore.

He choked the urge down ruthlessly. He had a job to do. There was no point even thinking about the future until McClain and the pair of wargs were dead, and no matter how much he liked her spirit, Riley wasn't going to be part of that future.

Riley dragged her shirt on – his shirt – and wrung the water out of her hair. The black cotton fell to mid-thigh, draping her lush curves in fabric. Lucius's gaze ran down her. He could smell his own scent on her skin. Her throat was grazed from his teeth, and the rough stubble along his jaw. He couldn't have marked her up any better. Some part of him had wanted his own brand on her.

A longing he'd best bury deep. It was time to focus his mind on the job in front of him. He'd thought it half-over, an ambush where he'd killed all of Cane's men, then locked him and Colton inside a cabin. One flick of the match and the house had burned merrily. He'd even toasted a fucking rabbit in the coals. Got himself drunk-sick on the bottle of vodka he'd been saving for the occasion.

Obviously, they'd gotten out somehow. This time, he was going to put a bullet between their eyes, or better yet, take an axe and decapitate them both. Make sure they were dead.

But McClain first.

Riley glanced over her shoulder as if she sensed him watching her, her dark eyes shadowed and oblique. Lucius realized he was standing there naked, just staring at her. Like a desperate man.

Forcing a dark little smile onto his face, he snatched his jeans off the sandy floor and shook them out before slowly dragging them over his wet legs. The worn denim was butter-soft and fit him like a glove. Taking extra care with the buttons, he kicked her own jeans up into his hand and held them out for her.

"It's the least I can do," he said, with mock gentility. "Considering I was cock-deep in you a few minutes ago."

She snatched the jeans out of his hands with a thin-lipped look. "You're an asshole." She dragged them on, fumbling them over her tanned thighs.

Time to shake out of this mood. He'd fucked her. Gotten what he wanted. That was enough. It had to be. Still, his gaze stayed with her, enjoying the sight of her naked skin for as long as he could before he shrugged. "I've been called worse."

"No doubt."

She wiggled the jeans over her hips and that was the end of it. No sign of their encounter, beyond the red marks at her throat and the aching echo of her teeth in the heavy muscle of his shoulder.

Knotting her long hair into a plait, she tied it off with a strand of cotton she picked from the sleeve of her shirt. Brown eyes met his. "You don't have to wait for me."

"Your shirt's gaping," he told her, excuse enough. But the desire for human company – *her* company – lingered. *Pathetic son of a bitch.* He scraped a hand over his tired face. He obviously needed more sleep; the few hours he'd snatched were evidently not enough.

Riley made a growling sound in her throat and pushed past. "You breathe a word of this, and you'll regret it."

"Who am I goin' to tell?" *The sad fucking truth.*

He followed her up the sandy passage, away from the pool and the play of memories.

The kid was awake, trying to drag himself into a sitting position with a wince. Bruises blackened both his eyes, and someone had broken his nose.

Lucius peered at him. "You look like a raccoon."

The kid went red. Not a great look with his flaming hair. "Fuck you."

A distant sound caught his attention. An engine. Lucius froze, the blood in his veins running ice-cold. Riley was bending over, trying to straighten the blankets, but she saw him still and her gaze lifted to his.

"What is it?"

He jerked the rifle into his hand and yanked a black cotton tank out of his bag. Tugging it over his head, he started for the mouth of the cavern. "I can hear cars. More than one."

Riley gasped, then he heard her pumping the shotgun. "Jimmy, hold this," she said. "I'll get the binoculars."

Lucius barely heard her, his gut trembling in anticipation. He eased against the mouth of the cave and peered out. A narrow dust cloud lined the plain below. Two jeeps heading straight for them. He jerked the rifle to his eye and peered through the sight, a frown dawning. Four men in each jeep, bristling with guns. But they were all human, and there was no sign of rust or gun turrets, like the vehicles he'd expected to see.

"They're not reivers."

"It's McClain," the kid said, just behind him.

Need swept through, white-hot and so vicious it almost blinded him. *McClain.* His hands clenched on the gun. Finally. So close he could almost smell the bastard.

Then his brain caught up.

Lucius turned. "How'd you—"

The butt of the shotgun smashed into his face. He went down hard, the right side of his face burning with pain. White light exploded in his head. *Need to move...* But he couldn't. Struggled up onto one elbow.

"Rigged up the two-way radio I found in a crate," the kid said, his voice sounding a million miles away. "Sent an SOS through to Absolution while you were gone." He smiled through the white haze and lifted the gun again. "Now who looks like a raccoon?"

The shotgun smashed down again.

Riley looked up as Wade went down, her heart leaping into her throat. Jimmy lifted the gun again, smashing Wade in the face. His body jerked and lay still, like a puppet whose strings had been cut.

"Jimmy," she whispered, dropping the binoculars and racing to his side.

He lifted the gun again, a vicious look on his face. Riley didn't think, just grabbed at it from behind. A quick knee to the back of his and she wrenched it from his hands, shoving him back against the cave wall as he fell.

"What the hell do you think you're doing?" she asked. A quick glance at Wade showed he still wasn't moving. Lights out.

Black shadows marred his skin, and a cut tore through his brow. The devil looked remarkably vulnerable lying there like that.

Jimmy shoved himself to his feet, staring at her in surprise. "I got him, Riley. I got the warg." Like he too couldn't believe what he'd done.

"You idiot!" She darted to the mouth of the cave. "What about the Reivers?"

"They aren't Reivers. It's McClain." Confidence puffed out his shoulders. "There's an old radio in his supply store. I used it to SOS them when you two were fetching water and washing." His mouth split into a grin, broken tooth still snarled. The movement made him wince. "We're safe, Riley. We've got him."

The jeeps sprayed to a halt, armored men pouring out of them. Riley looked down in dismay. What was she going to do? She'd made a mistake in the pool – a desperate, skin-hungry mistake – but she'd never meant for this to happen.

Wake up. She nudged Wade with her foot, but he only groaned.

There was no way she could get him out of there, no way he could escape. Why'd the son of a bitch have to drop his guard now?

"Jimmy!" A commanding voice she knew too well.

Riley flinched and spun on her heel. McClain stopped in the mouth of the cavern, his broad shoulders framed by the endless blue sky. She saw him four times a year at the trading fairs. Heard his rough-as-gravel voice on the radio.

But the sight of him still took her breath away.

Six and a half feet of solid muscle, more heavily set than Wade. He wore a black shirt rolled up at the sleeves, revealing bronzed forearms sprinkled with golden hair. An ammo belt tugged tight over his chest, and a pair of faded old jeans hugged his thighs. The black felt of a ten-gallon hat was pulled down low over his eyes, but she knew he was staring at her. She could feel it on her skin. Underneath her skin. Itching.

"Riley." His voice was husky. He looked down, raked the scene with a hard glance. Probably saw more than she did in that quick look. "Are you all right?"

"Course I am," she managed to say.

He nodded then gestured to the men following him. "Tie him up, then shove him in the warg cage. I want the perimeter secure. Where's Eden? Get her up here to check on 'em."

Eden was his sister, a healer. The one McClain Riley tended to get along with. She felt her shoulders droop in relief.

A slim young woman bounded up the narrow incline, dressed in a loose white shirt rolled to her elbows and a pair of jeans. She had the same dark brows and intense grey-green stare as McClain, but where her brother was all arrogance and command, Eden had a gentler nature.

Eden winced when she saw Jimmy's face. "Well, don't you look a sight?"

McClain grabbed her arm, turning her toward Riley. His whole posture was tense, voice hard. The pair of them shared a look. "Her first."

"I'm fine." Riley frowned. "The worst thing I have is blisters."

McClain didn't even bother to look at her. "Check her out," he commanded, then turned and went to oversee Wade's incarceration.

Eden stepped closer, and Riley went up on her tiptoes to see over her shoulder. One of the men grabbed Wade by the boot and started dragging him across the sand. His hands had been bound so tightly they were already going white.

"Oh, thank God!" Eden wrapped her arms around Riley and hugged her. "When you didn't come home that night, your folks radioed Absolution. We've been out hunting ever since. Adam's been unbearable."

"That's nothing new," she grumbled. He hadn't listened to her protests that she was fine, simply overrode her like he usually did. As if her opinion wasn't as valid as his.

A faint smile tugged at Eden's lips. "Come on," she said, taking Riley by the hand. "Come sit and we'll have a look at you."

Easing her onto a rock in a strangely gentle way, Eden knelt in front of her.

Riley caught her hand. "Seriously, Eden. There's nothing wrong with me that a good meal and a night's rest won't cure."

"The boy said you'd been kidnapped." A question flickered in her pretty eyes. "By a warg. We were out searching anyway, but as soon as Adam heard who the warg was, he insisted on racing here. I thought we were going to flip one of the jeeps."

"It wasn't... that bad."

She could see that Eden didn't believe her. The healer patted her knee as a grim little smile edged her lips. "It's okay. Won't be long, and we'll be back at Absolution. You can rest up, take your time...."

"Absolution?" Riley frowned. "No. I want to go home. To Haven."

The faintest of hesitations.

Riley grabbed Eden's hand. "What is it?"

Eden shook her head. "When they heard you'd been taken, Peg and Jem radioed Adam. He said it wasn't safe anymore. That they needed to come to Absolution where he could protect them—"

Her chest tightened. "That son of a bitch. I was gone three days!" She jerked to her feet. "Where is he?"

Eden tried to grab her, but Riley pushed past. "McClain!"

His head turned but he stayed where he was, arms crossed over his chest as he watched them shove Wade into the cage. Wade was starting to stir now. At the sound of her voice, he grabbed for the bars, then jerked his hand back as it touched the silver.

Riley scrambled down the slope, slipping and sliding on the gravelly soil. "You arrogant bastard! I turn my back for a second and you're there, trying to overrule me! You knew we wanted to stay at Haven!"

"It's not safe." Intense green eyes met hers, the hat's shadow carving half his face into darkness. His jaw was scraped clean, the skin smooth and tanned. Shadows lingered in the dip above his firm mouth as it thinned. "Your council agreed."

She got in his face, fists clenched. "Of course they did. Peg and Jem have wanted to leave all year. Madi and Dr. Rawlins didn't. I was the deciding vote. With you breathing down their necks, they wouldn't have been able to fight the order. It's our home, damn it, McClain!"

A flicker of frustration filled his eyes, though his voice stayed calm. "The reivers burned New Hope to the ground, Riley. Who did you think was next? Us? We've got rock walls fifteen feet high. You've got a timber fence."

"And they've never gotten past it," she reminded him with a nasty grin. "Haven's got high visibility and good defensive towers. Our stockpile can keep us under siege for over six months, and we've got shooters. We've killed more reivers than New Hope and Isolation did together."

He grabbed her by the shoulders with warm hands. Turned her to the west. A tiny pall of dark shadows blurred the horizon.

"Haven burned, Riley. This morning, I'd say."

The shock of it tore a gasp from her throat. "No." But the proof was on the horizon. She shook her head. "No, it can't have burned." It was her home. She'd lived there all her life, in her father's house. The only reminder she had left of him.

"We got everyone out yesterday, thank God...."

Riley spun on her heel and drove her fist into his gut. The impact bruised her knuckles, but she snapped up with her elbow, under his chin. "You bastard!" she screamed. "Of course they burned it!" Someone grabbed her from behind, tore her off him. She tried to kick out, but missed. "There was nobody there! Nobody to defend it! It was defensible, McClain! It wouldn't have burned if you hadn't taken everyone. You just want to control us! Like the rest of your little clan of sheep!" Tears blurred her vision and she yanked hard, trying to break free of the grip someone had on her.

"Riley! Riley." Soothing hands cupped her face, and then Eden was there. "Calm down. We're doing the best we can. Your council voted, it isn't Adam's fault."

"I took your people in," he pointed out.

Riley went crazy again, kicking and tearing. Hot tears burned her skin, but the arrogant prick just watched, like he'd done them a fucking favor. "This is your fault," she told him. "You look!" She stabbed a finger out toward the horizon, toward the dirty smudge where her home had been. "That's on you." Turning, she brushed at the hands holding her. One of McClain's men. "Get your hands off me. I'm not going to go after him."

Wrenching out of the grip, she turned back to the cave. Jimmy watched with wide eyes, but she stormed past, into the cool shadows. He tried to touch her shoulder, but she shook him off with a snarl. Even he'd betrayed her.

Collapsing in the corner of the cave, she tucked her knees up in front of her and wept. It was gone. All of it. Her whole life just torn apart and smashed, and McClain had the gall to stand there and tell her he'd taken them in. Done them a favor.

Tears tore through her, a hacking wrench in her chest. How she wished she hadn't woken up this morning. Then this day would never have happened.

The worst thing was all she could think about was what had happened in that pool of water.

And how... happy – no, that wasn't the word – how *right* it had felt compared to the rest of her shitty life.

And how much that scared her.

Her eyes fell on the tiny carved doll Wade had discarded and she picked it up, curving her fingers around it. "Stupid," she whispered harshly, but she tucked it in her pocket all the same.

seven

HIS FACE ACHED like a bitch.

Luc leaned back against the cage bars, his shirt protecting him from the silver's burn. Wind whipped through his hair, stinging the harsh cuts and bruises on his face. He'd been bested by a kid. The thought disgusted him. But worse was the fact that McClain – the man he'd spent the last six years hunting – was sitting two seats away, leaning casually against the seatback as if he hadn't a care in the world.

Luc glared at the back of the bastard's hat. A pretty turn of events. This was what happened when he went soft. When he helped people. He forgot what he was for a moment, but they didn't. The kid had done a number on him, to be sure.

He glanced at the red curls whipping back in the wind in front of him. He couldn't even find it in him to be pissed at the boy. Luc would have done the same in that situation. But then he knew he was a shifty bastard. The boy who'd nearly pissed his pants when Luc had kidnapped Riley had grown up a hell of a lot in the last few days.

Blonde hair swam into view and, as if she'd ensorcelled him by that pool, his gaze ran over Riley hungrily. The scent of her grief stained the air, forcing a heavy silence on the occupants of the jeep. A young woman, who had to be McClain's sister, sat beside her and kept looking at her guiltily, but Riley never noticed. She was exhausted. Luc had watched them carry her out of the cave. She'd hadn't looked at them, not even when McClain tried to talk to her.

If it wasn't for her, he wouldn't be in this cage.

Luc bit off a curse and looked away, out into the desert. Tough words. He couldn't even summon up any anger for her either. Her pain itched along his skin, made him edgy. He wanted to touch her but he couldn't, and no one would even look at him.

Caged. He reached out with his bound hands, ran a finger along the bars, and hissed. Movement shifted in front of him. Riley. Stilling, her head half-turning toward him as if she were just as aware of him too.

A taunt leapt to his tongue, but he ground his teeth over it. He didn't want to hurt her, strangely enough. Reaching through the bars, he caught a strand of that flyaway blonde hair and rubbed it gently between his fingers.

McClain looked up in the rearview mirror. Grey-green eyes met his own. Luc stilled, fury pumping through his blood. There was his anger, right there.

McClain's eyes narrowed, and Luc realized the man was staring at his hand, and the tendril of blonde hair Luc held.

Smiling lazily, he stroked his fingers over it and laughed. *You want it?*

McClain snapped at the driver, and the jeep screamed to a halt. Hurdling over the door, he strode toward the back of the jeep and slammed a fist through the bars.

Lucius was waiting for it. He twisted fluidly, grabbing McClain's hand in a wrist-lock and shoving his bare arm against the silver bars. McClain's eyes widened, and he hissed as his skin touched the silver.

"Don't ever presume that I'm helpless," Lucius snarled, and heat flashed through his arm. His claws sprang out, and he dug them into the tender flesh of McClain's soft forearm. Aiming for the vein.

It wouldn't kill him, but he'd take what he could get.

People were screaming. The sister was standing on the seat, her hands on her cheeks as she yelled her brother's name. He'd heard McClain speak of her years ago, but the only time he'd ever seen her had been from a distance. They'd ridden together as bounty hunters, shared water and more out there on the Rim, watched each other's backs. But by silent agreement, they'd never brought each other home to their families. That was like bringing the darkness, death, and destruction of the Rim home with them. When Lucius had been at the settlement, all he'd wanted to do was kiss his wife and forget about the things he'd done.

Riley watched with an emotionless face. She reached for something, coming up with a dart gun in her hand.

Lucius's eyes widened as it swung toward him. "Don't!"

Her eyes narrowed. The gun went off, and something bit into his chest. He looked down at the dart, warmth spreading out through the entry site, washing through his veins like molten honey. With a wordless gurgle, he slumped back against the bars, the back of his neck burning as he collapsed.

The last thing he saw brought a smile to his lips as he went under.

She'd turned the dart gun on McClain.

Absolution reared over the plain like an ugly, squat fortress.

Riley hated it on sight.

McClain was snoring in the front seat, his hat over his face and his arm bandaged by Eden. Similar snores came from behind. She'd dragged Wade's bare skin off the cage bars and jammed a spare shirt under his head as Eden tended her brother. Nobody had said a word.

In fact, nobody had said anything since she'd shot McClain with his own dart gun.

"Here we are," Eden murmured, shifting uncomfortably in her seat. "Home swe—"

"Don't say it," Riley interjected. Home was a word that made her heart ache. She was so tired she just wanted to curl up under her mother's old quilt in her bed and wish this was all a dream. But that would never happen again. Eden had told her that Madi had thought to bring her things from home, but it wasn't the same. Here at Absolution, she'd be assigned a cell to sleep in, at least until she could sort out her sleeping arrangements.

Or until McClain tried to do it for her. Her eyes narrowed.

The gates started to open as they crossed the barren wasteland in front of the walls. Barbed wire curled into the distance, and the ground was pitted from gunfire. A pang filled her chest. That, more than anything, reminded her of Haven.

But Absolution was nearly three times the size of her little settlement. At Haven, cattle and livestock roamed the dirt streets, and some of the women had coaxed lush little gardens to life in the walled-off yards behind their homes. Here, some of the streets were cobbled, the jeep bouncing under the shadow of the gates. And they were swept clean. There were no goats, no cats, not even a dog. Men moved with military efficiency along the walls, dressed in matching black and carrying ancient AK-47's. Every house was roofed in tile – a virtual luxury – and the walls were solid white adobe.

There was a square, squat building at the very heart of the settlement. The jeep roared up the hill toward it, curving around the roads. People lifted their heads, smiled and waved. McClain's name was on everyone's lips. As they saw the warg cage in the back, the smiles died, and the calls turned harsh.

"Kill it!" one old lady yelled.

Riley flinched back into the seat. The world changed, and she couldn't find her feet. Sleep was a luxury she didn't think she would have time for. She had to get to

Wade, had to talk to him, tell him she'd never meant for any of this to happen.

Find a way out of this mess.

Driving between a pair of rough-hewn barracks, the driver yanked the jeep to a halt. Jimmy winced as he tried to get out, but Riley just sat there, staring up at the main building. It was two stories high, the walls white stucco. Arrow slits lined the walls, places were a man could fire from if he needed, and the covered walkway along the top of the barracks overlooked the yard. Absolution had been designed for defense. A grudging part of her had to admit that McClain had done a good job; it would take a miracle for the reivers to take this place.

"Are you coming?" Eden asked in a quiet murmur.

Riley looked up. She didn't want to get out of the jeep. Getting out meant accepting what had happened. Accepting that Haven was gone for good.

But she was a big girl now. Throwing a tantrum would gain her nothing, and the fury that had burned through her back at the cave was gone.

Shooting McClain had been damned therapeutic.

Without a word, she opened the jeep door and stepped out. She knew it wasn't fair, but she couldn't help feeling as though Eden had taken her brother's side. As she would. He *was* her brother; Eden was bound to defend him.

"Is there a room I can use until I decide what I'm going to do?" Riley asked. Her voice came out cool and neutral.

"You're not staying here?"

"No." The answer was short but definite. "There's nothing here for me." She'd been part of the council at Haven, respected, her choices helping to define the colony. McClain had his own council, his own systems in place. She knew the way he worked. The men-folk at Absolution formed the military, regardless of desire. The women tended the homes.

If he gave her a needle and thread, she'd jam it in his arm. Or worse.

Behind her, a scuffle broke out. Three men were trying to drag the warg cage off the back of the jeep. Wade caught her eye through the bars as she turned, then made a swiping gesture at one of the guards. His claws were out, but the action was lazy. The guard leapt back with a yell, as if he thought Wade truly intended to claw him up, then lifted his shotgun and jammed it through the bars. It landed with a meaty thump.

"Come," Eden murmured, taking her by the upper arm. "Let's go inside."

Riley forced herself to walk away, gritting her teeth against the harsh grunts and curses behind her. Wade could have kept his claws to himself. The action had been designed to inflame, like most of his actions.

Still....

She made it almost to the lintel before a rough cry caught her ear. He'd never have cried out. Not Wade. Not unless they'd hurt him bad.

Ripping out of Eden's grip, she stormed back down toward the jeep. It shouldn't matter – she wasn't responsible for this – but she couldn't stop herself from reacting. Wade trembled in a heap in the cage, on his hands and knees and spitting blood. Bruises darkened his eyes, and he'd managed to get free of his bonds. Those bloody claws, she suspected. Sharp as knives.

The guard lifted the shotgun high.

Riley grabbed the end. "For God's sake! That's *enough*! He's down."

He turned on her with his arm raised, and she saw the blank look of fury in his eyes. Whoever the guard was, he'd lost someone to the wargs, she was sure of it. Hate didn't burn that hot for no reason. She flinched, wrestling for the gun.

"Walker," McClain's voice cut the air. "You hit the lady, and I'll strip you down and whip you myself."

The hand froze in mid-air.

Riley slowly let the barrel of the gun go. She didn't want to turn, to look, but her gaze was drawn regardless of her feelings.

McClain leaned against the jeep, his voice steady despite the fact his knees threatened to give out. His gaze ran over her, and she saw something there that made her uneasy. Emotions she didn't think she could name. Emotions *he* probably couldn't name right then.

"Besides, she's got a mean right hook," McClain said. "And if she gets that gun, she'll shoot you right where it hurts."

Riley arched a brow, a sweet little smile curling over her lips. "How's your ass, McClain?"

"Want to kiss it better?" His voice was cool. The look in his eyes wasn't.

"You bend over and I'll shoot you again."

He smiled. Took a wobbly step forward. The smile died. "That's the last time I leave a loaded gun near you."

Each step brought him closer. Tension grew, spreading down her spine with tingling fingers. She didn't miss the glance he gave the cage behind her. Subconsciously, she took a step back, between him and Wade.

"Riley, don't turn your back on him," McClain snapped. "The bastard's got his claws out."

"He's had three days to claw me up if he wanted," she replied. "And I'm not sure you're in the right state of mind to be dealing with him right now."

"*Is* there a right state of mind to deal with Wade?"

"With plenty of sleep, and a good slug of alcohol, I'd imagine," she shot back.

"A good slug, all right. I've got a fucking silver bullet with his name on it." McClain glared at her. "Get out of the way, Riley. I won't ask you again."

"That's the problem. You never *do* ask."

McClain sucked in a deep breath. "When you're in my settlement, you obey my rules. Wade's dangerous."

She took a deep breath. "He helped me get Jimmy out. That's got to count for something, doesn't it?"

If anything, McClain's gaze flattened. "And what about you, Riley? What'd he do to you?"

"As fascinating as this conversation is," Wade drawled behind her, "I'm afraid I'm going to have to cut it short."

A hand curled in the back of her shirt and wrenched her backward. Riley yelped as she lost her balance, hitting the bars. A second later, warm arms curled around her, one at her waist, the other settling its claws against her throat.

Déjà vu.

"Let me go," she snapped.

"You should have listened to the man," Wade murmured. "I let my guard down once, and got my fingers burned. I don't plan on doing it again. Humanity's for the humans."

"I've got shooters at your back," McClain said, drawing his gun.

"What are they packin'?" Wade asked lazily. "Better be careful it don't travel straight through me." His hand stroked down over her breasts, her stomach. "She's not as indestructible as I am."

Riley clamped a hand over his. "Damn it, Wade," she muttered through clenched teeth. "Let me go."

"This is my only chance out of here." The whisper steamed her skin.

"No, it's not." She twisted her neck, caught a glance of him out of the corner of her eye. "I made a promise," she whispered, barely audible. "I'll get you out."

Wade slowly smiled, looked up. "He's not going to let me out," he replied in a satisfied murmur. "Not now."

McClain's face had gone hard as steel. He stepped closer. "Let her go."

The silence thickened as the two men stared at each other. Wade tapped his claws against her throat in warning as McClain took another step. "How much do you want her?" Wade asked. "How much would it hurt if I dug these a little deeper?" The pressure of his claws hardened, almost pricking the skin of her throat. "To lose her the way I lost everything I gave a damn about? How much, McClain?" The last question was a snarl, his claws digging dangerously deep.

Riley froze. "Wade?"

His attention was no longer on her. She might not have even existed. Only McClain was there in his eyes.

She could smell the stink of his burning flesh as it brushed against the silver bars. "It's not worth it. He'll never let you live," she said.

"He never intended to." His voice rose. "Did you, McClain? That would mess with the little plan he's got going on here."

"What the hell are you talking about?" she asked.

A hard laugh. "Ask him. Or better yet, ask where your room is, darlin'. And then ask him why he wants to kill me so bad."

"That last one's fairly self-explanatory."

"Mmm." The hum shivered over her ear as he rested his chin on her shoulder. "McClain's never wanted to kill me before, have you? He wanted to save me from my evil self."

McClain had his gun trained on them. "Let her go."

"Why don't you tell her what's got you so worked up?" Wade laughed. "Or better yet, tell her why I've got such a hard-on to kill you. To hurt you." His hand stroked over Riley's stomach.

McClain shifted his stance slightly and squeezed the trigger.

Wade jerked away, and Riley screamed as the bullet whizzed past her face, burying itself in the wall behind the cage. Wade settled behind her again, on the other side.

"You asshole!" she yelled. "That could have hit me."

"I have excellent aim," McClain replied coldly.

"Yet this is the third chance you've had at me," Wade said. "And you missed again."

McClain's eyes narrowed. "This goes too far, even for you, Wade. You had your chances. I won't cry any tears this time. Sometimes, there's nothing left to save."

"I bet you I can *make* you cry. Tears of blood," Wade replied. "I just have to find the right buttons to push."

Claws rippled over her tank, sliding it up. Riley held her breath, looking down as the razor-sharp edge of them revealed her midriff to the world. "What are you doing?" she whispered, true fear starting to slide through her veins. What did she know about him? Really know? "Let me go. Please. Please, don't do this."

"Sorry, darlin'." His fingers slid over her smooth skin, claws skittering light enough to send a shiver down her spine. "Truly, I am."

Riley clamped a hand over his, looking down, her throat tightening. "Please, don't. *Please.*" She turned her head, glanced over her shoulder. His face was close to hers, so close she could feel his breath on her lips. His gaze slowly left McClain, locked on hers, and Riley willed him to *see* her. "I trusted you," she whispered.

Thought flickered in his blue eyes. "Then you put your trust in the wrong person."

"Did I?" she pressed. A tiny hint of doubt made his lashes shutter, and she leapt after it, tried to chase it. "My daddy got clawed up. Put a gun in his mouth before he could turn." Ruthlessly, she captured his gaze. "I'll do the same, Wade. I swear I will. I won't let you make me into that."

"A monster?" He smiled bitterly. "Like me?"

And there was her opening. "A monster. Like that warg at the gates to Black River. Like all the wargs out there on the plains, howling for flesh. You're not like them, Wade. You have a choice," she said harshly. "Do this and you're no better than they are. You may as well take off that charm and just tear us all to shreds. Humanity's for the humans, Wade, but you still want it, I know you do. Otherwise, you would have taken that charm off long ago."

His gaze hardened to blue steel. "You don't know shit about me."

Riley's voice dropped until only he could have heard it. "I know you held my hand, when I was scared of the dark. You helped me save Jimmy when you didn't have to. And I know you held me, wanting me to hold you back, in that pool of water. You wanted that more than you wanted the sex. So, yes, I think I know a little bit about you, Wade. You want to be human more than you want anything in your life, don't you? You think McClain took that from you somehow." His gaze locked on hers with an intensity that almost frightened her, but she pushed on. "But he didn't take it from you. You make this choice, and *you* do. You throw that dream away like it's worth nothing." His body trembled, claws threatening to slice into her flesh. Riley stroked the warm skin of his hand, forcing herself to believe. "Let me go, Wade. Please. For both our sakes. You'll hurt me more than you'll ever hurt him."

For a long, breathless moment, she held his gaze. Slowly, she felt his touch give way, his claws retracting into his skin. He laughed, and it was full of mockery, but she didn't think it was aimed at her.

Then she was able to slowly push his hand away from her trembling midriff.

His fingers came up, traced the smooth curve of her cheek. Fingertips brushed against her mouth, trembling, the spark of it shooting straight through her. Cupping her face, he dragged her close and kissed her. Hard and fast, his lips pressing against hers with a desperation she could feel through the steel core of his body.

She shoved at him and stepped back. His hand lingered on hers, keeping her between him and the shooters. Riley stared at him. *Why the hell...?* She pressed a hand to her lips, confusion slicing through her.

He smiled. Sharp-edged and bittersweet. "Goodbye, Riley. You almost make me believe there's something good left."

Then he shoved her away from him. Looking up, he smiled, arms held out in surrender.

Bullets hit him from every direction, tearing through his flesh. He jerked, his knees going out from under him as a scream tore from her throat.

Then he slowly crumpled to the floor of the cage.

eight

IT HURT.

Worse than he'd expected. Bright light washed over him, half-blinded him. Pain was a razor's edge. He felt like someone had punched holes in him with a silver knife. It burned. Noise crackled in his ears, almost undistinguishable.

Someone was shouting. McClain. "Stop shooting!"

A gasp. A woman. Then the cage was wrenched open and her hands covered his chest, shoving into the raw burning mess that he swore was silver-borne. He could see again. A blurred outline of a woman, her blonde hair a halo against the beating sun. Horrified. Cursing down at him as she tried to crush his heart beneath her hands. White light outlined her body, softening her face, her hair, until all he could see was a pair of serious brown eyes staring frantically down at him.

Luc made a gurgling sound. Couldn't breathe. Blood bubbling on his lips. Heart pounding in his ears. The strength went out of him, and his head rolled back.

"Come on, you bastard. Come on!" Words scraped his skin. Scraped it raw.

He flinched. Hurt. The hurt was bad. So blinding he drifted for a moment in utter painlessness, and then blinked as it wrenched back into his life with razor-sharp claws.

I'm sorry. I don't think I can.

And the damnedest thing was he tried. But the strength was draining out of him, taking her away from him. He could hear her yelling at him, telling him to get his ass back here. Wet tears spattered his parched face, like the rain after a long summer.

It all seemed so very far away.

Slowly, he let go. Floated.

And then he faded away.

"Damn it!"

Riley held her hands over the mess of Wade's chest. No matter how hard she pressed, she couldn't seem to stop the blood from welling. Her hands were wet, coated with the stuff. She didn't think she'd ever manage to wash it off if he died.

And when had her feelings about him changed so much that she'd care?

Riley ground her teeth together, heat springing up behind her eyes. *You almost make me believe there's something good left*. Why the hell had he pushed her away? He'd known what was going to happen. And he'd accepted it.

McClain slid to his knees beside the open cage, his face hard and composed.

"Jesus," he muttered. Looking up, he bellowed, "Eden!" As soon as Eden reached his side, he relinquished his post, gesturing sharply to his men. "Stand down. Get a stretcher here immediately." Another look down. That time, his composure shattered. Frustration edged with a very real pain filled his grey-green eyes.

Riley tore her gaze from him, confused. Eden nudged her to the side, taking Riley's hand and pressing it over the bubbles of blood from lower in Wade's chest. "Here," she said. "Put the pressure here. If he can't breathe he'll die."

"Is he going to die?" Riley didn't think she could handle that. It was her fault he was in this situation.

Eden's expression closed over. "I don't know, Riley. I don't know."

"He's a warg."

They could recover from almost anything. But... She looked at his chest, at the blood drenching his shirt.

Eden gave a helpless shrug. "He's lost a lot of blood." Her lashes lowered. "And I don't have the facilities to replace it."

"Come on." McClain grabbed her by the arm, drew her to her feet. "Let Eden do her job, Riley. You're shaken up. You need to rest."

He drew her away, his hand like a manacle around her wrist. Two of his men rested a makeshift stretcher on the ground beside Eden and bent to lift Wade onto it.

Riley tore her gaze from his battered body, her bloodied hands still held out in front of her.

"This is my fault," she said blindly.

McClain led her toward the main building. His eyes lit on her, strangely gentle. "Wade knew what he was doing, Riley. You weren't at fault in any of this." His lips thinned. "Though I did warn you not to turn your back."

I didn't think he'd hurt me.

And she'd been right. He hadn't, when it came down to it. Even knowing what was going to happen once he gave up his human screen, he'd chosen to let her live. Chose her life over his.

Heat flared behind her eyes. A hot, salty tear slid down her cheek, which McClain pretended not to see.

"Come on," he said, maneuvering her toward the door. "You've had a bad shock today. I'll help you clean up."

One last glance in Wade's direction. His foot lolled off the stretcher as they carried him toward the infirmary, Eden holding someone's shirt over the worst of the wounds.

Her heart clenched in her chest, and she staggered over the doorstep. She wanted to see him, but how could she help? She'd only be in Eden's way. Without any nursing skills, she was worse than useless.

But at least she'd be the one person who hoped he pulled through. At least she could stop Eden from giving up on him

"I want to go to the infirmary," she stated, reaching out and shoving against the wall to stop his inexorable drag. Her bloody hand left a perfect print on the walls.

McClain's body turned toward her, and Riley dug her heels in. "No," she said. "I don't want to go to my room. I want to be there. I want to make sure he knows I'm there."

"He can't hear you," McClain said slowly, searching her face.

"I want to be there," she repeated.

McClain's tawny brows lowered. "Riley, I know... it was hard out there. I know what he did to you, what happened... If you think—"

"What he did to me?"

McClain tipped her chin to the side, his fingers warm against her skin. He brushed them down her neck, against a spot that hurt at his touch. His eyes went dark with unsaid emotion. With fury.

She looked down, but couldn't see. There was a mirror in the hall, with a hat stand. Shrugging his hand off her, she crossed to the mirror.

Bruises marred the smooth skin of her throat. And where McClain had touched her lingered an unmistakable bite mark.

Heat flushed up her neck, into her cheeks. She met McClain's gaze in the mirror and looked away first.

"You don't have to tell me about it." His voice had an edge to it, and his arms were held stiffly at his sides. "I'll never ask. But I know you're not thinking right at the moment. Sometimes it happens, when a man kidnaps a woman."

Riley's gaze shot to his. "It's not that. You don't—" She made a gurgling sound, hating this. "Is that why you're so angry with him?"

No answer. But from the look on his face, she *knew*.

Hugging her arms across her chest, careless of the blood, she shook her head. It was both her secret shame and a moment of intense rightness in her life. She couldn't regret what had happened, but the fact that she'd enjoyed it... That she didn't know if she'd say no if she had the chance to live through it again... That was her shame, right there.

But if she didn't say anything, McClain would bury Wade where he stood. She could read his body language. He had no intentions of seeing Wade back on his feet. In his mind, Wade had done the unthinkable.

"It's not what you think."

His hat lifted, revealing just a hint of those stunning eyes. Hard-edged now. Lacking all emotion. "Riley, you don't have to—" He scraped his hat off his head, revealing close-cropped tawny brown curls. "I'm not the person for this. You want to talk about it, you need to wait for Eden. I can't hold your hand through this." His own fisted. Clenched. "I want to kill him right now. For daring to put his bloody hands on you."

Riley grabbed his forearm, feeling the muscles flex beneath her grip. "It wasn't rape," she blurted. "I said yes."

She might as well have hit him. McClain didn't flinch, but his entire body turned to stone, his head slowly swiveling toward her. She couldn't quite meet his eyes, focusing instead on the line of his mouth. Silence filled the air, thickened it. And within him, every muscle bunched, as if violence was but a thought away.

He let out a harsh breath. "Why?"

"I don't know," she snapped, backing away. There was blood on his arm in the shape of a handprint. Wade's blood. "You don't understand. It was crazy out there. Wade was an asshole, but he helped me get Jimmy back. He didn't have to do that. I don't even know why he did. He'd kidnapped me. All he had to do was overpower me and drag me back out into the desert, but he didn't." She met his eyes then, begged for him to understand. "I'm not saying he's one of the good guys. But... there were moments when he was almost human. I was so scared of the dark, of the revenants, but he helped me through it. Christ, he tucked me into my blankets like I was a kid. There's something there, McClain, that isn't all bad. And we'd been through so much that... I gave in. I said yes. Even knowing what he was, I said yes."

Her words were met with silence. McClain bristled. "Yet you never *once* allowed me to touch you."

Riley licked her lips. "Don't think I never considered it." Until he opened his mouth. "But you want more from me than I can give. You want me to be something I'm not. Maybe I could make you happy for a few months. Maybe I'd even be happy myself, but in the end we'd only hate each other. Wade and I... It didn't mean anything. It was just sex, just... someone to turn to after everything I'd been through, but it *was* consensual."

He lifted an unsteady hand and raked it through his hair. A harsh bark of a laugh erupted from his throat. "Fucking karma, that's what this is." Looking up, he focused a predator gaze on her. "He's going to die, Riley. We all knew it. Eden's just making him comfortable."

The blood drained out of her face. "He's a warg. He's strong, he can heal anything—"

"Not even a warg can heal after that much blood loss."

The words were brutal. They tore something deep inside her, an inexplicable pain. "No."

McClain stepped closer. "Just sex?" Another low, bitter laugh. "Don't fool yourself, Riley. If it was just sex for you, I'd have had you in my bed years ago." He reached out, brushed his fingers against her face. "You never let down your guard. Never."

A long moment of horrible silence. Because he was right.

Then he took a deep breath. "Clean yourself up. Then come to the infirmary. I'll meet you there, and we'll see what we can do."

"You said he needs blood," she whispered. "Where the hell are we going to get compatible blood from here?"

McClain turned on his heel. "Just get yourself to the infirmary. And keep your mouth shut."

A breathless knock.

Riley exchanged glances with the man guarding the door. His hair was cropped close to his scalp and he waited in a prepared stance, his hands crossed in front of him, biceps bulging.

The door opened just enough to reveal Eden's face. Her expression relaxed when she saw Riley, and she gestured her through a crack in the door Riley could barely squeeze through.

Her gaze went straight to Wade, as if something linked them. He was flat on his back on the hospice bed, his tanned skin drained of color, and a mass of white bandages around his chest. The sight punched her in the chest, and Riley dragged her wet hair over her shoulder, licking at her lips. She'd washed herself as quickly as she could, splashing cold water over her face before she came. It was enough to slough off the fog that slowed her movements, her thoughts. Enough to bring the stark reality to the forefront.

She didn't want him to die.

McClain had his back to her, sitting on this side of the bed, his hat dragged low over his eyes. The room was clean and sterile, with bloodied bandages overflowing the bin and a bowl full of crimson water on the table. Eden returned to the table, wiping her hands dry on a towel, weariness staining her features.

Riley noticed it... and said nothing of it. She couldn't stop her eyes from traveling back to Wade. She kept expecting him to sit up and arch a brow in her direction with a mocking quip. But he didn't. His body was as still as death, skin as waxen as a corpse. Bruises marred his face, and the bloody tear through his eyebrow had been stitched.

"Is he...?" She couldn't ask.

"He's still alive," Eden murmured.

Stepping closer, Riley saw the needle taped to the inside of his elbow, and the tube leading away from it. Red blood filled the clear tube.

The other end of the line ran up to McClain's elbow, and the butterfly-shaped clip there. Riley stopped in shock, and Eden bumped into her.

Without his hat, McClain looked almost approachable. He looked up, his expression tired. "Sit down," he said. "And shut your mouth."

Slowly, Riley moved around the bed and settled on the seat on the other side. She was right. McClain was giving Wade his blood.

But how? A frown drew her brows together. A warg wasn't human. Not any longer. Were they? "They can take human blood? His body won't reject it, will he?"

Eden examined her work carefully, keeping her mouth shut. Riley looked to McClain for the answers.

He didn't look at her. Instead, he stared at Wade emotionlessly. "With your background – your father – I never thought you'd take to the monsters. I didn't—" He looked down. "I never made a move. I didn't think you'd ever trust me enough." His head turned, pinned her with a gaze that made her shiver. "You might think it wouldn't have worked, but I'm not so sure. You never knew me, Riley." A soft laugh. "And it's my own damned fault."

Slowly, he reached inside his shirt and drew out the length of a chain, a heavy pewter amulet dangling from it.

Riley froze.

McClain dropped it against his shirt, his gaze returning to Wade and the identical charm around his throat. "He told you about it then. Told you how it works?"

"He said if he lost it, I had to run." Riley had to swallow to get the words out. McClain? A warg? The words smashed every preconception she'd had of him, and raised a thousand questions in their place.

"How?" She looked down, then realized the connection between them. "Who?" she asked. "Who turned who?"

And again, she answered her own question.

"It was you," she said. "You made him what he is."

McClain nodded slowly. "I'm not proud of any of it, Riley. You don't think seeing him like this doesn't hurt me? Luc and I rode together, out along the Rim. I had his back, and he had mine."

"That's why he wants to kill you."

Eden pressed a gentle hand against her brother's arm. "It wasn't your fault," she said fiercely.

"I made the choice," he replied. "I chose you over him." He closed his eyes, as if he couldn't bear to face the truth himself. "A man named Bartholomew Cane rode into town one day when Eden was sixteen. Didn't know it at the time, but he and his man Colton were wargs. Both of them carried charms like this one. Gave me a bad gut feeling, but what could I do? There were signs, but the moon didn't affect them. So Luc and I dismissed our intuition.

"They were after local men to help ride down a warg who'd done them wrong, they claimed. The money was good. I put my hand up. Wade's wife was pregnant, and he didn't want to leave her side, so I went out alone."

Eden's grip tightened, leaving white imprints on his arm. "Adam," she whispered. "It's okay."

His shoulders tensed. "Did you know he had a wife?"

Riley looked at Wade, at the silent figure on the bed. "He told me. Said her name was Abbie."

The feel of McClain's gaze on her face was like a palpable touch. She met it and saw a new question smoldering there, though he never gave voice to it. Instead, he shifted uneasily. "We hunted the warg down and executed it. He was wearing the same charm as Cane and Colton, but I didn't notice until I rolled him over. He'd never gone beast on us, not once. I couldn't stop myself from wondering, and Cane knew it. Tore me up, out there on the range. Told me the warg had been his third, that he'd tried to run and borne the price. I was to be his replacement."

Disgust flavored his tone. "They had a spare charm. Colton's got native blood, and his grandfather's a shaman, so he made 'em. I don't know how any of it works. It just does. Cane wanted one more to ride with him."

"Wade," Riley whispered.

"I said I wouldn't do it." McClain shook his head emphatically. "Cane tried to force me to his will the way he'd done to Colton, but... I wouldn't. Nearly broke me. You've never felt such pain, like he was ripping my mind apart. I woke up hours later, and Colton was just sitting there. Said I should have agreed. That Cane had ways of breaking a man."

Eden stroked a hand over his shoulder. "He came for me, while Adam was out of it." She shot a fierce glare toward Riley as if daring her to condemn him. "Tore the charm off Adam and shoved us in a room together." She licked dry lips. "Night was coming."

McClain held out his hands. "I could feel it. Like an itch under the skin. I'd never turned, not once, but I knew I wouldn't be able to hold it. So I told Cane I'd give him what he wanted. I'd lure Wade out if he let Eden go."

His words fell into silence. Riley tucked her knees up in front of her, far too aware of both men. McClain, rock-solid McClain, had a face like granite, but that didn't mean he didn't feel anything. The revelation made something ache within her. Sympathy. Would she have done the same in his position? Either way, the choice was hard – kill his sister with his own hands, or betray a friend.

"I can't blame him for his hatred," McClain said wearily. "I earned it. I betrayed him in the worst possible way. I've tried to make amends, but he won't hear of it."

Eden leaned on his shoulder. "It's not your fault. No man should have to make that choice."

Riley shook her head. "I still can't believe... How do you hide it? If the settlement knew—"

"The only way they'd find out would be if you told them." Harsh words. Untrusting ones.

She stiffened. "I wouldn't do that. A week ago, maybe." But the man on the bed had changed that, changed all of her perceptions.

And McClain knew it. "He's not the man he once was, Riley. What I did to him... it turned him hard, bitter. He walked away from Abbie, even though she'd just lost the baby. Walked away from... everything. He's spent the last eight years trying to kill me." Reaching down, he stroked the thin tube that fed directly into his vein. "This changes nothing. I don't even know why I'm doing this.

When he wakes, he'll come after me as sure as the sun rises in the east."

Eden scowled. "I'm not going to let him hurt you." A defiant look in Riley's direction. "I pity the man, but I won't let him take my brother. No matter what happened."

Riley's heart raced. Eden wouldn't hurt him, not in this condition. She was a healer, not a killer, but if she thought her brother was in danger there were ways she could manage that. Leave the door open to someone with a grudge against a warg. Or keep him incapacitated with drugs or herbs.

"Maybe he's not the man he once was," Riley argued. "But I don't think he's entirely lost."

McClain tensed. "Don't be a fool, Riley. He used you."

"Yes," she said. "He made no mockery of his intentions, but you weren't there." With a frustrated sigh, she spread her hands. "I'm not an idiot. This... This is misplaced guilt. Because he gave me what I wanted, and I reneged on my side of the bargain. I gave him into the hands of his enemy, and that led to this. I don't want him to die. I don't want it to be my fault."

An intense look that burned her to the core. Without his hat, McClain looked amazingly vulnerable. Tawny curls and eyes that threatened to drown her. Green eyes, she realized now, with flecks of silver through them. Eyes she'd once thought were a mysterious grey-green. He reached down, lips twisting angrily as he tugged the needle from his arm. Weariness stained his hard features. "I wish I believed you," he snarled, handing the needle to Eden.

Snatching a piece of gauze, he pressed it against the bleeding vein. "But I've never seen you soften. Not for any man."

Wrenching to his feet, he staggered slightly. Eden grabbed his arm, shooting Riley an exasperated glance.

"I'm fine," he snapped, warding her off. "I just need to sleep."

"You're not staying?" Eden murmured.

McClain shot Wade one last condemning look. "No. Let the bastard bleed out, or let him live. I don't give a damn anymore."

Without looking at her, he surged toward the door, tucking the charm beneath his shirt once more. The door slammed behind him, and Riley took a slow breath. The man drove her crazy, but she didn't doubt his charisma. His presence filled a room, pressed against the skin.

Silence fell, full of unspoken reprimand.

Riley settled back into the chair, finally able to relax. "I won't tell anyone about him," she replied. "I don't have it in me to be vindictive."

Eden sighed. "He's lying, you know."

"McClain?"

"He cares. He cares far too damned much." With one last enigmatic look in Riley's direction, she sat on the bed and took Wade's wrist in her hands, pressing her fingers to his pulse.

"I wish I did too," Riley whispered. "Maybe it'd be easier. I'm not saying I haven't thought about it. Your brother's an attractive man." Heat flushed through her cheeks. "Always so damned hard. If there'd been one hint that there was something else there, one hint of softness, maybe my feelings would have changed. Argh." She sank her head into her hands. "Men. Why did any of this have to happen?"

Eden shrugged. "At least you've got options."

A trace of their old relationship, of friendly banter. "I'll trade you," Riley muttered. "Two options for none." She looked down at the prone figure on the bed. What was she thinking? Maybe she wouldn't even have two options. And when had Wade been put on that list? Her voice softened, a faint tremble to it. "Will he live, Eden?"

"You know I don't give promises."

"Your bedside manner sucks."

Eden grimaced, then took her fingers off his pulse. "It's stronger," she said. "The bleeding's slowed, and he's got a few pints of blood back into him. There's a chance. That's all I can give you. Now, we just have to wait."

"Waiting's for the patient," Riley grumbled.

Eden settled into the seat McClain had vacated. "Maybe we could talk." She shot Riley a sidelong glance through thick lashes. "How are you feeling? Have you recovered from your ordeal?"

"I'm tired." She sank into the chair and rested her chin on her knees. "But I'm fine, Eden."

"Adam...." The healer hesitated. "He told me... Do you need some morning-after tea?"

A bitter brew most goodwives out here knew by rote. An herb that often kept a man's seed from taking root. Riley flushed. "Please. Just in case."

Eden rose and slipped toward the bench at the far end of the room. Hundreds of tiny drawers filled the woodwork, and she eased one open, taking out a sachet.

"Stay here with him. I'll go find some boiled water for this to steep."

Riley nodded and watched as the door closed behind her friend's slim shape. The quietness of the room draped over her skin. She could barely hear him breathing. Inching closer, she peered at him.

"Don't do this," she whispered. "Don't die. Don't make me hate you." Edging onto the bed, she slid her hand over his, weaving her fingers between his own. His flesh was cool to the touch. Unresponsive. Riley sucked in a sharp breath. His hand had been her anchor in the dark.

Perhaps hers could be his.

nine

LUC COUGHED, HIS lungs heaving with pain. He could taste old blood on his lips, and the memory of drowning on it suddenly assailed him, making him wrench for the edge of the bed. The world was dark and silent. Alone. He was alone. Panic clenched his gut muscles as pain shot through him.

Shots.

Half a dozen of them, drilling into his chest. A gasp tore from his lips, an almost inarticulate cry of pain and fear as he reached for the bed, tried to ground himself.

"Hush." Whispered words in the dark. The rich scent of a woman, one he almost didn't recognize. Perfumed soap clung to her skin, disguising the earthy smell he'd come to know. Riley. Hands trailed over his bare shoulders, and he felt the dip of the bed as she sat on it. Then her arms slid around his neck and he clung to her, his lungs heaving, the panicked rasp of breath slowly calming.

Lucius buried his face in her neck. Not alone. She was there, though he didn't know where he was, or what the devil had happened.

The smooth stroke of her hand through his hair came, gentle and calming. He clutched at her arm, needing to feel her skin beneath his.

"You're alive," Riley whispered, as if afraid to curse him by saying the words louder. Another lingering caress through his hair. "We're in the infirmary. Eden stitched you up, said your wounds were starting to heal. It's nearly morning." Her face lowered, words whispered in his ear. "She said you might be frightened if you woke. They wanted to chain you to the bed, but I didn't think you'd be a danger."

His fingers curled around her wrist. Damn him for a fool, for showing any sign of weakness, but she was right. Fear tasted bitter on his tongue, and he hadn't the energy to drive her away, let alone the will. The pain left him vulnerable, made him crave her touch. Anything but waking alone.

He opened his mouth, but nothing came out. Not enough breath to speak. Riley seemed to understand. She eased him back onto the mattress, her hair tangling over his chest as she leaned forward, the silky strands painfully sensitive against his skin. Lucius grabbed for her hand.

"I'm not going anywhere," she murmured. "You need to sleep. To heal." A hesitation came. "I promise I'll watch over you."

He clutched her hand tight, rested it against his abdomen. Riley stilled, then slowly lay down, easing her chin onto his shoulder. The heat of her body warmed him, her sweet breath whispering over his bare skin as she curled around him from behind.

"I'm angry with you," she said. "That's twice you've threatened to claw me. Twice I've forgiven you. No more, you understand?"

Lucius turned his head toward her. His eyes were slowly adjusting to the slits of moonlight that peeked through the curtains. It washed over her hair and skin, turning it silver. He could just make out the angry glint in her dark eyes.

Taking a deep breath, he rasped, "Tomorrow. Talk... tomorrow."

Blessedly, she fell silent, but that steely glint in her eyes didn't soften. "Tomorrow," she replied. Her fingers curled into his and she sighed, relaxing against his shoulder. "Thank God, there'll be a tomorrow."

The curtains opened with a jerk. Riley sat up sharply, flinching at the sudden light. Eden shot her a prim look, lips thinned. "Adam's on his way." A pointed look. "Maybe you'd best straighten up."

Looking down, Riley saw the indentation on the sheets where she'd lain, and the way her fingers were still clasped with Wade's.

"He woke," she said, feeling as though she owed someone an explanation. "You were right. He was frightened."

Easing off the bed, she scraped her imprint off the bed and straightened the sheet over Wade's bare hips. That done, she turned her attention to her hair, finger-combing out the snarls and straightening her shirt.

"Damn it, Riley," Eden murmured, stalking past. "What are you doing?"

I don't know.

She turned away just as the door banged open; McClain stepped through, followed by a pair of his men. His expression raked over her, missing nothing, she was sure. Those smoky green eyes hardened, and he gestured sharply. "Is he out of danger?"

Eden checked his pulse and breathing. Wade murmured sleepily, reaching out for something. Her hand, Riley thought guiltily.

"His signs are good."

"Then we move him." McClain nodded as if the matter was decided. "He can't stay here. He's too dangerous, and I'm not going to have him take out his vengeance on either of you."

"Where are you taking him?" Riley stepped in front of him.

McClain looked down, barely an inch between them. "There's a cage in the lab. Eden can monitor him from there."

"He's barely lucid," she snapped. "What makes you think he won't backslide?"

One hard look that left nothing to be negotiated with. "He's a warg."

"He's not indestructible."

"He'll survive. If only to plague me another day." McClain ignored her and glanced at Eden. "Any questions?"

She shook her head, lips compressed. Not taking sides, damn her.

"Then get him out of here, Jericho. Be gentle, but make sure he's locked up tight. I want a guard on the room at all times." Another piercing glare that turned Riley's spine to ice. "And apart from Eden, no visitors unless I expressly command it."

Then he strode past and left her fuming behind him.

⟶ — — — ⟶   ⟵ — — — ⟵

He had no right.

Riley tucked her hands under her armpits, stalking through the walled gardens behind the main building. Gravel tracks wound between the garden beds, revealing neat rows of herbs and vegetables. Not a single flower in sight. A few fruit trees offered welcome shade, but the garden was built for a purpose, not for pleasure.

She had a room there, a bare cell with a few of the things Madi had brought with her. The old faded quilt her grandmother had made for her, her clothes and boots, a few books that she'd spent a small fortune acquiring. It only reminded her of what it was not.

Home.

Sighing, Riley ducked under the sprawling greenery of a kumquat tree with its dark, bladed leaves and small, yellow fruit. The shade was a welcome respite from the morning sun. Heat baked the gravel paths, the small wilted herbs. It shimmered off the cobbles and gave a stark haze to the white stucco walls, making them look sun-bleached and bare. Like bone.

What was she going to do? She'd spent the whole night curled against Wade, her fingers interlaced with his. Giving the man comfort.

Christ. She dropped her head into her hands. Who was she fooling? Certainly not herself, and by the look in Eden and McClain's eyes, not them either.

Why the fascination with a man who'd threatened to claw her up twice now? If she was expecting anything more from him, then she ought to just excise that thought from her head. The only person Wade gave a damn about was Wade. Or even McClain, who he was so desperate to kill. There was no room there for her.

"Are you okay?" The quiet voice took her by surprise.

Riley yanked her head up, sucking in a sharp breath. A young girl stared at her from the path, her white cotton pinafore stained and smothered in dust. Tangles of baby-fine blonde hair curled down her back, and her eyes were as blue as the midday sky, framed by lush, dark lashes.

She'd be a beauty one day. And with that smile creeping over her lips, she'd no doubt break more hearts than she'd keep. A fat little puppy scratched at her side, stifling a yawn.

"I'm fine," Riley said. She looked around. "Are you supposed to be here?"

The girl shrugged. "Probably not. But Aunt Eden's busy. She usually keeps an eye on me, but they brought in a warg yesterday. She's been tending to him." Her nose screwed up. "Don't know why. Adam's only going to have to kill it."

World-weary words from a girl who couldn't have been more than ten. Still, that was the way it was out here. Every single family in the Wastelands had lost at least one person to the dangers that stalked them.

Riley eased back on her hands, eyeing the girl. *Aunt Eden?* The only sibling Eden had was McClain, and she'd never heard of him having a child. Her gaze searched the girl's face, hunting for signs of him, but there were none. Only eyes the color of a cloudless sky.

Riley frowned then held out her hand. Dirt imprinted her palm, and she shook it off. "Name's Riley. I'm from Haven."

The little girl shook her hand solemnly. "I'm Lily." She settled on the rock garden edge that Riley perched on, her white skirts in the dirt. The puppy leapt up with a yelp, licking at her face, and Lily giggled.

"So...." Riley stretched her feet out. "Won't your parents be looking for you?"

Just like that, the light went out on the girl's sunny features. She shook her head. "My mama died. Adam found me a few years ago and took me in."

"And your father?"

"He died when I was two. The wargs got him." Her expression tightened, though she gave a careless shrug. "I can't remember him."

The puppy sniffed at Riley's lap, then gave a growl. Riley shifted out of the way, but it followed her, butting its nose against her hands and nibbling. "Hey."

Lily grabbed him by the collar and hauled him back. "Sit down, Arthur." She sighed. "I'm not s'posed to have him out." Big blue eyes looked up, blinding Riley for a moment. "You won't tell Adam, will you? It's against the rules. They're s'posed to be hunting dogs, but Arthur's the runt of the litter. He'll never be a hunter."

"I won't tell Adam," Riley replied. She couldn't stop herself from smiling. "Adam likes his rules, doesn't he?"

Another sigh. "I like him. He's good to take me in, but he thinks girls should be clean and pretty. Eden's trying to teach me to sew."

"You never know when you might need to stitch something up," Riley replied.

Lily looked at her as if betrayed.

"Like a gunshot or a knife wound," she replied. "Maybe a piece of canvas, or Hessian sacking. I used to work in the stables when I was a girl, and knowing how to stitch came in handy."

Lily's eyes were wide. "You ever sewn up a knife wound?"

"Nope. I leave that to the experts. Just because I *can* do it doesn't mean I should. Doc Rawlins told me I stitch like a drunken sailor. If the patient wanted a scar like a country lane, he'd let me at it."

Lily laughed. "I don't like sewing," she confessed.

"So, what *do* you like?"

A thoughtful look. Not the type of kid who said the first thing that sprang to mind. "Puppies," Lily said. "I like working with the dogs. I'm good with them too, but Adam said" —a rueful grin and a roll of the eyes— "that they can be dangerous. They're bred to hunt a warg down, so I have to stay away from them."

"Except for Arthur."

"I sneak him out," Lily confessed. "Nobody pays me much mind anyway. They're all busy, and I know how to get around the barracks without anyone seeing me."

Riley stilled. "What about the examination room?"

"Nobody goes there." Lily frowned. "There's nothing there but the warg cage, and the examining table. It's Eden's realm."

"What if I didn't want Eden to know I was there?"

"Take the keys," Lily said. "Only Adam and Eden have the master sets, but I know where Eden keeps hers. They're in her desk."

Filing that information away for later – and cursing herself for thinking to use a child – Riley straightened. "Why don't we get something to eat? I'm starved."

Lily brightened. "Okay."

Leading the way to the kitchens, the child chattered on about Arthur's penchant for shoes. "Once, he stole one of Adam's boots!" she said. "He chewed it beyond recognition, and I had to sneak in once Adam was asleep and steal the other one so he wouldn't know. So he'd think he'd misplaced them—"

With McClain's hearing, he'd no doubt heard her, but Riley didn't want to burst Lily's wishful thinking. And the story made something tighten in her chest. Maybe she'd been too quick to judge McClain? Few men out here took on a child who wasn't their own, and despite Lily's chafing at the rules, Riley had the feeling he might look the other way at times.

Smuggling Arthur into the kitchens was easier than expected. Lily looked both ways then hurried across the courtyard to the kitchen's door. Long tendrils of grapevines clung to the timber support beams that covered the courtyard, creating a leafy haven. Riley tugged one of the grapes from the vine and bit into it. The sour taste made her wince, but she enjoyed the rare treat.

"There won't be many people about," Lily told her, easing open the kitchen door. "Most people nap this time of day. Mrs. Divens – the cook – she'll be in the pantry, but she likes to have a nip of spirits now and then."

Coolness washed over her as Riley followed her inside. The kitchens were enormous, dominated by a massive hearth on the far end of the wall and a weather-beaten table in the center of the room. The floors were tiled with terracotta, another luxury that reminded her of how different Absolution was to Haven.

From the pantry came the soft sounds of someone snoring. Lily winked, sneaking through the azure beads that shielded the door and snatching a loaf of bread, a wheel of cheese and a slab of cured ham from the hook it hung on. Avoiding the cook's feet, where she'd tucked them up on a chair, the little girl eased through the beads without disturbing them, then reached for one of the enormous butcher knives in the block.

Riley grabbed it off her in concern, earning a look that indicated that Lily had relegated her to just another overprotective adult. Slicing the ham and cheese, she made a pair of sandwiches for them to eat. Lily grabbed a piece of ham and tossed it to Arthur, who gobbled it up as if scared it would disappear.

"Come on." Replacing the stolen items in the pantry, Lily grabbed Riley's hand and led her deeper into the main building. "We'll go to my room. Nobody will be up there this time of day."

Aware that she was entering McClain's private domain, Riley followed reluctantly. Unease itched down her spine, and she looked for him, but Lily was right; the house was silent, its occupants busy elsewhere. The opportunity gave her a chance to observe more about the man.

Like most buildings out west, the rooms were sparsely furnished. There were few trees this side of the Great Divide, so the heavy slabs of furniture must have been shipped west at great cost. A lot of the world's flora had died off during the Darkening, and what was left had mostly come from seeds that either lay dormant or were kept by the survivors.

Embroidered cushions hinted at Eden's touch. Gauzy white curtains let soft light into the room, softening the stark walls and solid chairs. A fireplace was surrounded by a heap of chairs, and stairs at the back of the room ran up to the second level. Shelves nailed to the wall were covered in books, another rarity. From the look of the titles, Eden evidently had a taste for the lurid. They were old volumes, no doubt published pre-D.

A pair of heavy boots sat beside the largest chair in the room. It was practically a monstrosity, with a carved chessboard on the table between it and another chair. A bottle of whiskey rested beside it. Definitely McClain's throne.

Lily dragged her up the stairs. "Come on!" she said urgently. "No food in the rooms! If anyone sees…"

Smiling at the subterfuge, Riley darted through the door into the room Lily had disappeared into. Lily shut it behind her with an emphatic slam, listening intently. Evidently hearing no sign of pursuit, she grinned up at Riley, her sandwich dangling from her fingers.

Arthur took his chance.

"No!" Lily yanked back, but the puppy's sharp teeth tore most of the sandwich from her fingers. "Arthur, you're not supposed to take food until I tell you to!" She snatched at a piece of cheese, but Arthur darted under the bed with his prize.

"Damn it," Lily muttered.

"We can share." Riley broke her sandwich in half and gave the girl the other piece.

Lily sighed. "He's only hungry because the other dogs eat all the food first. It's because he's the runt."

"You know a lot about dogs." Riley took a bite of her sandwich, looking around. Whatever she personally thought of McClain, he'd done a good job in making the little girl feel at home. The narrow bed was painted white, with a pretty pink patchwork quilt, and a wardrobe in the corner was open to reveal a multitude of clothes. A shelf over the bed held a variety of dolls and toys.

Lily busied herself with the sandwich, tucking it between her teeth to keep her hands free as she swept a bunch of toys off the bed. Taking it out of her mouth, she gestured to the bed. "I spend a lot of time with them. The other kids are usually too busy." One tanned shoulder shrugged, and she dragged herself up onto the bed.

Riley got a hint of what life might be like for her. Slightly lonely, hungry for attention... The way she'd latched on to Riley told her all she needed to know.

With a smile, she crossed to the window and peered out. The main house stood on top of the hill, surveying the entire settlement below. There were so many houses. Maybe more than two hundred, most of them made of white adobe. The occasional jeep traversed the streets. Beyond the wall, rust-colored mountains loomed in the distance. The Blaspheme Mountains. Her chest constricted.

Clearing her throat, she looked away. Her gaze cut across the shelf above the bed, and Riley froze.

"So, do you have a room?" Lily asked, her voice sounding distant. "Because I could ask Adam for you if you wanted me to. You could have a room here, in the house. I'm sure he'd let you. I heard him and Eden talking last night about a woman named Riley. He was angry about something, but Eden calmed him down." A shy smile. "She told him to stop being stupid, and make a goddamned move. Before it was too late."

Riley took a slow breath, her gaze returning to the shelf. There were hand-sewn dolls, a stuffed bear that looked frayed and worn, but behind them... A trio of hand-carved wooden dolls, their faces delicately featured, and the patterns on their dresses so achingly familiar that Riley suddenly didn't know what to say.

Lily followed her gaze. "That's Julie, Greta and Liberty," she said. Standing on the bed, she plucked one of the dolls from the shelf and blew the dust off it. "This is Greta. She's my favorite. My father made them for me – my real father, not Step-daddy Greg. Mama said he used to make them just for me, before he died."

Riley reached out and stroked the doll's face. Her heart was pounding in her chest. It couldn't be. The coincidence was just too large. Or maybe it wasn't. Why else would McClain take in a little girl who had nobody else? Guilt was a harsh motivator.

"She's pretty," Riley said softly. "My daddy used to make toys for me too. I guess he must have loved you a lot."

Lily shrugged, but her fingers trailed wistfully over the doll's dress. "He was a hero. He used to hunt the wargs out near our settlement, and keep us safe. But they got him one day." Her pretty features tightened. "I hate them. I wish they were all dead. Adam's going to kill that one they brought in the other day. He won't let me watch, but I know a place I can see from. They always execute them in the Main Square, and I can climb up onto the roof."

Riley knelt down, horrified at the vindictiveness that filled the girl's voice. She wasn't certain – a lot of men knew how to carve, after all – but the patterns were almost identical. Taking the doll from Lily, she turned it over in her hands, feeling the fine tracery of its lines. "My daddy got taken by wargs." Taking a deep breath, she continued. "I used to hate them too."

Lily looked up. "You don't hate them anymore?"

"I killed the one that clawed him." She shivered at the memory. Her first-ever kill. She'd felt so righteous, so full of anger and fury that it had been almost too easy to pull the trigger. It was only afterward that tears blurred her gaze, and her stomach heaved. She'd thought she'd feel better if she finally killed it, but the truth was harder to take. It didn't feel better. Her father was still gone.

"But I don't... I don't know what to feel anymore," Riley admitted. "I've started thinking lately about what it would feel like to be like my dad. Knowing that you were going to hurt your family, your friends, knowing that when the monster had you in its grips at night, all you'd think about would be the killing. In the end, he was still a man. Maybe I feel a little sorry for them."

"I don't," Lily said emphatically. Tears glimmered in her eyes. So blue. So breathtaking. Eyes that Riley could suddenly see in another's face.

Another fist to the chest. She'd tried to tell herself that this couldn't be real, but the truth was staring right at her.

"What was your daddy's name?" Riley asked softly.

"Luc," Lily replied. "His name was Luc."

Riley's knees folded and she knelt on the bed, still clutching the doll like a lifeline. He didn't know. *I walked away from my wife. From everything that mattered to me....* He'd been talking about Lily then, and the baby his wife was carrying. The baby that had died.

Walked away and never looked back. For their sakes. No doubt he still thought his wife lived. Riley's grip tightened on the doll. That would be another blow.

"Are you okay?" Lily asked, patting her knee.

"I'm fine," she murmured, looking down. She had to stop this. Somehow, she had to find a way out of this mess for him. Trying to force a smile onto her lips – and failing – she asked, "Do you think I could borrow Greta for a little bit? Just to keep me company at night?"

Lily nodded with those solemn, very-blue eyes. "I'm too old for her now, but sometimes she... she looks after me at night too." Then she patted Riley on the shoulder and leaned back on the bed.

ten

THERE WAS NO point going to McClain.

Riley headed straight for the infirmary.

The afternoon sun was starting to ease up. Instead of broiling, it was now only baking the desert air. Sweat rimmed her temples, the air thick and hard to breathe. By the time she reached the infirmary, perspiration dripped down her spine and hugged her breasts.

She knocked sharply. "Eden? Eden, let me in."

A few scuffling footsteps, and then the door opened. Eden peered out, her body shielding the interior of the room, as though she didn't intend to let Riley past. "Riley," she murmured. "I'm sorry, but I'm busy."

"We need to talk." Riley rested her hand on the door and gave her friend a serious look.

Heat flushed through Eden's cheeks. "There's no point. Adam gave me his orders. You're not to visit Wade."

"Is he okay?" she asked.

At least Eden gave her that. "Awake and breathing," she replied with a sigh. "And not speaking to anyone."

"That could be a blessing," she muttered, looking around. "Eden, please. I need to discuss something with you."

The door gave beneath her fingers slightly, and Riley pushed her advantage. "Please?"

"Fine." Eden sucked in a sharp breath. "You have ten minutes. I've got to get down and see Mary Clemmons. She's nearly due to have her baby." Stabbing a finger toward Riley, she added, "And I'll warn you not to waste your breath. I'm not letting you in to see him."

"Thanks." She smiled as the door opened and Eden backed off. "I don't want to see him anyway."

The lie rolled off her lips easily, but Eden sighed and dragged her chair out. The bed he'd lain on was once again made, the sheets pristine. No sign of him left in the room.

Eden picked up a pen and jotted a note on a piece of paper. "What did you want to see me about?"

Riley could have argued, could have begged the other woman to have mercy. Instead, she reached inside her bag and dragged out Greta. "This," she said, resting her on top of the paper Eden was writing on.

Those green eyes locked on the doll as if Riley had threatened her. "A doll? That's my niece Lily's, isn't it?"

"Your niece?"

Eden looked her in the eye. And lied. "Adam adopted her three years ago. You'd know that if you'd bothered to talk to him."

"We never got past the egos-butting-heads stage," Riley admitted. "And I'll be generous enough to include myself in that too."

"She's a good child, but she keeps to herself. I've tried to—"

"Eden." Reaching inside the bag, Riley drew out the second carving. The one Wade had done in the cave. "She said her father carved Greta. And two nights ago, I watched Wade carve this." Plonking it down beside the first, she asked softly, "Tell me the same hand didn't carve them both? Tell me its coincidence that her father's name is Luc, and we just happen to have a warg called Lucius in the cage?"

Eden's shoulders slumped. "Yes, he's her father." She bit her lip. "Adam doesn't know what to do either. We never expected this. Adam always used to keep an eye on Abbie and Lily. Making sure they had enough to make do. He never met them – they liked to keep their home lives separate, he and Luc – but he had a man there who used to radio him occasionally if they needed help."

Riley let out the breath she'd been holding. "So Abbie's dead?"

"Three years ago, the reivers took the town. Adam barely got the radio message before his contact was killed. He rode there with a war party, and they found the town still smoking. Most settlements have places to hide, just in case the reivers attack. Lily was trapped in one of them."

"Adam sniffed her out?"

Eden nodded. "They'd killed the men, and half the women. The ones they can't sell down south at the slave markets. Adam found a dead woman in the home Abbie owned. The corpse was so badly burned he couldn't tell if it was Abbie, but when they finally tracked the reivers down, she wasn't among the slaves there."

"Shit." Riley kicked back in her chair. "And Wade doesn't know." She shook her head slowly. "You know what McClain will do in the end. The whole settlement's pushing for it."

"It's what we do to wargs."

"Not all of them," Riley countered.

Eden's glance dropped.

"So, how do you tell Lily that you just executed her father?"

"We don't." Eden pushed to her feet and paced the room. "You're the only one who knows. You, me, and Adam. So if you don't tell her, she'll never know."

Son of a bitch. Riley ground the heels of her palms against her eyes. "This is a nightmare. You can't let him die, Eden. He's her father."

"And if he lives?" Eden snapped. "He won't stop, Riley. He'll keep coming and coming until Adam is dead. I won't risk my brother."

"Not even for Lily?"

"She buried her father years ago. He's a myth to her. A legend. Don't bring up the past and you won't hurt her."

That rankled all the way to the bone. If Riley had had a chance – any chance – to bring her father home, she would have. To find out that someone had kept him from her... Eden was only trying to do what was right, but she didn't know what it was like to lose her father to the wargs.

Dumping the bag on the desk, she picked up the pair of carved dolls and settled them inside. A glint of silver caught her eye from one of the pigeonholes. Keys.

Lily had even told her where they were.

Her heart leapt into her throat. Eden kept pacing, her shoulders tight and defensive. Surely the other woman had to notice her distress, but Eden was too wrapped in her own problems, arguing with herself about the ethics of the situation.

Riley edged around the desk and sat on it, her fingers drumming against the edge. "She wants to watch his execution, Eden. She hates the wargs for what she thinks they did to her father."

Eden shot a look of horror at her. "Adam won't let her."

"She knows where she can see without being seen. She told me."

Raking her brown hair out of her eyes, Eden turned and stared out the window. "I'll... I'll make sure she doesn't see."

Riley slid her hand into the pigeonhole, her fingers sliding over cool metal. Her heart raced in her chest and she froze, almost *knowing* that Eden would turn and catch her in the act.

The smooth metal keys slid across the timber, and she stiffened. Eden's head drooped, and Riley closed her hand around them slowly so they wouldn't clink.

Come on. Come on.

She slowly drew her hand out, the ring of keys fisted in her palm. Each second felt like a year. Turning, she grabbed her bag, using her body to shield her hand as she slid the keys inside.

"I'm sorry, Riley. I'll do what I can." Finally, the other woman looked around and Riley nodded, slinging the bag over her shoulder.

"I just wish there was some other way," Riley murmured.

"So do I."

The door slammed open.

Lucius slowly opened his eyes, his legs folded and his hands resting on his knees. His chest still hurt like a son of a bitch, but the wounds had closed over, leaving nothing but the pale slickness of a new scar. It was inside that he wasn't sure had healed completely. It hurt to cough, and his lungs felt like they'd shrunk a few inches.

"Well," he drawled, his gaze lighting over McClain. "And here I was hoping to see the pretty face of your sweet little sister again."

He almost glanced over McClain's shoulder, but there was no one there. Not that he'd expected to see anyone else. They'd shoved him in the cage that morning, and apparently everyone had forgotten about him. So much for curious blondes.

"Not quite as sweet." McClain's teeth showed. It wasn't a smile.

Lucius eyed him. "True. She's all grown up, McClain. Tits and all."

McClain didn't take the bait. Instead, he paused in front of the cage, hands on his denim-clad hips, the black felt of his hat hauled down low over his eyes.

"Hiding something?" Lucius smiled. "If they only knew what they had in their midst...."

"Does it have to be this way?" McClain asked abruptly. "You're not going to goad me into getting close enough. You might as well talk to me."

"I'm not very interested in anything you have to say." Slowly, Lucius closed his eyes.

"Not even if it's got to do with a certain troublesome blonde?"

Lucius forced his body to relax. Taking a deep breath, he let it expand his lungs slowly. "No. I got what I wanted from her."

Let McClain make of that what he willed. He'd have been able to smell Luc's scent all over Riley when he rescued her, and seen the signs: the tang of sex, the graze of stubble that had left its mark on her dusky skin. She might want it to be their dirty little secret, but she hadn't counted on McClain's superior senses.

"Did you?" Instead of anger, the words were soft. Curious.

Lucius's lashes opened; he couldn't read the intent behind McClain's words. And they pricked at him, as McClain had no doubt intended.

"You want me to describe what she was like?" Lucius mocked, sitting forward until his nose almost touched the silver-coated bars. His fists curled around them, the stink of burning flesh making his nostrils flinch. "How sweet she tasted? The noises she made?"

A flicker in those icy green eyes. He'd scored a hit, and the thought made him smile.

"I keep looking for something human inside you," McClain said, staring at him long and hard. "But its not there. You've changed. You're not the man I knew."

"That man died. Got stabbed in the back by someone who was 's'posed to be watching it." He smiled and went for blood. "So you watch *your* back now, McClain. And you make sure you sleep with one eye open...." He opened his hands, showed the silver burn along the inside of his palms. Most wargs couldn't handle the feel of it, but he'd spent years in cages, slowly forcing himself to push past the pain. Not all of his warg life had been spent freely, and when the enforcers wanted to study you.... "This cage won't hold me for long."

McClain nodded slowly, before taking a step back. Not out of fear. Instead, a hard implacability filled his face. "So be it. I'm sorry it had to come to this, Luc."

Lucius watched him hungrily. "I'm not. I've been waiting for this moment for years, to come face to face with you again."

"And what about the settlement? These people need me."

"I don't give a shit." He'd softened once, and look where that had gotten him. In this fucking cage, because of a woman who tempted parts of him that he hadn't even realized still existed. He crushed that longing ruthlessly. The goal was clear. McClain was right in from of him. He just had to get at him. "I want you dead, McClain, and I won't stop until one of us is down."

McClain straightened. "I know." His lips thinned. Something that looked like hope died in his eyes, replaced by resolve. "Tomorrow at dawn. I'll give you the night to heal. Then you'll get your chance at me."

What? Lucius surged to his feet, grabbing the bars again. "You'll meet me in the ring?" He'd expected a bullet to the back of the head. Hope swelled as bitter vengeance burned through his veins.

McClain turned on his heel, toward the door. "Just you and me, Luc. My knife, your claws. One survivor."

"No rules," he called softly.

"No rules," McClain echoed.

Riley leaned back against the wall, tapping her palms restlessly against the stone as she peeked around the corner. She'd seen McClain go into the examination room. The keys were burning a hole in her bag, but she couldn't do anything. Eden might find them missing soon, but with McClain and the two guards at the door she was useless.

Butterflies swarmed in her stomach, and she looked each way down the corridor, checking for witnesses, certain she'd be caught at any moment.

The door jerked open and she bounced back onto the balls of her feet as McClain's voice echoed in the courtyard. The jingle of keys sounded as he locked the door, then he swore under his breath.

Riley shoved her hands into her jeans pockets to still them. With his heightened sense of smell, there was no point hiding. Stepping out into the courtyard, she waited for him to notice her.

McClain went still. "What are you doing here?"

She tipped her chin up, shrugged. "Eden said you were considering a reprieve. I wanted to know if that were true or not." A lie, but she had to know.

A breathless moment.

His eyes hardened. "No. I'm not." He turned and dead-locked the door, slipping the key into his pocket. "I intend to execute him, Riley. Tomorrow. At dawn."

Then he pushed past, leaving her staring blindly at the door, guilt burning in her throat like bile.

She had to do something.

Now.

eleven

STAGING A JAILBREAK was never going to be easy, so Riley had planned ahead. After she'd stolen Eden's keys, she'd swung by McClain's room for a few necessary items.

Taking the dart gun out of her bag, she raked her gaze across the windows of the main house to see if anyone was looking, then shot the guard in the back of the thigh. He grunted softly, his leg giving way beneath him.

McClain spun around, his eyes widening. "Riley!"

She bit her lip and pulled the trigger. "Sorry."

The dart bloomed high on his chest. McClain winced and ripped it out. The guard fell at his feet, already out to the world.

White teeth gleamed as McClain bared them. "This is... twice." His knees hit the stone.

Riley hurried to his side. He grabbed her leg, but the strength was going out of him.

"See? We'd kill each other within a week," she said, grabbing him by the shoulders and easing him onto his back. His furious gaze locked on hers, and Riley softened. "Let me do this, Adam." The first time she'd ever used his first name. Stroking his jaw, she watched those luminous eyes fluttering closed. His hat had fallen off. "For Lily. For me. For you. I know you don't want to have to kill him. Let me get him away. Solve all our problems."

"He's not... trustworthy."

Riley laughed. "I know that, remember?"

"What about you...?"

Fingers caught her sleeve, then dropped. He was going under.

"I'm going with him," she whispered. "I might come back when I can change his mind about this revenge scheme. I don't know."

"No!"

She patted his shoulder, then dragged the bag over her own. It was full of supplies and ammunition. She'd hidden a shotgun near the stables, and borrowed the keys to one of the jeeps. Once McClain was down, there'd be no one to stop her.

"Riley." The word was a whisper. McClain's eyes shuttered closed, and his head lolled.

"Sorry," she whispered, though he couldn't hear her. "I truly am." She straightened. "This is to save both your lives."

It was short work to drag both him and the unconscious guard into one of the sheds that lined the courtyard. She eased them onto the hay, then wiped her hands on her jeans. Time for part two.

Undoing the top two buttons on her shirt, she took a calming breath, palmed the dart gun against her thigh, and then started walking around the corner as if she belonged there. The guard was on the balls of his feet. No doubt he'd heard McClain's muffled words. Riley shot him her brightest smile and rolled her eyes. There was a piece of hay in her hair. Deliberately. She pretended to see it, then plucked it out with a gasp, her cheeks heating. "Sorry," she murmured. "Didn't think anyone was here." Licking her lips, she added, "You didn't hear anything, right?"

The soldier grinned. "Not a thing, ma'am."

"Good."

Riley lifted the dart gun and shot him in the arm. His eyes rolled up in his head and, with a muffled "Nghr," he went down hard.

She caught him under the arms and staggered. They were definitely eating better here than at Haven.

She planted the unconscious guard in the garden, beneath the cumquat tree, then returned to the corridor. No sign of anyone. Her hands started shaking. This was actually working. Nobody would ever expect one of their own to break a warg out.

Dragging the keys out, she nearly dropped them in her rush. Adrenaline pumped through her veins. She didn't know how long McClain would be out for. Who knew how fast a warg's metabolism burned?

"Come on," she muttered.

Finding the right key took a few more moments. Then the lock clicked, and she breathed a sigh of relief. Slipping inside the lab, she pressed the door closed behind her, her eyes slowly adjusting to the dim light.

Wade leaned back against the cage bars, his torn black shirt protecting his skin from the silver. Inky black hair tangled over his forehead, and he rested one arm on his knee as though he were reclining at ease instead of trapped in a cage. The knee of his faded jeans was ripped, blood spattering the hem.

A hot look speared her, eyes blue in his tanned face. Then he closed them as if disinterested, letting his head fall back against the bars.

"Didn't think you'd come," he announced in a bored tone. "I thought visiting hours were over."

"Stand up," she snapped. He wasn't wearing shoes. She hadn't counted on that. "We have to get moving."

Hurrying toward the cage, she snatched the cage keys off a metal hook and started rifling through them.

Wade watched her, understanding dawning on his face. A smile spread over his lips. "Does McClain know you're here?"

"Technically, yes." She jammed a key into the lock, but it was the wrong size. Trying again, she was rewarded with a triumphant click. Her eyes met Wade's and she smiled in relief, starting to swing the door open.

He caught it with a tanned hand and snapped it shut. Ripping the keys from the lock, he threw them across the room.

Riley watched them land. "What the hell are you doing?" she asked, turning back to him.

His eyes closed and he leaned back against the bars, completely at ease. "Go back to your little room – or McClain's, for all I care – and tuck yourself into bed. I don't need rescuing. I'm exactly where I want to be."

Her shoulders sank. "What do you mean?" Kneeling down, she grabbed his fingers. "He's going to execute you tomorrow!"

"He's going to get in the ring with me tomorrow." A faint smile edged his lips. "He *thinks* he's going to execute me."

Tugging at his hand, Wade rested it on his thigh, just out of her reach.

Riley growled in frustration. "He might just do it, you know. What then?"

"I die. McClain lives." A shrug.

Dumping the bag on the ground, she dragged a hand over her mouth. What the hell was she going to do? She was running out of time, and it wasn't as though she could shoot him with the dart gun and drag him out of there. Wade had a good four inches on her, and the body beneath that tight black shirt was hard and lean, rippling with muscle.

"But I don't plan on that outcome," he added. "If it gives your mind any rest."

"It doesn't," she snapped. "I don't want to see him die either!"

That drew his attention. He blinked sleepily. "I see. Got a taste for danger now, have you?"

If he wasn't in the cage, she'd have hit him. "Why do I bother?" she asked herself. "Stupid, arrogant men. This doesn't have to be this way! I can get you out."

"Why? So I only have to work out a way to get in again?"

This time, she did kick the bars.

Wade stilled, watching her through narrowed eyes. The thin slit of blue was almost glacial. "Go to bed, darlin'," he said softly. "You don't owe me anything. I'm where I want to be. This sees your end of our arrangement fulfilled. You did what I asked of you."

"Damn it, I don't want this."

Wade's eyes met hers, the bluest eyes she'd ever seen. The color almost reminded her of that pool of water, of the way the light had gleamed off it, off Wade's naked skin.

Riley shook the thought away. A moment in time she wanted to forget. A moment she knew she never would. A shiver ran down her spine.

"Why?" His voice was hard and intense.

Wade uncurled his large body with liquid grace and rested his hands on the shiny, silver-coated bars of the warg cage. Resting his body weight on them, he stared down at her, as if daring her to tell him. His hot blue gaze scoured over her. It made her nipples tighten, her abdomen clench.

Her body knew that look. Recognized it. For a second, she was back in that pool, his mouth on her throat, his cock thrusting like hot steel within her. Wetness coated her panties. Damn him.

"Why don't you want that?" His gaze raked her body, as if he knew exactly what was going through her mind. "Did I get to you, sweetheart? Or is it McClain?"

"You don't know what I want," she snapped.

A quick movement. Riley flung her hands up, but he'd reached through the cage, cupped the back of her skull in one warm hand. The grip was firm enough that she couldn't tear loose. Wade stared at her for long seconds before his hand slowly relaxed, fingers stroking the sensitive skin of her nape.

"*You* don't know what you want."

Her cheeks went hot, her body limp. She almost swayed toward him, hypnotized by his gaze, by the soft promise in his voice. Riley shut her eyes, trying to break the connection. But it was there in the gentle caress against her neck, in the whisper of his breath, flushed and ragged.

In the thump of her heart.

"Yes, I do," she whispered.

His other hand reached out, caressed her face. Long, steady strokes. So sure of themselves. So sure of her.

"Perhaps. Or perhaps you just don't want to admit it," he murmured.

His hands cupped her face. Slowly, he drew her toward him. Riley blinked, her hands coming up to grip the cage bars. She shook her head, but Wade's grip was like steel.

"No," she whispered.

He brought her face to the bars as his own lowered. "Yes," he said, the words caressing her wet lips.

The kiss was light enough to burn. Riley's heart erupted in her ears, her body going liquid in his touch. *Yes.* He was right. She knew what she wanted, but everything she'd ever known said this was wrong.

But it felt so good. A groan strangled in her throat as she pressed against the bars, the hard steel grinding against her breasts. Wade's touch deepened, his thumbs stroking her jaw as he kissed her with a lightness that made her gasp.

"Damn you." She reached through the bars and grabbed his shirt. "Kiss me."

Lifting on her toes, she opened her mouth to him. The cold bars left imprints in her cheeks, but she didn't care. Wade's mouth was hot, desperate, his hands firming on her face. She couldn't stop herself from wanting more of this. *And I tried... I did.*

This was the last man she should want.

The last man she should *need*.

Her heart thumped a crazed rhythm against her ribs as she finally admitted the truth to herself. She was hopelessly infatuated with him, deliciously captivated. Even knowing there was no hope for them, she couldn't help herself.

Her fists clenched in his shirt, her tongue dashing against his. Wade's hand cupped her ass, pressing her hips and breasts against the bars. She still couldn't get close enough.

A sob tore past her lips. She slid a hand into the inky blackness of his hair. "I don't want to see you die," she admitted breathlessly.

His fingers dug into the flesh of her ass. He pulled back, breathing hard. "Get the keys," he growled.

Riley scurried after them, barely able to catch her breath. Tearing through them, she jammed the right one in the lock, and it clicked open. "Come on!" she said, grabbing the bag off the floor and heading to the door.

His hand caught her wrist, fingers wrapping around it. An insistent tug and Riley found herself reeled back into the steel cage of his arms. The bag fell from nerveless fingers as he curled a fist in her hair and yanked her head back, his lips capturing hers.

Riley's eyes widened. *No time!* But he shoved her back against the cage, dragging her knee up around his hips. Hauling her up, he ground his hips between her thighs, locking her ankles behind his butt. Riley reached up, grabbing hold of the bars in surprise.

She twisted her face to the side. "We don't have time!"

"We've got all the time in the world." His hand skittered down over her breast, cupping it lightly before moving on. "I'm not going anywhere."

His lips possessed hers, his hips riding over the seam of her jeans. It rubbed against her wetness, bringing a groan to her lips. Heat welled behind her eyes. Wade had no intentions of going. He never had. Yet she found she couldn't argue. She didn't have the words. All they truly had was this, a passion that burned out of control, like someone had poured oil on the flames.

Or perhaps that was the hurt, deep inside. Demanding that she kiss him hard, rock her hips against him. Hungry to hold him, knowing this could be the last time. A tear slid down her cheek as he ate at her mouth. There was no gentleness now, no finesse. Just the hard steel of his body, and a desire that inflamed them both.

Tugging at her shirt, he slid his mouth down her throat. Riley threw her head back, her fingers lacing tight around the bars to hold herself up. His lips rode over the thin cotton of her bra, nuzzling at her nipple through the fabric. She gasped as he bit at her, tugging the hardened peak between his teeth until it almost hurt. She wanted that. She needed to feel the pain on her skin, and not just within.

Moaning, gasping, she urged him on. Wade's hands moved with exquisite skill, cupping, kneading. Bringing her almost to the edge before easing off. Riley heard herself begging, but it was like someone else had taken over her body.

"Take me," she whispered, curling her arms around his neck and nipping at his lip frantically. "Do it. Now."

Those blue eyes were hazy with pleasure. His lip curled in a snarl, and he turned and pressed her down over the examination table face-first. Tugging the buttons on her jeans open, he wrenched the tight fabric past her hips, and her panties too. Cool air met her wet, desperate flesh. Then he nudged a hard thigh between her legs, rubbing it against her skin as he slowly worked at his own buttons.

Riley clenched her fingers in the sheet. Sweet Lord, she was so close. Tension throbbed between her legs, and she cried out as his thigh withdrew, her hips lifting to beg for more.

Wade's fingers dipped between her legs, gliding through her slickness. "Darlin', I can't go easy." His other hand clenched in the flesh of her ass. "I need you."

She understood. The blunt head of his cock brushed against her, and Riley arched back, feeling it part her lush flesh. Wade gasped, entering her in one hard thrust. Everything within her tightened as he rode over something sensitive, and she couldn't stop herself from *falling*, her hips bucking hard and a tortured scream tearing from her lips.

Each thrust wrung her dry, left her certain she could take no more. Wade was ruthless. He owned her, possessed her with each plunge, hands digging into her hips. Pushing deep, he continuously rubbed over that sensitive spot, and Riley's eyes went wide as sensation shattered through her. She didn't think she had anything left to give, but each thrust of his hips shoved her higher and higher, orgasm wringing her to pieces.

Reaching back, she cupped a hand over his, their fingers interlocking. This time, it was she who begged for the connection, she who was desperate to find something else within this.

A harsh groan broke over his lips, and his hips shuddered. Riley wrapped her other hand in the sheet, her greedy body clutching his hard as he came. They both cried out, the sound mingling in the air. Then he was collapsing over her, breathing hard, sweat slicking both of them.

Wade withdrew, and she felt it keenly. Every muscle within her was bruised and pulsing. Riley took a shaky breath and loosened her hand from the sheet.

"I don't think I can move," she whispered. "So much for my getaway."

Hands helped her stand, then Wade picked her up and rested her bottom on the bed.

"I won't," he gasped, his forehead pressed to hers. Sweat dripped down his face, the sinews in his arms standing out as he held her tightly. "I won't do this, not even for you. This is all I have to live for."

Riley shook her head. "That's not true. It's all you've *lived* for. There's a world of difference."

He shuddered, eyes clenched hard as if to fight the words. "Kidnapping you was the worst decision I've ever made."

"Liar." She kissed his lips gently, nuzzled at his mouth. Her fingertips rasped over the stubble on his jaw as she stroked it.

A breathless laugh as he kissed her back. "Yes, it was." He drew back, eyes clouded with indecision. "Yes," he repeated firmly. "It was."

Yanking his jeans back over his hips, he did each button up with exquisite slowness. Riley hopped down off the examination table, feeling suddenly vulnerable. His expression hardened with each button, as though she'd stripped him bare, and he was slowly putting his armor back into place. Searching for her panties, she found them and stepped into them. The jeans were another matter. They were tight, and her thighs were bruised with their lovemaking.

The rustle of fabric was the only sound. Her anger built slowly. He'd made it clear she wasn't enough, that his quest for vengeance was more important than she was.

Gathering her hair, she knotted it back at the base of her scalp with harsh movements. "So it was only one last fuck you wanted?" She'd tried for blasé, but there was an edge to her words that she couldn't quite help.

Wade looked at her, his eyes hooded and flat. No emotion. Completely unreadable. "Doesn't a condemned man get one last meal?"

"Damn it!" Riley couldn't hold it in any longer. Punching her fists down against her body, she glared at him. "It doesn't have to be like that. You could come with me. Run away. Just the two of us."

Wade's shoulders stiffened. "You're going to stay with me?" Incredulous words. "Out there in the desert?"

Riley raked a hand back through her hair. "I don't know. I just know I don't have a place here."

"Yes, you do." The words were blunt.

Riley sucked in an angry breath. "Fuck you. You *and* McClain!" She jerked her shirt down and straightened it. "I don't know why I bother." She yanked the backpack up over her shoulder. "Do what you want. Goodbye."

Turning on her heel, she started for the door. She got two steps before he grabbed her around the wrist. She was spun around, Wade stepping close, his body hot, hard and stiff with tension.

"Do you think this is easy?" he snarled. "I've spent eight fucking years hunting McClain down. I've finally got him in my sights. I finally get a chance at him. And you want me to give it up?"

Riley looked down at his hand. At the tenuous link between them. "What then? Once he's dead?"

"I go after Colton. And Cane."

"And then?"

Silence. Wade vibrated with fury, the silver ring around his pupils expanding. "There is no 'then,'" he choked out.

Riley met his gaze. "You didn't come here to kill them, did you? You came here to die."

His mouth twisted. "Them first."

She shook her head wordlessly. "That's a shit dream to live for."

"I don't exactly get a chance at the family and wife bullshit anymore," he snapped.

"You could."

Wade stared her down. "No," he said succinctly. "I can't. I won't. I'd spare any woman that burden, and as for children...." His eyes hardened. "*No.*" The last whisper tore her to pieces.

Riley's heart hammered in her ears. He wouldn't come. Not for her. But there was still a chance at this. Her last gambit. One he'd never see coming.

"Is that what your wife thought?" she asked. "Or your daughter? That they were better off without you?"

"I didn't take the time to ask." Cold eyes, cold voice. He retreated into himself at her words, as if she'd stabbed him with them.

"So how do you know they're all right?" she pressed. "How do you know they *were* better off without you?"

Turning around, he yanked his shirt back over his head, dragging it down over that honeyed skin. "I walked away, Riley, but I didn't abandon them. I sent money back, regular-like, through a man I knew. He let me know if they wanted for something."

"And do you still send money back?" Riley took a step toward him, shaking her head. He didn't know. Her heart clenched, like someone had closed a fist around it.

"Yes."

"Recently?"

Wade stilled, his head turning so he could look at her. "Why?"

"Just answer the question."

"Yes," he bit out. "I still send money back. She was my wife, I owed her that. And my daughter...." He frowned, a harsh glint of silver light spreading through his gaze. "How'd you know I had a daughter? I never mentioned her to you. I never mentioned any children."

A bitter hand to play, but she played it. Anything to save his life. Reaching down, she dragged the little doll he'd carved out of her bag and solemnly handed it to him.

Wade looked down, his thumb smoothing over the rough-hewn carving. A desperate longing flickered across his face, then he banished it. "So?" he asked. "I get bored out there on the trail. Ain't much company, darlin'. I taught myself to carve. Doesn't mean shit."

"I wasn't finished," she replied. Gently, she lifted Greta from the bag.

Wade's eyes locked on the doll. The color drained out of his face, and he snatched at it. "Where'd you get this?" Looking up, he stepped forward, into her space, fury blazing in those silvery-blue eyes. "Where the fuck did you find this?"

Riley steeled herself, adrenalin pumping through her veins. His rage beat at her skin, tempting her to step back, to cower, but she'd dealt this hand. Time to deal with the consequences.

"I met a little girl," she told him. "In the gardens. Her name is Lily—"

At the name, he flinched. "Lily," he repeated hoarsely. Disbelief scoured the rage from his face. "No," he whispered. "No, you're lying."

"She's McClain's ward," Riley said. "Told me her daddy died when she was two. He got taken by the wargs, out by the Rim." Taking his hand, she peered earnestly up into his face. "Why would I lie? How would I even know such things?"

He searched for a plausible answer... and found nothing. She watched each thought chase itself across his face, desperate for this to be some lie, some game of hers.

"Abbie?" The broken word was a plea.

Riley slowly shook her head. "Reivers," she said, as gently as she could. "McClain heard about it when it was too late – seems he kept an eye on your family too. He got there just in time to save Lily. He's been looking after her ever since."

"No. *No*," he whispered, the whites of his eyes showing. "That bastard." A flush of silver-grey in his irises. "He did this," he said hoarsely, looking past her – *through* her – as if she no longer existed. "If it weren't for him I would have been there. I would have—"

Riley caught his arm, swallowing hard. This wasn't going precisely the way she'd planned. "I'm sorry, Wade. I shouldn't have—"

His head shot up, gaze turning with unerring focus toward the door. Something murderous crossed his face, an expression she'd never want to see turned on her.

"McClain!" he bellowed, revealing slightly elongated teeth. His eyes were no longer human.

"Wade," she warned, taking hold of his wrist. "Don't do this—"

The door slammed open, McClain staggering inside. Wade bared his teeth in a hiss and shoved her behind him. "You son of a bitch." He stepped forward, fingernails lengthening into claws. "My wife died because of you."

McClain's gaze locked on her. Narrowed. "Riley, get out."

"He won't hurt me."

"Do as you're damned well told!" McClain snapped, stepping forward.

His men fanned out behind him, reaching for the pistols holstered at their waists. New soldiers, she realized grimly. Not the ones she'd rendered unconscious earlier.

"Couldn't wait until morning?" McClain taunted him.

And that was enough. Whatever had held Wade back no longer restrained him.

"You fucking bastard!" Wade launched at McClain, plowing a fist into his gut. His other hand went for McClain's throat, shoving him against the wall, his claws out and digging into the strained tendons. "You selfish fucking prick, you killed her! If I'd been there, if none of this had happened, I could have saved her. My daughter wouldn't have had to watch her mother die!"

Rage burned in his eyes. Riley yanked at his arm, trying to find some trace of humanity in him. And failing.

"Wade!" she yelled. "Let him go!"

Someone grabbed her from behind and dragged her away. Riley kicked and swore, her gaze locked on the two men. Wade yanked his fist back and bellowed. Rivulets of blood traced down McClain's throat as his claws dug deeper.

"Stand... back!" McClain snapped hoarsely to his men. He grabbed Wade by the wrist and forced Wade's grip to slacken. Their eyes met, McClain's grim, and... full of guilt?

Wade screamed and smashed him across the face with his fist. McClain went down, and the two guards grabbed for Wade. He spun and hurled one into the wall with a sickening crack. The other wrapped his arms around Wade's chest from behind, locking his arms to his side, yet he jerked back with an elbow to the guard's face, then yanked him over his shoulder in a body slam. The guard hit the floor hard, the breath whooshing out of him. Wade met McClain's eyes, then slashed the guard's bare skin with his claws.

"No!" Riley screamed, slumping against the man holding her. She stared in horror at Wade, then slowly down at the man on the floor. The man slapped a hand to his bleeding throat. Shallow wounds. Barely deep enough to cut.

But deep enough to condemn the guard to his own fate.

McClain looked up, his face tightening with fury. He launched himself off the floor, hitting Wade at waist height. The pair of them staggered back into the wall — and through it.

Riley yanked at the restraining grip. "Let me go, let me go!" She dug her fingers into the nerve below the soldier's thumb and he yelped, letting her go.

There was nothing she could do for the injured man. The wounds wouldn't harm him, and no medicine on this ravaged earth could stop the curse from taking hold. Even now, the veins around the slash marks were darkening, each tracery like a fine road map in his skin.

Riley staggered to the wall and peered through the hole. The two men wrestled on the ground, Wade gaining the upper hand. His arm drew back, fist poised to deliver a massive blow.

Suddenly, she was shoved out of the way. Falling to her knees, she saw the soldier who'd held her leap through, shotgun lifted high. A sharp crack, and then a grunt. She scrambled back to the hole, watching in horror as Wade fell to the ground like a sack of wheat. The soldier turned his shotgun around and pumped it, aiming directly at the back of his head.

"Don't," McClain rasped, sitting up with a hand held out in restraint. "Stand down."

His eyes locked on Riley's, bleak and dull with grief. "Tell me there's anything human left," he demanded.

She thought of the pain in Wade's eyes as she'd told him of his wife and daughter, the way he touched her so gently when he kissed her, the hunger in him to be touched. "Maybe I see something you don't."

McClain shoved himself to his feet. Glanced down at the fallen form beside him.

"I'll give him his chance. Tomorrow. At dawn," he said bleakly. "Even though the bastard doesn't deserve it."

He jerked his head toward her as if she no longer existed in his eyes. "Dennis, make sure Riley goes to her room, and see that she stays there this time." He glared at her. "Even if you have to use a dart gun on her."

twelve

RILEY PRESSED HER knees tightly together, her hands clenched between them. The mood of the crowd was electric, pressing in on her from all sides. People laughed, smiled, made jokes. Children scampered across the stands, like this was a holiday.

Only she felt like someone had wrapped a hand around her intestines. The urge to throw up was strong. *This is my fault. All my fault.*

If I hadn't told Wade about Lily, he would have been calm. He wouldn't have tried to kill McClain then. Or the guard.

She stared miserably into the square. One of McClain's guards leaned against the rail next to her, his presence clear. He was there to stop her from doing anything more.

The Square was just that, a whole heap of wooden bleachers that surrounded a smooth gravel core. Someone had set up wire caging to protect the crowd for the day's purpose, but the arena could be used for anything – speeches, meetings, even celebrations.

And today, blood would stain the red sands.

Someone slid into the seat beside her and Riley flinched, her nerves rubbed raw. Eden's tense expression swam into view.

"What are you doing?" Riley murmured. "Where's Lily?"

Eden had promised the little girl wouldn't have to see this.

"She's being watched," Eden replied, shooting her a tense look. Her shoulders were stiff. "I had to be here. I have to… I have to make sure he's okay."

McClain.

Riley nodded, turning her eyes back to the arena. "There's no way…?"

"I tried to talk to him last night," Eden replied quietly, knowing what she was asking. "Adam can forgive a lot of things, but Wade deliberately clawed up Cole." She shook her head. "He won't back down. Not this time."

And neither would Wade.

The crowd suddenly roared as McClain appeared, flanked by a trio of guards. Clad in his typical black denim jeans and a black shirt rolled up the elbows, he strode with purpose through the gap in the crowd. Someone hauled the chain-link fence open and he strode through, leaving the guards behind.

"Kill the warg!" an old woman screamed behind Riley.

"Come on, Adam!" another girl cried.

Dragging his hat off his head, he tossed it without aplomb to one of his guards and raked a hand through his sweat-dampened hair. There was no vanity to the movement – there never had been – but Riley caught enough sighs in the crowd to understand his place in the community here. McClain might be focused solely on his purpose, but he looked like a hero –a god – to his people.

There was a knife sheathed at his hip. Just one, the edge wicked-sharp. The bile in Riley's throat rose at the sight, and she looked away. What could she do? She was guarded, and on the wrong side of the fence. Events had spiraled out of control, and she had no hope of reeling them back in.

Or did she?

Unable to sit and watch, she surged to her feet, toward the fence. "McClain!"

Despite the roar of the crowd, and the number of women calling his name, his gaze turned implacably to hers. His hard mouth thinned, and he hesitated on the balls of his feet before pushing off toward her.

"Don't," she pleaded. "Don't do this."

Up close, he didn't look so god-like. He looked tired, fine white lines webbing the corners of his eyes. Scraping a hand over his mouth, he surveyed the crowd. Anything not to meet her eyes. "I don't want to do this, Riley. You know that. But he crossed the line, and I can't forgive that. If I ever thought there was anything worth saving, then he took that hope away." His gaze cut to hers, locking on with an intensity that shivered through her. "This needs to end. Now. Before more innocents get hurt."

"And Cole?"

A haunted expression crossed his face. "In the warg cage. It was… a long night."

Riley understood. "Did you get any sleep?" she whispered.

A long, slow look, as if wondering how much he trusted her. "Why does it matter to you? You made your choice."

The words bit like barbed wire. "Adam…." If only she'd come to know him before. To see this side of him, before Wade eclipsed her thoughts. Grief bubbled in her chest. McClain was a hard man, but she was starting to see the walls he hid behind.

"I don't think there was ever a choice," she said helplessly. "Not a conscious one, at least. And it doesn't have to be like this."

"He made his choices." McClain's voice turned hard, and he took a step back.

"Wait!" Riley grabbed onto the silver-coated wires, her heart in her throat. McClain hesitated, and she said quickly, "This is my fault. I told him about Lily – about Abbie. I thought it might give him something to live for, but I was wrong. I'm the reason Wade lost his temper."

"He's a grown man, Riley."

"I know that," she said through clenched teeth. "I'm not absolving him. He made a stupid choice. A horrible, hurtful choice—"

"And Cole is the one who'll pay for it," McClain snapped. "He doesn't deserve this, Riley. He was an innocent. He's got a goddamned mother and sister to support."

Riley tipped her chin up. "Kinda ironic, isn't it?"

McClain shut his mouth, his lip curling. Their eyes met, then he shoved away from the fence, giving her his back.

Riley clenched her fist and smashed it against her thigh. *Stupid.* Saying something like that was never going to get her anywhere.

Turning around, she eyed the vicious crowd. The sight only made homesickness rear in her heart. At Haven, there'd never been a spectacle like this. Wargs were taken out back and shot. She could understand, after all of the loved ones people lost, how they'd want to see some of their own gotten back, but the fascination with this duel seemed somehow sickening.

Or maybe that was because she couldn't see Wade as a monster anymore.

Eden watched her with a sympathetic expression. "You don't have to be here, Riley."

Riley took her seat, her shoulders hunched. "I don't want to watch, but I have to."

"I know." Eden breathed out slowly. "Trust me, I know."

Riley reached down and slid her hand through the other woman's. No matter what happened today, one of them would be left reeling. Or maybe both, she thought. This wasn't a win-win situation for either of them. "I wish this didn't have to happen."

Eden squeezed her hand back. "Yeah."

The crowd suddenly erupted into a frenzy. Riley's head jerked up. Wade had been shoved into the arena, his feet bare, his jeans still torn at the knees. He looked just as tired as McClain did, heavy manacles hanging from his wrists. Silver-coated wire mesh covered his hands, keeping him from clawing anyone else. Riley could see the blood and raw flesh from where the wire had cut and burned him. A necessary precaution, but a cruel one.

She could barely see. Men and women were jumping up and down, shaking at the wire mesh of the fence. If there were no fence she half-suspected the crowd would go after him themselves.

Riley swallowed hard, tasting bile, and Eden squeezed her fingers in sympathy.

McClain lifted his arms, gesturing for everyone to settle. It could have been a dramatic moment, but he took no advantage of it. From the hard look on his face, he wasn't looking forward to this.

A pair of guards stepped forward with keys. One of them held a shotgun to the back of Wade's head, and the other nervously fumbled with Wade's manacles. He looked bored, his gaze raking the crowd as though McClain weren't even there.

Looking for someone?

Riley stilled as their eyes met. She couldn't breathe all of a sudden, shrinking back against the seat. The night seemed to have aged him. His gaze flickered to her right, then back again, and she knew what he was looking for.

Slowly, she gave her head a tiny shake.

The manacles fell away, and the guards scrambled back toward the safety of the gate. Wade let out a soft sigh, visible through the softening of his shoulders. "Thank you," he mouthed to her. As he looked away, she thought he was done with her. But he gave McClain a hungry, lingering look then glanced back, rubbing at the raw marks on his wrist.

It was as though he didn't know what to say or do. *This is what you wanted*, she wanted to scream, sitting stiffly on her bench. She couldn't look away. Neither could he. Thought raced across his face, in the way he opened his mouth as if to say something before thinking better of it.

Finally, he shrugged, as if there wasn't anything to say to her. "Look after her," he mouthed. "Please."

Look after Lily. Riley straightened, her heart pounding in her chest. What the hell did that mean?

"Most of the time, we don't offer anything more than an execution. You're here because I owe a debt to you," McClain called. "Do you have anything to say?"

Riley held her breath, and felt the crowd doing the same. Was McClain crazy? All Wade had to do was say one little sentence. Tell the crowd who'd clawed him up, and then this would be turmoil.

Wade eyed the crowd, his black hair tangling over his eyes. With his dark looks and bleak expression, he looked hard and mean. Dried blood crusted his skin, and his shirt was torn in so many places she could see the ripple of his abdomen.

"No," he said finally. "No more games. Let's get this over with."

Riley let out the breath she'd been holding, her heart sinking.

He sounded tired.

Claws out.

Lucius ignored the hiss of the crowd as he crouched low, trying to turn all his focus to McClain. This was the moment he'd spent eight years trying to get to. Why the hell did he suddenly want it over with?

Exhaustion stained him. McClain looked tired too, though no doubt for different reasons. McClain unsheathed his blade, the wicked ten-inch hunting knife strapped to his thigh, and settled into an aggressive stance. Waiting.

This was the man who'd taken his family away. Luc's lungs tightened at the thought. For a man who tried not to feel anything, the day before had been a mess of emotion. He'd walked away from Abbie to spare her – or maybe to spare himself. That hurt was an old one, but the news of her loss had torn pieces in him he'd thought he didn't feel. Guilt had kept him awake for long hours. If he'd been there, he could have saved her.

He could have saved Lily from seeing that.

As much as he wanted to hate the man in front of him, he found there was nothing left in him. Grief had burned him dry, left him hollow. And if he was honest with himself, as he rarely was, a part of him knew exactly whose fault Abbie's death had been.

If I hadn't walked away....

Whose fault was it? McClain's for betraying him? Or his own, for not trusting his wife to love the monster he'd become?

He didn't like the answer to that.

You never did, the devil on his shoulder whispered. *But it was easier to blame someone else.*

A long night. A lot of thinking. A *lifetime* of thinking. He was tired of it.

"Come on," McClain snapped, shifting the knife from hand to hand and leaving himself open just enough to invite attack.

Revenge.

A shitty thing to live for....

Lucius stepped forward, moving woodenly. He knew Riley was watching. He could feel her gaze on his skin, drilling into the back of his head. The crowd might as well not have been there, but he was hyper-aware of her. One quick glimpse burned her image into his brain – stiff-bodied, her lips thin, her blonde hair scraped back into a tight ponytail as she stared at him.

And for the first time in a long time, he knew there'd been something to live for. Something other than the mire his life had become.

Too late for that.... It was too late the moment he'd jammed his claws into that kid, and then looked down to realize what he'd done.

Luc's gaze narrowed on McClain. So he wanted to play defense, did he? Baring his teeth in a smile, Luc stepped forward, wondering how McClain would deal with the settlement's questions if Luc scratched him.

Sunlight gleamed off the blade and Luc watched it warily, half-hypnotized by the movement.

"Come on," McClain snarled. "This is the only chance you'll ever get."

So be it.

He danced under McClain's guard, going straight for the throat. McClain's eyes narrowed, and he swung out of the way, lashing out with the knife. It scored across Luc's forearm, the pain shooting through him, and yet strangely distant.

He couldn't seem to keep his mind focused. As he staggered past McClain, blood spattering across the sands, he saw Riley on her feet, her fists clenched at her sides, and her face pale. The crowd roared its pleasure.

Boots shuffled on the sand behind him. Too late, he turned. The knife darted like a stream of silver in the sunlight, straight for his chest. Luc blocked McClain's wrist, forcing the strike high over his elbow. Curling his other hand into a fist, he followed through with a punch.

McClain's head snapped back to the collective "ooh" of the crowd. McClain staggered back, gathering his feet, and shaking his head. It was the best chance Luc had, but somehow he lost it. The image of that kid's shocked face as Luc had slashed his throat flashed through his mind.

Blood trickled from a cut on McClain's lip. His eyes narrowed and he shifted his grip on the hilt, crouching low. Both of them had drawn blood now.

Luc had dreamed of this fight for years, playing each blow over in his mind, thinking about McClain's weaknesses and strengths. In his imagination, he'd been brutally focused, waiting only for the right opportunity before he could finally end this. He'd anticipated victory, the chance to stand over McClain's body with the weight lifted off his shoulders as he smiled. Instead, he felt hollow.

Each movement seemed to come from outside him. He felt as though he was watching as his hand lashed out, claws raking through McClain's shirt and catching nothing but fabric. Then the knife was in the center of his vision, the razor edge of it kissing his cheek with white fire. There was a chance for it to cut deeper, but Luc rolled his shoulder and threw the other man off him.

They fell apart, breathing hard. McClain had always been good at what he did. Quick, efficient and brutal. He'd approached each hunt with the focus of a man determined to finish his duty. Not once had Luc seen hesitation in his eyes, the way it was now.

And the grim truth. *He could have had me then.*

McClain stalked forward, the knife held low against his thigh, as if to disguise the movement. They danced around each other, ignoring the scream of the crowd. Then McClain came after him with a brutal swing of the knife.

Wade grabbed his wrist as he melted out of the way, using McClain's momentum against him. He smashed the other man against the silver-coated fence, face first. McClain flinched, jerking away with the wire-burn imprinted on his face.

The knife was gone. Luc's claws had somehow retracted. He shoved McClain's back against the fence and planted a fist in his gut. McClain wilted over the blow, his hands clinging to Luc's hips.

"You son of a bitch," Luc snarled. He smashed his knee into McClain's face, rewarded with a roar of pain and a gush of blood from the man's nose.

A foot hooked behind his own. McClain's eyes were hot with fury now, and he jammed an elbow into Luc's face. The world turned white for a moment, and then he hit the ground hard, McClain on top of him. They rolled, dust stirring up around them as each tried to gain the upper hand.

Light reflected off something at the corner of his vision. The knife. Luc looked down, his hands curled around McClain's throat as they came to a halt. McClain's hand shot out, reaching for it... and falling short.

This was it. His chance. Luc's claws slashed out and he lifted his hand high, gaze locked on McClain's.

"*No!*" a little girl screamed.

The word went through him like a spear of ice, freezing time and sound, taking him back years into the past. Luc's head lifted, as if in a dream, and he looked up through the wire mesh that surrounded the makeshift arena.

A little girl stood in the aisle, her blue eyes shining with tears, her fists clenched in the fabric of her skirts. The light gleamed off her blonde hair, tumbled carelessly over her shoulders. Perhaps nine or ten. Far too young to be there.

God, she looks like her mother.

His heart seized at the thought. He hadn't seen her since she was two, and yet he knew, with a father's knowing, that she was his. He'd rocked her to sleep as a baby, picked her up each time she fell, and kissed her bloodied knees.

"Lily," he whispered.

Her gaze wasn't on him at all. "Adam," she mouthed silently, her face twisting with grief.

The word struck him like a punch. What was he doing? He felt his claws retract again, his hand hovering in the air. In that split second, he realized something – Lily had lost her mother, and McClain was the only father she knew. Kill McClain, and she would hate him forever.

Her father died long ago. Let her believe that. Let me give her this, for all the times I've never been there.

Movement shifted. Luc looked down as McClain finally grabbed the knife and swung it up toward him. He could have stopped it. There was a moment there where he could have blocked the blow.

And didn't.

The knife slid into his side with a whisper. The shock of it clenched every muscle in his body as he slumped. He swore, hot blood splashing onto the sand. The world spun as McClain rolled them, grabbing Luc by the throat and lifting the knife again. The crowd roared. Someone screamed. Riley? Maybe... He couldn't tell. The world was growing hazy, his side a mess of heat and pain.

Then the knife froze. Luc's gaze jerked to McClain's, and his gut clenched as he saw the hesitation, the conflict.

"Do it," he whispered.

The hand at his throat was shaking. "You fucking bastard," McClain snapped. "You had me. You fucking had me."

Luc fumbled for McClain's hand. "Do it," he snapped. "Then you look after her. You look after them both."

The crowd was on its feet, chanting for McClain, who looked up, the knife lowering an inch. Luc saw the chance slipping through his fingers. "Don't," he said hoarsely. "I'll come again, you know I will. I'll make you regret this," he hissed desperately, mind racing for a reason to force McClain's hand. "I'll take Eden."

The knife lowered. McClain suddenly stabbed it viciously into the sand beside Luc's head. "No, you won't," he said hoarsely, and then staggered to his feet.

The weight of his body was suddenly gone. Luc sucked in a hiss as pain flooded through him. He curled up onto his side, holding the gash between his ribs. Blood wet his fingers, but he could see where it was clotting. Already healing.

"Come back," he called. *Damn you.*

"What's going on?" someone in the crowd yelled. "Kill it, Adam!"

McClain walked away from him.

No! "You fucking coward!" Luc shoved to his knees, watching McClain's wide back stiffen. In a sudden surge of thwarted rage, he grabbed the knife and wrenched it from the sand.

McClain turned as Luc staggered to his feet. Their eyes met. And McClain opened his arms in a gesture of surrender.

Calling his bluff.

"Here's your chance," McClain said quietly. "You either take it now, or you leave, and you don't come back."

The crowd fell silent. Luc looked around, his vision a blur. His gaze locked on Riley, who was clinging to Eden's hand. Those brown eyes met his, silently pleading with him.

"Please don't," she whispered, though the sound of it was lost in the growing murmur of the crowd.

He could barely feel the knife in his hand. His fingers were numb. Then they opened, and the dagger hit the sand beside his feet. He looked down, unable to comprehend what was happening. This was everything he'd wanted. Wasn't it? Panic suddenly choked him. If he couldn't have this, then what the hell did he have to live for?

A shitty way to live....

He couldn't breathe all of a sudden. The crowd blurred as he looked up, and he sought instinctively for Lily. She was crying as a man tried to lead her away, struggling to see over her shoulder if McClain was okay. Luc scraped a hand over his face. "Agreed," he choked out. For Lily's sake... and for Riley.

He took one last look at them. Riley shut her eyes and sagged back onto her seat in relief, and Lily was almost at the top of the stairs, her panicked gaze on McClain, her fingers clasped around the stranger's.

Luc didn't know what it was that set him off, but his gaze locked on the tanned hand gripping his daughter's, and then jerked toward the stranger's face. A dark hat shielded his face, like most of the crowd there, and his broad shoulders filled out his black shirt. A machete hung over his shoulder, and as the stranger paused at the top to glance behind him, Luc's gut fell.

"No!" he screamed, launching himself at the silver mesh fence.

Johnny Colton tipped his hat to him with a slight smile, then disappeared with his daughter.

thirteen

"DON'T SHOOT!" McClain roared.

Riley looked up in shock as Wade launched himself at the wire fence and scaled it as if the mesh barely touched him.

"What the hell?" Eden murmured.

He wasn't looking at her. He wasn't looking at any of them. Instead, he glared with deadly intensity toward the top of the arena behind her.

Riley spun, but there was nothing there. Only hot sunlight, and the last vestiges of the crowd. Her brows lowered as she turned to face him. He was almost to the top. One of McClain's men stepped forward with his shotgun and smashed the butt into Wade's left hand, then the right. With a snarl, Wade tumbled flat on his back into the arena, dust rising. He rolled to his feet, lip curled in a snarl and his eyes wild, but more of McClain's men had stepped closer to this side of the fence, ready for him.

In desperation, Wade looked to her. "Colton's here," he said. "He's got Lily."

Riley sucked in a sharp breath, her fists clenching. "I'll get her back." Then she turned and bolted up the stairs, shoving her way through the hysterical crowd.

"No!"

Luc made a snatch for the fence, but one of McClain's men warned him back. In frustration, he watched Riley disappear at the top of the steps, his heart sinking into his gut. *What the fuck had he done?* She was no match for Colton, and if Colton realized that she held some meaning to him....

The heat washed out of his face. Deep inside, something quivered – the beast, threatening to rise up and consume him. He curled over, fingernails digging into his palms as the fury roared through him. *Take my woman.... Take my daughter... Kill him...* The thoughts were primal and dangerously close to the surface. Heat filled his mouth, his gums, his spine bowing as the monster sought to fight its way free. He pushed back, trying to force it down.

Luc came to on his knees, screaming.

The crowd was silent, even McClain's men backing away from the fence with paling faces. Luc forced himself to push the beast deep. He couldn't lose control. The charm helped contain it but sometimes, in emotional moments, he came close to losing himself. Do that, and both Lily and Riley were as good as dead.

"Wade." McClain's scuffed boots stepped into his vision, moving slowly. McClain would recognize what was happening to him, knowing enough to be wary.

An enemy. He breathed deep through his nose, feeling the heat slowly dissipate from his gums. Or an ally?

Looking up, he met McClain's gaze, fingers clenching in the dirt. "He's got her." The words came from a hoarse throat. "Colton was here. He took... took Lily. Riley went after them."

The expression on McClain's face tightened, and he swore under his breath. "I thought he was dead."

Luc couldn't speak. He shook his head wordlessly.

"Close the gates!" McClain bellowed. "Sound the siren. I want the walls manned. We've got a warg loose in the city. He's taken Lily, and I want her back unharmed. Don't confront him. Just find him and sound the alert!"

A hand came out of nowhere, tanned and marked with calluses. Luc looked up, into hard grey-green eyes.

"Take it," McClain snapped. "I'm not your fucking enemy. He is. If we don't work together, then we don't get Lily back."

The last of the fury roared through him at the thought. Luc clenched his teeth together, then reached out and gripped McClain's hand. McClain hauled him to his feet, pressing the knife hilt into his hand. "This time, don't hesitate."

There was a guard outside the arena. Riley snatched his handgun from its carelessly unsnapped holster and darted past, ignoring his cry of "Hey!"

Ahead of her, a tall man in dark clothes and a black hat led Lily down the street calmly. He glanced over his shoulder at the cry, coal-black eyes meeting hers before they narrowed. As she blinked, he swept Lily up over his shoulder and bolted between houses.

"Stop!" Riley yelled, leaping after him.

She raced around the corner, directly into his outstretched arm. It hit her high in the chest and she went down hard, struggling to breathe.

"No!" Lily cried out, sinking her small white teeth into his neck.

Riley realized his attention was gone and swung out with her feet, hooking her ankle behind his. His eyes widened on her for a moment before he fell, landing with Lily half on top of him. Thrusting the girl aside, he lashed out with his foot, and Riley barely avoided the blow. She scrambled backward, her back hitting the wall. Then she shoved to her feet and aimed the pistol at him. "Don't move."

Grabbing Lily's hair, Colton yanked her against him, pressing gleaming sharp claws against the little girl's throat. "I'll do it," he said, in a cool, dark voice that sounded almost weary.

Riley froze. "Let her go."

"Put the gun down."

"No."

"Then I'll tear her throat out."

Bleak, uncompromising words. Who the hell was this man? Riley swallowed hard, trying to listen for any sign of pursuit. It divided her attention for a split second, and he used it to throw Lily toward her. Riley snatched her finger off the trigger, staggering back under the girl's weight. Her back hit the wall, and Lily cried out as she fell to the ground.

An arm came out of nowhere, smashing down across Riley's wrist. The blow numbed her arm, and the pistol flew to the cobbles. Riley didn't have time to look for it. She ducked as Colton's fist smashed toward her face, taking a glancing blow across the cheekbone that stunned her. Hell, he moved like lightning. Not even Wade had moved like that. Maybe he could, but it made her realize that he'd never truly tried to hurt her.

The pain shot straight up her jaw, toward her ear. Another blow – a chop of his hand – cut toward her throat, and she caught it somehow, deflecting the main thrust of it. The blow still slammed her head back. All she could see was sky, and then she was on the ground on her back.

"Colton!"

She blinked as the howl of utter rage swept through the alley. Then there was a blur of movement and Wade was there, shoving Colton against the wall, his expression a mask of fury and long, sharp teeth bared in his opponent's face.

Not fully human.

Lily screamed as the men grappled. Riley tried to sit up, her face aching. Colton threw Wade across the alley with remarkable ease, then swooped to pick up the pistol she'd dropped. He pointed it coolly at Wade just as McClain shoved around the corner.

The gun didn't waver. Colton turned it on McClain and pulled the trigger.

"Shit!" Riley scrambled across the ground as McClain went down.

McClain coughed, blood spattering across his face, his eyes wide and panicked. Blood soaked his black shirt and Riley tore at it, trying to see the damage. "Eden!" she screamed as bare flesh met her gaze. And blood. Lots of it. Shoving her hand over the hole in his chest, she looked around desperately. "Somebody help me!"

Behind her, Wade rolled to his feet. Riley watched helplessly as Colton grabbed Lily and yanked her back against him. This time, he put the muzzle to her forehead. Wade froze and Riley stilled. Beneath her hand, she could feel McClain's heart thumping in his chest, wetness leeching out over her hands, but the world seemed suddenly silent.

"Back away," Colton said coolly. "I don't wish to hurt her, but I will."

"Let her go." Wade held his hands up, still in a half-crouch.

"Cane wants her."

"Don't," Wade said shortly. "Don't do this. You know what he'll do to her."

Colton's dark eyes narrowed slightly. "He wants you. You have three days to come for her. I'll keep her safe until then, you have my word."

"Fuck your word," Wade snarled, taking a step forward.

The gun shifted to him. "My advice is to heal. And quickly." Then Colton lowered the gun and shot Wade in the knee.

Riley flinched as Wade went down. He arched on the dirt, teeth ground together in pain as he curled over his knee. She looked down, but blood was pumping through her fingers, and McClain's pupils were starting to dilate. She couldn't leave him. Wade would live.

Colton nodded shortly at her, "Don't do anything foolish." Then he swung the frightened girl gently over his shoulder and disappeared.

"Oh, shit." Eden staggered around the corner, falling to her knees beside Riley. "What happened?" She tugged Riley's hands aside, then shoved her own over the wound. "Damn it. *Damn it.* Adam," she called. "Don't you dare!" Her eyes were wild as she turned on Riley. "I need my medical bag!" she screamed.

The world was chaos. McClain's men pushed past, rifles raised. Riley pointed them after Colton, then met Wade's gaze. Pain twisted his features as he dragged himself into a sitting position against the wall, panting hard.

"Get her bag," Wade gasped.

fourteen

THE KNEE CAP was shattered.

Riley bit her lip and leaned over his leg, dragging the light closer. Wade sucked in a sharp breath as she probed at the wound. This needed Eden's attention, but at the moment it wasn't going to get it. They'd dragged McClain into the surgery, and the doctor was hastily working on her brother. Colton had shot to kill, and the bullet was lodged deep in his chest, having nicked the heart. He shouldn't have been alive. He very nearly *wasn't*. But nobody had the guts to tell Eden that.

Riley's heart clenched. She'd faced the same dilemma days ago when the man she loved lay still and bloodless on the table in front of her. "Why isn't McClain healing?" she whispered.

Wade looked exhausted. "McClain's men pack silver-tips," he said quietly. "His body can't heal while the bullet's still inside him."

"And?" She looked up. "There was an 'and' on the end of that."

His blue eyes locked on hers. "By that stage, it will probably be too late."

The thought made her feel ill. "If you gave him your blood—"

"It's not the blood loss that's killing him." Wade flinched as her tweezers slipped. "Give them here. You need to dig in and get the bullet out instead of playing with it."

"I'm not playing with it," she snapped, though the idea of digging inside his knee made bile rise in her throat.

He knelt over his leg. "Hold the fabric of my jeans out of the way." When Riley obeyed, he took a deep breath, then shoved the tweezers into the gaping hole in his knee.

"Jesus," she muttered, licking her lips as her stomach rebelled.

Sweat stained his face as he felt around. His lips quivered, and a small gasp escaped him as he pulled the bullet slowly from the wound. It was whole, though badly crushed, and he tossed both the tweezers and the bullet aside carelessly before collapsing back on the bed.

"*Fuck*," he said breathlessly, raking his hands back through his hair. The muscle in his abdomen twitched as his shirt rode up, and she could see the toll pain had taken on him.

"Its okay," she whispered, stroking a hand through his hair. "You got it all. You got—"

"It's not okay," he snapped. It was the first time he'd even remotely referred to Lily since the incident in the alley. His eyes closed, and he trembled. "Give me a minute. Then get me a crutch. And a gun."

Riley's hand stilled. "You're not going after him tonight. You can barely move."

Those luminous eyes opened, and she saw the mixture of pain and fear there. "I failed her once," he said, and light shimmered off the suspicious wetness in his eyes. "I am *not* going to fail her again."

"You never failed her," Riley protested, but he cut it off with a sharp jerk of the hand.

"I walked away," he said. "I left her and her mother alone without protection. I won't ever forgive myself for that, Riley." He dragged a trembling hand over his eyes. "I feel like I've made a lifetime of fucking mistakes, one after the other."

She could see this conversation wasn't going anywhere. Lips thinning, she sat up, reaching for the bottle of iodine and a bandage. The knee would heal itself better than any doctoring she attempted on it. "Tell me about Cane," she said. "Tell me why you're so afraid of him getting his hands on Lily."

He sucked in a ragged breath and visibly shuddered. "Cane's an evil man. I've seen some of the things he's done, Riley. If he sets you in his sights, he doesn't stop until he's torn apart your whole world. Colton tries to rein him in, but it's like trying to control a rattlesnake." Letting out a breath, he turned his head toward her, eyes stark. "He'll hurt her, Riley. Just to prove that he can. Just to hurt me. I have to get her back before it's too late. I swear, if he touches her—"

Anguish tore through her, and she slid her fingers through his. "We'll get her back. I promise."

Wade stilled. "We?"

"You don't seriously think I'm going to let you go after them alone?"

He rose onto his elbows. "No way. You're not coming. If Cane gets his hands on you—"

"He'll do nothing that he won't do to Lily," she snapped. "He's got at least two other wargs with him, and who knows how many reivers. You're not thinking clearly. You need help. Go in alone, and you're only going to get yourself caught, or killed." She squeezed his hand. "Then what happens to Lily?"

"No." Something hot and possessive burned in his gaze, and his fingers clenched hers back. He shook his head. "No, Riley. No. One man can get in and out alone. The same way Colton did."

Riley poured a capful of iodine over a piece of linen. "How are you going to fight with Lily there? She might need to be carried." What she didn't add was, *She might also be frightened of you.*

His lips thinned. Riley didn't let him speak, just gently swiped the iodine over his knee. With a hiss, he sucked his tongue between his teeth.

"And you're not going anywhere until you can stand," she warned. "Let alone fighting three wargs. You're an idiot."

"I don't have a choice," he snapped, glancing toward the open door to the surgery. "McClain can't back me up. Even if he would."

"You know he would," she shot back, sliding the bandage under his knee. She'd cut his jeans open horizontally, and the pieces flapped around his muscular calf. "And you don't need McClain. You have me. If we gather some of his men—"

"They'll shoot me the second I give them my back," he muttered.

Riley slowly wound the cotton bandage around his knee, then clipped it in place. He was right, of course; she'd had to stop one of the men from shooting him in the alley when he was down. "We'll deal with that when we get there."

"*We* are not going anywhere," he said between his teeth. "Here, help me up."

"You need to rest."

"Either you help," he told her, "or I'll do it myself."

Riley cursed and slid a shoulder under his arm. She helped him sit up, gently easing his leg over the side of the hospice bed. "Don't push yourself. You need to let that heal, or you won't be much use to anyone."

"I need to shift," he muttered.

Riley met his eyes, but he dropped his gaze. "I heal quickly in this form, but something in the shift regenerates the body. I'll be able to walk by morning."

When the moon no longer rode through his blood, forcing the beast to the surface.

He finally looked up, light gleaming off the silvery shine of his eyes. "I need a warg cage, Riley. And I need you to watch my back for the night. Make sure nobody takes it into his head to get rid of me while I can't protect myself."

"And in the morning, you'll let me come along with you?" She crossed her arms over her chest.

Another muttered curse. But that one sounded like defeat.

Riley smiled. "I'll watch your back," she promised.

The door of the warg cage clanged shut. Wade limped toward the center, a shudder running through his large body. He could feel Riley's eyes on him, but he didn't want to turn and look at her. It was hard enough doing this in front of her. If he didn't think someone would put a bullet in his head while he was trapped, he'd have never allowed it.

There were no windows in the room, but he didn't need one. The moon was rising. He could feel it in his blood, a shiver under the skin. A burning itch. Yanking the black shirt over his head, he tossed it through the bars and started working on his belt. The jeans were destroyed. No point bothering to remove them.

The itch spread, as if it knew exactly what was going through his mind. As his hand closed over the cool pewter of the charm, he flinched. A long time since he'd voluntarily removed it. Entrusting it to someone else for the night was the craziest thing he'd ever done, but he knew bone-deep that Riley would never betray him.

"Are you okay?" she asked softly.

He jerked his head in a nod, then slid the charm over his head. "If I get out, then make sure you shoot me."

"I will."

231

And he knew she would. He trusted her to do it in a way he'd trust no one else. With a sigh, he reached through the bars and held the charm out.

Soft footsteps crossed the floor. Already the itch was growing unbearable, as if ready to boil over his skin. Wade met her eyes. "Take the charm, and get as far across the room as you can. No matter what I say or do, don't come close to the cage. I'll be quicker than you, and you don't know how far I can reach when I want to."

The candlelight warmed the soft blonde halo of her hair. Riley gave him a shaky smile. "I know what to do," she said, the shotgun over her shoulder. Her fingers hesitated over the charm though.

"Take it," he said sharply. The fever was rising in his blood. He didn't think he could hold off much longer.

"Just one last thing," she whispered, and reached up on her toes to kiss him.

The shock of her hot mouth made him flinch. How could she do this, knowing what was about to happen? Luc groaned and reached for her, dragging her up against the bars, his fingers wrapped tightly around the charm. Her mouth was wet and eager, and he lost himself in it, his entire body quaking with the urge to restrain himself.

Pain lashed along his spine. Luc yanked back, feeling the heat in his face and gums. He shoved the charm at her hand and pushed her back several feet. "Get back."

The moment the pewter left his grasp, the itch turned into a conflagration. Luc screamed as pain laced him. It tore through his bones like molten lava, cramping through every muscle in his body. He was on his knees, the pain in his damaged one nothing compared to this as his body jerked itself into a new alignment.

His spine bowed, huge muscle tearing through his skin, which was sprouting fur. Teeth erupted in his mouth, and his claws shot out. The last thing he saw as the fury rose to take him was Riley's frightened face.

It seemed to take forever. Riley swallowed hard, her back to the wall as she watched him. Wade lay on the floor of the cage, breathing hard. Or the *thing* that used to be Wade.

Caught between man and beast, he whimpered in pain and stirred. Riley let out a shaky breath. Hell, he was huge. Muscle distorted his body, and it just looked... wrong. Like every nightmare cobbled together, and given flesh.

She'd seen wargs before, but never this close or in such clarity.

Another moan caught her ear as he tried to lift his head. Riley frowned. "Are you okay?"

No sign that he'd heard her. His massive shoulders bunched, and he lifted his head. His jeans were torn, hair sprouting through the rips. From the size of him, he would be close to seven and a half feet tall.

"Wade?" she whispered, edging forward. She couldn't take her eyes off him. Here was the monster every borderlander feared. But if he could be tamed, if he could be—

He snarled and sprang at the cage, his claws raking off the bars with a high-pitched screech. Eerie silver eyes narrowed on her as he shook the bars, howling at the sudden pain as his hands burned.

Riley scrambled backward, tripping over her feet and hitting the ground. Wade's lips curled back off his teeth, as if he sensed her sudden vulnerability. That time, the bars shifted, the steel warping as he tore at them. Her heart thumped madly and she scrambled across the floor for the gun, coming up with it in shaking hands.

He let go with a snarl, his palms curling toward his chest. Riley's finger jerked on the trigger then eased. She couldn't stay there. She was too frightened, and the fear was ratcheting up his hunger.

She'd been wrong. There was nothing human left in him tonight. The part of him that was Wade was submerged beneath nothing more than vicious need.

Jerking open the door, she slammed it shut behind her and jammed the heavy iron bar into place. Then she slid down the wall, her knees curling up in front of her. Her hands were shaking. She put the gun down and pressed her face into them, the tremble sweeping through her entire body. Inside the room, Wade howled in thwarted fury, a sound that chilled her to the core.

There was something hot on her cheeks. Riley dashed at the tears. "Damn it!" *Damn her.* She'd promised him she'd stay, but she hadn't been able to handle it.

Hadn't been able to handle the monster inside him.

And come morning, she would have to face him and she knew, deep inside, that he would remember that.

The howling rang on, low and eerie. An almost mournful sound.

Riley buried her head between her knees and tried not to listen. She'd tried to go back in, but Wade had gone berserk again, and she'd staggered back outside, slamming the door shut with a final clang. It had taken her a full hour to work up the courage, and as soon as he'd seen her all of her bravery had fled.

Nothing for it but to wait for morning.

Down the hallway, the infirmary door suddenly jerked open. Riley looked up as Eden staggered out, her pretty face ravaged with tears. As soon as she saw the healer, her heart gave a painful squeeze. "Eden," she called softly, pushing herself to her feet.

Eden didn't hear her. Instead, she kicked the wall viciously, then started pummeling it with her fists.

Shit. Riley's gut dropped. *No.* She ran toward the other woman, grabbing her upraised fists. "Eden! Eden, stop it! I'm here. Stop it, you're going to hurt yourself!"

The other woman turned into her arms with a sob and collapsed, her knees giving out. Riley caught her, staggering back into the wall at the sudden weight. "Adam," Riley said hoarsely. "Is he...?"

Eden cried out, shaking her head against Riley's chest. "I can't—I can't do anything," she sobbed. "He's dying, and I can't fucking do anything!" The sudden weight as she slumped took Riley by surprise.

Somehow, they ended up on the floor, on their knees. Riley locked her arms around the other woman, her eyes swimming with tears. *Christ*. She'd never gotten along well with him, but she'd never wanted *this*. The man had always seemed invincible, radiating such an aura of control that you knew he would never fail.

Stroking Eden's hair, she tried to crush her close, to somehow reassure her that everything was going to be all right. But it wasn't. Her tears turned bitter. Lily was in a monster's hands, Wade *was* a monster, and Adam was dying unless—

Unless—

She went so still she almost stopped breathing, Wade's words an echo in her ears. *Something in the shift regenerates the body....*

"Eden," she whispered, excitement a hot flutter in his chest. "Has he still got his amulet on?"

Eden shuddered, lifting her sticky face off Riley's shoulder, her eyes glazed. "What?" she croaked. "Of course he does."

Riley slid her hands to Eden's wrist and squeezed. "You need to listen to me. Is there another warg cage somewhere?"

"Of course. We always—" Eden's face suddenly drained of color. "No," she whispered. "No, I can't. He'll never forgive me."

"And if he's dead?" she asked harshly. "Can you live with that?" She eased her grip as Eden's face crumpled, feeling like a bitch. "Wade told me that something in the shift regenerates the body. If we can get McClain into a warg cage, and get the amulet off him, there might be a chance." Her gaze lifted to the windows at the end of the corridor. A faint softening on the dark horizon bore the testament of time. "We don't have long," she said. "The sun's going to come up soon. If you want to save his life, then we've only got an hour or so to do it."

Eden stared at her helplessly. Red blotches made a mess of her face, and her brown hair hung in loose tangles.

Riley ground her teeth together and dragged Eden to her feet. "Come on," she said. "Do you want to save him or not?"

The words jolted the healer. She drew a shaky breath and nodded. "Yes," she whispered.

Opening the infirmary door, Riley found a pair of guards watching over the bed. Bloodied bandages filled the wastebasket, and the bowl of water beside the bed was crimson. Stepping closer, she saw that McClain's chest had been sewn together with thick, dark thread, but he laid so still, his face so slack that for a moment, she thought he was dead already.

Eden ran a trembling hand over his shoulder. "Jory?" she asked softly.

"Ma'am?" One of the guards cleared his throat and stepped forward.

"I need the warg cage in the prison. Bring it here, and be quick."

His gaze flickered to Riley's as if questioning the order. She nodded sharply. "Bring it as fast as you can."

The two men left the room. Eden sagged onto a chair beside the bed and slid her hand into McClain's unresponsive one. "If he survives he'll never forgive me."

"Yes, he will."

"No." A fresh surge of hot tears slid down Eden's cheek, as she stared hopelessly at her brother. "You don't understand how he feels about this. I can't keep this secret. We can't do this by ourselves." Her lip quivered. "They'll know, and then they'll want him dead. We don't allow wargs to live here at Absolution. If they realize what he's been hiding all along—"

"Maybe," Riley said. She knelt on one of the chairs, watching the still form. His heart was barely beating. "Maybe not. You've lived here all along, so you don't see the way they look at him. They might forgive him." She shrugged a shoulder helplessly. "Hell, I didn't think I could ever forgive something like this, but..." A deep breath. "It's been a long, life-changing week."

"They won't," Eden whispered. "They won't change."

Silence as they waited, illuminated by the steady tick of the clock on the wall. Riley was half-tempted to tear it off and smash it by the time the men returned.

The knock at the door startled both of them. Riley crossed to it and eased it open, glancing down the hallway to where Wade raged. If she concentrated, she could still hear the rabid snarl.

Four men heaved a warg cage between them, faces straining. Riley stepped aside and gestured them in.

Four men.

Four witnesses.

No help for it.

Once Eden had the cage in place, she took a deep breath. "Put him in it," she said.

The man she'd called Jory frowned, "Ma'am, what's going on? What's—"

"Just do it," Riley snapped. "This is hard enough for her as it is."

His hooded gaze cut toward her, his lips thinning. With a jerk of his head, he stepped toward the bed. "Yes, ma'am."

McClain never moved as they eased him off the bed and into the cold bars of the cage. Riley shut the door with a loud clang and locked it. If this worked... *Please, let it work....*

Reaching through the bars, her fingers closed around the cold pewter charm. His skin was almost as cool to the touch, reminding her that they were running out of time. Even as she lifted the pewter from his skin, she saw a pulse thud heavily in the vein in his throat. Muscle crawled beneath her outstretched hand, like something obscene rippling under his skin.

"Mercy," Jory whispered in a horrified voice.

Riley jerked her hand back through the bars, tearing the chain from his throat.

The response was instantaneous. McClain's back arched off the floor, and his eyes shot wide as he screamed. "*No!*" A hollow, gut-wrenching sound of thwarted fury.

Riley leapt out of the way, just as Eden's knees gave out. Jory caught her as she fell, his gaze locked on the cage and the tableau within.

"Hell," one of the guards muttered in a sick tone. "He's a fucking warg."

McClain's skin tore along his arms, fur ripping through with a vengeance. The change was faster, far more violent than Wade's had been. His spine bowed, the scream in his throat thinning until it was almost a howl. His mouth elongated, teeth lengthening on a snarl, and as he turned his head she saw the desperation in his beautiful, still-human eyes.

Then it was gone. The monster tore itself free, shaking off its humanity as if it were a horrific butterfly emerging from its cocoon. His feet jerked, claws ripping through the skin, his jeans swelling as muscle bulged. They finally tore, and thick, tawny fur sprung through.

Finally, it was over. McClain lay on his side and panted, a vicious glitter in his eyes as he watched them. Riley didn't trust that look an inch.

"Oh, God," Eden whispered, taking a step toward him. "What have I done?"

Jory jerked her out of the way. "No," he said. "You can't go near him, not like this."

Another guard had his hand on the gun at his hip, indecision warring with violence on his face. Riley caught his gaze. "Leave," she suggested, her own hand dropping to her gun.

His lips worked, then he nodded, tearing his gaze away as he stormed from the room.

"Christ," one of the other men whispered, sinking onto his haunches and staring in horrified fascination at the cage. "What happened? Did that warg get him today?"

"No," Riley replied. She couldn't let Wade take the blame for this. And maybe Absolution needed to see that a warg could live amongst them safely, without any of them even knowing. "He's been like this for ten years."

The guards all looked at her, a medley of horror, fear and confusion written across their faces.

"How?" Jory asked.

Riley held up the pewter charm. "The same way Wade controls himself. With this, neither of them have to turn."

"Fuck this," one of them whispered. He shook his head, sidling toward the door, unable to tear his gaze from McClain. "You can't control this," he said. "You just can't."

As he left, Riley's heart sank. She met Eden's gaze, her lips thinning as she turned to the growling beast in the cage. She'd saved his life – McClain would live.

But at what cost?

SOFT, SILVERY SUNLIGHT streamed through the window.

Luc lifted his head, his arms shaking as the last of the pain left him. He sucked in a sharp breath, bringing with it the scent of rage and blood, and the lingering remnants of woman.

A soft intake of breath caught his attention. Riley. Luc stiffened, clenching his eyes shut against the horror of the night. There was an old story told in some settlements about how a warg could never remember the change, how each morning brought with it the fear of *what had he done*. How he wasn't responsible because the beast had made him do it.

Easier to think that. Easier to hope that when their fathers and brothers and sisters changed, they didn't have to live with the horror of what they'd done. That, secretly, a part of them didn't want to rape and slaughter.

But he remembered it *all*.

The rage. The fury. The need. Riley's face as she jerked away from him, horror printed all over her features as she ran, unable to bear it. The sound of her harsh breathing as she slammed the door behind her and locked it.

His fist clenched, nails scraping over the cold floor. Her expression was like a mirror, showing him just what type of monster he was. She'd said she could handle it, but she hadn't been able to. Pain choked him up and he bit it down sharply, along with everything else in his miserable life.

It didn't matter.

Lily mattered, and that was all.

"Are you okay?" she whispered, though she hadn't moved.

He nodded, opening his eyes and wiping the expression off his face. "I'm fine."

Fabric shifted as she pushed to her feet. Luc risked a glance, saw the stain of exhaustion on her features. His gaze sharpened. "Did you sleep?"

She shook her head, sorting through the keys sluggishly. "I couldn't." She jammed a key into the lock, and the door swung open with an iron squeal. "Eden's a mess, and—"

His lungs were a sudden vise as memory flooded back. "McClain?"

Riley wouldn't look at him. "You got your wish. Your revenge."

His mouth suddenly tasted like ash, and he stumbled as he stepped over the lip of the cage. "Mercy," he said, through a voice rough with grief. "I didn't—I never wanted—" Not truly.

Riley caught his arm, and Luc looked down. "I'm sorry," she said. "He's still alive. I didn't mean to make you think he'd died." She took a shuddering breath. "He *was* dying though. Then I remembered what you'd said about the shift regenerating the body."

The breath went out of him. "You took the charm off him?"

She nodded bleakly. "We put him in the cage, and took the charm off." A bitter smile tugged her lips. "It worked perfectly. One warg, not even a sign of the stitches in his chest."

The smile faded, and her eyes suddenly swam with tears. Luc slid a gentle finger over her cheek, and she turned into his body with a sudden sob, pressing her face against his chest.

His arms closed over her back slowly, stroking the soft silk of her hair. Her tears didn't come easy. It were as if she fought them, each racking sob tearing out of her in a way that made her whole body shake.

Hell. He clutched her tight, running desperate hands over her shoulders. "It's okay," he murmured. "He couldn't keep living the lie forever. Nobody can."

He'd never bothered to try.

As if becoming aware of where she was, Riley's shoulders tensed. He could feel it, running all the way through her, as if she suddenly fought not to push away.

Luc let her go. Stepped back. It was like a bullet to the chest.

Riley dragged a hand over her wet face, her nose running. "I know." She sucked in a huge breath, trying to ground herself. "I just feel responsible. It was my decision, and I pushed Eden into it. He was dying." Shadows swam through her eyes. "They've got him locked in the cage still."

"No chance of parole," Luc murmured. He knew the way of it. Something bitter soured his thoughts, but he fought it away. The world had changed in the last few days. Not even McClain deserved that. "Where do they think I am?"

She wiped her eyes, a hint of determination crossing her features. Trying to put herself back together. "In the cage. I told them I'd put you there."

"Then they're not likely to appreciate it if they find me out of it," he said. "Especially with tensions running high this morning. We need to move." He hesitated. "If you still intend to come?"

He didn't use the word 'want.'

"I'm coming." Her face firmed as she made her decision. "I haven't forgotten about Lily."

"It's going to be dangerous."

"I know." Riley's body stiffened, her voice softening. "I understand that now."

After she'd seen him in the cage. Guilt and self-hatred flared in his gut. How the hell could she stand to be near him after what she'd seen?

"But I can't leave her there," Riley added. "And I gave you my word."

Soft, quiet words. He wasn't the only one feeling the effects of the previous night. Luc sucked in a sharp breath, looking around for his clothes. If he kept it all bottled up inside, then maybe it wouldn't show on his face? The hope... shattered... that a woman could ever truly want a monster like him.

"Did you get what I asked for then?" His voice was cool. Distant. Inside, however, he was an inferno of emotion. This was why he'd walked away from Abbie. Not just because he was a danger to them, but because he'd never wanted to see on her face what he could see on Riley's.

"I got it. Packs are loaded in the jeep. We'll have to move quickly. The settlement's running high with tension, and nobody seems to know what to do, but that won't last long. I give us an hour to get out of here."

Luc turned away as he jerked his jeans on. There was a faint tremble in his hands. This was all the harsher because, for once, he'd actually started to believe that he could have a normal life.

No point dreaming of something he could never have. His only focus right now was Lily. And making sure that he got her back safely.

"Fine," he said sharply. "Just let me get dressed and we'll get going."

sixteen

THE HOT SUN pounded down on her skin as the jeep roared through the desert.

Riley drew her knees up to her chest as Wade drove, watching sightlessly as the scenery raced past. She was so tired her eyes burned, but she knew she couldn't sleep. Every so often, she glanced over her shoulder, checking for signs of pursuit.

Getting out of Absolution had been easier than getting in ever would be. Nobody had expected someone to steal a jeep and ride off with it. They'd idled through the streets to the main gates, a hat drawn down over Wade's face. When the guard at the gate asked for their identity cards, Wade had punched him in the face and knocked him out cold. None of the guards on the top of the gate had seen, as the jeep was parked underneath. Riley had winched the gate open and they'd driven through, Wade giving the guards on the top of the gatehouse a loose wave.

Thirty seconds later, they'd opened fire, no doubt finding the prone form of their fallen comrade.

If McClain were in charge, that breach would never have happened, but the town was abuzz with disorder. Almost everybody had been called to meet in the town square.

She didn't like leaving McClain behind to deal with the consequences of her actions, but she didn't have a choice. Lily needed her more than McClain did, though the last she'd heard, he was still in the cage.

Wade looked over at her as he steered the jeep through a gulch in the desert. He'd been quiet since they left, as if something were bothering him. Or, if she were truthful, she knew precisely what was bothering him.

She just didn't have the guts to confront it.

"It's not your fault," he said, referring to McClain.

"I know." Hollow words.

Another minute of silence stretched out, the wind catching her hat. Riley slapped a hand to it, tugging it back into place so the broad brim sheltered her skin. Her hair was tucked up beneath it, and she wore men's clothes, laced tight enough to fool anyone as to her gender. The backseat looked like an arsenal.

"I'm just trying to work out where this sense of duty comes from, why you feel like you need to take all of the blame? To shoulder burdens that aren't your own," he finally said, hands tight on the steering wheel. "You didn't have to come."

Riley nibbled on the hem of her sleeve, thinking about his question. It was the way her father had raised her. Abel Kincaid had been the leader of his community, and that meant responsibility, rather than entitlement. You did what needed to be done. Even if that meant going out alone to hunt a warg that had slaughtered a nearby homestead, when you knew your hands were beginning to shake, and you could barely lift the shotgun to your shoulder.

Sometimes, she wished her father hadn't shouldered his responsibility that one time, but to do that would have made him less of the man he was.

Riley shook off the melancholy thoughts of her father. Wade was speaking about the here and now. About her. "Would you have come? If that was my daughter out there?"

Long, long silence. "Yes," he finally said. He didn't take his eyes off the faint track in front of them. "But only for you."

Her breath caught. Whatever lay between them – this insane attraction, this invisible bond, this tension – she wasn't the only one who felt it.

"I'm not so sure about that." She leaned back against the side of the door, watching the stern line of his profile. Faint, tired lines creased at the corners of his eyes, his knuckles flexing and unclenching on the steering wheel. Small signs of a father's fear, despite the cool manner he spoke with. "Would you leave a little girl – or boy – in Cane's hands? Even if you didn't know them?"

The wind ruffled his hair, stirring the black cambric of his shirt. "No."

"You don't want to care, do you? But you do. And I don't think you're asking me the question you want to."

It was a dare. She'd felt the distance between them all morning. Riley shifted uneasily. Not even she was brave enough to bring up the night before, and her feelings about it. She didn't even know what she *did* feel.

Horror. Fear. An odd mixture of pain and grief. Wade was a monster, and she couldn't deny that. He would never be anything else. The only thing that let him cling to his semblance of humanity was the charm around his throat.

There was no cure for a warg. Only a bullet.

The thought hurt. She'd known from the start what he was, but somehow something had changed, and she'd started looking at him as a man.

If they ever had a life together, what type of life would it be? No settlement would take them in, unless they kept his secret, and she saw how that had turned out for McClain. Besides, Wade's tone indicated he wouldn't live that way. He couldn't hide what he was. Not without burying himself in bitterness.

Wade stared ahead. "You thirsty?"

Riley felt a surge of both disappointment and relief. He hadn't taken up her dare, and he wouldn't. The question would go unsaid. She wouldn't have to answer something she didn't know if she could answer. Yet the tension between them remained.

"No," she replied quietly. "I'm not."

The minutes ticked by. Wade steered the jeep through a crossroads with grim determination, barely even glancing down the other road.

"Do you know where he's going?" she asked.

"Did a lot of scouting when I first got here," he replied, his knuckles tightening on the wheel as they hit a pothole. "They'll need water and shelter, and they're running with reivers, which limits their options. The old Copperplate Mine's the only thing out this way that's big enough to support them." His lashes lowered. "Besides, I can see the tire marks from Colton's jeep. I know where he's going."

Impulsively, she slid her hand over his thigh. Hard muscle clenched beneath the dark denim. "We'll get her back, you know."

He nodded sharply, as if unable to speak.

The day stretched out, shadows lengthening. Wade drove like a man possessed, handling the jeep with one hand, his mirrored shades hiding any sign of emotion. His jaw was locked tight, knuckles white around the wheel; however, Riley didn't need to see his eyes to know what he was thinking.

"You used to be a bounty hunter out on the Rim," she murmured, to distract him. "You ever cross the Great Divide, head east? My father said they have cities out there, huge walled cities, not like the slaver trading towns down south, along the New Mérida border."

Wade glanced sideways. "Only once," he admitted. "I was hunting a pack of shadow cats, and they took me across the Divide." He shook his head. "It's a different world out there. This side of the Divide, everyone's scattered. Small settling towns, the occasional homestead... Timber's scarce in the Wastelands, but across the Divide you can see whole forests of bleached, calcified trees. Ghost Forests, they call them, from when the meteor first hit. And there's... people there too. They call them mutos, those who were exposed to all manner of shit when the meteor struck."

"And the cities?"

"Didn't get that far. The Eastern Confederacy's got roaming packs of enforcers running all the way along its state lines. They say they're building a wall too. Like that ancient wall in the Orient that I read about once. Only this one's to keep us out. The rabble, the reivers, and the revenants."

"They don't have revenants and wargs in the Confederacy?" she asked curiously. This far into the Wastelands, it wasn't often that news came from the east – or that anyone traveled for more than a hundred miles in their whole life. An envious stirring irritated her.

"No. They hunt 'em down, burn 'em out. The military controls the whole Confederacy, and when they're not fighting down along the New Mérida border, they send their troops out on scalping missions for warg packs, or revenants." Wade's lips twitched in a smile. "Why? You itching to leave the settlement?"

"No. I'm just... curious. I've never seen anything other than the Wastelands. I can't even imagine what a city would look like."

"Big," he said with a shrug. "Huge buildings, like the ones that brushed the skies before the meteor. Had an old man down in Lexton tell me most of them folk live in the cities, where it's safer. Call each other 'citizen' and they're only allowed to wear the confederacy colors of white and green. Anyone who disobeys the law is executed."

"Sounds kind of like what happens out here," she mused.

"Yeah, only without the cameras watching your every move."

She couldn't fathom the idea. Peg had once owned a camera, an old family heirloom that took hours to develop each photo, though she'd stopped taking them once she ran out of paper for it. Imagine having cameras everywhere, to take photographs of everyone who passed?

"We've got busybodies instead," she replied dryly. "Grateful to repeat every word they've heard, or anything they've seen. Whether it's true or not...." She shrugged. "Well, that's another story."

The jeep hit a bump, and Wade smoothed it out instantaneously. "Wouldn't know. You get that a lot?"

"I'm an unmarried woman," she said. "I have more people poking into my life than anyone else."

A long moment of silence stretched out. Riley surveyed the barren plains, but there was no sign of movement out there. Only the hoodoos jutting in the distance.

"And no doubt your pick of men." Soft words. He didn't look at her, but she could tell that he was focused on her.

"I could have had a harem," she replied. "That would have made the goodwives choke on their tea."

"No husband though."

"Never met anyone whose ideas meshed with mine." A lot whose ideas involved her in the house, cooking dinner while the men tended the settlement. A hard deal for a woman who'd been raised to follow in her daddy's footsteps. "Not that I'm against marriage or children," she added quickly.

Another glance that scoured her like fire. Riley pretended she hadn't noticed. "How long do you think it will take to get to the mine?"

"On these roads?" Wade cursed under his breath. "Probably noon tomorrow, if we're lucky."

His knuckles went white on the wheel again.

Orange flame crackled in the night, licking at the small twigs Riley fed into the fire. They'd come across a fallen tree – almost too good an opportunity to pass up out here – and decided to make camp for the night. Travelling in the dark was too dangerous, and although Wade was wound tighter than a child's top, even he admitted a few hours' rest would help him gain back his strength.

Turning warg took a lot out of a man, and he hadn't been able to hunt. The beast inside him was restless still, driven to the edge by the threat to his daughter.

"Sounds like it's more human than you realize," she'd muttered, which had earned her a sharp look.

"Maybe I'm not the one doubting," he shot back before striding out into the night to scout for danger, leaving her to stare after him.

Wade had been gone for over an hour. Riley stabbed a stick into the hot coals in short, angry movements. Just what had he meant by those words?

A twig snapped, and her head jerked up. Slowly, Wade came into focus, with an armful of smaller branches and brush – whitethorn by the look of it, and scrub oak. This close to the mountains, the trees began to appear, and even grow larger, with the occasional cottonwood grove. Out in the plains, the only thing one came across was agave, prickly pear, and cactus.

Wade dumped his armful by the fire, flame flickering over the silvery shine in his eyes. He wasn't even attempting to hide the feral cast to his features. Not fully human tonight. His cheekbones looked like they'd been carved with a hatchet, and veins distended along the back of his hands a forearms.

As if aware of her scrutiny, he shot her a look, a challenge. *Not human. Never will be. So what are you going to do about it?*

Riley scowled back and tipped her chin up. *Well, I'm not running. Even though I've seen you at your beastly worst.*

His gaze dropped away, and he rubbed his fist absently.

Coward.

"Sit," she said. "You're wearing me out with all that pacing."

He'd caught a Gila monster earlier, and Riley had carefully roasted it over the open flames. The meat sizzled, and she reached out and cut a chunk off, nearly burning her fingers. The first taste of it melted in her mouth. "Dinner's ready."

Wade sank onto a boulder on the other side of the fire – about as far away from her as he could get – and used his own knife to carve off a generous hunk of meat. Riley handed him the pack of flatbread she'd acquired at

Absolution, and they ate in silence, using the bread as both plate and a wrap for the meat.

"What time do you think we'll get moving?" she asked.

"Just before dawn. If we blow a tire or two, then we'll never make it in time," he replied, licking his fingers. Frustration darted across his face. He wanted to push on; so did she, but common sense had won out. The waiting was almost agonizing. Just ratcheting the tension higher.

Wade picked up a chunk of cottonwood and withdrew his knife. He started scraping the bark off the thick branch, his hands moving swiftly. Riley picked up her stick again and started drawing circles in the dirt at her feet.

Distraction.

"You couldn't move quicker in your other form?" she asked quietly.

"I could, but I wouldn't. I'm not in control when I'm in warg form." Those silvery eyes raked over her, as if to show her precisely how much the warg shone through tonight. "Most likely, I'd be distracted by the hunt. Or... other desires."

Her.

Riley stilled, the end of the stick trailing in the dirt.

"You look surprised." His words were another challenge. "Don't forget I'm a monster, Riley."

Her breath caught. "That's not fair."

Wade looked at her, cold light shining in those blue eyes. Holding himself back. "Isn't it? I remember the look on your face." His tone softened, and he looked down at his hands, the knife making a curl of wood. It dropped to the ground. "I remember how you ran from the room. Do you think I wanted you to see me like that?"

"No." Her voice was very small. "I knew what you were—"

"But you didn't understand it," he replied, carving another gentle curl in the wood, "until you saw it."

Silence. Not even a hint of warg-song tonight.

Riley slashed the end of the stick through the figure she'd been drawing. "Do you want the truth?"

His gaze jerked to hers. His hands stopped their smooth motion.

"Do you want to know what I felt?" she asked, her voice rising. "Why the hell won't you ask?"

His lips pressed tightly together.

She jerked to her feet. "Ask me! Why won't you ask me?"

Wade stood, tossing aside the knife and the half-made carving. "Maybe I don't want to fucking know," he snapped, turning on his heel, as if he were going to leave.

Riley didn't know what came over her. Leaping over the fire, she grabbed his arm and wrenched him toward her. "So you walk away? The way you always do?"

He spun, and the furious glitter in his eyes almost made her back away. "Don't!" he snarled, stabbing a finger at her. "Don't you fucking dare say that!"

"Or?"

His gaze half-shuttered. Slowly, his body turned toward her, every muscle bunching as if violence rode through him. "Fine," he snarled. "You want to know why I won't ask? Because I know the answer. I saw it on your face as I writhed in that goddamned cage. I was everything you hated, everything you feared, and you couldn't handle it. You *ran*."

Her chest was heaving. Riley stared up at him, smoke curling around them as the wind changed. "You weren't there," she said weakly. "That wasn't you."

"I was there," he snapped. "That's the thing nobody will admit, Riley. I was there. That was me. That's the true curse. That's why I hate it so much, because it's like admitting the worst part of yourself exists. Every horrible little thought you ever have swims to the surface, but multiplied a hundredfold, and you have to ride with it, aware of everything. I wanted blood, and I wanted flesh, and I wanted you." His hot gaze ran down her figure. "And I hate that more than anything. That I could hurt you, and not be able to stop myself."

The outbreak took her by surprise. Truth was there between them, and she realized that she hadn't been entirely truthful with him. She'd withheld, when he'd spat everything he felt out into the world.

"All right," she whispered. "You want to know how I felt? I was scared, and a part of me was horrified. You keep saying it was you, but it wasn't. I looked in your eyes, and you weren't there anymore, and *that* was what frightened me." She swallowed hard. "You were the monster that everyone out here fears, and yeah, maybe I'm still a little afraid, but I trust you. I *don't* believe that was you. That was your monster, your beast.

"And you know what? I'm still here. I haven't run, Wade, and I'm not going to." The words made her realize the truth as much as he did. They also made her aware of another truth. "I keep wondering how I'm going to make a life with you, but the question I don't ask myself is whether I *want* to make a life with you. I don't know when, but I made that decision somewhere along the way. Maybe that bloody pool of water."

He stared at her, shadows carving grim lines into his face. Hope flared in his eyes, then died. "And how long does that last?" Dropping his gaze, he turned away from her again. "No, Riley. You need to start thinking about your future, but I won't be in it."

Frustration reared. "Don't you dare walk away!" she yelled, looking around for something, anything to throw. "Or I swear I will brain you with this water canteen."

He stopped in his tracks. "Wargs don't have wives. They don't have lovers. I should never have touched you. I'm sorry for that."

"No, you're not!" She was so angry she wanted to hit him. "You're not sorry you touched me at all. You wanted it. I wanted it. You're just afraid to face the consequences of that action.

"You did your wife a disservice, Wade. You never gave her a choice to accept you. You walked away before she could face that fear. And now you're doing it to me!"

"She could have come after me," he said simply, his words floating on the wind.

True. Riley's fists clenched. "I would. I will."

Wade stared out into the desert night, his shoulders stiff. His head turned to the side, his stark profile standing out against the black desert night. "No." As if he just realized the challenge he'd thrown her.

"If I'm brave enough to face my fears, why can't you?"

"I don't want to talk about it." A soft growl lit his voice before he started walking into the darkness. "Go to sleep. I'll keep watch."

Her eyes narrowed. "Go to sleep, my ass," Riley muttered, stepping over a small log and sliding down the embankment after him. "You think it's that easy? You think you just say no, and I'll go on my way and forget you?"

She tripped on something in the dark and staggered forward, her hands out. Her palms met Wade's back, and he went down on one knee as she steadied.

She could barely see him, night-blind after the hot orange glow of the fire. The wind was cool now, cutting through her clothes and making her shiver.

Spinning around, Wade's hand caught her by the back of the leg. "Did you just shove me?" he asked incredulously.

The heat of his palm through her jeans did wicked things to her body, but Riley wasn't about to be distracted. "Maybe I did." And maybe she had. Could she have stopped herself? "What are you going to do about it?"

"This!" he snapped.

The world upended as he drove his shoulder into her midriff and strained to his feet. Riley cried out softly, punching her fist into his buttocks. "Put me down!" she yelled, straining and kicking. "You are not going to win this argument like this!"

Riley jerked on his shoulder, her legs swinging wildly. Wade turned and strode back up the hill, frustration and fear churning inside him.

You wanted a woman who'd fight for you, didn't you?

He ground his teeth together and dumped her on her outspread bedroll. She kicked herself up onto her knees as if she were going to tackle him, her eyes glittering hotly in the fire's gleam. Luc grabbed her by the shoulders and shoved her back down, pinning her wrists on the blankets and crushing her with his weight.

"Be still!"

She breathed hard, squirming beneath him. "Make me."

Luc sucked in a sharp breath. Bloody hell. Each little squirm impressed itself on his body, his hips sliding into the V of hers. He knew the instant she felt his erection, her body stiffening beneath him.

Their eyes met.

And then it was as if all the tension suddenly erupted, her mouth attacking his in the dark, even as his hands tore at her clothes.

He needed this. Wanted it so badly. And she was just as savage, her nails raking over his shoulders, fingers knotting in his hair.

The wildness within wanted to howl in glee. *His.* His cock thickened, aching in his jeans. Luc couldn't stop himself. He lifted his hips, tearing at the buttons. A needy little sound purred in Riley's throat, her teeth sinking into his lips.

"Want you," she gasped. "Want you so much. And I'm not letting go! No matter how far you run, no matter how fast...." Her hands slid between them, his cock falling free of his jeans into her hot palms.

Luc buried his head against her throat with a gasp, the heated silk of her hair brushing against his face. He thrust into her clenched fist, grabbing her by the ass and driving her against him. Not enough. He wanted inside her. Now.

The musky scent of her arousal told him she felt the same. Luc tugged at her jeans, tearing the buttons in his haste. Then he had them free, yanking them down her legs until she was wearing only her white cotton panties with the tiny little bow stitched onto them.

Kneeling between her legs, he grasped her hips and nuzzled his face between her thighs. Her scent was dizzying here. Delicious. Grasping the edges of her panties, he slid them lower, dragging them over her knees. Riley kicked free of them, then Luc grasped her thighs and held her open for him. Her blonde curls glinted in the firelight, her soft gasps lingering in the air.

She moaned as he covered her with his mouth, tasting the sweetness of her body. Tongue plunging into her, darting over her. *God.* He groaned. Couldn't get enough. His cock *ached.*

He could just feel her body start trembling as he broke his intimate kiss, and drove up over her. "You're mine," he whispered, bending her knee up and thrusting hard into the molten core of her. Just for a moment, he let himself pretend the dream was real. That the woman in his arms would never melt away.

Riley threw her head back as she came, a scream dying on her lips. "Luc!"

He felt every delicious little shudder of her body and drove into her harder, forcing her to ride the storm again. Skin against skin, the heels of her feet digging into his bare buttocks as he pinned her to the ground and took her.

He couldn't stop the fury, couldn't be gentle. He needed her. A starving man, desperate for one last taste. And she was just as eager, her hips undulating beneath his, little soft whimpers whispering in his ear. All she could do with her wrists pinned.

Or maybe not. The rasp of her teeth in the soft flesh of his earlobe drove him crazy. Her hot breath on his neck. Luc felt the flash-fire of pleasure tighten his balls, the surge of cum shooting up his cock.

"Yes... yes..." One of her hands tore free, clutching at the base of his scalp. He drove into her one last time, even as she whispered, "I love you."

Everything in the world went silent, orgasm screaming through him. Luc's grip on her tightened, her arms sliding around him as he collapsed with a shudder, sweat wet on his flanks. Riley's breasts rose and fell beneath him, her free hand rubbing gently up and down his spine.

"I meant it," she whispered. "Every word of it. I won't pretend a part of me isn't scared. Sometimes... sometimes, I think I'm just as afraid of this as of... the other. Afraid that you won't feel the same way. Not that I expect you to, not yet," she added hurriedly. "But one day, maybe."

He couldn't answer. Instead, his hold on her tightened, just a little. This was more than he'd ever hoped for, more than he'd ever dared consider. The tightness in his chest was unexpected, like a fist clenching. Those words changed everything.

And it scared the fuck out of him.

Because she was telling him that this was real. That she had no intentions of leaving him, no matter what he did, no matter what happened. No matter how much of a monster he was. And he actually began to believe it. For the first time in years, he felt like a human again. A man who just might have a future. Riley was hope. She was everything. And if he lost her, it would kill him.

"It's okay," she whispered, brushing her lips against his neck. "I know it seems crazy. Everything's happened so fast, but it feels so real."

Luc finally looked up, bringing his hand up to stroke the sweaty hair off her cheek. The fire crackled, its warm glow turning her skin to molten honey. Beautiful. Stubborn. Gloriously his. He withdrew from her body, but not her arms. He could stay there forever, he thought. No matter how scared he was about Lily, Riley's presence made it somewhat bearable. As if the fear could be overcome, the same way he would overcome Cane.

"You drive me crazy," he admitted.

A tiny smile played around her lips. "Crazy-good?"

"Crazy-good."

Luc rolled onto his side, taking her with him. Her head rested on his upper arm and he sighed softly, pressing his lips to her temple. Her body relaxed against his, fingertips tracing small circles on his chest. Slowly, the circles died. Her breathing softened as she fell asleep.

"It feels real," he admitted, knowing she didn't hear him.

seventeen

RILEY SIGHED.

Ahead of them, canyons loomed, carving huge red swathes out of the mountains. Ebenezer's Labyrinth, they called it, after the old settler who'd gotten lost in there and died. She eyed the canyon walls as Wade steered them down the narrow track. Perfect ambush territory, and barely a few hours' drive from the Copperplate Mine.

Tension raked through her, and she dragged a shotgun into her lap, her gaze riding high over the walls. Cool shadows washed away the blazing heat of the sun, and she slipped her hat back so her peripheral view was better.

"Can you hear that?" Wade murmured, his gaze flickering to the rearview mirror.

Riley cocked her head. Silence. "What?"

"We've got company," he replied. "Behind us."

A shot ricocheted off the canyon and Riley yelped, ducking low in the seat. She pumped the shotgun and peered over the back of the seat. A rusted-out jeep roared into view. It looked like someone had taken several cars, ransacked them, and welded bits and pieces onto the jeep. A heavy gun turret sat in the middle, with a reiver manning it, goggles in place. There were three more riding in back, and a pair in the front. Behind them, in the thick, choking dust trail, she could just make out a second vehicle.

"Shit." She yanked off her safety belt and knelt on the seat, putting the shotgun to her shoulder. "Can you get us out of here?"

"Hold on," Wade said, hitting the gas.

She aimed low and pulled the trigger, feeling the kick against her shoulder. Metal screamed as her pellets sprayed off the grill on the front of the jeep.

The reivers returned fire, spinning the gun turret toward them.

"Get down!" Riley yelled, throwing herself low in the seat. Bullets screamed overhead, cutting through the red rock of the canyon walls. She used the time to jack out the spent cartridges and reload.

Wade roared around a corner, flying over a rut in the road. Riley bounced, dragging herself upright with her hand on the door. She propped the shotgun on the headrest of her seat and waited for the reivers to follow.

Her first shot took out the man on the gun. He arched back into space and disappeared, another leaping forward to take his place.

"That's one down," she said grimly, her hands in a constant movement. Fire. Reload. Fire. Reload.

The gun on the turret spewed bullets as another reiver climbed up. Riley slid down onto the floor of the jeep as her headrest exploded in a cloud of dust and fabric.

"Think you can drive?" Wade yelled, looking at her.

"What?"

"Can you drive?" he repeated.

She nodded, her head hitting the dash as he hit a bump. "What are you going to do?"

"Take out that gun." His mouth was a grim line. "That one was too close for comfort."

Wade leaned back in the seat, slowing a fraction as he gestured for her to clamber between his thighs.

Riley left the shotgun on the passenger side and slid onto his lap, settling between his warm thighs. His hands slid around her, locking hers on the steering wheel.

"Be careful," he told her, pressing a swift kiss to the side of her neck. "Keep your head down."

His body started to slide out from behind her. Riley eased her foot onto the gas. "You too," she said, her heart fluttering in her chest. "You're not bulletproof."

Then he was gone, leaping into the back of the jeep.

Riley slid fully into the seat, peering through the dusty windshield. A flicker of movement in her mirrors showed Wade crouching in the back of the jeep, his knife glinting silver in his hand. He suddenly leapt high into the air, vanishing into the dust cloud behind her.

Riley sucked in a sharp breath. He knew what he was doing; she had to trust that. But a cold hand of fear shivered down her spine.

Gunfire barked, and then someone screamed behind her. Her eyes kept jerking from the path ahead to the mirrors, and that was dangerous. The canyon twisted and turned with exhilarating speed. She had to force her eyes to the road and concentrate on driving.

The canyon suddenly widened, a panoramic vista of sky spreading out in front of her. Riley's startled mind had a second to realize what was ahead – the old, dammed river far below – before she jerked the steering wheel hard. The canyon track hooked around a corner, running along the top of the cliffs, and the jeep teetered on two wheels as she forced it to corner hard.

Behind her, the reivers' jeep wasn't so lucky. She caught a glimpse of Wade, kneeling over the driver's body and forcing the wheel to lock. He held on right to the end, the reivers' jeep screaming through the half-rotted timber fence and out over the cliff face. Leaping high, Wade dove into a roll, coming up on the edge of the cliff.

Riley slammed on the brakes. "Get in!" she screamed as the wheels locked, red sand flying around them.

Wade rolled onto his knees, his dark hair failing across his eyes. He yelled something at her, making a furious gesture with his hand. What?

Then dust sprayed around the corner. Riley's gaze jerked to the second jeep, her eyes meeting the driver's. He braced himself, eyes widening as his jeep drove straight at her.

The impact smashed her forward and Riley hit the steering wheel hard, something slamming into her head. The world blurred, her ears ringing as the jeep skidded to the side until it finally crashed against something. She felt whatever it was give. Pain. God... She felt it all through her ribs and face, like some giant fist had smashed into both areas. The teeth on the right side of her face throbbed dully.

The jeep finally slid to a halt, rocking onto its side. The world stopped moving. She was breathing hard, each breath rasping over the side of her mouth and stinging. As her vision started to focus, she caught sight of the glass in front of her, a spider web of cracks snaking through it. She'd hit the front window.

The ringing in her ears began to dull. Through it, she should could hear someone screaming her name, a distorted sound as though it came from deep underwater.

"Urfm." She tried to lift her head, and realized the steering wheel was jammed under her ribs. Hand crunching on glass shards, she pushed away from the dash, trying to see what was happening.

The world shifted with a metal screech. Riley's hand clutched for the steering wheel, her eyes shooting wide open. And that was when the distorted voice finally began to make sense, "...n't move! Riley, don't fucking move!"

Blue and red met her startled gaze as she glanced over her shoulder. So much blue, light shimmering off it, glittering. Her mind finally made sense of the sight, and she froze, whimpering in her throat.

The river. She was staring at it far below. Or not so far, really. Just far enough that the fall would probably kill her.

Slowly, she looked around, not daring to move her body. She'd hit the fence that ran along the edge of the cliff, and the back half of the jeep was hanging over the edge, tilting toward the water below. Something lurched, and Riley screamed as the jeep slid another half-inch, dangling from whatever it was caught on. The remains of the fence, she suspected.

"Luc!" she screamed. He'd get her out. She knew he would.

"Hold on!" He roared back. "Don't move!"

A shotgun coughed, and she flinched. Turning her head and torso slowly, she wet her lips as the jeep quivered like a metal beast beneath her, threatening to throw her if she shifted so much as an inch.

Wade grappled with a reiver, wrenching the shotgun off the man. He smashed it across the reiver's face, then discarded it as the man fell, his hot gaze cutting to hers. In it, she saw anguish and desperation as he raced toward her. The certainty that he could get her out of this stuttered like a candle.

"Luc," she whispered.

"Don't move," he repeated tersely, sliding to a halt at the front of the jeep. The entire thing had slid around, the back end hanging remorselessly out over the cliff face. Gravity seemed to suck at her, as if it were slowly reeling her in.

Behind him, the second jeep was flipped over, the grill completely crumpled, its scattered reivers groaning on the sand. Or some not moving at all.

"Didn't think... it hit that hard," she murmured, a smile lighting over her lips then fading. Heat sprang up behind her eyes. Her left one was hot and puffy.

"I flipped it," he said, edging closer, as if he didn't quite trust his footing. "You're on loose sand." Frustration crawled over his face. "If you weren't, I could probably drag the jeep back in."

"But you can't get a grip," she replied soberly. "It's okay." A whisper. "We'll work it out."

"Why the hell did you stop?" Finally, he gave vent to some of his frustration, sneaking a little closer, his fingertips straining as he reached for the jeep.

"I was worried about you."

Their eyes met.

"I'm not human, darlin'." He frowned. "Next time, when I tell you to drive, you drive."

"Definitely." *Next time.*

"Are you hurt?"

Riley stroked a tongue over her teeth. They felt a little numb, but the pain wasn't quite as bad as she'd first thought. The shock of it, most like. "Nothing broken, I don't think."

"You've got one hell of a shiner."

The conversational tone almost made her smile. Almost.

"Luc, what are we going to do?"

He considered it, his fingers touching the edge of the jeep, as if to anchor it. As if he didn't dare put any firmer pressure on it. Slowly, he bent, peering under the hood before coming back up. "You're caught on the fence post." He frowned. "It's half-wrenched out of the ground, but it's holding. Just."

As if to taunt his words, something groaned.

Luc reached out. "I want you to move slowly. You're going to have to climb out over the front of the jeep."

His fingers seemed a mile away. She glanced back at the beckoning blue.

"Don't look at the water," he snapped. "Look at me. At my hand. As soon as you're close enough to reach, I can drag you to safety."

Riley's gaze locked on his fingers. "I'm scared."

"I know," he said. "But you've been scared before. Of the dark, remember? I got you out of there."

"I think I'm going to add a new phobia to my growing list. I feel like I'm getting a serious fear of heights." She tried to smile again and saw the faint echo on his own lips, trying to give her hope.

"Can you grab the frame of the window? Try and ease yourself up."

Getting over the half-smashed window was going to be a problem. She eyed the frame, then the side mirror. "Might be better to go to the side, I'm thinking."

"Just move slowly." He began to drag his shirt over his head. "I'm going to hold this out for you to grab." Twirling it into a semblance of a rope, Luc flipped the end toward her. It fluttered in the breeze, temptingly close.

Riley eased her foot up onto the seat of the jeep. Somehow, her body had draped itself over the steering wheel.

She put a little more pressure onto her foot and reached up, grabbing hold of the side mirror. Each move was infinitely slow. She could feel the wind plucking at her shirt, dancing over her skin. Like it wanted her to come play with it.

Her attention scattered at the thought, cold sweat springing up along her spine.

"Riley," Wade said calmly. "Riley, look at me." He stared at her as if the strength of his gaze alone could drag her to safety. "I am not going to let you die." He swallowed hard. "No matter what I have to do. Now, bring your hand up slowly, and reach for the top of the windshield."

It was a nerve-shattering reach, her fingers gripping the metal edge of the windshield. Glass pebbled under her fingers, hitting her jeans before flinging back into space. She didn't look. She couldn't. All she could do was stare into Wade's eyes and listen to that soothing voice, trust he would grab her.

Her toe edged onto the side of the jeep and she eased upward, balancing her weight on it. The shirt was barely inches away now.

"Nearly there, darlin'." He stretched out further, as if the extra inch could help. "I want you to reach—"

An ominous cracking sound shattered the silence. Riley froze as the jeep shifted.

"Oh, Jesus," she whispered, her heart thundering in her ears as she balanced precariously on the edge of the jeep. Her gaze cut to Wade's.

He'd frozen too, his lips thin and white. "Don't move," he whispered.

Sand trickled into space. Riley's fingers clutched around the thin metal ridging of the windshield, the glass cutting into her bare flesh. Another faint shift, with a low, creaking groan. Like the cracking of an arthritic man's fingers.

"It's moving," she blurted. "I can feel the whole thing shifting."

"You're almost there. Just don't move, let it settle—"

Riley screamed a little as the jeep slid. The entire vehicle teetered backward, as if balanced on the edge of the cliff face. A child's seesaw, the weight slowing tipping in one sure direction.

"Oh, my God," she whispered, sucking in a sharp breath and looking back. "Oh, my God, oh, my God—"

"Riley! Look at me! You're going to have to jump."

"I can't." Riley clenched her eyes shut, paralyzed.

"You have to! Open your bloody eyes and look at me!"

"I can't."

"You can!"

Slowly, she looked at him. Wade seemed further away now, fear carving stark lines in his face. In his expression, she saw the hopeless truth.

"It'll tip if I jump," she whispered.

He looked her in the eyes. "It's going to tip anyway. You need to trust me. I won't let you die." His nostrils flared, his chest heaving. Slowly, he dropped the shirt. "You need to jump. Trust me, Riley."

"I won't make it. You're too far away."

He shook his head. "I know." A faint, sad smile slid over his mouth. "Can you swim?"

The jeep slowly tilted back, her weight pulling on the windshield. Tears sprang into her eyes. Her thoughts raced, the words coming a mile a minute. "It's too far. The impact will kill me."

"Riley," he barked. Again, the sound drew her attention back to him. "It won't kill *me*. Trust me. Jump. You need to angle away from the jeep so we don't land on it."

"We?" she babbled. She could feel it going. It was only a matter of seconds. A scream caught in her throat. All she could see were Wade's devilishly blue eyes as he crouched low, the muscles in his thighs bunching.

"Jump!" he yelled, and launched himself at her.

eighteen

RILEY SCREAMED AS she pushed away from the jeep.

It was finally going, and she threw herself back into space, her heart in her throat and her ears tight and ringing. *Trust. Trust him.* It was all she had.

The world was weightless. Airless. No pull on her, no greedy gravity sucking at her.

For a few seconds, all was beautiful. That quivering moment where her motion propelled her through space, and then the world came rushing back, and she was falling, arms flailing, her mouth wide in a silent scream as she tried desperately to fly.

And failed.

Wade came flying out of nowhere, cutting over the edge of the cliff in a flawless dive. He gained on her, inch by precious inch. Riley couldn't breathe. The air around her was a vacuum – she was going too fast. No oxygen, her lungs heaving desperately in her chest. Somehow, she turned her head to the side and sucked in a short breath. The blue beneath her was growing bigger as she tumbled onto her front, staring directly at it. Her eyes watered at the sudden stream of air, her swollen cheek screaming with pain as her cheeks pulled back from her mouth and rippled.

Then Wade hit her hard, strong arms wrapping around her waist and sending them into a free-falling somersault. Legs, arms, sky, water.... She couldn't make sense of herself.

"...got you..." he bellowed, dragging her into his grasp.

They flipped again until she was on top and was breathing into his chest, his arms wrapping around her like steel, drawing her own in tight between them. She caught a glimpse of the jeep, cart-wheeling beside them.

"Hold on!" he screamed.

The world stopped as they smashed into the water, Wade's grip on her loosening. Then she was under, her body slowing as it tore from his grip, her head spinning at the impact. Nostrils full of water, choking, air... Needed air... Which way was up?

She clawed and kicked, trying to orient herself. The world was tinged with gold, and bubbles streamed past her as she tried to find the surface. Up. A shimmering disc of molten light burned above her. Riley tried to reach it, her body a world of hurt.

She broke the surface with a gasp, her lungs burning as she coughed and choked. Water spewed from her nostrils, then it was dragging her back under as the weight of it filled her clothes and boots.

She came up again, the cold of it starting to seep in. So cold her lungs felt like a vise squeezed them. Or maybe that was the fall.

Air. She sucked it in. Choked again. Wade. Where was he? Riley's lungs were burning so badly she thought she was going to vomit, but she couldn't see him. Panic squeezed tight, making it even harder to breathe. The slam of the impact had hurt so much, and she'd been on top.

What if...?

Sucking in a lungful of air that burned within, Riley dove back under. Her body was so weak it fought her, but she strove beneath the surface, hunting furiously for him. A warg could survive a fall like that, maybe. But a warg could also drown.

Luc.

No sign of him. She came back up, gasping in another mouthful of sweet, precious air before she dove again. That time, she went deeper. The water was colder there, the pressure of it tightening over her skin and chest as the murky depths came closer. Ears ringing, Riley was just about to surface again when she saw him.

He floated slowly, his body sinking toward the dark bottom. Riley lashed out with her feet, her chest constricting as she fought to reach him. The faint light from above gleamed golden on his bare chest, the only reason she'd seen him.

Each stroke was a struggle. Her lungs were starting to burn, her vision narrowing. The ringing in her ears was almost screaming at her, pressure clamping tight over her nostrils and sinuses. Her fingers brushed wet denim. She fought on, her hand clamping around his ankle. Elation flooded her, then the weight of him dragged at her, and she had to kick hard to get them moving up.

Riley fought as she'd never fought in her life. To hold on to him, to herself, to the ringing in her ears as her kicking slowed, thrashing violently toward the surface. She could almost feel the warmth now, the bright light of the sun spreading across her vision. Ripples spread in the water, and she broke the surface with a gasp.

One breath. Not enough. Lungs still burning.

But she had to drag him to the surface too. He'd been down longer than she had.

Sliding her arms under his armpits, Riley kicked hard and they both broke the surface. Her vision narrowed in and out, little dizzy spots dancing across the center as she sucked in as much air as she could breathe. Her entire body quivered, her muscles wanting to just seize and give up. To sink below the cold, cold water and enter the silent depths below again.

No.

Riley kicked with weak legs, turning Wade's face to the side. Water spilled from his mouth, but his chest hadn't moved. *No. No, not this.* She'd brought him to the surface. *Breathe, damn you.*

Snuggling his back against her chest, she locked her fingers together and brought them up under his ribs. His chest was so broad she could barely keep her fingers laced.

One hard yank, forcing his body back against hers. His head rested against her shoulder, wet hair spilling against her skin like silk.

"*Come on,*" she whispered, her lips starting to quiver. If she lost him... Hot tears welled in her eyes.

Riley gave another hard yank, forcing the water out of his lungs. Wade jackknifed in her grip, turning his head violently to the side as he coughed. Hard fingers clenched in her forearm, as if he didn't know where he was.

The tears spilled then. Riley pressed her lips to the side of his throat and cried loudly, her nose running, lungs burning with abuse.

"I'm here," she said hoarsely. "I've got you."

His fingers eased on her arm. Wade sucked in a rasping breath that rattled in his throat, and it was the most beautiful sound she'd ever heard.

"I've got you," she whispered again, resting her head back in the cool water as her tears spilled down her cheeks.

No matter what she had to do, no matter who she had to fight, she would never let him go again.

◆━━━━━━━━▶   ◀━━━━━━━━◆

They collapsed on a narrow sandy strip, barely making it clear of the water.

Riley made sure he was breathing all right, then crumpled onto the wet sand, her body finally giving out. She didn't think she could ever move again. It had taken everything she had to swim them to shore.

She woke – or came to – hours later, as someone pulled her up the beach. Panic made her dig her nails into the sand, then Wade lifted her in his arms, half-crawling with her, half-dragging her as he got them to dry sand.

Night was coming, the sun fading into the horizon in a hot, coppery puddle. Wade moved himself into a sitting position then helped her up, her back to his chest. Riley shivered with the cold, her entire body aching from exertion.

"Here," he said hoarsely, rubbing stiff hands down her arms to bring some heat back into her flesh. The chafe hurt, but some of the muscle ache eased. She cried again, not sure why, as he held her and kissed the top of her head, slowly rubbing the heat back into her damp skin.

"Need... to get warm," Riley breathed. Her throat burned like she'd been doing shots of pure acid, and her lungs felt like someone had punched her in the chest several times. "Desert... night... coming."

And with it, a chill so cold she almost began crying again. They might have survived the fall and the water, but the cold was the next true danger.

"Let me warm you," Wade whispered, his clammy hands picking at her shirt. He pried apart a button, then another. At her back, the heat of his body began to seep through, as if finally penetrating the chill of his skin.

At least there was no wind here, tucked high against the base of the cliffs, and the sand was dry and silky. Riley lay limply in his arms as he stripped the wet, chilly shirt from her body and the tank she'd borrowed from Eden. It was harder for him to get her jeans off, dragging them down over her damp legs and tugging them impatiently. His hands shook as he fought the wet material, and she thought he was going to tear it.

"You just... want to get me naked," she said through chattering teeth, as he laid her back on the sand.

A smile danced over his face. "Always." He cupped her fists in his hands and blew on them, hot breath curling over her skin as he pressed a kiss to her knuckles. He sobered a little as he straightened. "But I don't think either of us is up for what comes after I get you naked."

Stripping off his own jeans, he tossed them aside and knelt over her, his body thick with shadows. Scraping the sun-warmed sand up around her, he slowly knelt down, muscles straining in his forearms with fatigue as he pressed his body flat over hers.

Riley soaked in the heat of the sand, shivering uncontrollably. His skin was chilly to the touch, but as they both dried, she could feel that heat deep within him start to soak through again.

The sun slowly set, the indigo blackness of the sky sweeping across the heavens. Riley clutched him tight to her, drowsy against his chest as he pressed his weight down onto her. She was starting to feel all of her hurt now, her cheek and side aching from the crash. The events of the day just seemed too surreal to take in fully.

"You saved my life," she whispered, remembering that moment when he dove over the cliff after her.

"You saved mine." His hand stroked the left side of her face and cupped her cheek. He pressed a kiss to her hair.

"Even?"

A rumble sounded in his chest. "If I start a fire, will you owe me?"

Riley almost shivered again. "I will do anything you want if you get a fire blazing."

"Anything?"

"Anything," she whispered sleepily.

Flames crackled.

Riley pried her eyelids apart, staring at the dancing flames in front of her. Wade knelt in front of it, slowly feeding larger pieces of wood into the crackling inferno.

Stars gleamed overhead and the moon was halfway across the sky. Riley could barely move she was so exhausted. Instead, she stared at the flames, her mind blessedly blank as the heat licked over her skin.

Drifting in pleasant dreams of nothingness, she gave a start when warm hands helped her up. Then naked skin was sliding over hers, and Wade lowered her down near the fire, pressing his chest against her back. The heat was so delicious she tried to stretch a hand out toward it.

"Rest," he whispered, curling his arms around her. "We're safe and dry and alive."

"Thank you," she murmured, her eyes drifting shut.

Warm lips against her bare shoulder. "You don't owe me anything, darlin'. Just sleep. And let your body heal."

Sunlight heated his skin. Wade stretched sleepily, feeling the body in his arms murmur and turn toward him. He could smell smoke and ash, but as he cracked his eyes open, he realized the fire had died down long ago.

Rolling onto his back, he ground his teeth together against the pain and peered up blearily at the sun. Had to be nine, or thereabouts. Luc scraped an unsteady hand over his face, his stomach growling. Every part of him ached from the fall. The night was a seeming blur as he'd hauled himself up off Riley once she'd stopped shivering, setting out to find enough wood to make her a fire. He could barely remember collapsing against her back once more.

With a wince, he rolled up into a sitting position. As much as he'd like to stay here and heal, he couldn't. Lily was out there somewhere, and he had this one last day to get to her. The thought hardened him. No matter how much his back hurt, he had to find her.

Rolling onto his knees, he slid a hand over Riley's shoulder. "Hey," he murmured.

She pushed at his hand and growled something under her breath that sounded like, "Go 'way."

Wade looked up at the sun's position. They had a long way to go. "You have to get up, darlin'. We have to get movin'."

Riley blinked up at him, her velvety brown eyes disoriented with sleep, and her silky blonde hair tumbled around her shoulders. His heart clenched in his chest at the sight. His golden warrior. He could scarcely believe she'd dragged him out of the water. This was the type of woman who'd never let him go.

No matter what the danger was to herself.

His heart clenched again, this time in pain. He'd almost gotten her killed because he hadn't been strong enough to tell her not to come. He'd wanted someone by his side so desperately that she'd nearly died.

Selfish.

The right thing to do would be to get her back to Absolution before she got hurt. But it was too late now.

Today was the third day, the last to find Colton. He couldn't leave her behind, unprotected in the desert, and he didn't have time to get her safely back to Absolution. He would have to take her with him.

Straight into Bartholomew Cane's lair.

"If you're thinking what I think you are, you can forget it," Riley said suddenly.

The world around him came back into focus, Riley's warm brown eyes narrowing at him as she shook out her shirt with stiff movements. "What am I thinking?"

"About Cane. About me. Leaving me here." She dragged her bra and tank on, wincing as she had to reach over her shoulders. One eye was swollen and black, her cheekbone grazed, and her ribs were a mass of bruises.

That she read him so well bothered him. "You're hurt."

"So are you."

"I'll heal," he reminded her.

"So will I."

Luc's lips thinned. "I'll heal by tonight."

"Tonight. Tomorrow." She sat down to drag her jeans up her long, smooth legs. "What difference does it make? I dare say I look worse than I feel."

"Riley," he warned. Each of her movements was slow and precise. She was hurting, she just wouldn't admit it.

"You're not going to win this argument. You don't think I can track you, wherever you go? And you said yourself we're heading for the old Copperplate Mine."

Luc shoved to his feet, knowing when the battle was lost. "I had this idea," he told her, reaching for his own jeans. "A week ago now, though it feels more like several of them... Here's a pretty little blonde, practically begging to be kidnapped. Perfect bait. Just what I need to lure McClain to me—"

"How did it all go so wrong?"

"Precisely. I wish I could go back in time. Talk some sense into myself. Say, 'Luc, old man, you are going to regret this. This pretty little piece of ass is going to make a mule seem reasonable. She's going to send you up against revenants, reivers, and settlers waving pitchforks. She's going to take every single plan you had and smash them to pieces, like a child with a tower of blocks.'"

"She is going to change your life."

"She is going to make your life hell," he countered.

"She is going to give you some of the hottest sex you've ever had." Slowly, Riley stood up, her face admirably blank. "Finished feeling sorry for yourself?"

He had no argument to that. "The sex is good."

An arched eyebrow.

"Amazing," he amended.

"Just the sex?"

Luc dragged his shirt on and looked around for his boots. The leather was ruined and still damp, but it would do. "Maybe more than just the sex. You're pretty easy on the eyes too."

"You say the sweetest things."

Another taunt sprang to mind, but he stared down at her, those molten brown eyes meeting his. Luc stepped forward and cupped her jaw with both hands. "Riley, you are the devil," he whispered. "And I would sell you my soul gladly, if you didn't already own it." His face lowered, lips brushing against her own.

A soft kiss, full of promise. Tongue darting against hers teasingly before he drew back, knowing she was in pain. And there was nothing he could do about it.

The sweet rush of Riley's breath stirred against his damp mouth. "Then stop trying to leave me behind. You're right, Luc. You belong to me," she whispered, hands sliding up his chest and curling around his collar. Hot brown eyes met his. "I'm not going to let anyone take what's mine. Not Cane. Not Colton. Not the reivers."

His hands dropped from her face, but she didn't let him go. "How do you plan to stop them? We've got no guns, no ammunition, no food, and no water. All of that was in the jeep."

"You're right," she said, looking at the cliffs above them. "But I'll sure bet the reivers had those supplies."

Luc smiled. "That's my girl."

nineteen

THE CLIMB WAS torture.

Riley started out gamely, knowing that if she gave any sign that she was hurting, he'd try and leave her behind to rest. The road wound back and forth like a snake's trail as it worked its way up the sheer cliffs. Soon, she was dripping with sweat and staring directly at her feet. Didn't seem so much of an angle then. She could almost pretend that she was walking on flat ground.

Almost.

The right side of her face ached in the searing sun, her teeth throbbing. Nothing broken, thank God, but just the thought of running her tongue over them to check made her wince. Soon it was all she could do just to put one foot in front of the other. Her vision blurred until she blocked out the world, the pain, everything but each step at a time.

"Here we go." A hand curled around her arm, helping her the last few steps.

Riley looked up. They'd reached the top. She could have cried.

Luc stared down at her through narrowed eyes. Riley tried to smile, but it died on her mouth as the movement screamed through her cheek.

"I'm okay," she muttered.

He hesitated. "Maybe you should rest."

The words hit her like the sight of a desert oasis, but if she sat down she'd never get up. Riley shook her head.

Though concern warmed his eyes, he didn't say anything. Simply helped her forward, his large body blocking out the sun.

"So, how old are you?" he asked suddenly.

"Twenty-four," she replied. "Why?"

"Figured we ought to get to know each other." A small crooked smile curled over his mouth. "Considering we skipped the first date and all. Besides, you keep talking about not letting me go. What if I suddenly realize you snore like a warg, can't cook, and have plans for thirteen children?"

"I know the important things," she replied. "I know you'd risk anything to keep me safe, even your own life. I know no matter what happened to me, you'd come for me. You wouldn't give up on me. I know that, when life gets rough, you'd be there to hold my hand and take away all of my fears. The rest's just trivial."

"Humor me."

She knew what he was doing. Trying to keep her mind off her pain. Riley took a deep breath. "I like to cook, and I'm good at it," she said. "My daddy could only make beans and steak, and you get sick of that pretty quickly, so someone had to learn. A little girl like me, without a mother? Why, I had dozens of my mother's friends clucking over me, showing me the best way to fry cornbread, or roast Gila. Used to drive me crazy."

"What happened to your mother?"

It still hurt, though not as much as it had once. "She died when I was seven. Lost the baby in birth, and never recovered. Would have been a brother for me. Instead…" She shrugged, clenching her fists. She could never forget that night. The cries getting weaker, then finally stopping. The midwife coming out with a pale face and red-rimmed eyes. *'I'm sorry, honey. I've got some bad news for you…'* And her father, locking himself away for days until he finally emerged, stinking of liquor.

"And you became your father's son?" Wade's words jerked her out of the memories.

Riley swallowed hard. "I was always my father's son. Picked up my first shotgun when I was five. He taught me to drive when I was eight and butcher a cow when I was nine."

"You can cook and kill. Handy skill-set."

"So I'm passing the wife interview?" she asked teasingly, pushing away the memories of her mama's loss.

Luc glanced at her sidelong. "Give a girl an inch, and she starts planning the wedding."

Riley's lungs caught. "I didn't mean—"

"I know." He smiled, staring straight ahead. "I'll ask you one day. Don't like the thought of other men thinking you're still available." Eyes narrowing. "McClain in particular."

Riley had nothing to say to that. The road stretched out ahead, dusty and barren. "So, do you snore?" she asked quickly. "I've been too tired every night to hear."

"I don't snore. Sometimes I get hairy though."

Despite herself, she breathed out a laugh. It was the first time he'd ever come close to joking about his curse.

The questions continued as they walked, and Riley found the distraction welcome. It was comfortable to talk to him, sharing things she'd never really talked about with anyone else. Some of his answers surprised her; he could cook, sew if necessary, and turn his hands to most things. He liked to gamble, didn't drink, and preferred animals to humans. When he'd been a boy, he'd bred warg-hunting dogs with his father, and he enjoyed dancing to slow music, with a woman pressed tight against him. He liked making love even slower.

"So, am I passing the husband test?" he asked dryly, humor creasing the fine lines around his eyes.

Riley smiled as they turned a corner, the jeep coming into view. "I make your odds about even."

A hand slapped her bottom, then Luc strode ahead. Riley's laughter cut off as she realized he was scanning for danger. "Anything?"

"Nothing alive." Still, he didn't relax as they approached the jeep, keeping his body between her and any sign of danger.

He'd never be an easy man to live with, she thought as she watched him circle the vehicle. Some of her friends would struggle to accept his nature, and they'd never be able to live in a large settlement. But he'd protect her with his life, and he'd never expect her to be something she wasn't.

Besides, she needed someone to argue with. Someone who challenged her to stand at his side, not just step in front of her to protect her. Someone who pushed her to be the woman she knew she could be, not just the type of woman he wanted.

"You passed the test," Riley admitted, watching as he slid his hands under one side of the jeep, the muscles in his thighs bunching.

A quick glance from scorching blue eyes and then he ground his teeth and lifted, biceps straining. The jeep shuddered, metal groaning, and then it slowly lifted on its side as he tipped it over.

A cloud of dust swooshed out from underneath as it landed on all four wheels. The grill was dented, the front window smashed clean out. There was more rust on the panels than green paint, and the gun turret was painted with dried blood.

A body slumped over the wheel, flies buzzing. Luc's lip curled and he yanked the door open, cutting the safety belt with his claws. The flies disappeared as he jumped into the back of the jeep and kicked the body out onto the ground at her feet.

"Any water?" she asked, wincing a little. Every part of her body ached.

"Got a canteen." He rifled through a pack. "You're not drinking it though. Not until I can get something fresh for you."

Her mouth was so dry she almost didn't care. Then she glanced down at the reiver, with his cracked lips. A leather aviator's cap covered his hair, and his goggles cut into his swollen white flesh as he gaped at nothing.

"I'm not drinking it," she agreed. Wouldn't take them that long to find fresh water. Not with the dammed river below.

There were three packs in the back of the jeep. Wade held out a hand to help her up, then knelt down and rifled through them, discarding useless – or disgusting – items, and stockpiling the rest.

"You ever been up to Copperplate?" he asked.

"Once," Riley admitted, sorting out the pile of ammo. "It's the sort of thing we kids used to do, before the reivers started hitting the settlements hard. Sneak out, go up to Copperplate or out to the salt marshes, and race the jeeps, climb the hoodoos, drink applejack we'd filched from home. It was a while ago now."

Wade swiftly filled her in on the details he'd found while scouting. Riley was impressed, and commented on it. She'd never have expected him to be so organized, almost military proficient.

"Only smart bounty hunters survive out there on the Rim of the Great Divide," he said with a shrug. "It's a different world to this one." A hard laugh. "Makes the Wastelands look like a kid's playground. Lot of caves and caverns in the Great Divide. Maybe the meteor carved 'em out, don't know. Means there's a lot of revenants, a lot of shadow-cats. Not that you ever see them. Just their tracks. My uncle taught me to hunt, and he didn't suffer fools lightly. Used to be a Confederate frontline scout before he bailed. Tough as nails."

She was curious. "And your parents?"

Wade's expression softened. "My father was a rancher. Mom... She was a bit like Uncle Robert. Fleeing from something. She never said what, but you could see it in her eyes. Used to prowl the house at night. Never slept well. Hid under the bed during thunderstorms. My father passed when I was eight, so Uncle Robert mostly had the raising of me."

"He taught you well, then."

Wade's hands hesitated on the pile. "He would have shot me, if I'd come home like this. So I didn't. Knew he'd look after Abbie and Lily. Didn't want to see that look on his face, you know?"

Riley knelt down, taking the full pack from him. "Sounds a lot like my daddy. I think he'd be proud of you though, Luc. Not everyone would have fought the way you have."

"Maybe." The answer was non-committal, expression locked down tight. "Think you can find the keys to this thing?"

There was no sign of them. "I can do better."

"Riley Kincaid," he tsked, as she climbed into the front seat and pulled the cover off the steering column, revealing the car's wires. "I thought you were a good girl."

"Oh, I am. I'm good at a lot of things."

"That you are." He slung the pair of packs into close reach behind the seats and shoved a shotgun into a premade holster that had been attached to the door. Grimly, he slid into the seat beside her. "Let's do this."

The realization of what was about to happen made her heart start pounding. "Nervous?" she asked, noting the stiff line of his shoulders as he stared toward the east.

"Scared." His gaze cut to hers. "I've never had anything to lose since I turned warg. Don't know whether that's a blessin' or not."

Riley's breath caught.

Looking down, she stripped the insulation from the battery wires and twisted them together. Then she carefully sparked the ignition wire against them. The jeep's engine kicked, and a rumble started deep under the hood. Once more, jamming her foot down to rev the engine a couple of times, and it growled to life.

Slowly, Riley eased it into gear, the movement tearing through her ribs. The crash the day before had wrought damage to the jeep, but mostly it was superficial.

Kind of like her, she guessed. Battered, bruised, trembling with exhaustion, and fueled by determination.

"You got a plan?" she asked.

"Something along the lines of Black River," he replied. "This can't be a full frontal assault. I won't risk Lily. Or you."

"And if they don't give us any choice?"

He cut her a sharp look. "Then I'll make a deal. Myself for Lily. I won't fight them, as long as they let you get away with her cleanly."

The words hit Riley like a punch to the chest. "Son of a bitch," she swore. "That's the only reason you let me come, isn't it?"

The look on his face was answer enough.

The mine was high in the Altera Mountains. Some said you could even see the edge of the Great Rift from the highest peak, if you had a pair of binoculars, but then those were rare in the settlements. A gun scope was the better alternative.

The last time she'd been here, she'd been all of fifteen, and reivers were barely a threat this far out. They'd moved in swiftly in the last few years, driven north by the slave-traders along the border of New Mérida, and possibly the abundance of reiver packs that supplied the slavers down south.

Wade guided her along an old canyon track that seemed more of a path to bighorn or the native goats out here than an actual road. Huge ruts made the bottom of the jeep scrape several times, and she was aching all over from the muscle needed to fight the vehicle in the direction she wanted. Finally, the wheels locked in a crevice and spun, spraying up sand and gravel behind them.

Riley took her foot off the gas and sighed. "I think this is as far as we go."

For obvious reasons, they couldn't take the main road to Copperplate, but Wade seemed to know the mountains like the back of his hand. He nodded, a swift glance at the sun betraying his tension. It was mid-afternoon.

"We've got about three miles to hike. Think you're up to it?"

Riley stared at the winding track that climbed ahead of them. "I can do it," she said, though she didn't particularly want to. Sitting for so long had stiffened her up.

"First, let me get this damn thing free," he muttered, "just in case we need to get out of here in a hurry."

We. She took comfort from that. After his little bombshell earlier, she'd been too afraid to even examine what she'd do if that were the only option available to them.

Wade forced the jeep out of its ruts, and together they backed it into the side of the mountain, his biceps straining. The tight black shirt he wore was torn in several places, leaving part of his chest bare.

Between them, they got the jeep turned around, ready to leave, and Riley unhooked the battery wires. Fuel gauge wasn't optimistic, but it might get them back to Absolution.

"We'll circle around and come from the east," Wade said, offering her his hand. "Copperplate's riddled with tunnels."

"Great. Because I hadn't quite had enough dark caves."

Riley eased out of the jeep, feeling as stiff as an old man. Carefully, she stretched, trying to hide as much of her wince as she could. They both knew she was in no real condition to make a run for it, if she needed to. Desperation was the only thing keeping her at his side. He couldn't do this alone, and she wouldn't let him.

Wade shouldered his pack and helped slide her own over her shoulders. It was as light as they could make it, and even then the straps cut in. But the only other option was to head out into the mountains with no spare ammunition, food, or water, and she might as well cut her wrists now.

Riley judged the sky, forcing herself to suck it up. "It's about two or three hours until the sun starts hitting the horizon."

He nodded tersely. "It's not a good situation," he admitted. "But I'm running out of time."

"We," she corrected, stepping past him and starting up the narrow trail. The sawed-off shotgun was a welcome weight in her hands, despite the signs of neglect on it.

That he let her go first surprised her, until she felt his hand on her back to help her as gravel slipped beneath her boots. And she was aching enough that she didn't try to push herself. *Slow and steady... Or I'll never make it.*

"No sign of wargs," Wade murmured after the first mile. "At least that's one blessing. Cane and his crew must have cleared them out."

Riley nodded, her legs trembling so badly that she didn't even bother to answer. If she looked up, she could see miles of trekking in front of them, the red cliffs above rising seemingly forever.

Scrambling up trails made for bighorn was a nightmare. Wade was the only thing keeping her going, his hand and steady presence at her back helping her up each steep incline. Riley had never cursed her body so much. Being human sucked.

"At least you have crazy super-healing powers," she muttered as Wade forced her to stop and take a drink of warm water from the canteen. It spilled over her lips in a welcome wave.

Concern filled his eyes. Hesitation. "Maybe you should head back."

Riley lowered the water canteen and glared at him.

He held his hands up in surrender. "Even I know some fights are never going to be won." His lips twisted. "I just hate seein' you hurt, darlin'."

"The second I stop is the second I start stiffening up. Tomorrow's probably going to be worse." A grim thought. Riley capped the bottle. "Let's move."

She didn't know how long they climbed, but she was finally staring at a cave. Water spilled out of it in a trickle, rusted metal bars covering it. Shadows had fallen as the sun slowly dipped toward the horizon. They were running out of time.

"Spillway," Wade announced quietly, stepping into the water. He bent low and hauled at the edge of the bars. Metal squealed as it curled back upon itself until there was a gap wide enough for her to fit through. "We're at the back of the mine. This should bring us into the heart of it. We'll come at them from within. I'll track Lily down, and maybe we can get out before they even know we've been."

Maybe. There was wishful thinking.

Riley staggered into the water, the biting cold sweeping through her and bringing much needed clarity. Ducking beneath the bars, she waited for Wade to follow, her nerves peaking. *Caves. Jesus, why did it have to be more caves?* Already she could feel the heavy press of the earth above.

Unstrapping the shotgun from over her shoulder, she pumped a few rounds into it.

"Don't shoot unless you absolutely have to," Wade warned. "It wouldn't surprise me if Cane's got a few surprises up his sleeve. Doesn't seem like him, leaving the back door unguarded like this."

"Maybe we got lucky." But she didn't believe it any more than he did.

Wade led the way forward, clicking on the flashlight they'd found in the reiver packs. He handed it to her, to keep his hands free. Carrying both it and the shotgun was awkward, but she managed to handle them both.

Following the spillway, they made their way deeper into the mine, eventually coming out into an intersecting tunnel. This one had rail tracks.

"Right or left?" she whispered.

"Left. Air smells fresher." A small frown played over his brow. "People have been through here recently. Smells like gasoline and tobacco."

"How much gasoline?"

He shook his head. "Not enough for him to be trying to burn us alive. A small drip from a container, I'm thinking." He cocked his head again, color draining from his tanned face. "Can you hear that?"

Riley fell silent. "Nothing—" And then... Whispers in the darkness. A shuffling sound that echoed through the tunnels.

Riley's head shot up. She didn't need to ask, but the words tumbled from her lips anyway. "What the hell is that?"

twenty

"REVENANTS. FUCK!" WADE bared his teeth, the light gleaming off them. "I knew this was too easy."

Riley lifted the flashlight. Her heart ticked in her chest, her mouth dry. She didn't want to go further, didn't want to let the darkness, or the reivers, sweep her up.

But a little girl was waiting at the end of this. Wade was waiting. And he'd done the same thing for Jimmy, when he didn't have to.

Their eyes met. Wade knew exactly what she was thinking.

Somehow, she forced a smile to her lips, though it probably looked more like a grimace. "Of course there have to be revenants. And Cane has to know, which means they're probably here on purpose. Locked in the mines to protect his back. With our luck, they've probably been starving them for days." She licked her lips. "Lay on, MacDuff."

"Mac what?" The tension eased out of his shoulders.

"Old play my dad had that survived the Darkening. Only vice he ever had, buying books and useless things." Riley shrugged.

The silence stretched out. Through it, she could hear that silent whisper of clothing and rotting flesh. The heat drained out of her face, and she clutched the shotgun tighter.

"You're one hell of a woman," Wade murmured, his eyes alight with a silvery glow. He stepped closer, hands cupping her face. "I'll make sure you get out of this, Riley. I promise." Then he kissed her, slow and deep. A kiss that promised the world and more.

When he drew back, her fingers tightened in the collar of his shirt. Just for a moment. She didn't want to let go, because she had the horrible, sneaking suspicion that this just might be the last time she ever got to touch him.

Don't think like that. This isn't the worst corner you've both been backed into.

She took a deep breath, slow and steady, her fingers unlocking from his shirt. "Don't get yourself killed." Voice huskier than it ought to be.

His hand came up, brushed her cheek. A considering look in his eyes. "This was easier last time we had to do this." He let out a slow breath. "*Don't* get bitten."

"Or you'll shoot me yourself?"

The look on his face showed her he found nothing to laugh about at her black humor.

Riley sobered fast. "Okay. How do we do this? We start shooting, and we'll bring the whole molehill down upon us."

Wade stared down the left tunnel, his nostrils flaring. "Got an idea. Wait here, I'll check out if my hunch is correct."

"Awesome," she muttered, her hands sweaty on the shotgun. "I'll stay here. In the dark. With the revenants."

Something groaned in the darkness. Riley tensed, but that had sounded almost metallic. Not something that probably wanted to eat her.

Shining the flashlight down into the tunnel, she let out a relieved sigh when the silver-shine of Wade's eyes lit up. He was pushing a heavily laden trolley cart up the short incline, using the old rail tracks. Muscle strained under his shirt, proving just how heavy the trolley was.

"Son of a bitch." Riley stepped back, eyeing the cart, which was full of gasoline tanks. "Guess you found a supply station."

"Cane's, by the look of it," he agreed happily. "Had a chance to have a look around. Don't think he trusts his reivers enough to leave fuel out in vulnerable places. This was all locked up in a caged storeroom back there." He jerked his head back over his shoulder and eased to a stop beside her.

"They're going to know we're here," Riley reminded him. "This is going to go boom in a major way."

Wade's teeth flashed white in the darkness. "You have no idea. Guess what else I found. Check my pack."

Riley unzipped the bag over his shoulders and whistled under her breath. "Dynamite?"

"It's old," he warned. "No leakage, so it must have been turned frequently enough. Found it in Copperplate's stockroom. Might even be pre-Darkening."

"It should still work." She zipped the bag back up. "You've got a plan."

"I've got a plan," he agreed. "Stealth was never going to work anyway. So now, we're going to create a hell of a lot of confusion and use it to cover our tracks. First though, I need to do some scouting. Find out where they're holding Lily." He looked at her. "Do you think you can start some minor preparations while I'm gone?"

Alone. Riley swallowed.

"I had a look around," he said quickly. "This tunnel loops back on itself. In the middle's an enormous pit, where they keep the revenants. They're trapped down there for now. Didn't want them free to wander, is my guess. You won't come across any, and I'll be quick."

Riley nodded. She was starting to feel a little numb to it all by now. And fear would keep her sharp.

"Good." He kissed her swiftly. "Here's what I want you to do…."

Five minutes later, she was swiftly laying out the cord to the dynamite along the edges of the pit. Wade had been right; below, she could hear the rasp of clothing and clawing fingers scrabbling at the sides of the pit as the revenants reached for her. A quick sweep of the flashlight gleamed off dozens of opaque eyes.

"Fuck," she whispered. "Fuck, fuck, fuckity fuck." *They're down there, you're up here. Stop sweating it,* she told herself.

One misstep and she'd be down there with them.

"Thank you, optimism," she muttered. Swiftly, she bound the cord together and began stepping backward, toward the main tunnel.

"What the hell's going on here? Colton?" The voice came out of the tunnel.

Riley froze. A flashlight gleamed in the tunnel, bobbing as it came toward her. She could just make out the heavy set of a pair of rugged shoulders, and a black felt hat. *Shit.*

The other warg.

And she was standing on a narrow ledge with no place to go.

A quick glance over her shoulder showed the gaping maw of the tunnel on the opposite end of the ledge, the one she hadn't had time to check out. Riley darted toward it, flicking off her flashlight as she pressed her back against the cold cave walls inside the shadowy tunnel. Her heart was pounding through her chest, so loudly she almost thought the strange warg might hear it over the sound of the revenants' sudden frantic shuffling below.

A rock skittered against her boot. Riley knelt down and palmed it, licking her lips. What the hell was she going to do? Run deeper into the mine? Who the hell knew what was down there? With her luck, she'd probably come out right in the heart of the pit below.

The warg flashed his light over the revenants as he stepped free of the opposite tunnel. "What's set you bastards off, huh?" He spat over the edge. "Creepy fucking deadheads." He glanced down, and she stiffened as she saw the moment he realized someone else had been there.

"Or maybe something else?" he muttered, kneeling down and picking up the cord she'd been fusing together. Tattoos swirled on his bare arms in the light. Slowly, he looked up, silver-shine creeping through his irises. He sniffed the air, a smile crawling over his fleshy mouth.

"There you are," he whispered. "Almost didn't smell you over that stink." He stood up, gaze searching the dark and locking on her tunnel. "Pretty girl," he whispered. "I smell you."

One step toward her. Another. His heavy boots crunching on shale.

Nowhere to run. Nowhere to hide. Riley stuck the flashlight in her pocket, then hefted the shotgun. No way he'd think she'd attack.

She stepped out of the darkness with the shotgun lifted high. The warg's eyes widened in surprise, his flashlight dropping as he tried to catch the shotgun butt. He grabbed it with both hands just as Riley stepped in to him and thrust a boot into his chest.

Wrenching the gun from her hands, he fell backward with a surprised "Oof."

Riley didn't waste time trying to get her gun back. She leapt over him and ran, reaching down to snatch at her pack from the shadows of a rocky outcrop as she darted across the ledge. Beneath her, the revenants hissed.

"Bitch!" The snarl came from behind as the warg found his feet.

Riley flicked her flashlight on and sprinted. Or tried to. Everything hurt, and she wasn't anywhere near fast enough. *Shit*. What the hell was she going to do? She was only halfway through the setup Wade had asked of her.

He'd taken half the charges to plant on his way, but there'd barely been time for him to get them in place either.

A shotgun roared, pellets spraying the walls beside her. Riley screamed, throwing her hands over her head as she ran. Bastard was shooting at her!

Ahead, the trolley loomed, stacked high with gasoline tanks. She had the matches in her pocket, old ones Wade had found in the storeroom. A quick glance showed the warg stalking up the tunnel behind her, feeding two shells into the shotgun with steady hands.

Riley skidded to a halt beside the trolley. She could run, but she wouldn't get far. Not once he got those shells in. Fingers scrambling for the matches, she ripped them from her pocket and jerked one free of its pack. "Come on, come *on*...." Bloody fingers. So frigging useless all of a sudden. She dropped the pack, and half of the matches spilled across the ground.

Bending down, she scrounged for the matches and swiftly lit one. Where the hell was Wade? Surely he'd heard that shot. Surely he'd come for her....

Until then, she'd just have to deal with this herself.

Looking up, she met the warg's eyes, just as he pumped the shotgun. Riley flicked the match inside the trolley, and it exploded into flame from the gasoline she'd poured over the jerry cans.

Scrambling behind it, she yelped as the shotgun roared again, pellets pinging off the heavy metal cart. Setting her shoulder against it, Riley pushed hard. A second where its weight resisted, then it moved a fraction of an inch. Faster. Gaining momentum. She felt the moment that gravity kicked in, and the downward velocity of the rail tracks caught it. Suddenly, it was racing down the tunnel toward the warg, picking up speed as it went. A raging inferno of flame with enough spare fuel to really kick off the party once the jerry cans exploded.

The warg's eyes widened, and he slammed his back flat against the wall. It wasn't enough – his size worked against him. The trolley would clip him, possibly tip off the tracks, and he knew it. Glaring at her, he turned and ran, tossing the shotgun aside carelessly.

The burning whoosh as the cart hit the end of the sheared-off tracks and soared out over the pit echoed in the narrow tunnel. Riley took a step back, her eyes glued to the spectacle as the trolley launched into space, leaving its fiery afterimage burned into her retinas.

A lingering moment of quiet.

Then the sudden coughing roar as a fireball bloomed. *Shit.* She hadn't quite counted on that, hadn't….

The dynamite.

Riley's eyes went wide. She spun around and raced up the tunnel, fists pumping at her sides, the flashlight's beam bobbing sporadically in front of her, and the pack slapping against her back. Her ribs gave an aching squeeze, but adrenaline had kicked in, dulling it to an almost tolerable pain.

Light gleamed off a warg's cat-shine eyes, and then Wade was sliding to a halt in front of her, relief taking the sharp edges from his face. "Riley." Hoarseness turned his voice to granite-edged tones. "What the hell?"

"Run!" she screamed.

He glanced over her shoulder, grabbed her wrist and turned, sprinting at her side. "What did you do?"

"There was another warg."

The explosion ripped through the world, like a massive hand shoving her in the back. Both she and Wade went down hard, Riley grimacing as the pain in her side gave a sharp aching stab. Ears ringing. Hair whipping around her head as debris rained down, and the earth beneath them shook.

Then suddenly a heavy weight settled over her. "—iley—"

And fire bloomed.

It rolled over the top of them in an enormous fiery cloud, sucking all of the oxygen from the air, searing her lungs. The hard body covering hers flinched.

Seconds that seemed like hours. Then she could breathe again, her lungs dry-baked, coughing, racking, choking for air—

Wade shuddered and threw himself off her, rolling onto his back. The flames in his clothes smoldered out, and Riley lifted her head, fingertips grazing the floor. She blinked hard, trying to get some moisture back into her eyes. "You okay?"

Wade bared his teeth in a grimace. "Becoming a spit-roast is not exactly what I had in mind."

The tunnels trembled. Riley pushed herself to her knees somehow. Her hands were shaking. "Sorry. Didn't have much time to plan that." She held out her hand to him, and he dragged himself upright with a wince.

The stink of burnt flesh stained the air. Riley reached for his shoulder. "Let me—"

He shook her off. "No time. I'll heal." A quick glance up the tunnel. "We need to get moving. Set off the rest of the charges. I know where they're holding Lily."

Riley bit her lip. *Stubborn ass...* She held out a hand to help haul him to her feet.

Wade gave her a look that seemed to say, *Takes one to know one.* Then he pushed himself upright. "Where's the shotgun?"

She jerked a thumb over her shoulder. "Probably melted into the stone right now."

With a grunt, Wade settled a hand in the small of her back. "Remind me not to leave you alone again."

Riley flinched. Like she'd fucked up. "I didn't have a choice."

"Wasn't talking about that," he replied gruffly. His fingers flexed on her back. "Heard the shotgun go off. Gave me a minor heart attack. I'm not cut out for this shit. It was so much easier without a partner."

So much easier not to care.

Riley bit back her retort. He was struggling with this so much more than she was. But then, he'd never expected to find someone to care for. Neither had she, but she'd at least hoped.

"Cut the light," he instructed curtly, leading her to an intersection. A warm hand slid into hers. "You'll have to trust me to lead you. And keep your voice down, we're getting closer to the surface."

Blackness veiled the tunnels as she followed Wade with careful steps. Shouts came from nearby. Confusion.

"Good," he whispered. "Got 'em all on the run. Let's stir the ant nest a little more." He fiddled with something in his jeans pocket, and a little box rattled. His matches.

The darkness began to yield to faint light. Cool air on her face, like a ghostly whisper. The tunnel mouth yawned ahead of them, the sky a fading patchwork that melted into indigo in the east. Stars flickered.

Wade stopped her by the tunnel opening and knelt down, gesturing her close to his side. The spicy warmth of his scent curled through her nostrils. "Lily's being held over there," he said, pointing to a small adobe building that melted into the cliff. The entire cliff face was pocked with small caves and adobe structures that had been built into the sides of the actual mine.

Reivers ran across the open ground in front of it, thundering up the scaffolding that led to the upper levels, or scrambling up rope ladders. Riley had never really seen them so closely, only through the sights of a rifle, or howling across the bloodied sands toward Haven, and even then she'd been concentrating on other matters. Like the best place to drill a hole through one of them.

It was easy to pick the strata among the pack, just by their clothes. Reivers worshipped strength, and several big men roamed through them, lashing out here and there with chains, and wearing their leather and metal-plated vests like a crown. Others wore open, crusted sores, scraps of rags and leather, and the bare patches of their skin revealed concave chests. These were the mongrels who fed at the edges of the pack. Clothing and weaponry was scarcer among them, and they were easy to pick out by the smearing of red clay across their skin, to protect it from the heat. Red dogs some of the Wastelanders called them, the howling, maniacal reivers who attacked first and were often cut down in the first flight. Bullet fodder on motorbikes. The ones in leather were those to be found in the jeeps, where they had slightly more protection – and authority.

There were several women among them too; some were chained to the iron-link fence along the cliff face, their bodies naked, and their shoulders drooping in dejection, as if all the care in the world had been crushed from them. Slaves. Others strutted the sands like their male compatriots, their heads shaved on the sides, and fierce plaits running down the center line of their scalps. Where the male reivers were a mixture of prime fighters and mad lackeys, the female reivers were all hard, their gazes showing a specific flatness, as if, to survive this world, they'd had to give up any concept of emotions or weaknesses.

Dozens of rusted jeeps were parked haphazardly below, with gun turrets gleaming in the dying light. Wade talked Riley through the layout of the compound. The circular cliffs provided a natural barrier with only one way in. "They know we're down here now though," he murmured. "Give me a moment to set the charges to confuse them. Then we'll make a direct hit on the building holding Lily."

Riley surveyed the compound. "There are dozens of reivers. What if they recover?"

"Then I'll kill them." Matter-of-factly.

Plus two wargs, and God knew how many guns.

Riley bit her lip and pointed. "That jeep there. See the gun turret? Someone's left the ammunition belt there."

"Lazy bastards."

"Reivers," she said with a snort. "Not known for hygiene, sanity, or discipline. Let me take the jeep. I'll keep anything off your back while you go for Lily."

He considered it, a dark look creeping into his eyes. "Don't like it," he finally said, but a quick glance at the skyline and the dawning crimson colors there revealed his unease. Night was starting to beckon.

"But you know it's the smart option." Riley leaned close, brushed her lips against his. Anything to take his mind off what was coming. "Whoever would have thought the cold-hearted warg who kidnapped me would be so protective?"

The kiss deepened, turned smoldering. His hand cupping the back of her nape, his tongue darting over hers. Just enough to set the slow burn in her blood, then Wade drew back, his breath whispering over her cheeks.

"I love you, Riley Kincaid," he whispered in her ear. "You gave me a piece of myself back. Just you remember that." Then he was stepping back, melting into the shadows. All business, while she was still trying to process the words he'd whispered. Had he really whispered them, or was it just her imagination? "Let me set the charges. Then run for the jeep when everything goes off. Try not to draw attention to yourself until then. I'll meet you by the jeep with Lily. It'll give us something to escape in too."

Her heart leapt, then squeezed. Again, it sounded like he didn't think he was going to get out of this. *Like hell.*

She grabbed a handful of his hair, stepped in to him. Her desperate mouth seeking his in the semi-dark. Drinking him in, fists curling in his hair, tongue toying with his own. They were both breathing hard when she stepped back, the press of his erection against her midriff.

"You get in, and get her out," she whispered, voice smoky-rough. "Then come back to me. That's an order."

"Yes, ma'am," he said, his voice just as rough as hers.

twenty-one

LEAVING RILEY BY herself again was the hardest thing he'd ever had to do.

He knew she was strong and resourceful, knew that she could more than take care of herself. That wasn't the problem. The problem was the choking fear that rose in him at the thought of everything that could go wrong. One stray bullet. Too many reivers rushing her. Cane somehow slipping behind his back....

If they got out of this, he was never going to leave her alone again.

In the chaos following the explosions he'd rigged, it was easy to slip across the wide expanse of the cavern floor relatively unnoticed. The afternoon's shadows had lengthened, predicting an hour or two until dusk, and fire still burst in gouts from the main mine shaft as other pockets of leftover dynamite went off. Reivers howled and screamed as each explosion hammered at their eardrums, laughing maniacally as several of their compatriots caught fire. They streamed toward the mine like ants, frantically trying to get inside. The bait was taken.

Adobe gleamed in the sunlight as Luc focused on the building where he'd scented his daughter. There were two reivers on duty, but most of their attention was on the pair of reivers rolling around in the dirt, trying to put their smoldering clothes out. Running past three more, he ducked behind a pair of armored trucks and wove between several canvas tents.

No sign of Colton or Cane yet.

Luc's eyes narrowed as he paused behind a jeep, squatting low. Riley would make for the gun turret, but hold off until needed. The longer they could use stealth as a weapon, the better.

Stealing a glance behind him, he caught a flash of movement as Riley slid to her ass in the dust beside the jeep with the gun turret. Their eyes met, and she smiled grimly.

Luc nodded, then turned his attention back to the job at hand.

Barely ten feet from the adobe hut where Lily was hiding. Luc licked dry lips, gathering his thighs beneath him for a short sprint. Leaning low, he took a steady breath and then gunfire ripped through the clearing, spraying off the jeep he was crouched beside.

Ping-ping-ping. Luc threw himself flat and rolled under the jeep, his heart hammering in his ears.

Fuck. He risked a look, and someone drilled another three holes into the dirt beside his face. Luc jerked back, sweat dampening his skin. Lily's hut was so close....

But then, that was the point, wasn't it?

To let him get close enough to scent his daughter, to almost picture wrapping her up in his arms, before pulling the rug out from under him. Cane was nothing if not pure bastard. Luc had spent two months tracking him and Colton, before he thought he'd burned them alive, and in every town the story was the same. Whores with burn marks on their skins, men who were goaded into fights that ended up being assassinations, settlements that were raided and burned out, the bodies left bloated in the sun... A monster in human skin. Cane didn't need night to fall for his true nature to emerge.

"Welcome to Copperplate, Wade!" Bartholomew Cane bellowed, his voice ringing clear through the canyon and echoing. "You made it further than expected."

Bullets haphazardly pinged off the metal flanks of the jeep, just enough to keep him pinned down. Fucking bastard. Luc bared his teeth.

Cane's laughter lasted all of three seconds. Then the semi-automatic gun on the back of the reivers' jeep drilled the cliffs where the shots had come from with bullets. Screams cut the air, and Cane fell silent.

"Go, Luc!" Riley screamed, pausing just briefly. "I've got your back!"

The ricochet started up again.

From the sound of it, she was raining hell down upon the cliffs where the reivers were pinned down. Luc rolled out from under the jeep on the far side and launched himself into a sprint. All he could see was the faded blue door that led to where his daughter was being kept. He threw himself at it and rebounded hard, but the latch broke, timber splitting down the center. Another bullet sprayed white chips of adobe as he flung his arms up to protect his head, slamming his shoulder against the door again.

Hope soared through his chest as it splintered in half; he kicked the timber slats free, and barreled through.

"No further," Colton warned, holding a pistol against Lily's head.

Luc froze.

The other warg's eyes were narrowed and he sidestepped, keeping Lily between them. There was a gag around her mouth, and her eyes watered as she looked up at him helplessly. Everything in him urged him to leap forward, to kill the bastard and protect her. A father's instincts, reignited after years of neglect.

But Colton's pistol never wavered.

Colton wasn't the same type of man as Cane – Luc knew that. When he'd hunted them, witnesses spoke of how Colton had tried to restrain Cane's darker ambitions at times. That didn't make him an ally. There was some kind of bond between them, Colton following at Cane's heels, a slave to his whims.

"You don't have to do this," Luc said in a low, soothing voice, his gaze flickering to the pistol and back.

Colton swallowed. "Yeah, I do." His nostrils flared. "You don't understand. I have to do what he says. I have to. He's had me too long, and he's in my head. I can't disobey him."

They stared each other down. "So, you're just a whipped dog?" Luc asked. "When he tells you to kill little kids, you just go out and do it."

"You think I want this?" Colton snapped. His hand shook on the gun, and Lily whimpered as the barrel pressed harder against her temples. "I can... fight his orders sometimes. Sometimes it's long enough. Sometimes it's not."

"Easy." Luc eyed the other man's trigger finger.

"You're too late," Colton said. "You lost. You should never have come here. You just gave him everything that he wants."

"Me."

"No. Not you."

Gunfire fell silent in that second, and a shiver of premonition rasped along his nerves. *Riley.* The heat drained out of his face.

"That's how he works," Colton said. "There's a sickness inside him. And you nearly burned him alive, once upon a time. He can't forgive that, not now. He wants to take everything you have from you." The gun lowered, but Colton kept a grip on Lily. "But he won't do it himself. He'll make you hurt her instead."

That shiver became a bone-encompassing dread. "He won't get inside my head."

"He doesn't have to." Colton's gaze flickered toward his amulet. "Night's not so far away now. It's his favorite game."

Fuck.

"And he'll make you choose," Colton warned. "The girl. Or the woman."

Lily's face swam into view. She was terrified. And he'd failed her once already. It wasn't a choice, not really, but he knew that Riley wouldn't think it was a choice either.

He knew what stirred the beast – rage, fury, hunger, thoughts of hot, delicious fear dripping through the veins of its prey... The scent of fear was like a five-course buffet in his nose. The warg within him wasn't cruel. It was hungry. Hungry for flesh, or blood, or sex. Animalistic in the extreme. All of its desires were simplified. If it wanted, then it took. Even now, something trembled inside him at the thought. Claws sprang forth from his fingers, and he shook as he forced them back within his skin, reminding himself that he was part human too.

This wasn't always the case. It didn't have to be. He could fight this, if he had to. He could. But he had to do it smartly.

He'd seen wargs hunt and tear bodies apart, just for fun. He'd seen them defend their territory against intruders, or other wargs. The nature of the creature was primal. It wanted to be alpha, wanted to be the only warg standing, or to have others cringe at its feet in fear. No point in pretending that he wouldn't see Riley as prey. He would. What he had to focus on was the other part of his nature.

Make the warg see that she was his *territory*, to be defended and protected against other wargs. Focus on the hate and the rage, and direct it at the ones who deserved it. Then maybe, maybe – if Riley didn't panic – they might get through this.

"Wade!"

The bellow cut across the open valley of the mine, and Luc risked a glance over his shoulder through the open door. This was his weakness. Riley stood arched up onto her tiptoes, with Cane wrapped around her, his claws digging into her throat.

Shouldn't have brought her... Should have come for Lily myself.

Indecision haunted him. His daughter would always be his priority, but to move now would cost Riley her life, and she knew it. He could see it in her eyes as she met his gaze.

Those determined brown eyes narrowed, her lips firming as she tipped her head up slightly. "Go," she mouthed, trying to take the decision away from him.

Because that was who Riley was. A woman who'd sacrifice herself, no matter what the cost was. A hero. A leader. A woman whose worth wasn't measured in gold, but in deeds.

Her father would have been proud, and Luc had a moment of doubt. How could he ever be worthy of her?

'Humanity's for the humans,' he'd said once. And he believed, *truly* believed that he was no longer welcome in those ranks. But staring at Cane, knowing what the bastard would do to her....

A monster would walk away from her right now, without a care, except for his daughter. And a hero would make one last suicidal attempt to save Riley, because that was what heroes did.

But Luc was no hero. He was also no monster.

And Riley was the strongest, bravest woman he'd ever met.

His half-formed plan was risky and dangerous, and driven by Colton's words. His first instinct was to reject it, but what else could he do?

It was a gamble, no doubt. He knew what type of man Cane was. That was the monster, right there, and to do this meant pitting both of them against each other, in the most dangerous game of all. Even now, he could still feel the flicker of cold sweat dance over the back of his neck, because there were no guarantees that he could pull this off, that Riley would make the right moves... But he had to trust her, and his own instincts.

Did he have the strength of will to do this?

You are what you are, a little voice whispered. *Nobody's hero.*

But then, that wasn't what was needed, right at this instant.

Luc's nostrils flared, and then he spread his feet in a wide stance, dropped the knife, and swept his hands up behind his head. "I surrender."

"No," Riley whispered, as she saw the resolve form in Luc's face. She struggled weakly against Colton's hold on her, but she might as well have been wrestling with steel.

"I surrender," Luc said, in an eerily calm voice. "That's what you want, isn't it? Me? Let Lily go, as you promised, and you can do whatever you want to me. Riley can take her with her."

"Let them go?" Cane laughed. "Maybe I will let them go, out there in the desert. How far do you think they'll get with no supplies, and a hungry pack of wargs out there?"

Luc's face paled, but his eyes only narrowed slightly.

Not the result that Cane wanted. Riley could see the hungry look on his face swiftly denied, replaced by something more feral. It was as though he fed on emotions, on the bitter, gut-wrenching twist of them, and Luc had somehow denied him. "Grab him," he bellowed, striding forward. "And bring the woman," he snapped over his shoulder at Colton.

Reivers lunged forward and snatched at Wade as if he were a rabid dog, they a pack of hyenas. One of them had some sort of whip made of chains and lashed him across the middle, sharp, jerky movements that made him grunt as they pinned him to the floor, a swarm of bodies burying him in their midst. Maybe he didn't dare fight back, but she could see the rage in his expression, the way he had to clench his jaw not to.

"What are you going to do with her?" Luc growled, dragging himself to his feet with a swarm of reivers clinging to him.

"Something special. Put him in the cage!"

Tarps dropped from around the tray on a clapped-out old truck, and a silver warg cage gleamed. Luc was thrown unceremoniously inside, and the door clanged shut.

Cane paused beside the jeep, then reached out to finger a lock of her hair. Riley jerked away, but her hair pulled taut and she winced, then froze.

"Let her go," Luc demanded, the words soft.

Riley was dragged to her knees in front of the cage, every root in her hair screaming against her scalp as Cane hauled her against him. Thick fingers curled around her throat, and he licked her cheek. "I can see the appeal."

Wade threw himself at the bars. "You fucking touch her, and I'll kill you!"

Smoke curled out from where his fists were clenched around the bars, flesh sizzling. He almost, almost managed to stretch the bars half an inch.

Riley strained. "Stop it, Luc! You're hurting yourself."

He let go with a snarl, but he was breathing hard. "Nothing will keep me in here. You hear that? Nothing. Let her go."

Cane released her and Riley collapsed onto her hands and knees, touching her scalp tentatively. His boot stepped beside her and she flashed a seething look at it, wishing she had a knife. Wouldn't be so fucking smug if she jammed a blade into his foot. Fear burned hot in her throat though. There were a lot of things a warg and a pack of reivers could do to a woman.

"Nothing, huh?" Cane laughed. "Maybe *I* won't be doing anything to her at all."

Riley looked up and caught the faint silvery gleam in Luc's blue eyes. Their gazes met, and she felt like he was trying to tell her something.

A gunshot went off in the cliffs surrounding them, and something soared into the sky before exploding with a flash of brilliant bright light. Twilight was beginning to fall, and the flare gleamed like the first star in the sky.

Cane looked up, an ugly expression crossing his face. Maybe glee. "Looks like we got company, boys!"

Hoots went up around them, reivers ululating in their throats like animals and shaking shotguns here and there. Some of them had clay smeared across their cheeks and faces in red stripes, and it looked like dried blood. One or two of them wore masks, with empty goggle eyes glinting in the sunlight. Animals. All of them animals. Or no, that wasn't fair, for she'd never seen real animals behave like this. These were scavengers and, like a pack, they were shaking with the excitement of the hunt.

Because that's what this was. A reiver scout had seen something out there on the plains. For a second, Riley thought it might even be some of the guards from Absolution, but then McClain's face sprang to mind. Absolution had lost its compass. Would those men and women there come after her and Wade? Would they take a risk like this? For two strangers?

Not strangers. No, she was forgetting something – Lily had lived there. As far as the people of Absolution knew, Lily was one of them, and she was just a little girl. Absolution might be all shook up, but it looked out for its own.

"Lock 'em up," Cane told Colton, as an aside. "Everybody else, mount up! We've got scalps to claim!"

"Remember what I told you," Luc demanded, eyes wild-shot with silver, not quite human. "I'm still there."

Riley was shoved past him, into a small, squat building beside the one in which Lily had been kept. "What?" Her gaze danced between him and Cane, but the taller man was gloating as he and Colton manhandled the cage closer.

There was something in Wade's eyes. An intensity that she couldn't quite understand. Or a demand.

Trust me, his gaze seemed to say. *I need you to trust me.*

And then the cage door opened and Luc was stumbling toward her, Cane's hand ripping something from his neck at the last second. They collided, and Riley went down as Luc tried to grab her. Every part of her body ached from the toll the last few days had taken, and the adrenaline was only just strong enough to take the edge off it. The world spun as she righted herself, but Wade didn't help her up. There was no hand stretched out to her, no words to quell her fears.

Instead, he was on his knees, his fingers curled as he clutched at his head. In pain? Or... something else. Riley didn't know why, but every hair along her arms lifted as if her instincts knew something that she didn't.

"Lock the girl up next door," Cane told Colton, then smiled. "Have fun, Wade. I'll see you in the morning." Cane took one last look at them, and then he slammed the door shut.

"No... fear..." The words were a twisted, guttural grunt that could barely be called language. "No... matter... what..."

Riley froze, her blood running cold.

Because the face that had uttered them wasn't entirely human.

Not anymore.

twenty-two

"WADE," RILEY WHISPERED, backing up against the bed as the warg overtook him. There was no answer in his glittering gaze, no sign of the man she knew. "Luc?"

No sign that he even heard her. Black hair spilled from his entire body as the change overtook him, his features twisted and deformed, half-animal, half-man. His lip curled back off his dangerously sharp teeth, and he advanced with a menacing step.

What had he said before? *I'm still there.* He was aware of everything that happened when the fury of the beast had him in its grip. That meant he was somewhere in there, somewhere inside. She just had to find him.

It was terrifying, but he'd known. And he'd allowed it, which meant he believed that he might get through this without killing her, as Cane no doubt intended. It all came down to her though, and how she reacted.

Strong emotions set him off, made it harder for him to keep control. And that was when he was *human*.

"I'm not afraid that you'll hurt me." Riley swallowed the hard lump of fear in her throat and forced herself to meet his silvery gaze. "Luc," she called. "I know you won't hurt me. I know you can do this. You can hold it off. Control it. You can win. And in the morning, we can kill Cane for this."

A growl erupted from his throat, and she almost flinched.

Keep going. Keep him listening.

"I love you," she blurted, as he started toward her. "I want you to know that. No matter what happens." Swallowing hard, she added, "It's okay. This is not your fault. I love you."

A rippling shudder went through the massive form, a slight hesitation. Riley leapt on it, her breath hitching in her throat, almost a cry of fear. Oh, God. What if she couldn't get through to him? What if, no matter how hard he fought, he couldn't control himself?

"I love you," she said again, fear making her trip on the words. He hesitated again, then shook it off. Riley closed her eyes, the heated scent of wolf musk filling the room. "You're a stupid, arrogant idiot, but I love you. I love you because you held my hand in the dark, and helped me rescue Jimmy. I love you because you kissed me in that pool, and for the first time in my life, I realized that it wasn't just sex. I love you because I can yell at you, and you don't care if I'm just a woman."

He was listening. Oh, God, he was listening.

Riley kept going, trying to think of every little memory she had of him, anything to bring Luc back to her. "You drive me crazy. You're everything I shouldn't want, but I do. I want to be with you forever. I want... I want children," she blurted. "A place together. I know it's only a dream to you, but I think we can do it. Maybe just the two of us – or three, because I know you want Lily with us. We could do it. We could be a family."

The monster stopped in its tracks, breathing hard. Riley didn't dare hope. One slip and it could be on her, its awful claws rending.

"Do you remember when I held your hand?" she whispered. "When you were hurt? I was so afraid I was going to lose you, and I knew how scared I'd been when I was lost in the dark. I held your hand all night, even though I was afraid of you – not of what you were, but of how I felt. I was so confused, because this is against all of the rules I grew up with."

A quiver ran through that enormous body. Riley forced herself to be brave. Taking a step toward him cost her everything she had. She licked her lips as his head jerked, watching the movement. "Easy," she whispered, slowly lifting her hand. "I just want to touch you." She sucked in a breath, inches trembling between her hand and his arm. "You like it when I touch you," she reminded him. The distance narrowed. Her fingers brushed the black fur that covered his lean, sinewy form. She almost yanked them back then, but any sign of fear or rejection would only destroy this tenuous connection.

"I love you," she whispered, sliding her hand over his arm.

He flinched, breathing harshly through his nostrils. Nearly eight feet of monster. Riley's hand firmed on his fur. "Your fur's soft," she whispered in surprise. He was quivering, but he'd made no move. Slowly, she lifted her hand and stroked his arm, running her fingers through the thick silky pelt.

"You like that, don't you?" she whispered, lifting her other hand and brushing the backs of her fingers down his chest. She didn't dare believe she'd won. Wade quivered beneath her touch so violently she knew it was taking everything in him to control this.

I want blood. I want flesh.

If either of them let go, he'd hurt her, she knew it. Breathing deeply, she slid her hand into his, feeling the threatening pinprick of his claws as she slid her fingers between his. "Shush," she murmured as he twitched. "I just want to hold your hand, like I did last time you were hurt." She ran her other hand over his chest. "I'll hold it all night, Luc. You just have to stay with me. I'll be your anchor. Just stay with me."

Another shudder, fighting against his instincts.

"You can do it," she breathed, pressing on his shoulder. "Let's sit down. Let's rest. Come, my love."

Slowly, he went to his knees, a soft growl curling through his throat. Riley's hand began to shake as he pressed himself against her, burying his muzzle against her abdomen. She tensed, then slowly lowered her hand to the soft fur on his scalp. If she didn't think too much, it was almost hypnotic, the slow, steady stroke of her hand through that warm fur.

Without thinking, she started humming, the same old lullaby he'd hummed in the cave that night, when he carved a doll for the child he'd thought he'd lost. Though he didn't move, she could tell he was listening, a rumble of satisfaction curling through his chest.

"That's it," she whispered, a feeling of absolute incredulity rushing through her blood. Her head swam. She'd done it. She'd brought him back to himself.

Now she just had to hold him until dawn.

And a glance at the window showed her dawn was a long time away.

twenty-three

A LONG, MOURNFUL howl filled the crisp pre-dawn. A smile stretched over Bartholomew Cane's lips at the sound, and he kicked his heels down off the chair in front of him, almost spilling his wine.

"There it is." He laughed. "The son of a bitch is starting to realize what he did."

Tossing back the last gulp of wine, he glared across the room. Colton sat quietly on the sofa, the little girl curled up beside him. Cane had demanded she be given a room away from Colton's overly protective hovering, but Colton had defied him. No amount of pressure, no force he applied, would change Colton's mind. It was the first time his second had openly defied him.

I gave my word she wouldn't be hurt.

But Cane hadn't. His gaze narrowed on the girl. She'd been nothing to him but leverage, but now that she'd caused his second to defy him, it was personal. The girl would have to die. Preferably in front of both Wade and Colton.

Colton needed to learn who his master was again, and Wade... Wade needed to be destroyed, for daring to try and kill him.

His good mood evaporating, Cane tossed his glass into the fireplace. It shattered and the girl woke with a start, flinching into the sofa. Colton looked up, meeting Cane's gaze, his own dark eyes hot and aggressive.

Cane shoved to his feet, locking their gazes with his will. "You want to push me?" he asked, dangerously soft. "I own you. And, by God, I'll show you by the time this day's over." His gaze drifted to the girl again, and she cowered with a whimper. "But for now, I have Wade to deal with. Consider this a reprieve."

"Don't be afraid," Colton murmured, squeezing her hand. "I won't let anyone hurt you."

That last comment with a sharp look at Cane.

Fucking ungrateful little shit. Cane bared his teeth and strode toward the door.

A reiver on guard yawned in his face at the top of the stairs. Cane snarled and kicked him in the chest. The man's eyes widened, and he screamed as his body arched back into space and disappeared. A meaty thud sounded as he landed far below.

That put a smile on his face.

Cane stretched, turning his face toward the horizon – and dawn. He could feel it under his skin, the itch that he could never escape subsiding at least. Both his and Wade's appropriated charm hung around his throat, forcing the beast inside him down. The last few months had been awful as his charm began to fail – never knowing when he was going to lose control, never knowing if he'd ever change back to a man. He'd needed another, and with both Wade and McClain in this area, the chances were good. Besides, he had some unfinished business with the pair of them.

A scream of inhuman rage came from the west, from Wade's prison. The reivers on duty all spun toward the sound, some crossing themselves to an ancient God. Pathetic little pissants.

The loss in the warg's voice was beautiful. A goddamned symphony.

Cane grabbed the edges of the thin ladder and slid down to the bottom. Above him, dawn light silvered the adobe of the house someone had long ago carved into the cave system, and he'd since taken over. Dust stirred around his boots, and Cane scuffed his hands against his jeans as he turned.

Packs of reivers slunk out of his way as he stepped over the body of their fallen comrade. Nobody would dare say a word, even if they thought to. Cane had bought them a lot of good luck, his wargs taking over Isolation, New Hope, and Haven within months. The reivers had more food – and slaves – than they knew what to do with.

No, no one would dare say a word about the body.

He crossed the hard-packed dirt of the center of the mine, listening to the unearthly scream within the building in front of him. It was almost human now, if a human had ever felt a loss that deep.

"Wade!" he bellowed.

Another scream of rage shook the building in response. Cane climbed the wooden steps and paused on the ramp outside the door. The scent of hot, coppery blood washed through his senses, making his mouth water and his heartbeat accelerate. A tingle ran over his skin, the hairs on his arms standing up. Cane looked down. *No.* The extra charm was supposed to stop this.

He'd questioned Colton about the charms not long ago, needing to know if the shaman magic in them was fading, or if it were something else. Colton had dared to say that it wasn't because there was a monster inside him, it was because he *was* the monster. So close to the creature he despised that he would never be able to keep it hidden.

He'd made Colton bleed that day. The one good thing about a warg's healing powers – you could slice them to shreds, and they'd still be able to hunt at your command the next day.

Silence fell. Cane looked up sharply, and drew his gun. Shoving open the door, he came to a halt on the threshold, his incredulous gaze roving the room.

Hell. Wade'd done a number on her. Blood splashed the walls like raindrops, and the bed was crushed, the legs crumpled beneath it. Wade knelt in the center of the room, naked, clutching the bloodied ruins of the woman's black shirt and whatever was left of her. His back quivered, his hands shaking as he sucked in a sharp, pained breath.

Cane took a step inside the room. He smiled. "Did you like that, Wade? Did she taste good?" He breathed in deeply, the woman's scent so strong he could almost sense her. "Did you get one last fuck in before you tore her to shreds?"

"I'll kill you," Wade whispered hoarsely.

Cane lifted the pistol and put it to the back of the man's head. He clicked the safety off, the sound echoing in the room. Wade stiffened. The seconds dragged out.

Cane laughed and aimed the gun high, clicking the safety back on. "Don't think it's that easy. I don't do mercy of any kind. You live with this, and you remember." His laughter turned huskier, as if the very thought of it aroused the monster inside.

Movement shifted behind him. The door slammed shut. Cane half-turned, just as something heavy smashed him across the face. The blow spun him off his feet, his hand losing the pistol. Somehow, he ended up flat on his back, staring up at a blonde, blood-spattered woman with one of the timber bed legs in her hand.

"Surprise." The woman smiled before lifting her boot and kicking him in the face.

"Bitch," Cane snarled.

Riley's eyes narrowed and she kicked at him again, the toe of her boot digging into his ribs with a satisfying crunch. Cane snarled, catching her leg against his side and tearing her off balance.

Shit. She went down hard, landing awkwardly on the bed leg. The spear of pain through her ribs made her head spin. As her vision swam, she saw Cane leer up over her, his teeth bared in a grimace of fury, blood dripping down his face. Her own blood ran cold at the expression on his face; he might've still been a man, but a monster stared back at her, wanting only to hurt.

"Riley!" Wade came out of nowhere, barreling into Cane. They smashed against the wall, smearing some of the blood Wade had flicked on the adobe to fool Cane.

Riley rolled to her side with a wince. *Get up!* But her brain and body weren't quite connected at the moment. The toll of all her injuries and exhaustion were finally starting to take its payment from her. Bearing her teeth, she pushed up onto her knees, moving slowly.

Cane and Wade wrestled backward, the muscles in Wade's naked arms tensing and flexing as if he were struggling. He took a step back. Then another, his teeth bared in fury.

"Colton!" Cane roared. "Get in here!"

Riley's gaze locked on the shut door. If Colton arrived, the odds were grim. She saw Cane's pistol on the floor and scrambled for it in ugly, jerking movements, just as the door kicked open with a bang.

Colton came through, Lily cradled in front of him, his gun held low against his thigh.

Riley lay flat on her back, the gun in her hands trembling as she aimed it at his head. "Don't move," she said coldly, wincing a little at the ache in her side.

Those liquid black eyes glanced her way, then back to Cane. Like a well-heeled dog.

Wade smashed Cane against the wall with a roar, his hands curled around the other man's throat. Cane grabbed his wrist, his face twisting in effort as he tried to haul Wade away. His eyes rolled toward Colton.

"Shoot—" He managed to say, spittle spraying over Wade's arm. "Shoot... erm."

Colton lifted the gun, his expression cool and distant. His other hand wrapped around Lily's chest, holding the frightened girl in place.

"Don't!" Riley screamed, her finger twitching on the trigger.

Gunfire spat. Once. Twice. She screamed as Colton jerked back into the wall, her shot taking him high in the chest.

Someone fell. She rolled to her knees, and then onto her feet as Wade and Cane both went down. "Luc!" With a sharp, wary glance at Colton, she grabbed Wade's arm and rolled him off Cane. There was blood all over him, and his eyes were glassy.

Oh, God. Oh, God, oh, God. Heat sprang up behind her eyes as she went to her knees beside him. "Where is it? Where'd he get you? Are you all right?"

Wade coughed and pushed at her. "Riley—"

"I'm so sorry—"

He caught her wrists. "Riley! I'm fine."

Fine. Her eyes went wide and she froze, melting into him. Wade cupped her face with a trembling hand, giving her a tremulous smile. Then he pushed her away. "He wasn't shooting at me."

She looked down. Cane stared sightlessly at the roof, his arms akimbo in a way that wasn't natural, a bullet hole gaping in his temple. The gleam of a pair of pewter amulets sparkled around his throat.

There was no way Colton could have missed that shot. She looked up, just as Colton bared his teeth in a pained hiss, trying to drag himself into a sitting position against the wall. Their gazes locked.

"Have to be careful—" Colton swallowed "—with giving indirect... orders." Leaning his head back against the wall, he laughed under his breath, a pained hacking sound. "Finally got the fucker." Looking up, he focused on Lily, who was curled into a ball behind the door. "Pardon the language, darlin'."

Wade slowly drew to his feet, grabbing the sheet off the bed and wrapping it around his naked waist. He held out a hand and Riley stood up slowly, her ears still ringing. At his questioning look, she realized she must have winced.

"Fell hard," she muttered. "Just my ribs."

He nodded. Then he looked past her, his gaze locking on the tiny little girl in the corner with an absoluteness that blocked everything else out. "Lily," he said quietly, holding out his hand. "Lily, it's okay. We'll get you out of here."

The little girl's eyes swam with tears and she swallowed, looking between him and Riley. Seconds ticked past, and then Wade realized she wasn't going to come to him. His hand slowly dropped, his expression shuttering completely.

"Hell, Luc," Riley said, shouldering past him with deliberate lightness in her voice. "You're covered in blood, and she's been through an awful lot. She probably doesn't even know where she is right now."

Squatting down, she put her hands on her knees and stared at Lily. "You okay, sweetheart? Nobody hurt you, did they?"

Lily's face screwed up, and she started crying. Riley dragged her into her arms, feeling the tiny body wrap itself around her so tightly she could barely breathe. Fire lanced through her ribs, but she couldn't let go.

"It's okay," she murmured, running a hand through that silky-fine hair. "We came to take you home. Everything will be all right now. Your daddy's here to make sure you're okay." She met his gaze over Lily's head, "Nothing can hurt you now that he's here, because he's bigger and meaner than anything else, and he'll do anything to keep you safe because he loves you."

Wade tore his gaze away then, his jaw tightening. "Can you carry her? We need to get moving."

"Lily," she whispered, feeling the pain of his rejection. "Lily, are you okay to move? We can't stay here. We have to go."

The little girl's grip tightened around her neck.

"I'm not leaving you behind, honey." Riley struggled to her feet, her side aching. "Luc," she called. "I don't think I can carry her."

He'd picked up the remnants of his jeans and was dragging them on underneath the sheet. At her words, his fingers slowed on the buttons. "Can she walk?" Hoarse words.

"Lily." Riley took a step, and gasped as pain tore through her. "I can't carry you. You either have to walk or let your daddy carry you."

Lily shook her head against her throat, sobbing helplessly. "No."

Visibly steeling himself, Wade crossed toward them, and reached out for her. "Come on, Lily. You're hurting Riley."

Taking her by the arms, he gently tugged. Lily looked up in horror and yanked at Riley's shirt. Riley gasped and clapped a hand to her side as Wade gently took the little girl.

His broad arms wrapped around his daughter as she fought him. Setting his teeth grimly, he crushed her against his massive chest. "Shush, Lily. I've got you. You're safe now."

The little girl's sobs slowly died, and his hands relaxed a little. The expression on his face nearly tore Riley's heart out of her chest as his quivering hand came up to stroke his daughter's hair. Turning his face, he breathed in the scent of her, as if he couldn't quite believe she was there.

"I've missed you," he whispered.

Riley stooped to collect Colton's gun, keeping a wary eye on him. Colton stared back at her, baring his teeth in a bloody grimace. One hand was clapped high against his chest, his shirt wet with blood. His long, dark hair tumbled over his shoulder, the sharp angle of his nose welted with bruises.

He'd heal, though it would take him most of the day.

Wade stepped up beside her, lifting his own gun as he cradled Lily against him with the other hand. His expression was bleak as he stared down at Colton.

Colton stiffened.

"No, don't!" Lily cried out, grabbing Wade's wrist. "He looked after me. He stopped the other man from hurting me."

Wade looked at her beneath his lashes. Slowly, his gun lowered. "That's the only reason I won't do this. Don't follow us."

Colton slumped back, giving a pained wheeze that might have been a laugh. "No... intentions of...." He looked down, lifting his bloodied hand to examine the wound. As if the effort strained him, his head flopped back. "Leave me... a gun. For that pack... of hyenas... out there."

Wade tucked the pistol in the waistband of his jeans. "Riley, can you fetch my amulet?"

She quickly retrieved the pair of polished charms, tucking them into her pocket. Wade had stepped past Colton with his bare feet, his body shielding Lily as he peered through the door. "They've gone to ground."

"For the moment," she murmured, glancing at Colton. It was clear Wade had no intention of sparing him a weapon.

A split-second decision. She clicked the safety off her own pistol and dropped it in his lap.

Colton looked up at her in surprise.

"Don't make me regret it," she told him, then slipped out after Wade.

epilogue

One month later...

LUC SHIFTED in bed, a warm armful against his chest hampering his movements. Riley grumbled sleepily, then brushed her lips against his bare chest.

"Morning," she murmured.

"Morning," he replied with a bemused smile. Of all the things he'd learned about her in the last month, the one that never failed to amuse him was this: she was barely human until after ten in the morning. "You said you didn't snore."

"If I recall, I don't believe I ever actually answered that question. I asked if *you* snored," she grumbled sleepily, but the drum of his fingers along her hip was starting to wake her up. Riley shifted, brushing her ass against his cock.

Luc inhaled sharply. "Temptress."

"Demon," she whispered.

"Crazy woman."

"Kidnapper."

"Best mistake of my life."

Riley laughed. The sound of it thrilled him, sending his heart soaring. These were the moments between them that he enjoyed the most.

Turning her face toward the door, she cocked her head, listening. "Lily's not up yet?"

Lily. His smile faded. "I can hear her shifting. She's not quite awake."

Noticing the sudden stiffening of his shoulders, Riley stroked a hand over his chest. "Give her time," she said. "She's been through a lot."

He knew that. But knowing it didn't stop the ache in his chest whenever his daughter's gaze slid away from his. He let out a slow breath. Lily was getting better, slowly starting to respond to his questions, and letting him help her when she needed it. But he was fully aware that without Riley there to act as buffer between them, he wouldn't have had a hope. As far as Lily was concerned, her father had died when she was two, and he was the warg who'd tried to kill her Uncle Adam. The fact that he *was* her father had been a nasty shock for her.

Riley pressed a gentle kiss to his throat, in order to distract him. It might have been a whirlwind courtship, but she knew his moods well. Luc's hand slid over hers, giving it a squeeze. That was one thing that was right about this new life of his. He didn't know when it had happened – when Riley had become the part of his life that he never wanted to lose – but he was glad it had.

Wargs don't get happy-ever-afters. Wargs don't have a future.

They were words he'd spent years telling himself, and they still struck at odd moments, but he knew them for the lies they were now.

"This is my happy-ever-after," he whispered, rolling Riley onto her back, and coming over her.

Her smile was slightly mysterious, but also happy. "Do I even want to know?"

That smile. It killed him. Wrapped a hand tight around his heart and wouldn't let go. His gut tightened with nervousness, but he leaned forward and brushed his mouth against hers. A fleeting kiss, just a tease, and then she drew back with that wicked gleam shining in her whiskey brown eyes.

Soft lips brushed against the slope of his shoulder, nibbling up to his neck. Those fingertips traced burning circles on his hip. Lower. Lower. Not quite low enough.

"Again?" she whispered.

"Helps keep control," Luc replied quickly.

"Really?" The word came out dry. "You wouldn't just be telling me that in order to get me into bed?"

"I'm already in your bed," he said. Those teasing fingers trailed down his flank, growing lighter and lighter until they broke from his skin, just before she reached the thatch of hair between his thighs. "I want to be inside you."

"You already are," she whispered, kissing his soft mouth. Taking his hand, she pressed it between her breasts. "You're in here. You'll always be in here."

Luc stilled above her, a shudder running through him. "You don't know how much I fucking love hearing those words."

Riley laughed, pressing her head back into the pillow and exposing her throat. Oh, she knew, all right; he could see it. A fierce urge came over him and he bit her throat, nipping at the skin, and then easing enough for him to press a kiss there. Riley moaned, her thighs falling apart and welcoming him between them.

He took her slowly, filling her with one sure thrust, and then sliding sensually within her. When she moaned, he captured her mouth with heated kisses. "Quiet," he whispered.

Riley shuddered beneath him, biting her lip as she tried to obey. The walls at Haven were solid stone, but there were some things he didn't want his daughter hearing. Somehow, the secretiveness of these encounters made them even more thrilling. He lost himself in her, and she in him, skin on skin, biting, licking, fucking....

Afterward, they lay entangled, with Riley's head resting on his chest and her breasts pressed against him. Luc dozed, idly untangling her hair. These little moments were the most precious to him.

A door creaked open elsewhere in the house, a sign that Lily was up and about. Riley sighed softly as he eased her head off his shoulder. "Time to be up and about, love."

"You've worn me out." She stretched and yawned.

"Hardly." Luc laughed, slipping from the bed. "Come on, sleepyhead. This place isn't going to rebuild itself."

The sun soared in the sky by the time Luc set about his duties. He could hear Riley talking to Lily in the little room they'd managed to scratch out of the burned mess she'd once called home, and were now using as a kitchen. Haven had been hit hard by the reivers, but he liked the feel of the place. There was a natural spring in the center of town, around which sprang up a grove of cottonwood trees, and most of the buildings were still standing, as they'd been built from stone. Plenty of room for pens for some goats, or whatever Riley wanted to rear, and enough space in the lush garden at the back of her home so Lily could play safely all day.

Of course, they were all alone out here, but that was the way he liked it. The rest of the townsfolk originally from Haven had stayed at Absolution, though some of them had ridden out after him and Riley when they'd discovered Lily was missing. Eden had led the charge, despite what the Council of Absolution had argued for. A rescue party made up of settlers, not soldiers, but he'd been grateful to see them when he, Riley and Lily made their dusty escape from Copperplate.

Of course, that gratefulness had changed when they'd arrived back in Absolution.

The soldiers on the gates had refused to let him in, eyeing him with hard, flat eyes. The distrust had probably been earned, but the rejection had come hard on the heels of his daughter's. Luc had taken one step back, not quite certain what he was going to do, when Riley came to the rescue, taking Lily by the hand and telling him she'd be back with their things.

So he'd sat on the hot sand outside Absolution's walls and waited, wondering if both of them would return. Eden had brought him water, perhaps out of pity. Perhaps out of a sense that her own brother was facing the same rejection. Or perhaps just because that was the type of person she was.

When Riley and Lily returned with their bags, he'd almost been surprised. He shouldn't have been, however; Riley wasn't the type of person to go back on her word. With a smile, she'd slipped her hand inside his and gestured for the keys to one of the jeeps from Eden. "I know exactly where we're going to go," she'd said.

Haven.

It felt strange to think of the place as his new home. He'd moved around so much in the past eight years that he could barely remember what it felt like to have a place of his own. He liked it. Every day was long and hard, but at least he could sit back as dusk settled in the sky, looking out over what he'd done for the day with a solid sense of achievement.

Squatting low, Luc took hold of a heavy beam of fallen timber, grit his teeth together, and began hauling it out of the way. Sweat trickled down his spine, and he dropped it in the pile of lumber that was still good enough to re-use. Dusting off his jeans, he paused. An engine's roar echoed faintly on the breeze.

Two shadows leapt to life across the blistering haze of the plain surrounding Haven. Two men on motorbikes, by the look of it. Luc headed for the shotgun he'd propped against the porch and yelled, "Riley! Visitors!"

"Friend or foe?"

"Don't know!" he replied.

Stalking out into the street, he squinted through the hot sunlight. Tension eased from his shoulders when he recognized the lead rider. McClain. A different kind of tension filled him, but he lowered the shotgun, waiting for the pair of them to arrive. At McClain's side was a lean young man, whom he recognized as Cole, the soldier he'd cut up at Salvation. They eased to a halt, McClain raking the buildings around them with a hard glare.

Silver winked at the kid's throat – the amulet that Luc had taken from Cane and given to him at Absolution when they'd returned with Lily. It had been the least he could do, though judging from the narrowed look Cole shot him, the gesture hadn't granted him forgiveness.

Not that he blamed him.

Cole's hand strayed to his hip, and Luc tensed—

And then a hand slid into his, tugging at it to get his attention. Lily stepped between them, giving Cole her back as she held up her hands to Luc.

It was the first time she'd made some sort of overture toward him. And even though it cut his heart fair out of his chest, he tried to steer her back toward the house, where Riley stood watching, with a shotgun slung over her shoulder."Honey, you shouldn't be out—"

"Up," she said, tugging at his hand again and glancing over her shoulder toward Cole.

The kid looked like a kid again, barely a man, but old enough to look chagrined. "Ain't here for vengeance, Lily."

"Good," she said, and somehow Luc found his arms full of his daughter, with her legs slung over his hip. She was far too big to carry, but he didn't let her go. The last time he'd held her like this, she'd been two.

McClain eased in beside him, riding on the brakes. "Wade. Riley." He tipped his head in a nod. "Got any water a man could borrow?"

"This way," Riley said, stepping forward with a wary smile. She gestured to Cole. "I'll show you where the spring is. Lily, do you want to help?"

"Hey, Adam!" Lily waved, then slipped down his hip and took off after Riley and Cole.

"He won't—"

"He won't hurt them," McClain said, watching them both go. He arched a brow at Luc as the tension eased out of him. "He's a good kid. Not your biggest fan, but then I've explained matters."

Something wriggled in the saddlebags slung over McClain's bike. Light flashed off the solar panels that decorated the metal body of it. Gasoline was getting scarce – and expensive – and most vehicles out here were equipped with both sources of fuel.

"You bought a housewarming gift?" He could smell it.

McClain actually grinned, then flipped open the bag and hauled out a fat, wiggling pup. He handed him over, and Luc was forced to take it. The ball of fluff wriggled its little body, then licked him.

"You might as well put him down," McClain said. "He'll follow Lily."

Doing as he said, Luc watched the pup shoot off in the direction the others had gone. Damn dogs. The pup vanished behind the wall Luc had patched the day before, and then let out a few happy yips. Two seconds later, Lily cried out in delight, "Arthur!"

"Let me guess, I have another mouth to feed now?" he asked drily.

"You don't have to." McClain shrugged.

Yeah, right. He could hear the sound of his daughter's happy laughter. It wasn't really a choice. Checkmate to McClain.

"So Cane's dead," McClain said, slinging his leg over the bike and kicking out the rusted old kickstand. "And Colton?"

"Probably still alive to haunt me." Luc scowled. "I couldn't shoot the bastard. He saved my life, shot Cane himself."

A humorless snort from McClain. "Guess he finally broke free of that alpha bond Cane had on him. I'd still watch my back if I were you."

"Always do."

"Different now you've got family to watch over though," McClain said. "It makes it harder, when you care for them. Takes away that edge you always had."

"You should know."

"I did know." McClain's voice held a soft note of what was in the past. He looked away, surveying the burned buildings that Luc and Riley had been slowly cleaning up, but it was clear that he didn't see them.

"So, they let you out of the cage?" Luc said. "What now?"

McClain shrugged. "Seemed a good time to head out, perhaps see a bit of the world. I know where my skills lie. Could turn my hand back to bounty hunting. At least it's one thing I'm good for, cleaning up shit like that."

Shit like us remained unsaid.

"You could stay here, if you wanted," Luc said, even though the offer wasn't entirely a great one. "Lily still thinks you're her uncle. She asks about you sometimes."

McClain shook his head. "Don't think so. Thanks." And his gaze drifted to the wall, where Riley, Cole and Lily had disappeared behind.

"A couple of months ago, all I ever wanted was to see you dead," Luc admitted. "So I won't pretend that we're friends again. But... You ever need a place to stay, you remember that the offer's there."

"And all I wanted was to make up for what I'd done to you, to find some way to bring you back. Just can't wrap my head around it, that Riley'd be the one who saved you."

"Some things are worth fighting for. Riley's one of them."

A shared nod.

"Yeah, I get that," McClain said, and there was bitterness in his voice. "Thought that myself. Once upon a time." He sighed, slipping his hat off and raking a hand through his short-cropped hair. "I can't even be pissed at you for it. She's different with you than she ever was with me. And I'm glad... Glad that someone got through to you. I guess you could say that giving her up is my penance for what I did to you. I won't begrudge you for it."

Luc snorted. "Perhaps. But then you never had her."

McClain's eyes narrowed, but then he laughed. "You always did have a mean mouth on you."

"I always told the truth, whether or not you wanted to hear it."

"Then tell me this," McClain locked hard green eyes on him, suddenly serious. "It never goes away, Luc. The monster... It's always there, lurking inside me, inside us... How can you risk it? How can you stay here, with her and Lily, knowing it might come out one day?"

"How did you stay there?" he replied. "All those years, with all those people, even your sister?"

McClain shuddered. "That was the second time I ever turned, did you know that? The second time. I think I managed to bury it for so many years, once I put the amulet on, that I forgot how hard it was. I had this... this illusion that I controlled it. Keeping it locked up never hurt as much as it does now. I feel like the monster got a taste of what it feels like to tear through my skin, and breathe the hot, scented air of a desert night. It could smell the people around it, and my mouth was watering at the taste of flesh. At the idea of eating my *friends*." His voice roughened. "It's still there, and it's hungrier than it ever was. It yearns now. It remembers what it feels like to be *free*." McClain swallowed, his voice breaking. "How do I ever risk finding a home again? How can I ever hope... for anything... when it lurks inside me?"

"Because it's not uncontrollable," Luc admitted.

McClain breathed a bitter laugh. "Then what happens when one night it breaks free and you tear your wife to pieces, Wade? You want truth? That's the truth, staring you right in the face, even if you won't admit it. You can't lock the warg away within you forever."

That was fear talking.

"I always used to think that too. I was so afraid to destroy the people I loved, that I walked out on my wife and daughter. For years, I never considered that there could be another option." Luc sighed, reluctant to even remember that night when Riley had held a monster's hand and lived to tell of it. That memory would haunt his dreams forever. "But I've made my peace with myself, and the truth is this: I'm not afraid to live a life with Riley. I'm not. Because I've stared that fear in the eye, and I got through it." McClain shot him a hopeless look, but Luc powered on. "You want the truth? Cane locked me in with Riley, and took my amulet. All night."

McClain's eyes sharpened. "And you didn't turn?"

Luc shook his head. "I turned. I can't even explain it. You know we're always there inside the warg, or at least a part of us is. It scared the hell out of me, that I could lose... lose the one woman I loved, at my own hands. For the first time, I was in control of the beast. I was the one holding the reins as it lurked deep inside me, even when I wore its skin."

McClain breathed out a laugh. "Fuck." He looked utterly haggard. "It's like a dream."

"No, it's not," Luc said. "It was a nightmare, McClain. If Riley had shown a single hint of fear, she'd be dead. The monster would have roused at the scent of it, and overridden me. And I had someone else that I was saving all of its rage for. We were lucky. But... I understand now."

Their eyes met. "I don't blame you for what you did to me, not with your own sister locked in the cell with you."

He looked away, toward where his daughter was smiling at Cole, trying to trap the kid's hand in a cat's cradle as they walked around the corner. Lily laughed, and his throat thickened. "You didn't have a choice, and in the same situation I admit now that I might have chosen the same path. And I made my own choices in response to what I'd become, decisions that I could rue until the day I die, if not for the fact that there's no point. You can't second-guess yourself. I can't go back and stop myself from leaving Abbie and Lily, and if I'm honest, my uncle probably would have shot me anyway. Then I'd still not be there when the reivers killed Abbie.

"So I don't blame you anymore. You did what you had to, and then you tried to make amends. Thank you for looking after Lily for me."

McClain's face wore a hard mask. "It was the least I could do."

Both of them stared at each other.

"Even?" Luc suggested.

McClain nodded gruffly. "Even."

Riley walked back out into the yard with a jug of water drawn from the well. Hot sunshine turned the blonde of her hair into a gleaming halo, though Luc had no aspirations that she was anything angelic. Grumpy, fearless, protective, stubborn, brave, and kind... That was his woman. The type of woman who wouldn't back down when those who belonged to her were threatened.

He couldn't help but notice that he wasn't the only one watching her.

"She suits you," McClain said simply. "And you suit her. I'm not going to lie. I don't understand it."

Because he'd wanted her too, and when weighed against each other, who was the better man? Luc's lips thinned. "The problem is you never understood her. You wanted her to be something she's not."

Another laugh. "You're probably right." McClain's voice dropped into wistfulness. "I'm glad she found you. She did what I could not."

"She believes in me." And more than that... "She makes me feel like I'm not just a man, but a good one. She's my everything."

Silence swelled between them.

As if they'd spoken enough on matters that bordered on personal, McClain looked around at the rubble of Haven. "You're going to stay here?"

"It's Riley's home," he replied. "And I like it here. I can keep the reivers and wargs at bay, and Riley's going to see if some of the others from Haven want to return."

"They won't want to live with you in their midst, Luc."

He shrugged. "Then they can stay at Absolution. Their choice." He looked up. "You're going then?"

McClain nodded. "Not much left for me here."

"You made them what they were."

"I'm a warg, Luc." It was hard to meet those eyes. There was none of the forgiveness there that he had found. "And I lied to them. That trumps everything. I'm no longer McClain, the man who built a haven for them. I'm the monster that hid in their ranks. The Council made a decision. For the services I rendered—" His voice thickened with bitterness "—they'll let me live, on the condition that I never return. I'll take Cole with me, perhaps head south."

"What about Eden?"

"What do you mean?" Riley asked, pausing beside them and offering McClain the jug of water. "What's up with Eden?"

"She doesn't know you've left, does she?" Luc asked, sliding an arm around Riley's waist.

"It's not safe for her out here," McClain said promptly, taking a mouthful of water and nodding a thanks at her.

"Does she think the same?" Riley asked.

McClain shrugged and looked away, tracking the horizon with his gaze. "Cole and I left before dawn. I've risked her life enough, I think."

"Man, you really don't understand women, do you?" Luc said.

That earned him a hard look. "What would you have me do? I know what her choice would be."

"Then let her make her choice," Riley said.

"No. At Absolution, she has a place, a voice on the Council, and the prospect of more... A husband, children. I want that for my sister."

McClain didn't say what else he was thinking, but it was clear in the tone of his voice – he wanted that for himself too. Luc knew what that felt like, the longing for something you didn't think you were worthy of. Finding it had come when he'd least expected it, but accepting it had only happened when he'd laid the demons of his past to rest.

He still wasn't certain he deserved it, but he was damned sure he wasn't going to let the chance slip away from. He squeezed Riley a little tighter.

"I'll keep an eye on Eden," Luc told him. "As payback for what you did for Lily."

A sharp nod. McClain didn't thank him, but then that had never been the way they'd worked. "We'd best get moving then," he said. "Before Eden sends out a search party."

"If she does, then I'm going to tell her exactly where you went," Riley muttered, taking the jug of water back from him.

"Wouldn't expect anything else," McClain said dryly.

Cole joined McClain, and they both kicked their starter motors over.

Lily's hand slipped into Luc's again as she watched McClain get on his bike. It filled him with hope. Each small gesture was a step forward for their relationship.

"Hope you find what you're looking for," he said softly, knowing McClain would hear him.

McClain gave them all one last nod, waved good-bye, and then he and Cole headed out into the Wastelands.

Luc didn't bother to watch them go, turning his little family back to the half-ruined house. The past was done. He was only looking forward from now on.

coming 2017...

If you enjoyed *Nobody's Hero*, then get ready for *The Last True Hero*! Book two in the Burned Lands series, it will be available in early 2017, so make sure you sign up for my newsletter at www.becmcmaster.com to receive news and excerpts about this release!

Can't wait for more Burned Lands action and romance? Check out my *London Steampunk* series. I recommend starting with *Kiss Of Steel*. Not only is it the first book, but it also features a cocky, bad boy anti-hero who captured my heart from the very first moment he came onscreen. There's humour, heroes to die for, dangerous plots, sexy corsets, kick-bustle heroines, duels, steamy kisses (not-just-kisses), and vampires. They may not be your regular sexy vampires either.

Thank you for reading *Nobody's Hero*! I hope you enjoyed it. Please consider leaving a review online, to help others find my books.

Not ready to leave the Burned Lands? Read on for a preview of what's next for Adam McClain...

The Last True Hero

BOOK TWO: THE BURNED LANDS SERIES

Sometimes the monsters aren't so easy to see...

In the drought-stricken Wastelands that arose out of an apocalypse, Adam McClain never thought himself the hero. Kicked out of the town he created, and shunned by his friends and former allies when they discovered what he was, he's managed to find work as a bounty hunter. After all, who better to hunt the wargs and reivers that haunt the Badlands, than one of the monsters themselves?

She's the woman he can't have

Mia Grey learned the hard way that men can't be trusted, and when McClain strides into her bar she knows that trouble just walked in. The rugged bounty hunter is her greatest weakness—but he's hiding something, and the last time a man kept secrets from her, she got her fingers burned. Tempting as he is, Mia's staying far away.

But when a horde of reivers strikes her town and captures her sister, the only one Mia can turn to for help is McClain. Together they might be able to rescue her sister from the slavers, but what will happen when Mia learns what McClain is hiding? Can she ever trust him again? And when the man who broke Mia's heart in the first place discovers the same secret, will McClain survive?

Eight years ago...

THE FIRST TIME Adam McClain put the gun in his mouth, he couldn't pull the trigger. He'd found a nice lonely spot out in the Badlands, far enough away from his sister that she wouldn't find the body, and one with a beautiful view over the Great Divide, which split the continent in half.

He didn't want to die. Maybe that was what stopped him. Or maybe it was the thought of his sister, Eden, who would be left alone in a harsh world, with no one to protect her. Or maybe it was his shame—the knowledge that he was not alone in feeling this way. The partner he'd once ridden with, Lucius Wade, would be staring at the same sky, feeling the same rush of blood through his veins that Adam felt as the moon became a glint on the horizon.

And it was because of Adam that Wade shared the same predicament.

So he took the coward's way out. He pulled the gun out of his mouth, and dropped it to the ground. Night was slowly falling, and with it came the heat in his blood, the moon's curse. He could feel it whispering through his veins, as the monster within fought to free itself.

Thou shalt not suffer a warg to live. That was the first law he'd ever learned, at the knee of his stern bounty hunter father. Adam had followed in his footsteps, hunting the wargs and shadow cats that lurked in the shadows of the wastelands, and it was only now that he recognised the irony.

As muscle ripped and bones tore themselves in half and reformed, he screamed his rage out into the empty night. It was the first time he'd shifted, and the agony of it was blinding. Soon there was nothing more than a monster remaining, and the man that Adam was, lay buried deep inside the brutish beast's heart.

When the sun rose in the morning, he found himself a man again, naked and panting on the blistering sands of the desert floor, with blood on his hands, and the taste of it in his mouth. It was a long walk back to where he'd been, his feet healing even as the harsh rocky floor tore them apart.

Adam put the gun in his mouth again. This time he knew the bone deep truth of what he'd become. His hands shook. Eden flashed into his mind again.

'Promise me, you'll watch over her, boy,' his father's voice whispered in his mind, from a memory long ago, when his father had ridden out that last time.

Adam had always kept his promises, even if he'd had to stab his best friend in the back to do so. His hands were shaking so hard when he pulled the gun out of his mouth the second time, that he actually crushed the handpiece.

A wink of pewter caught his eye from the black bag he'd brought with him. Adam stared at it for a long time, knowing that he didn't deserve it. The amulet was a promise too. A dream of another life. He'd taken it from Bartholomew Cane, the man who'd changed him into... this. Cane wore one himself, as did his warg partner, Johnny Colton. Though Adam wanted both their heads, he'd wanted what the amulet represented more.

A way to keep the beast at bay. A way to hide what he was in a crowd of humans. A means to pretend that nothing had changed, that he was still the man he'd always been.

Wade had promised them all vengeance. That was the only thing that kept his once-partner sane after what had happened between them. But Adam had something else to live for.

Atonement.

So he dressed himself in the spare clothes he'd bought—perhaps he'd known he couldn't really do—and then he started back toward the beaten up old motorcycle that had brought him here.

Eden would be wondering where he was, and Adam had promises to keep...

ABOUT THE AUTHOR

Bec McMaster is the award-winning author of the London Steampunk series. A member of RWA, she writes sexy, dark paranormals, and adventurous steampunk romances, and grew up with her nose in a book. Following a life-long love affair with fantasy, she discovered romance novels as a 16 year-old, and hasn't looked back.

In 2012, Sourcebooks released her debut novel, *Kiss of Steel*, the first in the London Steampunk series, followed by: *Heart of Iron, My Lady Quicksilver, Forged By Desire*, and *Of Silk And Steam*. Two novellas–*Tarnished Knight* and *The Curious Case Of The Clockwork Menace*–fleshed out the series. She has been nominated for RT Reviews Best Steampunk Romance for *Heart of Iron (2013)*, won RT Reviews Best Steampunk Romance with *Of Silk And Steam (2015)*, and *Forged By Desire* was nominated for a RITA award in 2015. The series has received starred reviews from Booklist, Publishers Weekly, and Library Journal, with Heart of Iron named one of their Best Romances of 2013.

In 2016, she debuted the Dark Arts series with *Shadowbound*, as well as the Burned Lands series with *Nobody's Hero*.

When not poring over travel brochures, playing netball, or cooking things that are very likely bad for her, Bec spends most of her time in front of the computer. She lives in a small country town in Victoria, Australia, with her very own Beta Hero; a Staffordshire terrier named Kobe, who has perfected her own Puss-in-boots sad eyes–especially when bacon is involved; and demanding chickens, Siggy and Lagertha.

For news on new releases, cover reveals, contests, and special promotions, join her mailing list at www.becmcmaster.com

ACKNOWLEDGMENTS

This story has lived in my head for at least six years, and it all started with Riley, a feisty heroine in a dystopian world, and McClain, the true-blue hero who would be her man. Halfway through chapter one, Luc Wade swaggered onstage and kidnapped her, in order to settle a debt with McClain. McClain was supposed to come to the rescue. Wade was supposed to get his comeuppance. The problem? The chemistry between he and Riley was scorching off the page, and Wade decided nope, he's not just the bad guy here. That's why this book is called *Nobody's Hero*. Because Wade was never, ever meant to be the one who got the girl.

As for McClain, he was just as important a part of Wade's story as Riley was, and I loved delving into this tale of a man who was honest, loyal, true, and yet kept a very dark secret from the world... He and Wade had a real bromance from the start, and I couldn't resist their scenes together.

I enjoyed every second of writing this book, but as with every project I take on, I couldn't have done it without a lot of help from these amazing people:

I owe huge thanks to my editor Kristin from Hot Tree Editing for her work in spit-and-polishing this manuscript until it gleamed; my wonderful cover artists from Damonza.com for taking everything I described and giving me the cover of my dreams; and Marisa Shor and Allyson Gottlieb from Cover Me Darling for the print formatting.

To the ELE, and the Central Victorian Writers groups for keeping me sane, and being my support groups! Special thanks to my family, and to my other half—my very own beta hero, Byron—who has always been unabashedly proud of this dream of mine, even when I didn't know if I could do it.

Last, not least, to all of my readers who support me on this journey, and have been crazy vocal about their love for the London Steampunk series, and anything else I write! I hope you enjoy this crazy little detour into a dark, sexy world!

CPSIA information can be obtained
at www.ICGtesting.com
Printed in the USA
LVOW07s1807061217
558856LV00005B/769/P